PENGUIN BOOKS

GABRIEL'S RAPTURE

Sylvain Reynard is a Canadian writer with an interest in Renaissance art and culture and an inordinate attachment to the city of Florence.

Books by Sylvain Reynard

GABRIEL'S INFERNO
GABRIEL'S RAPTURE

Gabriel's Rapture

Sylvain Reynard

PENGUIN BOOKS

PENGUIN BOOKS

Published by the Penguin Group
Penguin Books Ltd, 80 Strand, London WC2R 0RL, England
Penguin Group (USA) Inc., 375 Hudson Street, New York, New York 10014, USA
Penguin Group (Canada), 90 Eglinton Avenue East, Suite 700, Toronto, Ontario, Canada M4P 2Y3
(a division of Pearson Penguin Canada Inc.)
Penguin Ireland, 25 St Stephen's Green, Dublin 2, Ireland (a division of Penguin Books Ltd)
Penguin Group (Australia), 707 Collins Street, Melbourne, Victoria 3008, Australia
(a division of Pearson Australia Group Pty Ltd)
Penguin Books India Pvt Ltd, 11 Community Centre,
Panchsheel Park, New Delhi – 110 017, India
Penguin Group (NZ), 67 Apollo Drive, Rosedale, Auckland 0632, New Zealand
(a division of Pearson New Zealand Ltd)
Penguin Books (South Africa) (Pty) Ltd, Block D, Rosebank Office Park,
181 Jan Smuts Avenue, Parktown North, Gauteng 2193, South Africa

Penguin Books Ltd, Registered Offices: 80 Strand, London WC2R 0RL, England

www.penguin.com

First published in the United States of America by Omnific Publishing 2012
Published in the United States of America by Berkley Books 2012
First published in Great Britain by Penguin Books 2012
002

Copyright © Sylvain Reynard, 2012
All rights reserved

The moral right of the author has been asserted

Printed in England by Clays Ltd, St Ives plc

ISBN: 978-1-405-91243-3

www.greenpenguin.co.uk

Penguin Books is committed to a sustainable
future for our business, our readers and our planet.
This book is made from Forest Stewardship
Council™ certified paper.

ALWAYS LEARNING   **PEARSON**

To my readers,
with gratitude.

Dante following Virgil up the mountain.
Engraving by Gustave Doré, 1870

"And of that second kingdom will I sing
Wherein the human spirit doth purge itself,
And to ascend to heaven becometh worthy."

—Dante Alighieri, Purgatorio, Canto I.004-006.

Prologue

Florence, 1290

The poet dropped the note to the floor with a shaking hand. He sat for several moments, motionless as a statue. Then, with a great clenching of teeth, he stood to his feet and swept agitatedly through the house, ignoring tables and fragile items, disdaining the other inhabitants of his home.

There was only one person whom he wished to see.

He strode quickly through the city streets, almost breaking into a run on his way to the river. He stood at the end of the bridge, their bridge, his moist eyes eagerly scanning the adjacent riverbank for the barest glimpse of his beloved.

She was nowhere to be found.

She would never return.

His beloved Beatrice was gone.

Chapter One

Professor Gabriel Emerson was sitting in bed, naked, reading *La Nazione*, the Florentine newspaper. He'd awoken early in the Palazzo Vecchio penthouse of the Gallery Hotel Art and ordered room service, but he couldn't resist returning to bed to watch the young woman sleep. She was on her side facing him, breathing softly, a diamond sparkling on her ear. Her cheeks were pink from the warmth of the room as their bed was bathed in sunshine from the floor-to-ceiling windows.

The bed covers were deliciously rumpled, smelling of sex and sandalwood. His blue eyes glimmered, traveling lazily over her exposed skin and long, dark hair. As he turned back to his newspaper, she shifted slightly and moaned. Concerned, he tossed the paper aside.

She brought her knees up to her chest, curling into a ball. Low murmurings came from her lips, and Gabriel leaned closer so he could decipher what she was saying. But he couldn't.

All of a sudden, her body twisted and she let out a heart-wrenching cry. Her arms flailed as she wrestled with the sheet that shrouded her.

"Julianne?" He placed a gentle hand on her bare shoulder, but she cringed away from him.

She began muttering his name, over and over again, her tone growing progressively more panicked.

"Julia, I'm here," he raised his voice. Just as he reached for her again, she sat bolt upright, gasping for air.

"Are you all right?" Gabriel moved closer, resisting the urge to touch her. She was breathing roughly, and under his watchful gaze, she fanned a shaking hand over her eyes.

"Julia?"

After a long, tense minute, she looked at him, eyes wide.

He frowned. "What happened?"

She swallowed loudly. "A nightmare."

"What was it about?"

"I was in the woods behind your parents' house, back in Selinsgrove."

Gabriel's eyebrows knit together behind his dark-rimmed glasses. "Why would you dream about that?"

She inhaled, drawing the sheet over her exposed breasts and up to her chin. The linen was full and white, swallowing her petite frame whole before billowing cloudlike over the mattress. She reminded him of an Athenian statue.

He ran his fingers gently over her skin. "Julianne, talk to me."

She squirmed under his piercing blue eyes, but he would not let her go. "The dream began beautifully. We made love under the stars, and I fell asleep in your arms. When I woke up you were gone."

"You dreamed I made love to you, then abandoned you?" His tone cooled to mask his discomfort.

"I woke up in the orchard without you once," she reproached him softly.

The fire in his belly was instantly quenched. He thought back to the magical evening six years ago when they first met, when they simply talked and held each other. He'd awoken the following morning and wandered away, leaving a sleeping teenage girl all alone. Surely her anxiety was understandable if not pitiable.

He unwound her clenched fingers one by one and kissed them repentantly. "I love you, Beatrice. I'm not going to leave you. You know that, right?"

"It would hurt so much more to lose you now."

With a frown he wrapped an arm around her shoulder, pressing her cheek to his chest. A myriad of memories crowded his mind as he thought back to what had transpired the evening before. He'd gazed on her naked form for the first time and initiated her into the intimacies of lovemaking. She'd shared her innocence with him, and he thought he'd made her happy. Certainly it had been one of the best evenings of his life. He pondered that fact for a moment.

"Do you regret last night?"

"No. I'm glad you were my first. It's what I wanted since we met."

He placed his hand on her cheek, tracing her skin with his thumb. "I'm honored to have been your first." He leaned forward, his eyes unblinking. "But I want to be your last."

She smiled and lifted her lips to meet his. Before he could embrace her, the chimes of Big Ben filled the room.

"Ignore it," he whispered fiercely, his arm stretching across her body, pushing her to recline beneath him.

Her eyes darted over his shoulder to where his iPhone lay on the desk. "I thought she wasn't going to call you anymore."

"I'm not answering, so it doesn't matter." He kneeled between her legs and lifted the sheet from her body. "In my bed, there's only us."

She searched his eyes as he began to bring their naked bodies into closer contact.

Gabriel leaned forward to kiss her, but she turned her head. "I haven't brushed my teeth."

"I don't care." He lowered his lips to her neck, kissing across her quickening pulse.

"I'd like to clean up first."

He huffed in frustration, leaning on one elbow. "Don't let Paulina ruin what we have."

"I'm not." She tried to roll out from under him and take the sheet with her, but he caught hold of it. He gazed over the rims of his glasses, his eyes sparkling with mischief.

"I need the sheet to make the bed."

Her eyes traveled from the white fabric that was clutched between her fingers, to his face. He looked like a panther waiting to pounce. She glanced over the side of the bed at the pile of clothes on the floor. They were beyond her reach.

"What's the problem?" he asked, stifling a grin.

Julia blushed and gripped the material more tightly. With a chuckle, he released the sheet and pulled her into his arms.

"You don't need to be shy. You're beautiful. If I had my wish, you'd never wear clothes again."

He pressed his lips to her earlobe, gently touching the diamond stud. He was certain his adoptive mother, Grace, would have been happy that her earrings found their way to Julia. With another brief kiss, he turned away, sliding over to sit on the edge of the bed.

She slipped into the washroom but not before Gabriel caught sight of her alluring back as she dropped the sheet just outside the door.

While brushing her teeth, she thought about what had transpired. Making love with Gabriel had been a very emotional experience, and even now her heart felt the aftershocks. That wasn't surprising considering their history. She'd wanted him since she spent a chaste night with him in an orchard when she was seventeen, but he'd been gone when she awoke the next morning. He'd forgotten her in the aftermath of a drunken, drug-induced haze. Six long years passed before she saw him again, and then, he didn't remember her.

When she encountered him again on the first day of his graduate seminar at the University of Toronto, he was attractive but cold, like a distant star. She hadn't believed then that she'd become his lover. She hadn't believed it possible that the temperamental and arrogant Professor would reciprocate her affection.

There were so many things she hadn't known. Sex was a kind of knowledge, and now she knew the sting of sexual jealousy in a manner she'd never experienced before. The mere idea of Gabriel doing what they'd done with some other woman, and in his case many other women, made her heart ache.

She knew that Gabriel's trysts were different from what they'd shared—that they were assignations not brought about by love or affection. But he'd undressed them, seen them naked, and entered their bodies. After being with him, how many of those women craved more? Paulina had. She and Gabriel had maintained contact over the years since they conceived and lost a child together.

Julia's new understanding of sex changed her view of his past and made her more sympathetic to Paulina's plight. And all the more guarded against losing Gabriel to her or to any other woman.

Julia gripped the edge of the vanity as a wave of insecurity washed over her. Gabriel loved her; she believed this. But he was also a gentleman and would never reveal that their union had left him wanting. And what of her own behavior? She'd asked questions and talked when she expected that most lovers would have been silent. She'd done very little to please him, and when she tried he'd stopped her.

Her ex-boyfriend's words came screaming back at her, swirling in her mind with condemnation:

You're frigid.

You're going to be a lousy lay.

She turned away from the mirror as she contemplated what might happen if Gabriel was dissatisfied with her. The specter of sexual betrayal reared its maleficent head, bringing with it visions of finding Simon in bed with her roommate.

She straightened her shoulders. If she could persuade Gabriel to be patient and to teach her, then she was confident she could please him. He loved her. He would give her a chance. She was his as surely as if he'd branded his name on her skin.

When she stepped into the bedroom she caught sight of him through the open door to the terrace. On her way, she was distracted by a beautiful vase of dark purple and paler, variegated irises sitting on top of the desk. Some lovers might have purchased long-stemmed red roses, but not Gabriel.

She opened the card that was nestled amongst the blossoms.

My Dearest Julianne,
Thank you for your immeasurable gift.
The only thing I have of value is my heart.
It's yours,
Gabriel.

Julia reread the card twice, her heart swelling with love and relief. Gabriel's words didn't sound like they were penned by a man who was dissatisfied or frustrated. Whatever Julia's worries, Gabriel didn't seem to share them.

Gabriel was sunning himself on the futon, his glasses off, his chest gloriously exposed. With his muscular, six-foot-two frame, it was as if Apollo himself had deigned to visit her. Sensing her presence on the terrace, he opened his eyes and patted his lap. She joined him, and his arms enveloped her as he kissed her passionately.

"Why, hello there," he murmured, brushing a stray tendril back from her face. He peered at her closely. "What's wrong?"

"Nothing. Thank you for the flowers. They're beautiful."

He brushed his lips against hers. "You're welcome. But you look troubled. Is it about Paulina?"

"I'm upset that she's calling you, but no." Julia's expression brightened. "Thank you for your card. It said what I desperately wanted to hear."

"I'm glad." He squeezed her more closely. "Tell me what's bothering you."

She toyed with the belt to her bathrobe for a moment, until he took her hand in his. She looked at him. "Was last night everything you'd hoped for?"

Gabriel exhaled sharply, for her question had taken him by surprise. "That's a strange question."

"I know it had to be different for you. I wasn't very . . . active."

"Active? What are you talking about?"

"I didn't do much to please you." She blushed.

He stroked the flushing skin lightly with the tip of his finger. "You pleased me a great deal. I know you were nervous, but I enjoyed myself tremendously. We belong to one another now—in every way. What else is troubling you?"

"I demanded that we switch positions when you would have preferred me on top."

"You didn't demand, you *asked*. Frankly, Julianne, I'd like to hear you demand things of me. I want to know that you want me as desperately as I want you." His expression relaxed, and he drew a circle or two around her breast. "You dreamed about your first time being a certain way. I wanted to give that to you, but I was worried. What if you were uncomfortable? What if I wasn't careful enough? Last night was a first for me too."

He released her, pouring coffee and steamed milk from two separate carafes into a latté bowl and spreading the tray of food between them on the banquette. There were pastries and fruit, toast and Nutella, boiled eggs and cheese, and several *Baci Perugina* Gabriel had bribed a hotel employee to run out and purchase along with the extravagant bouquet of irises from the *Giardino dell'Iris*.

Julia unwrapped one of the *Baci* and ate it, eyes closed with pure pleasure. "You ordered a feast."

"I awoke ravenous this morning. I would have waited for you but . . ." He shook his head as he picked up a grape and fixed her with a sparkling eye. "Open."

She opened her mouth, and he popped the grape inside, tracing his finger temptingly across her lower lip.

"And you must drink this, please." He handed her a wine glass filled with cranberry juice and soda.

She rolled her eyes. "You're overprotective."

He shook his head. "This is how a man behaves when he's in love and he wants his sweetheart healthy for all the sex he plans on having with her." He winked smugly.

"I'm not going to ask how you know about such things. Give me that." She grabbed the glass from his hand and downed it, her eyes focused on his, as he chuckled.

"You're adorable."

She stuck her tongue out at him before fixing herself a breakfast plate.

"How do you feel this morning?" Gabriel's face grew concerned.

She swallowed a piece of Fontina cheese. "Okay."

He pressed his lips together firmly, as if her answer displeased him.

"Making love changes things between a man and a woman," he prompted.

"Um, aren't you happy with, uh, what we did?" The pink of her cheeks faded immediately, leaving her pale.

"Of course I'm happy. I'm trying to find out if you're happy. And based upon what you've said so far, I'm worried that you aren't."

Julia picked at the fabric of her robe, avoiding Gabriel's probing gaze. "When I was at college the girls on my floor would sit around and talk about their boyfriends. One night they told stories about their first times." She nibbled at the tip of one of her fingers.

"Only a few of the girls had good things to say. The other stories were awful. One girl had been molested as a child. Some of the girls had been forced by a boyfriend or a date. Several of them said that their first times were completely awkward and unfulfilling—a boyfriend grunting and finishing quickly. I thought, if that's all I can hope for, I'd rather stay a virgin."

"That's horrible."

She fixed her eyes on the breakfast tray.

"I wanted to be loved. I decided it would be better to have a chaste affair of the heart and mind through letters than a sexual relationship. I had my doubts that I would ever find anyone who could give me both. Certainly, Simon didn't love me. Now I'm in a relationship with a sex god, and I can't give him anything like the pleasure he gives me."

Gabriel's eyebrows shot up. "Sex god? You've said that before, but believe me, I'm not—"

She interrupted him, looking him straight in the eye. "Teach me. I'm sure last night was not as, um . . . fulfilling as it usually is for you, but I promise that if you are patient with me, I will improve."

He cursed obliquely. "Come here." He pulled her around the breakfast tray and into his lap again, wrapping his arms around her. He was quiet for a moment, before sighing deeply.

"You assume that my previous sexual encounters were completely fulfilling, but you're wrong. You gave me what I've never had—love and sex together. You're the only one who has ever been my lover in the true sense."

He kissed her gently in solemn confirmation of his words. "The anticipation and the allure of a woman are crucial to the experience. I can safely say that your allurements and my anticipation were like nothing I've ever experienced before. Add to that the experience of making love for the first time . . . Words fail me."

She nodded but something about her movement disquieted him.

"I promise I'm not flattering you." He paused as if he were pondering his next words carefully. "At the risk of being *Neanderthal*, I should probably tell you that your innocence is tremendously erotic. The thought that I can be the one to teach you about sex . . . that someone so modest is also so passionate . . ." His voice trailed off as he looked at her intently. "You could become more skilled in the art of love by learning new tricks and new positions, but you can't become more attractive or more sexually fulfilling. Not to me."

Julia leaned over and kissed him. "Thank you for taking such good care of me last night," she whispered, her cheeks turning pink.

"As for Paulina, I'll deal with her. Please put her out of your mind."

Julia turned her attention back to her uneaten breakfast, resisting the urge to argue with him. "Will you tell me about your first time?"

"I'd rather not."

She busied herself with a pastry as she tried to think of a safer subject. The financial woes of Europe came readily to mind.

He rubbed at his eyes with both hands, covering them briefly. It would be far too easy to lie, he knew, but after all she'd given him, she deserved to know his secrets. "You remember Jamie Roberts."

"Of course."

Gabriel lowered his hands. "I lost my virginity to her."

Julia's eyebrows shot up. Jamie and her domineering mother had never been very pleasant to Julia, and she had always disliked them. She had no idea that Officer Roberts, who had investigated Simon's attack on her a month previous, had been Gabriel's first.

"It was not the greatest of experiences," he said quietly. "In fact, I would say it was scarring. I didn't love her. There was some attraction, of course, but no true affection. We went to Selinsgrove High School together. She sat next to me in History one year." He shrugged. "We flirted and messed around after school and eventually . . .

"Jamie was a virgin but lied and said she wasn't. I wasn't attentive to her at all. I was selfish and stupid." He cursed. "She said it didn't hurt much, but there was blood afterward. I felt like an animal and I've always regretted it." Gabriel cringed, and Julia felt the guilt radiating from him. His description made her almost ill, but it also explained a great deal.

"That's horrible. I'm so sorry." She squeezed his hand. "Is that why you were so worried last night?"

He nodded.

"She misled you."

"That's no excuse for my behavior, before or afterward." He cleared his throat. "She assumed we were in a relationship, but I wasn't interested. That made it worse, of course. I graduated from being merely an animal to being an animal *and* an asshole. When I saw her at Thanksgiving, I hadn't spoken to her in years. I asked her to forgive me. She was remarkably gracious.

"I've always felt guilty for treating her badly. I've stayed away from virgins ever since." He swallowed noisily. "Until last night.

"First times are supposed to be sweet, but seldom are. While you were worrying about pleasing me, I was worrying about pleasing you. Perhaps I was too careful, too protective, but I couldn't have borne it if I'd hurt you."

Julia put her breakfast aside and stroked his face. "You were very gentle and very generous. I've never known such joy, and that's because you loved me with more than just your body. Thank you."

As if to prove her point, he kissed her deeply. Julia hummed as his hands tangled through her hair, and she wrapped her arms about his neck. He slid his hands between them to the front of her robe, parting it hesitantly. He lifted his head, his eyes questioning.

She nodded.

He began whispering kisses against her neck and drew his mouth up to tug at her earlobe. "How do you feel?"

"Great," she whispered as his lips skimmed down to her throat.

He moved so he could see her face while one of his hands traveled to rest atop her lower abdomen. "Are you sore?"

"A little."

"Then we should wait."

"No!"

He laughed, his lips curling up into his signature seductive smile. "Did you mean what you said last night about making love out here?"

She shivered at the way his voice inflamed her but returned his smile, winding her fingers in his hair, tugging him closer. He opened her robe and began to explore her curves with both hands before dropping his mouth to kiss her breasts.

"You were shy with me this morning." He pressed a reverent kiss over her heart "What changed?"

Julia brushed against the hint of a dimple in his chin. "I will probably always be a little shy about being naked. But I want you. I want you to look into my eyes and tell me you love me as you move inside me. I will remember that as long as I live."

"I'll keep reminding you," he breathed.

He divested her of her robe and positioned her on her back. "Are you cold?"

"Not when you're holding me," she whispered, smiling. "Wouldn't you rather have me on top? I'd like to try it."

He threw off his robe and boxer shorts quickly and covered her body with his own, placing a hand on either side of her face. "Someone might see you out here, darling. And I can't have that. No one gets to see this beautiful body except me.

"Although the neighbors and passersby might be able to *hear* you . . . for the next hour or so . . ." He chuckled as she inhaled sharply, a tremor of pleasure coursing all the way down to her toes.

He kissed her, pushing her hair away from her face. "My goal is to see how many times I can please you before I can't hold back anymore."

She grinned. "I like the sound of that."

"So do I. So let me hear you."

The blue sky blushed to see such passionate lovemaking, while the Florentine sun smiled down, warming the lovers despite the gentle breeze. Beside them, Julia's coffee and milk grew stone cold and sullen at being ignored.

❁ ❁

After a brief nap, Julia borrowed Gabriel's MacBook to send an email to her father. She had two important messages in her inbox. The first was from Rachel.

> Jules!
> How are you? Is my brother behaving himself? Have you slept with him yet? Yes, it is COMPLETELY inappropriate for me to ask that question, but come on, if you were dating anyone else you would have told me already.
> I'm not going to volunteer any advice. I'm trying not to think too much about it. Just let me know you're happy and he's treating you properly.

Aaron sends his best.

Love you,

Rachel.

PS. Scott has a new girlfriend. He's been secretive about her so I'm not sure how long they've been dating. I keep bugging him to introduce me but he won't.

Maybe she's a professor.

Julia snickered, glad that Gabriel was showering and not reading over her shoulder. He'd be annoyed at his sister for posing such personal questions. She took a few moments to phrase her response before typing her reply.

Hi Rachel,

The hotel is beautiful. Gabriel has been very sweet and gave me your mother's diamond earrings. Did you know about that?

I feel guilty about it, so please let me know if this upsets you.

As to your other question, Yes. Gabriel treats me well, and I am VERY happy.

Say hi to Aaron for me. Looking forward to Christmas.

Love, Julia. XO

PS. I hope Scott's girlfriend is a professor. Gabriel will never let him hear the end of it.

Julia's second email was from Paul. It could be said that he pined for her, but also he was grateful to have maintained their friendship. He would rather keep his longings to himself than to lose her entirely. And he had to admit that since she'd begun seeing her boyfriend Owen, her very skin glowed.

(Not that he would have mentioned it.)

Hey Julia,

Sorry I didn't get the chance to say good-bye before you went home. I hope you have a good Christmas. I have a gift for you. Would you give me your address in Pennsylvania so I can send it?

I'm back at the farm trying to find time to work on my
dissertation in between large family gatherings and getting up
early to help my dad. Let's just say my daily routine involves a lot
of manure . . .
Can I bring you something from Vermont?
A Holstein of your very own?
Merry Christmas,
Paul.
P.S. Did you hear that Christa Peterson's dissertation
proposal was accepted by Emerson?
I guess Advent really is the season of miracles.

Julia stared at the computer screen, reading and re-reading Paul's
postscript. She wasn't sure what to make of it. It was possible, she
thought, that Gabriel accepted Christa's proposal because she threatened him.

Julia didn't want to bring up such an unpleasant topic during their
vacation, but the news troubled her. She typed a short reply to Paul, giving him her address, then she emailed her father, telling him that Gabriel was treating her like a princess. She closed the laptop and sighed.

"That doesn't sound like a happy Julianne." Gabriel's voice sounded
behind her.

"I think I'm going to ignore my email for the rest of our trip."

"Good idea."

She turned to find him standing in front of her, wet from the shower,
hair tousled, a white towel wound around his hips.

"You're beautiful," she blurted before thinking.

He chuckled and pulled her to her feet so he could embrace her.
"Do you have a thing for men in towels, Miss Mitchell?"

"Maybe for one particular man."

"Are you feeling all right?" He raised his eyebrows expectantly, his
expression hungry.

"I'm a little uncomfortable. But it was worth it."

His eyes narrowed. "You need to tell me if I'm hurting you, Julianne.
Don't hide things from me."

She rolled her eyes. "Gabriel, it doesn't hurt; it's merely uncomfortable. I didn't notice it *during* because there were other things on my mind—*several* other things. You were very distracting."

He smiled and kissed her neck loudly. "You need to let me start distracting you in the shower. I'm tired of showering alone."

"I'd like that. How are you feeling?"

He pretended to ponder her question. "Let's see—loud, hot sex with my beloved inside and *outside* . . . Yes, I'd say I'm great."

He hugged her close, and the cotton of her robe absorbed some of the water droplets from his skin. "I promise it won't always be uncomfortable. In time, your body will recognize me."

"It already recognizes you. And misses you," she whispered.

Gabriel moved the top of her robe aside so he could kiss the slope of her shoulder. With a gentle squeeze, he walked to the bed, retrieving a bottle of ibuprofen and handing it to her.

"I have to run over to the Uffizi for a meeting, then I have to pick up my new suit at the tailor's." He appeared concerned. "Would you mind shopping for a dress by yourself? I'd go with you, but my meeting won't leave me with much time."

"Not at all."

"If you can be ready in half an hour, we can walk out together."

Julia followed Gabriel into the bathroom, all thoughts of Christa and Paul forgotten.

After her shower, she stood in front of one of the vanities, drying her hair while Gabriel stood at the other. She found herself glancing over at him, watching as he carried out his shaving preparations with military precision. Finally, she gave up putting on lipstick and simply leaned against the sink, staring.

He was still naked to the waist, the towel now low on his hips, as he painstakingly shaved in the classical style. His brilliant blue eyes narrowed in concentration behind his black glasses, his damp hair impeccably combed.

Julia suppressed a laugh at the degree to which his quest for perfection was manifested. Gabriel used a shaving brush with a black wooden handle to mix European shaving soap into a thick lather. After spreading the foam on his face with the brush, he shaved using an antiquated safety razor.

(For some professors, disposable razors simply aren't good enough.)

"What?" He turned, noticing that she was perilously close to ogling him.

"I love you."

His expression softened. "I love you too, darling."

"You're the only non-British person I've ever heard use the term *darling*."

"That isn't true."

"It isn't?"

"Richard used to call Grace that." Gabriel gave her a sad look.

"Richard is old-fashioned, in the best sense." She smiled. "I love the fact that you're old-fashioned too."

Gabriel snorted and continued shaving. "I'm not so old-fashioned, or I wouldn't be making mad passionate love with you outside. And fantasizing about introducing you to some of my favorite positions from the *Kama Sutra*." He winked at her. "But I *am* a pretentious old bastard and a devil to live with. You'll have to tame me."

"And how shall I do that, Professor Emerson?"

"Never leave." His voice dropped, and he turned to face her.

"I'm more worried about losing you."

He leaned over and kissed her forehead. "Then you have nothing to worry about."

Chapter Two

Julia stepped out of the bedroom, feeling nervous. Gabriel had made arrangements for her to shop on his account at the local Prada boutique, and she'd chosen a Santorini-blue V-necked, sleeveless dress made of silk taffeta. Its A-line shape boasted a full pleated skirt and was reminiscent of the kind of dress worn by Grace Kelly in the 1950s. It suited Julia perfectly.

However, the boutique manager had wanted the accessories to modernize the dress, and thus she chose a sleek silver leather clutch and a pair of tangerine patent leather stilettos that Julia found perilously high. To complete the ensemble, a black cashmere wrap was provided.

She stood hesitantly in the sitting room, her hair long and loosely curled, her eyes bright and shining. She wore Grace's diamond earrings and her string of pearls.

Gabriel had been seated on the sofa in the living room, making last minute changes to his lecture notes. When he saw her he took off his glasses and stood.

"You're stunning." He kissed her cheek and twirled her so he could admire her dress. "Do you like it?"

"I love it. Thank you, Gabriel. I know it cost a fortune."

His gaze drifted down to her shoes.

She blinked. "Is something wrong?"

He cleared his throat as his attention remained riveted to her feet.

"Um . . . your shoes . . . they're—ah—"

"*Nice*. Aren't they?" She giggled.

"They're a good deal more than nice." His voice grew thick.

"Well, Professor Emerson, if I like your lecture, perhaps I'll continue wearing them after . . ."

Gabriel straightened his tie a little and gave her a cocky grin. "Oh, I'll see that you like my lecture, Miss Mitchell. Even if I have to deliver it to you personally, between the sheets. And it isn't my bedroom, it's *our* bedroom."

She blushed, and he pulled her into his arms.

"We should go," he said, pressing a kiss to her hair.

"Wait. I have a present for you." She disappeared and returned with a small box that had *Prada* emblazoned across the top.

He seemed surprised. "You didn't have to do that."

"I wanted to."

Gabriel smiled and carefully lifted the lid. He pulled back the tissue paper to find a lightly patterned Santorini-blue silk tie.

"I like it. Thank you." He kissed her cheek.

"It matches my dress."

"Now everyone will know that we belong to each other." He immediately removed his green tie, tossing it onto the coffee table, and began tying Julia's gift around his neck.

Gabriel's new suit had been custom made by his favorite local tailor. It was black and single-breasted with side vents. Julia admired the suit a great deal, but even more so, she admired the attractive figure in it.

There is nothing sexier than watching a man put on a tie, she thought.

"May I?" she offered, as Gabriel struggled in the absence of a mirror.

He nodded and bent forward, placing his hands around her waist. She adjusted his tie and fixed his collar, running her hands down his sleeves until they rested on the cufflinks at his wrists.

He gazed at her curiously. "You straightened my tie when I took you to Antonio's. We were sitting in the car."

"I remember."

"There's nothing sexier than having the woman you love fix your tie." He took her hands in his. "We've come a long way since that first night."

She reached up to kiss him, taking care not to sully his masculine mouth with her lipstick.

He brought his lips to her ear. "I don't know how I'm going to keep the Florentine men at bay this evening. You'll have to stay very close to me."

Julia squealed as he put his arms around her, lifting her so he could kiss her properly, which required Julia to reapply her lipstick and both of them to check their appearance in the mirror before they left their room.

Gabriel held her hand during the short walk to the Uffizi and even after they were whisked to the second floor by a rather pudgy gentleman wearing a paisley bow tie who introduced himself as Lorenzo, *Dottore* Vitali's personal assistant.

"*Professore*, I'm afraid we have need of you." Lorenzo glanced between Gabriel and Julia, his eyes darting to their conjoined hands.

Gabriel tightened his grip.

"It's for the—how you say—on the screen? PowerPoint?" Lorenzo gestured to the room behind them where guests were already congregating.

"Miss Mitchell has a reserved seat," said Gabriel pointedly, irritated that Lorenzo was ignoring her.

"Yes, *Professore*. I shall accompany your *fidanzata* personally." Lorenzo nodded respectfully in Julia's direction.

She opened her mouth to correct his characterization, but Gabriel pressed a kiss to the back of her hand, murmuring a promise against her skin. Then he was gone, and Julia was escorted to her place of honor in the front row.

She took in her surroundings, noting the presence of what looked like members of Florence's *glitterati* mingling with academics and local dignitaries. She smoothed the skirt of her dress, enjoying the whispering sound of the taffeta beneath her fingers. Given the appearance of the other guests, along with the presence of a bevy of photographers, she was glad that she was well-dressed. She didn't want to embarrass Gabriel on this most important occasion.

The lecture was being delivered in the Botticelli room, which was devoted to the finest of his works. In fact, the lectern was situated in between the *Birth of Venus* and the *Madonna of the Pomegranate*, while *Primavera* hung to the audience's right. The artwork on the wall to the audience's left had been removed, and a large screen had been hung, on which Gabriel's PowerPoint slides would be projected.

She knew how unusual it was to have a lecture in such a special space and silently said a prayer of thanks for this incredible blessing. When she'd spent her junior year in Florence she'd visited the Botticelli room at least once a week and sometimes more often. She found his art both soothing and inspiring. As a shy American undergraduate, she never would have imagined that, two years later, she would be accompanying a world-renowned Dante specialist as he lectured in that very room. She felt as if she'd won the lottery a thousand times over.

More than one hundred people crowded into the room, some even spilling into the standing area at the back. Julia watched Gabriel as he was introduced to various important looking guests. He was a very attractive man, tall and ruggedly handsome. She especially admired his glasses and the way his sleek, dark suit fit perfectly.

When he was blocked from her view by other people, she focused her attention on picking out his voice. He chatted amiably, switching seamlessly from Italian to French to German and back to Italian again.

(Even his German was sexy.)

She grew warm as she remembered what Gabriel looked like under his suit, his form naked and strained above her. She wondered if he was having similar thoughts whenever he looked at her, and in the midst of her private musings, he made eye contact and winked. His momentary display of playfulness put her in mind of their interlude on the terrace that morning, and a pleasant tremor traveled up and down her spine.

Gabriel sat politely through *Dottore* Vitali's introduction, which took no less than fifteen minutes as he painstakingly rehearsed the professor's accomplishments. To the casual observer, Gabriel appeared relaxed, almost bored. His nervousness was telegraphed by the way he unconsciously shuffled his lecture notes, notes that were merely an outline to the remarks that would come from his heart. He'd made a few last minute changes to his lecture. He couldn't speak of muses, love, and beauty without acknowledging the brown-eyed angel who'd bravely given herself to him the evening before. She was his inspiration, and she'd been so since she was seventeen. Her quiet beauty and generous goodness had touched his heart. He'd carried her image with him as a talisman against the dark demons of addiction. She was everything to him, and by God, he'd say so publicly.

After much flattery and applause, he took his place behind the po-dium and addressed the crowd in fluid Italian. "My lecture this evening will be somewhat unusual. I am not an art historian, yet I will be speak-ing to you about Sandro Botticelli's muse, *La Bella Simonetta*." At this, his eyes sought Julia's.

She smiled, trying to suppress the blush that threatened her cheeks. She knew the story of Botticelli and Simonetta Vespucci. Simonetta was referred to as the *Queen of Beauty* in the court of Florence, prior to her death at the tender age of twenty-two. To be compared to Simonetta by Gabriel was very high praise, indeed.

"I am tackling this controversial topic as a professor of literature, choosing Botticelli's artwork as a representation of various female ar-chetypes. Historically speaking, there have been many debates as to how close Simonetta was to Botticelli and to what degree she was the actual inspiration for his paintings. I hope to skirt some of those dis-agreements in order to focus your attention on a straightforward visual comparison of a few figures.

"I shall begin with the first three slides. In them, you will recognize pen and ink illustrations of Dante and Beatrice in Paradise."

Gabriel couldn't help but admire the images himself, transported as he was to the first time he'd welcomed Julianne into his home. That was the night he'd realized how much he wanted to please her, how beauti-ful she looked when she was happy.

As he gazed at the quiescence of Beatrice's expression, he compared her countenance with Julia's. She sat with rapt attention, her lovely head turned in profile as she admired Botticelli's handiwork. Gabriel wanted to make her look at him.

"Notice Beatrice's face." His voice grew soft as his eyes met those of his sweetheart. "The most beautiful face . . .

"We begin with Dante's muse and the figure of Beatrice. Although I'm sure she needs no introduction, allow me to point out that Beatrice represents courtly love, poetic inspiration, faith, hope, and charity. She is the ideal of feminine perfection, at once intelligent and compassion-ate, and vibrant with the kind of selfless love that can only come from God. She inspires Dante to be a better man."

Gabriel paused a moment to touch his tie. It did not need straightening, but his fingers lingered against the blue silk. Julia blinked at the gesture, and Gabriel knew that he'd been understood.

"Now consider the face of the goddess Venus."

All eyes in the room except Gabriel's focused on the *Birth of Venus*. He looked over his notes eagerly as the audience admired one of Botticelli's greatest and largest works.

"It appears that Venus has Beatrice's face. Once again, I'm not interested in a historical analysis of the models for the painting. I'm simply asking you to note the visible similarities between the figures. They represent two muses, two ideal types, one theological and one secular. Beatrice is the lover of the soul; Venus is the lover of the body. Botticelli's *La Bella* has both faces—one of sacrificial love or *agape*, and one of sexual love or *eros*."

His voice deepened, and Julia found her skin warming at the sound.

"In the portrait of Venus, the emphasis is on her physical beauty. Even though she represents sexual love, she maintains a venerable modesty, clutching part of her hair in order to cover herself. Notice the demure expression and the placement of her hand across her breast. Her shyness increases the eroticism of her portrayal—it doesn't diminish it." He removed his glasses for dramatic effect and fixed Julia with an unblinking eye. "Many people fail to see how modesty and sweetness of temper compound erotic appeal."

Julia fidgeted with the zipper on her purse, resisting the urge to squirm in her seat. Gabriel replaced his glasses.

"*Eros* is not lust. According to Dante, lust is one of the seven deadly sins. Erotic love can include sex but is not limited to it. *Eros* is the all-consuming fire of infatuation and affection that is expressed in the emotion of *being in love*. And believe me when I say that it far outstrips the rivals for its affections, in every respect."

Julia couldn't help but notice the dismissive way with which he'd pronounced the word *rivals*, punctuating his expression with a wave of his hand. It was as if he were casting aside all previous lovers with a mere gesture, while his blazing blue eyes fixed on her.

"Anyone who has ever been in love knows the difference between *eros* and lust. There's no comparison. One is an empty, unfulfilling shadow of the other.

"Of course, one might object that it is impossible for one person, one woman, to represent the ideal of both *agape* and *eros*. If you will allow my indulgence for a moment, I will suggest that such skepticism is a form of misogyny. For only a misogynist would argue that women are either saints or seductresses—virgins or whores. Of course, a woman, or a man for that matter, can be both—the muse can be lover to *both* soul and body.

"Now consider the painting behind me, *Madonna of the Pomegranate*."

Again, the eyes of the audience shifted to one of Botticelli's paintings. Gabriel noticed with satisfaction the way Julia intentionally fingered one of her diamond earrings, as if she understood his revelations and received them gladly. As if she knew he was revealing his love for her through art. His heart swelled.

"Once again, we see the same face repeated in the figure of the Madonna. Beatrice, Venus, and Mary—a trinity of ideal women, each wearing the same face. *Agape, eros,* and chastity, a heady combination that would make even the strongest man fall to his knees, if he was fortunate enough to find one person who manifests all three."

A cough that sounded suspiciously as if it were covering a derisive remark echoed throughout the room. Angry at being interrupted, Gabriel scowled in the general direction of the second row, over Julia's shoulder. The cough was repeated once more for dramatic effect and a testosterone fueled staring contest began between a clearly annoyed Italian and Gabriel.

Conscious of the fact that he was speaking into a microphone, Gabriel resisted the urge to curse and, with a scathing look at his detractor, continued.

"Some have argued that it was a pomegranate and not an apple that tempted Eve in the Garden of Eden. With respect to Botticelli's painting, many have argued that the pomegranate symbolizes the blood of Christ in his suffering and his subsequent new life through the resurrection.

"For my purposes, the pomegranate represents the Edenic fruit, the Madonna as the second Eve and Christ as the second Adam. With the Madonna, Botticelli hearkens back to the first Eve, the archetype of femininity, beauty, and female companionship.

"I'll go further, by asserting that Eve is also the ideal of female friendship, the *friend* of Adam, and thus she is the ideal of *philia*, the love that emerges out of friendship. The friendship between Mary and Joseph manifests this ideal, as well."

His voice caught, so he took a moment to sip some water before continuing. Something about the comparison between Julia and Eve made him feel vulnerable, naked, hearkening back to the night he'd given her an apple and held her in his arms under the stars.

The audience began murmuring, wondering why a polite pause to take a drink had extended into a break. Gabriel's color deepened as he raised his eyes to look at his beloved once again, desperate for her understanding.

Her ruby lips parted into an encouraging smile. Instantly, Gabriel exhaled.

"Botticelli's muse is a saint, a lover, and a friend, not a cardboard cutout of a woman or an adolescent fantasy. She is real, she is complicated, and she is endlessly fascinating. A woman to worship.

"As I'm sure you're aware, the preciseness of the Greek language allows one to speak more perspicuously about the different kinds of love. A modern treatment of this discussion can be found in C.S. Lewis's *The Four Loves*, if you're interested."

He cleared his throat and smiled winningly at the room.

"Finally, consider the painting to my left, *Primavera*. One might expect to see the face of Botticelli's muse reflected in the central figure in the painting. But consider the face of Flora, on the right. Once again, she bears a similarity to Beatrice, Venus, and the Madonna.

"Surprisingly, Flora appears twice in the painting. As we move from the center of the painting to the right, you see Flora pregnant, swollen with Zephyr's child. Zephyr is on the far right, hovering amongst the orange trees with the second depiction of Flora, as a virgin nymph. Her expression is marked with fear. She's fleeing the arms of her prospective lover and gazing back at him in panic. However, when she's pregnant, her countenance is serene. Her fear is replaced by contentment."

Julia flushed as she remembered how kind Gabriel had been to her the night before. He'd been tender and gentle, and in his arms she'd felt worshipped. Remembering the myth of Flora and Zephyr she shuddered, wishing that all lovers would be as tender with their virgin partners as Gabriel had been.

"Flora represents the consummation of physical love and motherhood. She is the ideal of *storge,* or familial love, the kind of love manifested from a mother to her child, and between lovers who share a commitment that is not based solely on sex or pleasure, but is between married partners."

No one but Julia noticed the white knuckling as he held the edge of the podium with two hands. No one but Julia noticed the slight tremor in his voice as he pronounced the words *pregnant* and *motherhood.*

His eyebrows furrowed as he collected himself, shuffling his papers for a moment. Julia recognized his vulnerability for what it was, fighting the urge to go to him and embrace him. She began tapping one of her tangerine colored stiletto heels in anticipation.

Gabriel caught her sudden movement and swallowed hard before continuing. "In early writings on *Primavera*, Flora was asserted to be the likeness of *La Bella Simonetta,* Botticelli's muse. If that is true, just on visual inspection alone, we can assert that *Simonetta* is the inspiration for Beatrice, Venus, and the Madonna, for all four ladies share the same face.

"Thus, we have the icons of *agape, eros, philia,* and *storge* all represented by a single face, a single woman—*Simonetta.* To put this another way, one could argue that Botticelli sees in his beloved muse all four types of love and all four ideals of womanhood: saint, lover, friend, and spouse.

"In the end, however, I must return to where we began, with Beatrice. It is no accident that the inspiration behind one of Italy's best-known literary works was given Simonetta's features. Faced with such beauty, such goodness, what man wouldn't want her by his side not just for a season, but for a lifetime?"

He gazed around the room gravely.

"To quote the Poet, *now your blessedness appears.* Thank you."

As Gabriel ended his lecture to enthusiastic applause, Julia blinked back tears, overcome with emotion.

Dottore Vitali retook the podium, extending his thanks to Professor Emerson for an illuminating discussion. A small group of local politicians presented him with several gifts, including a medallion depicting the city of Florence.

Julia remained in her seat for as long as possible, hoping that Gabriel would come to her. But he was deluged with members of the audience, including several officious art historians.

(For it was considered brash if not egotistical for a mere literature professor to analyze the crown jewels of the Uffizi's collection.)

Reluctantly, she trailed behind him as several members of the media plied him with questions. She caught his eye, and he gave her a tight, apologetic smile before posing for pictures.

Frustrated, she wandered around some of the adjoining rooms, admiring the paintings until she arrived at one of her favorites, Leonardo da Vinci's *Annunciation*. She was standing close, too close really, noting the detail in the marble pillar, when a voice sounded in her ear in Italian.

"You like this painting?"

Julia looked up into the eyes of a man with black hair and very tanned skin. He was taller than her, but not overly, and was of a muscular build. He wore a very expensive black suit, with a single red rose pinned to his lapel. She recognized him as one of the guests who sat behind her during the lecture.

"Yes, very much," she responded in Italian.

"I have always admired the depth that da Vinci gives to his paintings, particularly the shading and detail on the pillar."

She smiled and turned back to the painting. "That's exactly what I was studying, along with the feathers on the angel's wings. They're incredible."

The gentleman bowed. "Please allow me to introduce myself. I am Giuseppe Pacciani."

Julia hesitated, for she recognized his last name. He shared it with the man suspected of being Florence's most famous serial killer.

The man appeared to be waiting for her to respond to his greeting, so she suppressed the urge to run.

"Julia Mitchell." She extended her hand in a polite gesture, but he took her by surprise when he grasped it between both of his hands and drew it to his lips, looking up at her as he kissed it.

"Enchanted. And may I say that your beauty rivals that of *La Bella Simonetta*. Especially in light of this evening's lecture."

Julia averted her eyes and swiftly removed her hand.

"Allow me to provide you with a drink." He quickly flagged down a waiter and took two champagne flutes from his tray. He clinked their glasses together and toasted their health.

Julia sipped the Ferrari *spumante* gratefully, as it gave her a distraction from his intense stare. He was charming, but she was wary of him, not least because of his name.

He smiled at her hungrily.

"I am a professor of literature at the university. And you?"

"I study Dante."

"Ah, *il Poeta*. My specialization is Dante, also. Where do you study? Not here." His eyes wandered from her face to her body to her shoes, before traveling to her face again.

She took a generous step back. "At the University of Toronto."

"Ah! A Canadian. One of my former students is studying there right now. Perhaps you are acquainted." He stepped closer.

Julia elected not to correct him about her citizenship and stepped back once again. "Toronto is a large university. Probably not."

Giuseppe smiled, showing very straight white teeth that glinted strangely in the museum light.

"Have you seen Piero di Cosimo's *Perseus Frees Andromeda?*" He gestured to one of the adjacent paintings.

Julia nodded. "Yes."

"There are Flemish elements in his work, do you see? Also, notice the figures standing in the crowd." He gestured to a grouping on the right side of the painting.

Julia stepped to one side so she could take a better look. Giuseppe stood beside her, a good deal too close, watching her study the painting.

"Do you like it?"

"Yes, but I prefer Botticelli." Stubbornly, she kept her eyes on the painting, hoping he would tire of standing closer to her and move away.

(Preferably across the Arno.)

"Are you a student of Professor Emerson's?"

Julia swallowed noisily. "No. I—I study with someone else."

"He is considered to be good by North American standards, which is why he was invited here. However, his lecture was an embarrassment. How did you come to discover Dante?"

Julia was about to argue with Giuseppe about his characterization of the lecture, when he reached out to touch her hair.

She flinched and immediately retreated, but his arms were long and his hand followed her. She opened her mouth to reprove him when someone growled nearby.

Giuseppe and Julia turned their heads slowly to see Gabriel, sapphire eyes flashing, hands on hips, flaring out his open suit jacket like the plumes of an angry peacock.

He took a menacing step closer.

"I see you've met my *fidanzata*. I suggest you keep your hands to yourself, unless you're prepared to lose them."

Giuseppe scowled before his face smoothed out into a polite smile. "We've been speaking for several minutes. She never mentioned you."

Julia didn't wait for Gabriel to rip Giuseppe's arms from his sockets, thus sullying the Uffizi's pristine floors with his blood. Instead, she stood between the two men and placed a hand on Gabriel's chest.

"Gabriel, this is Professor Pacciani. He's also a Dante specialist."

A look passed between the two men, and Julia realized that Pacciani was the man who'd rudely interrupted Gabriel's lecture by muttering and coughing.

He lifted his hands in mock surrender.

"A thousand apologies. I should have realized from the way you looked at her during your . . . speech that she was yours. Forgive me, *Simonetta*." His eyes moved to hers and rested there, his mouth parting in a sneer.

At the sound of his sarcasm, Gabriel took a step closer, his fists clenched.

"Darling, I need to find somewhere to put my glass." Julia shook her empty champagne flute, hoping it would distract him.

Gabriel took the glass and handed it to Pacciani. "I'm sure you know where to put this."

He grabbed Julia's hand and quickly pulled her away. The guests parted like the Red Sea in front of them as they made their way through the Botticelli room.

Julia saw person after person stare at them and she blushed even more deeply.

"Where are we going?"

He led her into the adjoining tiled corridor and began walking toward the end of it, far beyond earshot of the other guests. Pushing her into a dark corner, he positioned her between two large marble statues perched high atop plinths. She was dwarfed by the towering forms.

He grabbed her purse and tossed it aside. The sound of the leather hitting the floor echoed down the corridor.

"What were you doing with him?" Gabriel's eyes flamed, and his cheeks were slightly red, which for him was a rare occurrence.

"We were just making small talk before he—"

Gabriel pulled her into a searing kiss, one hand tangling in her hair and the other sliding down her dress. The force of the contact propelled her until she felt the cold wall of the Gallery against the naked skin of her upper back. His hard body aligned with hers forcefully.

"I don't want to see another man's hands on you again."

He parted her mouth roughly, penetrating with his tongue, while his hand slid over the curve of her backside, massaging the flesh with his fingers.

Julia realized instantly that he'd been careful with her every other time he'd touched her. He wasn't careful now. Part of her was inflamed, desperate for him. Another part of her was wondering what he would do if she said *stop* . . .

He lifted her left leg, pulling her thigh around his hip and pressing against her.

She felt him through the fabric of her dress, hearing the silk taffeta rustle like a breathless woman. The dress clearly wanted more.

"What do I have to do to make you mine?" he groaned, mouth against mouth.

"I *am* yours."

"Not tonight, it seems." He tugged her lower lip backwards into his mouth, nipping it with his teeth. "Didn't you understand my lecture? Every word, every painting was for you." His hand slid up her dress, teasing the skin of her thigh until it reached the string that stretched across her hip.

He pulled back to see her face. "No garters tonight?"

She shook her head.

"Then what's this?" His fingers tugged at the very thin string.

"Panties," she breathed.

His eyes glinted in the semi-darkness. *"What kind of panties?"*

"A thong."

He smiled dangerously before pressing his lips to her ear. "Am I to assume that you wore this for me?"

"Only for you. Always."

Without warning, Gabriel lifted her, pressing her against the cold wall. His lips on her neck, he pushed their hips closer. The long, thin heels of Julia's tangerine stilettos caught the curves of his ass. He fixed her with wild, blue eyes.

"I want you. Right now."

With one hand, he tugged at the string until it tore. Suddenly, she found herself bare. He reached back to stuff the thong in his jacket pocket, and her heels shifted, digging into his ass so much that he winced.

"Do you know how difficult it was for me to control myself after the lecture? How I longed to take you in my arms? Conducting small talk was torture when all I wanted was this.

"I wish you could see how sexy you are with your back against the wall and your legs wrapped around me. I want you like this, except I want you panting my name."

Gabriel dipped his tongue in the hollow at the base of her throat and Julia's eyes closed. Her passions were struggling with her mind, which urged her to push him away and take a moment to think. In a mood such as this, Gabriel was dangerous.

All of a sudden, Julia heard voices echoing down the hallway. Her eyes flew open.

The sound of footsteps and merry laughter grew closer. Gabriel lifted his head, bringing his mouth to her ear. *"Don't make a sound,"* he whispered. She could feel his lips curve up into a smile as they pressed against her.

The footsteps stopped a few feet away, and Julia heard two male voices conversing in Italian. Her heart continued to race as she strained her hearing for any sign of movement. Gabriel kept stroking her gently, swallowing her sounds with his mouth. From time to time, he'd whisper sensual things to her—phrases that made her flush.

One of the male voices laughed loudly. Julia lifted her head in surprise, while Gabriel took that opportunity to kiss her throat, nibbling at the delicate skin.

"Please don't bite me."

The murmuring voices echoed around them. It took a moment, but eventually the import of her words sliced through his aroused, frantic state. He lifted his face from her neck.

With their chests pressed so tightly together, he could feel her heart. He closed his eyes, as if entranced by its staccato rhythm. When he opened them again, most of the fire was gone.

Julia had carefully concealed Simon's bite mark with makeup, but Gabriel found it with his finger, tracing its perimeter lightly before kissing it. He exhaled slowly, very slowly, and shook his head.

"You're the only woman who has ever said no to me."

"I'm not saying no."

He looked over his shoulder and spied two older gentlemen, deep in conversation. They were close enough to see him if they looked in his direction.

He turned back to Julia and gave her a sad smile. "You deserve better than a jealous lover taking you against a wall. And I'm not in favor of being caught by our host. Forgive me."

He kissed her and traced below her swollen lower lip with his thumb, removing the slight smear of crimson lipstick from her pale skin.

"I'm not about to undo the trust I saw in your eyes last night. When I'm in my right mind and we have the museum all to ourselves . . ." His expression darkened as he fantasized. "Another time, perhaps."

He removed her heels from his backside and placed her on her feet, leaning over to straighten the skirt of her dress. The taffeta rustled breathlessly at his touch and then forlornly, was silent.

Fortunately, *Dottore* Vitali and his companion chose that moment to return to the party, their footsteps growing fainter and fainter as they walked away.

"The banquet is supposed to begin shortly. I can't insult them by leaving. But when I get you home . . ." His eyes fixed on hers. "The wall just inside our room will be our first stop."

She nodded, relieved that he wasn't angry anymore. Truthfully, she was somewhat nervous but very excited about the prospect of *wall sex*.

He adjusted himself through his trousers and buttoned up his suit jacket, willing his body to calm. He tried to smooth his hair but only succeeded in making it look more like he had dragged his lover into a dark corner for museum sex.

Museum sex is a peculiar compunction of certain academics. (But it should not be disdained without trying it.)

Julia fixed his hair and straightened his tie, checking his face and collar for lipstick. When she was finished, he picked up her clutch and her sweater, handing them to her with a kiss. Smirking, he adjusted her panties in his suit pocket so they were no longer visible.

She took an experimental step forward, finding the absence of her panties surprisingly liberating.

"I could drink you like champagne," he whispered.

She reached up on tiptoe to kiss his cheek. "I wish you'd teach me your tricks of seduction."

"Only if you will teach me how to love as you love."

Gabriel escorted her through the empty corridor and down the stairs to the first floor, where the banquet was just beginning.

❦ ❦

Professor Pacciani stumbled back to his apartment by the Pitti Palace in the wee hours of the morning. This was not an unusual occurrence.

He fumbled with his keys, cursing as he dropped them, and entered the flat, closing the door behind him. He walked to the small room in which his twin four-year-old sons were asleep, kissing them before shuffling to his study.

He smoked a leisurely cigarette as he waited for his computer to boot up, then he logged into his email. He ignored his inbox and composed a short message to a former student and lover. They had not been in contact since her graduation.

He mentioned meeting Professor Emerson and his very young Canadian *fidanzata*. He mused that although he'd been impressed with Emerson's monograph with Oxford University Press, the Professor's lecture smacked of a pseudo-intellectualism that truly had no place in a professional academic lecture. One should either be intellectual and academic, or one should be a public speaker and entertaining, but not both. Pacciani queried churlishly if this was what passed for excellence in North American universities.

He ended his email with an explicit and detailed suggestion of a prospective sexual rendezvous, possibly in the late spring. Then he finished his cigarette in the darkness and joined his wife in their matrimonial bed.

Chapter Three

Christa Peterson had a privileged upbringing, so really, there was no excuse for her vicious nature. She had two parents who loved each other and their only daughter very much. Her father was a well-respected oncologist in Toronto. Her mother was a librarian at Havergal College, an elite, private girl's school that Christa attended from kindergarten through grade twelve.

Christa went to Sunday school. She was confirmed as an Anglican. She studied Thomas Cranmer's *Book of Common Prayer*, but none of these actions touched her heart. And when she was fifteen years old she discovered the immense power of female sexuality. Once she discovered it, it became not only her currency but her weapon of choice.

Her best friend, Lisa Malcolm, had an older brother called Brent. Brent was handsome. He looked like so many other graduates of Upper Canada College, a private boy's school that catered to Canada's old moneyed families. He had blond hair and blue eyes and was tall and fit. He was a rower for the University of Toronto's men's team and could easily have starred in a J.Crew commercial.

Christa had admired Brent from afar but because of the four-year age difference, he'd never noticed her. But then, late one night while sleeping over at Lisa's house, Christa ran into Brent on her way to the bathroom. He'd been extremely taken by her long dark hair, big brown eyes, and youthful, nubile form. He'd kissed her gently in the hallway and brushed tentative fingers across her breast. Then he'd taken her hand and invited her to his room.

After thirty minutes of making out and feeling one another through their clothes, he was eager to take things further. Christa hesitated, because she was a virgin, so Brent began making wild and extravagant promises—gifts, romantic dates, and finally, a Baume & Mercier stainless steel watch that had been a present from his parents on his eighteenth birthday.

Christa had admired his watch. She knew it well, for Brent treasured it. In truth, she wanted it almost more than she wanted him.

Brent fastened the watch on her wrist, and she stared at it, marveling at the coolness of the steel against her flesh and the way it slid easily up and down her narrow forearm. It was a token. A sign that he desired her so intensely, he was willing to give her one of his most prized possessions.

It made her feel wanted. And powerful.

"You're so beautiful," he whispered. "I won't hurt you. But God, I want you. And I promise I'll make you feel good."

Christa smiled and let him place her on his narrow bed like an Incan sacrifice on an altar and gave her virginity up to him in exchange for a three-thousand-dollar watch.

Brent kept his word. He was gentle. He went slowly. He kissed her and softly explored her mouth. He paid homage to her breasts. He prepared her with his fingers and tested her to ensure that she was ready for him. When he entered her, he did so carefully. There was no blood. Just large hands rubbing circles on her hips and a low voice that murmured instructions on how to relax, until her discomfort disappeared.

As promised, he made her feel good. He made her feel beautiful and special. And when it was over he held her closely all night. For he was not an entirely vicious soul, driven as he was by carnal needs.

They would repeat this act many times over the next three years, despite other romantic entanglements. Before Brent entered her, he would always place a gift in her hand.

He was soon followed by Mr. Woolworth, Christa's grade-eleven Math teacher. Christa's encounters with Brent taught her much about men, how to read their wants and desires, how to tantalize and provoke, and how to string along and tease.

She teased Mr. Woolworth unmercifully until the man cracked and begged her to meet him at a hotel after school. Christa liked it when men begged. In the plain hotel room, her teacher surprised her with a silver necklace from Tiffany. He placed the delicate links around her neck and kissed her flesh softly. In exchange, Christa let him explore her body for hours until he fell asleep, exhausted and sated.

He was not as attractive as Brent, but he was far more experienced. For every subsequent gift, she would allow him to touch her in old and new ways. By the time their affair ended and Christa moved to Quebec to attend Bishop's University, she'd amassed an enormous amount of jewelry and an extensive knowledge of sexual relations. Moreover, Christa had become one of few women who viewed the role of the man-eating seductress as something to emulate.

When Christa completed her master's degree in Renaissance Studies at the *Università degli Studi di Firenze,* her pattern of relationships was fixed. She preferred older men, men in positions of power. She was excited by forbidden affairs—the more remote, the more improbable, the better.

She tried for two years to seduce a priest who was assigned to the *Duomo* in Florence, and right before graduation, she succeeded. He took her in the single bed of his tiny apartment, but before he touched her, he wrapped her long, warm fingers around a tiny icon that had been painted by Giotto. It was priceless. But so, she reasoned, was she. Christa would allow men to have her, but only at a price. And she'd always bedded the men she wanted—eventually.

Until her first year of PhD coursework at the University of Toronto when she met Professor Gabriel O. Emerson. He was by far the most attractive and sensual of all the men she'd ever met. And he appeared very sexual. His raw, smoldering carnality oozed from every pore. She could almost smell it.

She watched him hunt at his favorite bar. She noted his stealthy, seductive approach and the way women reacted to him. She studied him the way she studied Italian, and she put her knowledge to good use.

But he spurned her. He never looked at her body. He would gaze into her eyes coldly, as if she wasn't even female.

She began to dress more provocatively. He never glanced below her neck.

She tried to be sweet and self-deprecating. He was impatient.

She baked him cookies and took to leaving anonymous culinary treats in his mail box at the department. The treats would remain untouched for weeks until Mrs. Jenkins, the departmental secretary, threw them into the garbage, worried about a potential infestation of vermin.

The more Professor Emerson rejected her, the more she wanted him. The more she became obsessed with having him, the less she cared about receiving gifts in trade. She would give herself to him freely if he would only look at her with desire.

But he didn't.

So in the fall of 2009, when she had the opportunity to meet him at Starbucks and discuss her dissertation, she was eager to see if their meeting could turn into dinner and possibly a visit to Lobby. She would be on her best behavior, but she would be alluring. Hopefully, he would stop resisting her.

In preparation for her meeting, she spent six hundred dollars on a black Bordelle chemise, along with garters and black silk stockings. She disdained the matching panties. Every time the garters pulled across the surface of her skin, she felt inflamed. She wondered how it would feel when Professor Emerson released her stockings from their bonds, preferably with his teeth.

Unfortunately for Christa, Paul and Julia had chosen to inhabit the same Starbucks at the same time. Christa knew without doubt that any impropriety on her part would be eagerly watched and noted by her fellow students. The Professor would know this too, and thus be far more professional than usual.

So when Christa confronted Paul and Julia, she was beyond pissed. She wanted to insult the two of them so they would leave before the Professor arrived. She did her damnedest to make sure that happened. Nevertheless, her attempt at intimidating her fellow graduate students went horribly awry. Professor Emerson arrived earlier than expected and overheard her.

"Miss Peterson." Gabriel pointed toward an empty table far away from Paul and Julia and indicated that Christa should follow him.

"Professor Emerson, I bought you a venti latté with skim milk." She tried to hand it to him, but he waved it aside.

"Only barbarians drink coffee with milk after breakfast. Haven't you ever been to Italy? And by the way, Miss Peterson, skim milk is for wankers. Or fat girls."

He spun on his heel and walked over to the counter to order his own coffee while Christa tried valiantly to hide her rage.

Damn you, Julianne. This is all your fault. You and the monk.

Christa sat in the chair that Professor Emerson had pointed out, feeling almost defeated. Almost, for from her vantage point, she had a lovely view of Professor Emerson's ass in his gray flannel trousers. Rounded like two apples. Two ripe, delicious apples.

She wanted to take a bite out of them.

At length, the professor returned with his own damn coffee. He sat as far away from her as possible, while still technically sitting at the same table, and gazed at her harshly.

"I need to speak to you about your behavior. But before I do, let me make one thing clear. I agreed to meet you here today because *I* desired a coffee. In the future, we will meet in the department as we normally do. Your transparent attempts at engineering social engagements between the two of us will be unsuccessful. Do you understand?"

"Yes, sir."

"One word from me and you'll be finding yourself a new dissertation director." He cleared his throat. "In the future you will address me as *Professor Emerson*, even when speaking of me in the third person. Is that clear?"

"Yes, Professor Emerson." *Ohhhh, Professor. You have no idea how much I want to scream your name. Professor, Professor, Professor . . .*

"Moreover, you will refrain from making personal remarks about my other students, especially Miss Mitchell. Is that clear?"

"Clear."

Now Christa was beginning to seethe a little, but she kept her reaction to herself. She placed all the blame on Julia. She wanted to drive Julia out of the program. She simply wasn't sure how to do that. Yet.

"Finally, anything you hear from me about another student or person connected with the university will be deemed to be confidential, and you will not repeat it or else you will find yourself another dissertation director. Do you think you are intelligent enough to comply with these very simple instructions?"

"Yes, Professor." She bristled slightly at his condescension, but truth be told, she found his grumpiness sexy. She wanted to tease it out of him. To seduce him into doing unspeakable things to her, to—

"Any more abuse directed toward MA students will be brought to the attention of Professor Martin, the department chair. I believe you are well aware of the regulations governing the behavior of graduate students. I don't need to remind you about the prohibitions against hazing, do I?"

"But I wasn't hazing Julia, I was—"

"No sniveling. And I doubt that Miss Mitchell gave you permission to use her first name. You will address her properly or not at all."

Christa bowed her head. Threats of the sort he was making were not sexy. She'd worked very hard to get into the PhD program at the University of Toronto, and she wasn't about to let it all slip through her fingers. Not for some pathetic little bitch who had something cooking with the Professor's research assistant.

Gabriel saw her reaction but said nothing, slowly sipping his espresso. He felt no remorse and was beginning to wonder what else he could do to make her cry.

"I'm confident you are well aware of the university's policies governing harassment. Those policies work both ways. Professors can file a complaint if they believe they are being harassed by a student. If you cross the line with me, I'll drag you to the Dean's Office so quickly your head will spin. Do you understand?"

Christa lifted her chin and gazed at him with wide, frightened eyes. "But we—I thought—"

"But nothing!" Gabriel snapped. "Unless you're delusional, you'll realize that there is no *we*. I won't repeat myself. You know where you stand."

He glanced at Julia and Paul one last time. "Now that we have dispensed with today's pleasantries, I'd like to tell you what I thought about your last dissertation proposal. It was rubbish. In the first place, your thesis is derivative. In the second, you've made no attempt to provide a literature review that comes close to being adequate. If you cannot amend your proposal to address these issues, you will need to find another director. If you choose to submit a revised proposal, you will need to do so within two weeks. Now if you'll excuse me, I have a meeting that is actually worth my time. Good afternoon."

Gabriel departed Starbucks abruptly, leaving a rather shell-shocked Christa staring off into space.

She heard part of his speech, of course, but her mind was focused on other things. First, she was going to do something to get back at Julia. She didn't know what and she didn't know when. But she was going to shank that bitch (metaphorically speaking) and cut her (also metaphorically speaking).

Second, she was going to rewrite her dissertation proposal and hopefully win Professor Emerson's academic approval.

Third, she was going to redouble her efforts at seduction. Now that she had seen Professor Emerson angry, there was nothing she desired more than to see him angry with her—*while naked*. She was going to change his mind. She was going to break through his harsh exterior. She was going to see him kneeling before her, begging for her, and then . . .

Clearly, the four-inch heels and the Bordelle lingerie weren't enough. Christa was going to head over to Holt Renfrew, and she was going to buy herself a new dress. Something European. Something sexy. Something by Versace.

Then she was going to Lobby to set her third scheme in motion . . .

Chapter Four

In the penthouse of a boutique hotel in Florence, clothes had been tossed haphazardly across a sitting room floor, trailing like breadcrumbs from the doorway toward a wall that was no longer blank. Groans and obvious rhythms floated in the air, wafting over a man's fine handmade shoes, a black bra, a tailored suit tossed wantonly over a coffee table, a taffeta dress puddled into a Santorini-blue pool . . .

If one were a detective, one would notice that the lady's panties and shoes were missing.

The air was thick with the smell of orange blossoms and Aramis, mingled with the musk of sweat and naked flesh. The room was dark. Not even the moonlight streaming in from the terrace reached the wall where two nude bodies clung to one another. The man stood upright, supporting the woman, who had her legs wrapped around his hips.

"Open your eyes." Gabriel's plea was punctuated by a cacophony of sound—skin sliding over skin, desperate cries muffled by lips and flesh, quick gulps of oxygen, and the slight thud of Julia's back against the wall.

She could hear him as he groaned with every thrust, but her ability to speak had withdrawn as she focused on a single sensation—*pleasure*. Every movement of her lover pleased her, even the friction between their chests and the grip of his hands as he held her aloft. She danced on the very edge of satisfaction, breathless with anticipation that the next movement would push her over. Building, building, building, building . . .

"Are—you—okay?" He was breathing hard, his last word leaving his mouth as a cry as the slightest turn of her ankles pressed her sharp heels into his flesh.

Julia threw her head back and let out a few incoherent sounds as she climaxed, intense waves radiating out from where they were joined and speeding along her nerves until her entire body vibrated. Gabriel felt it, of course, and followed soon after; two deep thrusts and he cried her name into the crook of her neck, his body shaking.

"You worried me," he whispered afterward. He lay on his back in the center of the large, white bed while his sleepy beloved curled into his side, her head resting over the surface of his tattoo.

"Why?"

"You wouldn't open your eyes. You wouldn't speak. I was worried I was too rough."

She moved her fingers along his abdomen to the few hairs that trailed down from his navel, tracing the texture lazily.

"You didn't hurt me. It felt different this time—more intense. Every time you moved, the most incredible feeling passed through me. I couldn't open my eyes."

Gabriel smiled to himself in relief and pressed his lips to her forehead.

"That position is deeper. And don't forget all our foreplay at the museum. I couldn't keep my hands off you during dinner."

"That's because you knew I'd lost my panties."

"That's because I want you. Always." He offered her a half-smile.

"Every time with you is better than the last," she whispered.

His expression grew wistful. "But you never say my name."

"I say your name all the time. It's a wonder you haven't come up with a pet name you'd rather I use, such as Gabe, or Dante, or *The Professor*."

"That's not what I meant. I mean you never say my name—when you come."

She lifted her chin so she could see his face. His expression matched his tone, wistful and momentarily vulnerable. The confident mask had slipped.

"For me, your name is synonymous with orgasm. I'm going to start calling them *Emgasms*."

He laughed loudly, a hearty, chest-bouncing chuckle that required Julia to sit up. She joined him in his laughter, grateful that his moment of melancholy had passed.

"You have quite the sense of humor, Miss Mitchell." He tilted her chin upward so he could worship her lips once more before relaxing into the pillows and drifting off to sleep.

Julia stayed awake a little longer as she contemplated the anxious, insecure little boy who revealed himself at rare and unexpected moments.

The following morning Gabriel treated Julia to her preferred breakfast at Café Perseo, a fine *gelateria* in the Piazza Signoria. They sat inside because normal December temperatures had returned and it was rainy and cool.

One could sit by the square all day, every day, and watch the world walk by. There were old buildings on the perimeter—the Uffizi was around the corner. There was a tremendously impressive fountain and beautiful statues, including a copy of Michelangelo's *David* and a statue of Perseus holding the dismembered head of Medusa in front of a lovely loggia.

Julia avoided looking at Perseus as she ate her gelato. Gabriel avoided looking at the legions of beautiful Florentine women in order to watch his beloved. Hungrily.

"Are you sure you wouldn't like a taste? Raspberry and lemon are great together." She held out a spoon where the two flavors commingled.

"Oh I want a taste. But not of that." His eyes glinted. "I prefer something a trifle more *exotic*." He nudged his espresso aside so he could take her hand in his. "Thank you for last night and this morning."

"I think I'm the one who should be thanking you, Professor." She squeezed his hand and busied herself with her breakfast, such as it was.

"I'm surprised there isn't an outline of my body vaporized onto the wall of our room." She giggled, holding out a small spoonful of the frozen treat.

He allowed her to feed him, and when his tongue darted out to lick his lips, she found herself light-headed. A bevy of images from earlier that morning flashed through her mind. And one remained.

O gods of sex-god boyfriends who enjoy pleasuring their lovers, thank you for this morning.

She swallowed hard. "You know, that was my first time."

"It won't be your last. I promise." Gabriel licked his lips provocatively, eager to make her squirm.

She leaned over to give him a peck on the cheek. But he was having none of that. He snaked a hand to the back of her neck and pulled her closer.

Her mouth was sweet with gelato and the unique taste that was Julia. He groaned when he released her, wishing he could take her back to the hotel for a repeat of last night's performance, or perhaps to the museum . . .

"Can I ask you something?" She busied herself with her bowl so she didn't have to meet his gaze.

"Of course."

"Why did you say that I was your fiancée?"

"*Fidanzata* has multiple meanings."

"The primary meaning is *fiancée*."

"*Ragazza* doesn't express the depth of my attachment." Gabriel wiggled his toes in his new, tight shoes. His mouth twitched as he contemplated what to say next, if he should say anything at all. He elected to remain silent, shifting uncomfortably in his seat.

Julia noticed what she perceived to be his physical discomfort. "I'm sorry about my heels."

"What's that?"

"I saw the marks on your backside when you were getting dressed this morning. I didn't mean to injure you."

He grinned wickedly. "Occupational hazard for those obsessed with high-heeled shoes. I wear my love scars with pride."

"I'll be more careful next time."

"No, you damn well won't."

Julia's eyes grew wide at the sudden flash of passion in his eyes.

He captured her lips with his before whispering in her ear, "I'm going to buy you a pair of boots with even higher heels, then I'm going to see what you can do with them."

As they strolled across the Ponte Vecchio under a shared umbrella, Gabriel persisted in pulling her into shop after shop, trying to tempt her into accepting an extravagant gift of jewelry—Etruscan reproductions,

Roman coins, gold necklaces, etc. But she would only smile and decline, pointing to Grace's diamond earrings and saying that they were more than enough. Her lack of attachment to material things only made him want to heap them at her feet.

When they reached the center of the bridge, Julia tugged at his arm and led him to the edge so they could gaze out over the Arno.

"There *is* something you could buy for me, Gabriel."

He peered over at her curiously, the crisp Florentine air flushing her cheeks. She was goodness, light and warmth and softness. But terribly, terribly stubborn.

"Name it."

Julia paused to run her hand over the barrier that separated her from the edge of the bridge. "I want my scar removed."

He was almost surprised. He knew that she was ashamed of Simon's bite mark. He'd walked in on her applying concealer that morning, and she'd grown teary when he asked about it.

She avoided his eyes and continued. "I don't like looking at it. I don't like the fact that you have to look at it. I want it gone."

"We could find a plastic surgeon in Philadelphia, while we're home for Christmas."

"Our time at home is so short. I couldn't do that to my dad. Or to Rachel."

Gabriel shifted the umbrella to his other hand and pulled her into a hug. He kissed her, trailing down to her neck until he made contact with the mark.

"I will gladly do this for you and more. You just have to ask. But I would like you to do something for me."

"What?"

"I would like you to talk to someone. About what happened."

Julia lowered her eyes. "I talk to you."

"I meant someone who isn't an ass. I can hire a doctor who will remove the scar from your skin, but no one can remove the scars on the inside. It's important for you to realize that. I don't want you to be disappointed."

"I won't be. And stop calling yourself names. It upsets me."

He conceded her point with a nod of the head. "I think it would help if you had someone to talk to—about everything. Tom, your mother, *him*, and me." He gave her a pained look. "I am a difficult man. I know that. I think if you had someone to talk to, it would help."

She closed her eyes. "I will, but only if you agree to do the same thing."

He stiffened.

She opened her eyes, speaking quickly. "I know that you don't want to, and believe me, I understand. But if I'm going to do this, you need to do it too. You were really angry last night, and even though I know you weren't angry with me, I had to bear the brunt of it."

"I tried to make up for it afterward." He gritted his teeth.

She reached up to stroke his agitated jaw. "Of course. But it bothered me that you were so upset over an unsolicited pass from a stranger. And that you thought that sex would relieve your anger and mark me as yours."

Gabriel's face registered shock, for he had never interpreted his actions in that way.

"I would never hurt you." He squeezed her hand.

"I know."

Gabriel looked upset, and the panic in his eyes didn't abate when Julia reached up to pet his hair a little.

"We're quite a pair, aren't we? With our scars and histories and all our problems. A tragic romance, I suppose." She smiled and tried to make light of their situation.

"The only tragedy would be losing you," he said, kissing her lightly.

"You'll only lose me if you stop loving me."

"I'm a lucky man then. I'll be able to keep you forever."

He kissed her once more before wrapping his arms around her.

"Therapy was required when I went into rehab. I continued meeting with a therapist for a year or so afterward, in addition to going to weekly self-help meetings. It isn't as if I haven't gone down that road."

Julia frowned. "You're in recovery and you don't go to meetings. I haven't said much about it before, but that's a serious problem. On top of that, you still drink."

"I was a cocaine addict, not an alcoholic."

She paused, searching his eyes. It was as if she'd uncovered an old medieval map that outlined the edge of the world with the words *here there be dragons.*

"We both know that Narcotics Anonymous strongly suggests that addicts don't drink." She sighed. "As much as I will try to help, some things are beyond me. As much as sex with you pleases me, I don't want to become your new drug of choice. I can't fix things."

"Is that what you think? That I use sex to fix things?" His question was in earnest, and so Julia resisted the urge to respond with sarcasm.

"I think that you used to use sex to fix things. You said as much to me once, remember? You used sex to combat your loneliness. Or to punish yourself."

A dark shadow passed over Gabriel's features. "It isn't like that with you."

"But when a person is upset, old patterns of behavior emerge. It's true of me too, except my coping mechanisms are different." She kissed him softly but long enough for his panic to recede and for him to kiss her back.

When they pulled apart they stood wrapped around one another until Julia decided to break the silence. "Your lecture last night reminded me of something." She pulled her phone from her purse and quickly scrolled through some pictures. "Here."

He took the phone from her hand and gazed at an exquisite painting. In it, St. Francesca Romana cradled an infant child with the assistance of the Virgin Mary, while an angel looked on.

"It's beautiful." He returned her phone.

"Gabriel," she said softly. "Look at the painting."

He did. And the strangest feeling passed over him.

She began to speak in a low voice. "I've always loved this painting. I thought it was because there are similarities between Gentileschi and Caravaggio. But it's more than that. St. Frances lost some of her children to the plague. This painting is supposed to portray one of her visions of what happened to those children."

She searched Gabriel's eyes to see if he grasped her meaning. But he hadn't.

"When I look at this painting, I think of your baby, Maia. Grace is holding her, surrounded by angels." Julia pointed to the figures in the painting. "See? The baby is safe and loved. That's what Paradise is like. You don't have to worry."

Julia looked up into his face. His pained, beautiful face. Gabriel had tears in his eyes.

"I'm sorry. I'm so sorry. I was trying to comfort you." She wrapped her arms around his neck, gripping him tightly.

Eventually, he wiped at his eyes. He hid his face in her hair, feeling grateful and relieved.

The following afternoon, the rain stopped. So the couple took a taxi up to the *Piazzale Michelangelo,* which provided a sweeping view of the city. They could have taken a city bus like regular people, but Gabriel was not like regular people.

(Few Dante specialists are.)

"What did Rachel say in her email?" he asked as they admired the tiled roof of the Duomo.

Julia fidgeted with her fingernails. "She and Aaron said hello. They wanted to know if we were happy."

Gabriel's eyes narrowed. "Is that all?"

"Um, no."

"So?"

She shrugged. "They said that Scott had a girlfriend. That was about it."

"Good for Scott." He chuckled. "Was there anything else?"

"Why do you ask?"

He cocked his head to one side. "Because I can tell when you're hiding something."

He began to run his fingers up and down the soft flesh at her waist, a particularly ticklish spot.

"You aren't going to do that in public."

"Oh, yes I am." He grinned and began moving his fingers with purpose, trying to tickle her.

She started giggling and trying to wriggle out of his grasp, but he held her close.

"Come on, Julianne. Tell me what Rachel said."

"Stop tickling," she gasped, "and I'll tell you."

Gabriel stilled his hands.

She took a deep breath. "She wanted to know if we'd, um, slept together."

"Oh, really?" His lips turned up into a half-smile. "And what did you say?"

"I told the truth."

He searched her eyes. "Anything else?"

"She said she hoped you were behaving yourself and that I was happy. And I said yes—on both counts." She waited for a moment, thinking about whether or not she should mention the email from a certain Vermont farm boy.

"But there's something else. Go ahead." He was still smiling indulgently.

"Well, Paul emailed me."

Gabriel scowled. "What? When?"

"The day of your lecture."

"Why didn't you mention this before?" he fumed.

"Because of this." She gestured to the irritation visible on his face. "I knew it would upset you, and I didn't want to do that when you had to speak in front of a room full of important people."

"What did he say?"

"He said that you passed Christa's dissertation proposal."

"What else did he say?"

"He wished me a Merry Christmas and said that he was sending something to me in Selinsgrove."

Gabriel's nostrils flared. "Why would he do that?"

"Because he's my friend. It's probably maple syrup, which I will gladly give to my dad. Paul knows that I have a boyfriend and that I am very, *very* happy. I'll forward the email to you, if you like."

"That won't be necessary." Gabriel's lips thinned visibly.

Julia crossed her arms in front of her chest. "You were eager to have me spend time with Paul when Professor Pain was around."

"That was different. And I don't particularly wish to discuss *her* ever again."

"Easy for you to say. You don't keep running into people I've slept with."

Gabriel glared.

Julia clapped a hand over her mouth. "I'm sorry. That was a terrible thing to say."

"As you may recall, I have run into at least one person with whom you've been sexually involved."

He turned and walked away, approaching the edge of the lookout. She gave him a moment or two to himself, then she stood beside him and cautiously wrapped her little finger around his. "I'm sorry."

He didn't respond.

"Thank you for rescuing me from Simon."

Gabriel scowled. "You know that I have a past. Do you intend to keep bringing it up?"

She lowered her gaze to her shoes. "No."

"That remark was beneath you."

"I'm sorry."

He kept his eyes trained on the city that was spread out before them. Red tiled roofs shone in the sun, while Brunelleschi's dome dominated the view.

Julia decided to change the subject. "Christa was behaving strangely at your last seminar. She seemed resentful. Do you think she knows about us?"

"She's sour because I haven't welcomed her outrageous advances. But she met the deadline for her revised proposal and her work was acceptable."

"So she wasn't—blackmailing you?"

"Not every woman is your rival for me," he snapped, pushing away her hand.

Her eyes widened in surprise. "That remark was beneath *you*."

After a moment, the anger seemed to seep out of him. His shoulders slumped. "Forgive me."

"Let's not waste our time together arguing."

"Agreed. But I don't like the idea of Paul emailing you. Although I suppose you could be friends with worse persons." Gabriel sounded unusually prim.

She smiled and pressed her lips to his cheek. "There's the Professor Emerson I know and love."

He pulled out his phone so he could take her picture against the background of the beautiful view. Julia was laughing, and he was taking picture after picture when his phone began to ring. The not so dulcet tones of London's Big Ben sounded between them.

Julia gave him a challenging look.

He grimaced and pulled her into an intense kiss. He cupped her face with his hand, determinedly parting her lips with his own and gently slipping his tongue inside.

She kissed him back, wrapping her arms around his waist to pull him closer. And all the while, Big Ben chimed.

"You aren't going to answer it?" she finally got a chance to ask.

"No. I told you earlier, I wasn't going to speak to her."

He pressed his lips to Julia's once again, but only briefly.

"I feel sorry for her," Julia said.

"Why?"

"Because she created a child with you. Because she still wants you, but she's lost you. If I were to lose you to someone else, I'd be devastated."

Gabriel huffed impatiently. "You aren't going to lose me. Stop that."

Julia smiled weakly. "Um, I need to say something."

He moved back.

"This is coming from my concern for you. I want you to know that." She looked at him in earnest. "I feel sorry for Paulina, but it's clear that she's been holding what happened over your head in order to keep you in her life. I'm wondering if she gets into trouble just so you'll rescue her. I think it's time for her to develop an emotional attachment to someone else. Someone she can fall in love with."

"I don't disagree," he said stiffly.

"What if she can't be happy until she lets you go? You let her go and you found me. It would be a mercy on your part for you to let her go so she can find her own happiness."

Gabriel nodded grimly and kissed her forehead but refused to say anything more on the subject.

The rest of their stay in Florence was a happy one, a counterfeit honeymoon of a sort. They frequented various churches and museums during the day, in between returns to their hotel, where they would make love sometimes slowly and sometimes madly. Every evening Gabriel would choose a different restaurant for dinner, and they would walk home afterward, pausing on one of the bridges to make out like teenagers in the cool evening air.

On their last evening in Florence, Gabriel took Julia to Caffé Concerto, one of his favorite restaurants, which was positioned on the banks of the Arno. They spent several hours over a multi-course dinner, leisurely talking about their holiday and their burgeoning sexual relationship. They both confessed that the past week had been an awakening of sorts—for Julia, an awakening to the mysteries of *eros;* for Gabriel, an awakening to the mysteries of the four loves intertwined.

In conversation, he finally revealed his surprise. He'd rented a villa in Umbria for their second week of holidays. He promised to take her to Venice and Rome on their next vacation, possibly in the summer after they visited Oxford.

After dinner, Gabriel led her one last time to the Duomo. "I need to kiss you," he whispered, pulling her body close to his.

She was going to reply, she was going to tell him to take her to the hotel and mark her body in a deeper way, but she was interrupted.

"Beautiful lady! Some money for an old man . . ." A voice called to her in Italian from the front steps of the Duomo.

Unthinkingly, Julia leaned around Gabriel to discover who was speaking. The man continued, begging for money so he could buy something to eat.

Gabriel caught her arm before she could approach the steps. "Come away, love."

"But he's hungry. And it's so cold."

"The police will come around and carry him off. They don't like panhandlers in the city center."

"People are free to come and sit on the steps of a church. *Sanctuary . . .*" she mused.

"The medieval concept of *sanctuary* no longer exists. Western governments abolished it, starting with England in the seventeenth century." Gabriel grumbled as she opened her purse and withdrew a twenty Euro note.

"So much?" He frowned.

"It's all I have. And look, Gabriel." She gestured to the man's crutches.

"A clever ruse," he complained.

Julia fixed her lover with a very disappointed look. "I know what it's like to be hungry." She took a step in the beggar's direction but Gabriel pulled her back.

"He'll spend the money on wine or drugs. It isn't going to help him."

"Even a drug addict deserves a little kindness."

Gabriel flinched.

She looked over at the beggar. "St. Francis of Assisi didn't make his charity conditional. He gave to whoever asked."

Gabriel rolled his eyes. There was no way he was going to win an argument with Julianne when she invoked St. Francis. No one could win against that kind of argument.

"If I give him something, he will know that someone cared enough to help him. No matter what he does with the money that will be a good thing. Don't deprive me of an opportunity to give." She tried to step around Gabriel but he blocked her path. He took the bill from her hand and added something to it from his own pocket, then he handed the money to the beggar.

The two men had a quiet exchange in Italian, and the poor man blew kisses to Julia and tried in vain to shake Gabriel's hand.

He retreated, taking her arm and leading her away.

"What did he say?"

"He asked me to thank the *angel* for her mercy."

Julia stopped him so she could kiss at his frown until it morphed into a smile. "Thank you."

"I'm not the angel he was referring to," he growled, kissing her in return.

Chapter Five

The next morning, a limousine met the happy couple at the train station in Perugia. The driver conveyed them down the winding roads to an estate near Todi, a medieval village.

"Is this the villa?" Julia was in awe as they traveled up the long, private drive to what looked like a mansion on a hill. It was a three-story stone structure that sat on several acres of land dotted with cypress and olive trees.

As they drove, Gabriel pointed out a large mixed-fruit orchard that in warmer weather grew figs, peaches, and pomegranates. Nestled beside the villa was an infinity pool surrounded by a bed of lavender. Julia could almost smell the fragrance from inside the car, and she vowed at that moment to gather a few sprigs to perfume the sheets of their bed.

"Do you like it?" He searched her face eagerly, hoping that she would be pleased.

"I love it. When you said you were renting a villa, I didn't think it would be so opulent."

"Wait till you see inside. They have a fireplace and a hot tub on the upstairs balcony."

"I didn't bring a bathing suit."

"Who said anything about needing a bathing suit?" He moved his eyebrows suggestively, and Julia laughed.

A black Mercedes sat in the driveway so they could visit the neighboring villages, including Assisi, which was a destination of particular interest for Julia.

The housekeeper of the villa had stocked the kitchen with food and wine in anticipation of their arrival. Julia rolled her eyes when she discovered several bottles of imported cranberry juice in the pantry.

Professor Gabriel "Overprotective" Emerson strikes again.

"What do you think?" he asked, settling his hands on her waist as they stood together in the large, fully equipped kitchen.

"It's perfect."

"I was worried you wouldn't like being in the middle of Umbria. But I thought it would be good for us to spend some quiet time together."

Julia arched an eyebrow. "Our times together usually aren't quiet, Professor."

"That's because you drive me mad with desire." He gave her an impassioned kiss.

"Let's stay in tonight. We can cook together, if you like, and maybe relax by the fire."

"Sounds good." She kissed him once again.

"I'll carry the luggage upstairs while you explore the house. The hot tub is on the terrace just outside the master bedroom. I'll meet you there in fifteen minutes."

She acquiesced with a smile.

"Oh, and, Miss Mitchell . . ."

"Yes?"

"No clothes for the rest of the evening."

She squealed and scampered up the stairs.

Not only was the house tastefully decorated in various shades of cream and white, but it boasted a very romantic master bedroom on the second floor that was punctuated by a canopy bed. Julia found herself trying the bed out just for a moment before taking her toiletry case into the washroom.

She unpacked her makeup and placed her shampoo and bath gel in the large, open shower. She pinned her hair up and took off all her clothes, wrapping herself in an ivory towel. She'd never skinny-dipped before, but she was looking forward to it.

As she folded her clothes and placed them on the vanity, she heard music coming from the bedroom. She recognized the song "Don't Know Why" by Norah Jones. Gabriel thought of everything.

His voice outside the bathroom door reconfirmed that. "I brought up some *antipasti* and a bottle of wine, in case you're hungry. See you outside."

"I'll be there in a minute," she called.

Julia looked at herself in the mirror. Her eyes were bright with excitement, and her cheeks were a healthy pink. She was in love. She was happy. And she was (she thought) about to christen the hot tub with her beloved underneath a darkening Umbrian sky.

On her way to the terrace, she saw Gabriel's discarded clothes hanging over the back of a chair. The cold evening breeze wafted in through the open door, ruffling her hair, making the pink of her skin pinker still. Gabriel was naked and waiting for her.

She walked out onto the terrace and waited until she had his complete attention. Then she dropped the towel.

Near Burlington, Vermont, Paul Virgil Norris was wrapping Christmas presents at his parents' kitchen table: presents for his family, for his sister, and finally, for the woman for whom his heart pined.

It was, perhaps, surprising to see a two-hundred-pound rugby player with bolts of Christmas wrap and Scotch tape, painstakingly measuring before he put scissors to paper. A bottle of maple syrup, a stuffed toy Holstein, and two figurines were proudly arranged in front of him. The figurines were a curiosity, something he'd found in a comic book store in Toronto. One was supposed to be Dante, dressed as a crusading soldier with St. George's cross on his chain mail chest, while the other was a blond-haired, blue-eyed anachronism of a Beatrice in the garb of a medieval princess.

Sadly, the toy company neglected to make a Virgil action figure. (Virgil, apparently, was not worthy of *action*.) Paul begged to differ, and so he decided to write to the toy company to alert them to their regrettable oversight.

He wrapped each item carefully and placed them in a cardboard box with bubble wrap. He signed a Christmas card with a few words, trying desperately to sound casual in order to disguise his growing feelings, and taped the box shut, neatly addressing it to Miss Julianne Mitchell.

❀❀❀

After a very enjoyable time in the hot tub, Gabriel prepared an Umbrian dinner. *Bruschetta con pomodoro e basilico,* tagliatelle with olive oil and black truffles from the villa's estate, and a cheese course with local artisan cheeses and bread. They ate their fill, laughing and drinking a fine white wine from Orvieto in the candlelight. After dinner, Gabriel made a nest of blankets and pillows on the floor in front of the living room fireplace.

He plugged his iPhone into the sound system so they could continue enjoying his *Loving Julianne* playlist. Then he took her into his arms as they sat on the floor, finishing their wine, while the sounds of medieval chant swirled around their heads. They were naked, wrapped in blankets, and unashamed.

"The music is beautiful. What is it?" She closed her eyes as she focused on the female voices, which were singing *a cappella.*

"'Gaudete' by The Mediaeval Baebes. It's a Christmas song."

"That's quite the name for a music group."

"They're very talented. I saw them live the last time they came to Toronto."

"Oh, really?"

Gabriel smirked at her. "Are you jealous, Miss Mitchell?"

"Should I be?"

"No. My arms are full. Completely."

Their talking ceased against the backdrop of celestial voices as their kisses began. Soon their bodies were tangling naked next to the fire.

In the glow of the orange flames, Julia pushed Gabriel down on his back and straddled his hips. He grinned as he let her lead, welcoming her newfound confidence. "It isn't so scary, being on top, is it?"

"No. But I'm more comfortable with you now. I think the wall sex back at the hotel shook loose my inhibitions."

He wondered silently what other inhibitions he could shake loose with various kinds of sex—shower sex, for example. Or perhaps, the holy grail of domestic coupling—*kitchen table sex.*

Her voice interrupted his thoughts. "I want to please you."

"You do. So much."

She reached a hand behind her and lightly touched the top of his groin. "With my mouth. I feel badly that I haven't been able to reciprocate. You've been so generous."

His body reacted to her low whisper and hesitant hand. "Julianne, there's no *quid pro quo* here. I do things with you because I want to." His lips curled up into a half-smile. "But since you're offering . . ."

"I know men prefer it."

He shrugged. "Great sex will always be better. In comparison, everything else could only be an *amuse bouche.*" He winked at her wickedly, squeezing her hip for emphasis.

"Is this position okay? With you lying down or . . .?"

"It's fine," he whispered, his eyes suddenly alight.

"I suppose it's better than me on my knees." She watched his reaction from the corner of her eye.

"That's right. I, on the other hand, am happy to kneel before my Princess in order to pleasure her. As I have already demonstrated."

Julia laughed softly. Then her smile disappeared. "I need to tell you something."

He gazed up at her expectantly.

"I have a gag reflex."

A furrow appeared between his eyebrows. "I'd be worried if you didn't."

Julianne avoided his probing expression as her hand slipped lower. "Mine is kind of strong."

His hand closed over hers.

"It won't be an issue, darling. I promise." He squeezed her hand.

She moved farther down, and he began to weave her hair around his fingers, tugging playfully.

Julia froze.

For an oblivious moment, he toyed with her long, silken hair. Then he realized that she wasn't moving. "What's wrong?"

"Please don't hold my head down."

"I wasn't going to." He sounded perturbed.

She remained perfectly still, waiting. For what, he didn't know. He let go of her hair so he could lift her chin. "Sweetheart?"

"Um, it's only because *Idon'twanttothrowuponyou.*"

"What was that?"

She ducked her head. "I've—thrown up—before."

He stared at her incredulously. "What . . . after?"

"Um, no."

Gabriel was silent for some time, then his eyes narrowed. "Were you sick because of a gag reflex, or because that bastard held you down?"

She cringed, her head moving in the slightest of nods.

Gabriel swore, his anger burning blue. He sat up swiftly, rubbing his face with his hands.

In the past, he hadn't been tender with his sexual conquests, although he'd prided himself on maintaining some vestige of good manners. Less so when he was doing cocaine. Despite the *Bacchanalia* that he'd participated in, parties that had approximated the decadence of Rome on occasion, he'd never, *ever* held a girl's head down until she vomited. Nobody did that. Not even the drug dealers and addicts he used to hang around with did that, and they had no boundaries or moral compunctions at all. Only an incredibly sick, twisted, misogynistic motherfucker would get his kicks from humiliating a woman that way.

To do such a thing to Julianne—with her gentle eyes and beautiful soul. A shy creature who was ashamed of having a gag reflex. The senator's son was lucky he was hiding in his parents' house in Georgetown under a suspended sentence and a restraining order, or Gabriel would have appeared on his doorstep in order to continue their previous altercation. And he would have ended their conversation with more than a few punches.

He shook the murderous thoughts from his head, lifting Julia to her feet and wrapping her in a blanket. "Let's go upstairs."

"Why?"

"Because I can't sit here after what you just told me."

Julia's cheeks reddened with shame, and her large eyes filled with tears.

"Hey." Gabriel pressed his lips to her forehead. "It isn't your fault. Do you understand? You didn't do anything wrong."

She smiled thinly, but it was clear that she didn't believe him.

He led her upstairs and through the bedroom to the en-suite, ushering her in before closing the door behind them.

"What are you doing?"

"Hopefully, something nice." He traced the curve of her cheek with his thumb.

Gabriel turned on the shower, testing the temperature of the water until he was satisfied. He adjusted the flow until it was gently falling from the tropical rain showerhead. He slowly removed the blanket from her body and held the shower door open, waiting for her to step inside before he followed her.

She looked confused.

"I want to show you that I love you," he whispered. "Without taking you to bed."

"Take me to bed," she pleaded. "Then our evening won't be ruined."

"Our evening isn't ruined," he said fiercely. "But I'll be damned if anyone hurts you again." He used both hands to caress her hair, parting and moving it so every strand grew wet.

"You think I'm dirty."

"Far from it." He took her hand and pressed it over the tattoo on his chest. "You're the closest thing to an angel I'll ever touch." His eyes held hers without blinking. "But I think we both need to wash away the past."

He moved her hair to one side, pressing a kiss to her neck. Stepping back, he poured some of her vanilla-scented shampoo into his palm. His fingers worked the liquid into her scalp, rubbing slowly, and eventually sliding down the locks to the ends. He was careful in his movements. If he ever had one moment, one act, to demonstrate that his love for her was much deeper than a sexual infatuation, now was that moment.

As Julia began to relax, she thought back to one of the few happy memories she had of her mother. She was a little girl and her mother washed her hair in the bathtub. She remembered the two of them laughing. She remembered her mother smiling.

Having Gabriel wash her hair was far better. It was a deeply affectionate, deeply intimate experience. She was naked before him, as he washed away her shame.

He was naked too, but was careful not to crowd her, or to allow his slightly embarrassed arousal to brush up against her. This was not about sex. This was about making her feel loved.

"I'm sorry I've been so emotional." Her voice was quiet.

"Sex is supposed to be emotional. You don't have to hide your feelings from me." He wrapped his arms around her waist, hugging her. "I feel very deeply about us as well. These past few days have been the happiest of my life."

He rested his chin on her shoulder. "You were shy when you were seventeen, but I don't remember you being so wounded."

"I should have dumped him the first time he was cruel." Her voice shook. "But I didn't. I didn't stand up for myself and things got worse."

"It wasn't your fault."

She shrugged. "I stayed with him. I held on to the times when he was charming or thoughtful, hoping the bad times would disappear. I know that what I told you made you sick, but believe me, Gabriel, no one could be as disgusted with me as I am with myself."

"Julia," he groaned, turning her to face him. "I'm not disgusted with you. I don't care what you did; no one deserves to be treated that way. Do you hear me?" His eyes flamed a brilliant, dangerous blue.

She covered her face with her hands. "I wanted to do something for you. But I couldn't even get that right."

He pulled at her wrists, lowering her hands. "Listen to me. Because we love each other, everything between us, including sex, is a gift. Not a right, or an entitlement or an exaction—a gift. You have me now. Let him go."

"I still hear his voice in my head." She brushed away a stray tear.

Gabriel shook his head, shifting them so they stood in the center of the downpour, the hot water spilling over them. "Do you remember what I said in my lecture about Botticelli's *Primavera?*"

She nodded.

"Some people think that *Primavera* is about sexual awakening—that part of the painting is an allegory for an arranged marriage. At first, Flora is a virgin and she's afraid. When she's pregnant, she appears serene."

"I thought Zephyr raped her."

Gabriel clenched his jaw. "He did. He fell in love with her afterward and married her, transforming her into the goddess of flowers."

"Not a very good allegory for marriage."

"No, it isn't." He swallowed noisily. "Julia, even though some of your sexual experiences were traumatic, you can still have a fulfilling sexual life. I want you to know that you're safe when you're in my arms. I don't want you to do anything you don't enjoy, and that includes oral sex."

Gabriel wrapped an arm around her waist, watching the hot water as it traveled over their naked bodies before splashing to the tile at their feet. "We've only been sleeping together for a week. We have our whole lives to love each other, in multiple ways."

He silently and lovingly soaped the nape of her neck and across her shoulders with a sponge. Then he traced the lines of her shoulders and the individual bumps of her spine, pausing regularly to place his lips where the soap had been rinsed away.

He washed her lower back and the two little dimples that marked the transition to her backside. Without hesitation, he soaped each cheek and massaged the backs of her legs. He even washed her feet, grasping her hand and placing it on his shoulder to steady her as he soaped between her toes.

Julia had never felt more cared for in her life.

He attended the front of her neck and the slope of her shoulders. He washed and caressed her breasts with his hands, putting the sponge to one side as he kissed them. Then he was gently touching between her legs, not sexually but reverently, rinsing the suds that accumulated among her dark curls and finally pressing his mouth there as well.

When he was finished, he took her into his arms and kissed her like a shy teenager, chastely and simply. "You are teaching me to love, and I suppose I'm teaching you to love too, in a way. We aren't perfect, but we can have happiness. Can't we?" He pulled back so he could read her eyes.

"Yes," she murmured, her eyes filled with tears.

Gabriel clutched her to his heart and buried his face in her neck as the water rained down on them.

Emotionally exhausted, Julianne slept until noon the following day. Gabriel had been so kind, so loving. He'd foregone what Julia had always thought was a man's basic need—oral sex—and given her what could only be described as a cleansing of shame. Gabriel's love and acceptance had its intended, transformative effect.

As she opened her eyes, she felt lighter, stronger, happier. Carrying the secrets of how *he* humiliated her had proved to be a very heavy burden. With the weight of guilt lifted, she felt like a new person.

She thought it was probably blasphemous to compare her experience with that of Christian in *The Pilgrim's Progress*, but she saw an important resemblance between their respective deliverances. Truth sets one free, but love casts out fear.

In her twenty-three years, Julia hadn't realized how pervasive grace was and how Gabriel, who considered himself to be a very great sinner, could be a conduit of that grace. This was part of the divine comedy—God's sense of humor undergirding the inner workings of the universe. Sinners participated in the redemption of other sinners; faith, hope, and charity triumphed over disbelief, despair, and hatred, while the One who called all creatures to Himself watched and smiled.

Chapter Six

Gabriel awoke in the middle of their last night in Umbria to an empty bed. Dazed, in a semi-dreamlike state, he extended his arm to Julianne's side. The sheets held no warmth.

He swung his legs to the floor, wincing as his bare feet touched the cold stone. He pulled on a pair of boxer shorts and made his way downstairs, scratching at his bed-mussed hair. The light was on in the kitchen, but no Julianne. A half-drunk glass of cranberry juice sat on the counter next to a remnant of cheese and a crust of bread. It looked as if a mouse had been there for a nocturnal feeding but had been surprised and scurried off.

Walking into the living room, he saw a dark head resting on the arm of an overstuffed chair next to the fireplace. In sleep, Julianne looked younger and very peaceful. Her skin was pale, but her cheeks and lips had a rosy hue. Gabriel would have loved to compose a poem about her mouth and resolved to do so. In fact, her appearance reminded him of Frederick Leighton's *Flaming June*. She was clad only in an elegant ivory silk nightgown. One of the thin straps had fallen off her right shoulder, leaving the beautiful curve bare.

Gabriel couldn't help himself as the pale, smooth skin called out to him. He kissed her shoulder and crouched near her head, floating a hand over her hair and petting her softly.

She stirred and opened her eyes, blinking twice before smiling at him.

Her slow, sweet smile set his heart aflame. He actually felt his breathing speed. He'd never felt this way about anyone before, and the depth of feeling she drew from him consistently surprised him.

"Hi," he whispered, smoothing her hair away from her face. "Are you all right?"

"Of course."

"I was worried when I reached for you and you weren't there."

"I came down to get a snack."

Gabriel's eyebrows knit together, and he rested his hand lightly on the top of her head. "Are you still hungry?"

"Not for food."

"I haven't seen this before." He traced a finger across the neckline of her nightgown, skimming the tops of her breasts.

"I bought it for our first night together."

"It's beautiful. Why haven't you worn it?"

"I've been wearing all those things you bought me in Florence. What did the clerk call them? *Basques* and *body suits?* Your taste in women's lingerie is surprisingly old-fashioned, Professor Emerson. Next you'll be buying me a corset."

He chuckled and kissed her. "I'll remember to look for one. You're right, I tend to favor items that leave more to the imagination. It makes the *unwrapping* so much more enjoyable. But you're equally lovely in everything and nothing."

Julia reached over to touch his face and pulled him close for a deeper kiss. She dragged her lips across his jaw line until she was whispering in his ear. "Come to bed."

She took his hand and led him past the kitchen table, exchanging a saucy smirk with him before walking upstairs. She moved him to sit on the edge of the canopied bed while she stood before him, pausing.

She pushed the straps of her nightgown over her shoulders. It pooled at her ankles, leaving her naked.

In the semi-darkness of the room, he drank in her tempting curves. "You are an argument for God's existence," he murmured.

"What?"

"Your face, your breasts, your beautiful back. St. Thomas Aquinas would have had to add you as his Sixth Way if he'd ever been blessed enough to see you. You must have been *designed* and not merely made."

Julia lowered her eyes and blushed.

He smiled at her pink cheeks. "Am I making you shy?"

As if in answer, she took a step closer and pulled one of his hands so it cupped her breast.

He squeezed her softly. "Lie beside me and I'll hold you."

"I want you to love me."

He divested himself of his boxer shorts and moved so she could join him. Still cupping her breast, he began to kiss her, gently tangling his tongue with hers.

"*I breathe you,*" he whispered. "You're everything. You're the air." He teased her breasts with his fingers and planted gentle kisses down her neck, feathering up and down while she urged him on with confident fingers.

Julia pushed him to recline on his back and straddled his hips. He kissed between her breasts and took one of her nipples in his mouth as his hand glided across the surface of her skin, moving down to test her.

He released her breast in order to shake his head. "You aren't ready."

"But I want you."

"I want you too. But I want to set your body on fire, first."

Julia's desire was countered by Gabriel's commitment to see that each of their sexual encounters was pleasurable for both of them. He'd rather delay entrance and satisfaction until she was mad with want, rather than speed along before her body was sufficiently aroused.

When they finally came together, she looked down into open blue eyes, their noses only a whisper apart. She moved atop him painstakingly slowly, her eyes closing as she focused on the pleasurable sensation, before opening again. It was an intense connection. Dark blue, heavy with emotion, gazed up unblinkingly into wide chestnut. Every movement, every yearning was reflected between the couple's eyes.

"I love you." He nuzzled her with his nose as she gradually increased her pace.

"I love you too—" Her last word was interrupted by a low moan.

She reached down to catch his mouth as her movements sped. Their tongues explored one another, groans and confessions interrupting their connection. He touched her ribs and smoothed over her waist. He slipped his hands under the curve of her bottom so he could lift her slightly, increasing his leverage.

She'd become addicted to this, to him. She adored the way he looked at her in these intimate moments and the way in which the world fell out of focus around them. She longed to feel him loving her, moving inside her, for he always made her feel beautiful. She would have said that any orgasm was an extra gift in addition to the way she felt when they were conjoined.

Making love, like music or breathing or the tempo of one's heartbeat, was based on a primordial rhythm. Gabriel had come to read her body and to know the pace that matched it, like a glove that fits a lady's hand. It was the sort of knowledge that was at once personal and primary, the kind of knowledge King James's translators had been referring to when they wrote of Adam *knowing* his wife. The mysterious sacred knowledge that a lover had for his beloved—knowledge that was perverted and maligned in less holier couplings. Knowledge that deserved a marriage in more than name.

Julia put her new knowledge to good use, delighting Gabriel with her body again and again. And the way it felt when he was inside her— warm and thrilling and tropical and perfect.

He was close, oh, so close. He searched her expression and saw that her eyes were opened. Every motion of hers was reciprocated by him. Every motion brought both of them pleasure.

As they stared, a great moan erupted from her chest, and then in a twinkling instant she was throwing her head back and calling his name. It was a glorious thing for him to see and hear. Julianne finally called his name. Soon he was falling, groaning aloud as his body tensed and then released, the veins in his forehead and neck straining and relaxing.

A joyful, tender coupling.

She didn't want to let him go. She didn't want to feel him leave her body, and so she curled on top of him, watching his expression.

"Will it always be like this?"

Gabriel kissed her nose. "I don't know. But if Richard and Grace were any indication, it will only improve with time. I'll see the reflection of all our shared joys and experiences in your eyes, and you will see the same in mine. Our history will make it better, deeper."

She smiled at what he said and nodded; then her face grew sad.

"What is it?"

"I'm worried about what will happen next year."

"Why?"

"What if I don't get accepted into the PhD program at Toronto?"

He frowned. "I didn't know that you applied."

"I don't want to leave you."

"I don't want you to leave me either, but Julianne, the Toronto program is not for you. You'd have no one to work with. I can't supervise you, and I doubt Katherine would take on a multi-year commitment."

Julia's countenance fell.

Gabriel stroked her cheek with his finger. "I thought you wanted to go to Harvard."

"It's so far away."

"Only a short flight." He looked at her thoughtfully. "We can see each other on weekends and holidays. I applied for a sabbatical. It's possible that I could come with you for the first year."

"I'll be there for six years. Or more." She was close to tears now. Gabriel saw them swimming and shimmering in her eyes and his heart ached.

"We'll make it work," his voice grew rough. "Right now, we need to enjoy the time we have together. Let me worry about the future. I'll make sure we aren't separated."

She opened her mouth to protest, but he kissed her.

"The advantage to dating an older, more established man is that he can give you room to focus on your own career. I'll find a way to make my job fit around yours."

"That isn't fair."

"It would be grossly unfair to expect you to give up your dream of being a professor or to have you enroll in a program that is subpar. I won't let you sacrifice your dreams for me." He grinned. "Now kiss me, and let me know that you trust me."

"I trust you."

Gabriel held her in his arms, sighing as she rested her head on his chest.

Chapter Seven

Christa Peterson sat in her parents' house in north Toronto, check-ing her email a few days before Christmas. She'd been ignoring her inbox for a week. A relationship she had cultivated in addition to her pursuit of Professor Emerson had run its course, which meant that she wouldn't be skiing in Whistler, British Columbia, with her erstwhile lover over the Christmas holidays.

The banker in question had broken up with her via text message. This was in poor taste, to be sure, but what would be in even poorer taste would be the follow-up email that was sure to be waiting for her, like a ticking bomb lurking in her inbox.

Having steeled herself with a glass or two of vintage Bollinger cham-pagne, which she had purchased as a gift for the schmuck who was sup-posed to take her skiing, she checked her account. And there, sitting in her email, was a bomb. However, it was not the bomb she'd expected.

To say that she was surprised by the content of Professor Pacciani's email would have been an understatement. In fact, she felt as if the rug had been pulled out from under her.

The only Canadian woman she had ever seen Professor Emer-son show even restrained affection to was Professor Ann Singer. Yes, Christa had seen Emerson with various women at Lobby, but never the same woman twice. He was friendly with other female professors and staff, but only professionally so, greeting them always and only with a firm handshake. Professor Singer, in contrast, was rewarded with a double kiss when he greeted her after his last public lecture.

Christa did not want to rekindle her relationship with Professor Pacciani. He was sorely lacking in a particular physical respect, and she had no wish to return to the previous intimate encounters that had always left her frustrated and wanting. She had standards, after all, and any man who did not *measure up* to at least the size of her personal service accessory was not worth screwing.

(And she would have said you could quote her.)

Since she wanted more information about Professor Emerson's fiancée, she feigned interest in a spring rendezvous with Professor Pacciani and subtly asked for the fiancée's name. Then she went downstairs and finished off the rest of the champagne.

The day before Christmas found Julia sitting at the counter of Kinfolks restaurant in Selinsgrove, having lunch with her father. Gabriel was doing some last minute shopping with Richard while Rachel and Aaron drove to the grocery store to pick up the turkey. Scott was still in Philadelphia with his girlfriend.

Tom had faithfully delivered Julia's gift from Paul. She'd placed it on the floor at her feet, and now it was staring up at her, begging for attention like a puppy.

She opened it, deciding it was better to display its contents to her father than to her boyfriend. She gave the bottle of maple syrup to Tom with a smile, she giggled at the toy Holstein and kissed it, but when she unwrapped the Dante and Beatrice figurines her face grew pale. It was almost as if Paul knew. And yet, he couldn't have known that Gabriel and Julia were Dante and Beatrice, at least to each other.

While Tom ate his blue plate special—turkey with stuffing and mashed potatoes—Julia opened Paul's card. It displayed children engaged in a snowball fight and the typical *Merry Christmas* emblazoned on the front. But it was the words that Paul wrote in his own hand that brought a lump to her throat.

> Merry Christmas, Rabbit.
> I know it was a rough first semester and I'm sorry I didn't do a better job of helping you when you needed it. I'm proud of you for not quitting. With a big Vermont hug from your friend, Paul.
> P.S. I don't know if you've heard Sarah McLachlan's "Wintersong," but part of it made me think of you.

Julia didn't know the song that he was referring to, so the lyrics he omitted did not run through her mind as she examined the card's art-work more closely. In the center of the image of a snowball fight stood a little girl with long, dark hair in a bright red coat, laughing.

The quotation, the picture, the card, the gift—Paul had tried to keep his feelings secret, she thought, but he'd betrayed himself. It was all in the picture of the laughing girl and the song that she would listen to later.

Julia sighed and placed everything back in the box and set it at her feet.

"So, Gabriel treating you right?" Tom broached the topic of Julia's relationship in between bites of turkey.

"He loves me, Dad. He's very good to me."

Her father shook his head as he reflected on how Simon had had the appearance of being good and Gabriel had the reality of being good—and how he had failed to recognize the difference.

"You let me know if he isn't," he said, tasting the mashed potatoes.

Julia almost rolled her eyes. Yes, it was a bit late for Tom to play the part of the overprotective father, but better late than not at all.

"When Gabriel and I drove into town this morning we went by the house. I saw the sign on the lawn."

Tom wiped his mouth on a napkin. "I put it up for sale a couple of weeks ago."

"Why?"

"Why not? I can't live in a place where my daughter doesn't feel safe."

"But you grew up in that house. What about you and Deb?"

He shrugged and hid his expression behind a cup of coffee. "It's over."

She gasped. "I didn't know. I'm sorry."

Tom sipped his coffee stoically. "We had a difference of opinion. And her kids don't like me."

Julia fidgeted with her silverware, lining them up so their ends were even.

"So Deb sided with Natalie and Simon?"

He shrugged again.

"It was a long time coming. Truth is, I'm relieved. It feels good to be a free agent." He winked at her conspiratorially.

"I'm looking to buy a smaller house. I'd like to use some of the money I make to pay for your education."

Julia was surprised. Then she was angry. Her conflict with *him* had cost her and her father so much—too much to be remedied by a criminal record and some community service. She was scarred and her father lost his prospective wife and the Mitchell family home.

"Dad, you should use the money for your retirement."

"I'm sure there will be enough for everything. And if you don't want to use my money for school, then use it to buy beer. From now on, it's just you and me kid." He reached out a hand to ruffle Julia's hair, his preferred gesture of affection.

He excused himself to use the men's room, leaving her alone to contemplate her half-eaten cheeseburger and her changed father. She was deep in thought, fingering the glass of ginger ale in front of her, when someone moved to occupy the stool next to her.

"Hello, Jules."

Startled, Julia turned and found her former roommate, Natalie Lundy, sitting next to her.

There was a time when Julia had laughingly called her former friend *Jolene,* for her beautiful and voluptuous features perfectly matched those described in the song. But that was before Natalie had betrayed her. Now her beauty seemed harsh and cold.

As Julia stared at her, she noticed something painful about the way she was dressed—the vintage designer coat with the slightly frayed cuffs, the expensive boots that were worn and second-hand. On first glance, she looked rich and well dressed. But Julia glanced twice and saw what others could not see—the small town girl who was ashamed of her blue collar roots and wished to leave them far behind.

"Merry Christmas, Natalie. What can I get for you?" Diane, the waitress, leaned over the counter.

Julia watched as Natalie transformed from cold and sullen to cheerful and sunny, slipping into the local accent.

"Merry Christmas, Diane. I'll just have coffee. I can't stay long."

The waitress smiled and poured coffee, then moved to wait on a group of Tom's fellow volunteer firemen at the far end of the counter. As soon as her back was turned, Natalie's demeanor changed. She glared at Julia with hate-filled eyes.

"I need to talk to you."

"You have nothing to say that I want to hear." Julia moved to stand, but Natalie subtly gripped her wrist.

"Sit down and shut up, or I'll make a scene." Her voice was low, barely above a whisper. She smiled artificially. No one would know by looking at her that she was threatening Julia, who swallowed noisily and sat back down.

Natalie released her arm with a punishing squeeze. "We need to talk about Simon."

Julia's eyes darted toward the men's room, hoping that her father would reappear.

Natalie continued. "I'm going to assume that your recent misunderstanding with Simon was unintentional. You were upset; he said some things he shouldn't have, you called the police.

"Because of that misunderstanding, Simon now has a criminal record. I'm sure I don't need to explain why that record needs to disappear before he runs for state Senate. You need to fix the misunderstanding. Today."

Natalie smiled and flipped her hair behind her shoulder, acting as if she and Julia were engaged in a friendly conversation.

"There's nothing I can do," Julia mumbled. "He's already plea-bargained."

Natalie took a sip of her coffee. "Don't treat me like I'm stupid, Jules. I know that. Obviously, you need to tell the District Attorney that you lied. Explain that it was a lover's quarrel gone awry, you got your revenge, and now you feel bad about having made the whole thing up." She laughed a little too loudly. "Although, I don't understand how anyone believed that Simon could be interested in you. Look at you, for God's sake. You're a mess."

Julia bit back a harsh retort, deciding prudentially that silence was best.

Natalie leaned toward her, pulling the crewneck of Julia's sweater away from her throat with icy fingers. She examined Julia's neck carefully.

"There isn't a mark on you. Show the D.A. your neck and tell him you lied."

"No." Julia moved out of Natalie's reach, resisting the urge to show her the bite that she'd slathered with concealer that morning. She pulled her sweater further up her neck, pressing a hand over the place where Simon had bitten her. It was a phantom pain, she knew, but she could still feel where his teeth had broken skin.

Natalie dropped her voice to a whisper. "I'm not asking—I'm telling you." She pulled her BlackBerry out of her large handbag and placed it on the counter between them. "I hoped I wouldn't have to do this, but you leave me without a choice. I have pictures of you that Simon took. They're very . . . colorful."

Julia's eyes darted to the phone. She tried to swallow, but her mouth went dry. With a shaking hand, she lifted her glass to her lips, frantically trying not to spill her drink.

Natalie smiled, clearly enjoying the torture she was able to inflict on her former rival. She snatched up the cell phone eagerly, scrolling through the pictures. "I could never figure out how he set up the shots without you knowing. Or maybe you knew but didn't care." She tilted her head to one side, narrowing her eyes at Julia. "Do you care if everyone in Selinsgrove sees these pictures on the internet?"

Julia scanned the eyes of the townspeople around them, hoping they hadn't heard Natalie's threat. At least no one was looking in their direction. Her first instinct was to run, to hide. But that strategy hadn't saved her from her mother when she was younger. Her mother always found her. It hadn't saved her from Simon, either. He'd been stopped only because Gabriel hit him back.

Julia was tired of hiding. She felt her spine stiffen.

"Simon's record is your fault. He came to see me to get the pictures. But you've had them all along."

Natalie smiled sweetly, but didn't deny the accusation.

"Now you want me to clean up your mess. But I'm not going to do it."

Natalie laughed. "Oh yes, you are."

She looked at the screen again, making a show of bringing it close to her eyes. "God, your tits are small."

"Did you know that Senator Talbot wants to run for President?" Julia blurted.

Natalie tossed her hair behind her shoulder. "Of course I know. I'm going to work for the Senator's campaign."

Julia gave Natalie a long look. "Now I understand. Simon's record will be a problem for the Senator, so you need it to go away. You screwed up."

"How's that?"

"If you release those photos, Simon will dump you so fast your head will spin. And you'll never get out of this town."

Natalie waved a dismissive hand. "He won't dump me. And the Senator will never know about the pictures."

Julia felt her heart beginning to race. "If I'm in those pictures, Simon is too. What will the Senator think of that?"

"Haven't you heard of a little program called Photoshop? I can edit Simon out and edit someone else back in. But I won't have to because you're going to be a good little girl and do the right thing. Aren't you, Jules?"

Natalie flashed a patronizing smile as she placed her BlackBerry back in her purse and stood to leave, but Julia stopped her.

"He'll never introduce you to his parents. He told me that. You can do better than being Simon's dirty secret."

Natalie's expression faltered, then hardened. "You don't know what you're talking about," she snapped. "He's going to give me *exactly* what I want and so are you. If you don't fix this problem today, I'm posting the pictures online. Enjoy your Christmas."

She started to walk away but Julia called after her. "Wait."

Natalie paused, looking at her former friend with undisguised contempt.

Julia took a deep breath and gestured to Natalie to come closer. "Tell Simon to make sure the Senator renews his subscription to *The Washington Post*."

"Why?"

"Because if you release those pictures, I'll call Andrew Sampson at the *Post*. You remember him, don't you? He wrote an article last year about Simon's DUI arrest and how the Senator intervened."

Natalie shook her head. "I don't believe you."

Julia clenched her fists stubbornly. "If you release the pictures, I have nothing to lose. I'll tell the newspapers that Simon assaulted me, then sent the girl he keeps on the side to blackmail me."

Natalie's green eyes grew very wide then narrowed into serpentine slits.

"You wouldn't," she breathed.

"Try me."

Natalie stared in furious surprise before setting her teeth. "People have been walking all over you for years and you've done nothing. There's no way you're going to call up a reporter and spill your guts."

Julia lifted her chin, fighting to keep her voice steady. "Maybe I'm tired of being walked over." She shrugged dramatically. "If you release the pictures, you'll never work for the Senator's campaign. You'll just be part of an embarrassing scandal they'll sweep under the rug."

Natalie's ivory skin flushed a deep, dark red.

Julia took advantage of her silence and continued. "Leave me alone, and I'll forget about both of you. But I'm never going to lie about what he did to me. I've lied to cover for him too many times, and I'm not doing it anymore."

"You're just angry that Simon chose me over you," Natalie spat, her voice becoming louder. "You were this pathetic, weak little girl who didn't even know how to give a decent blow job!"

In the awkward silence that ensued, Julia realized that the other restaurant patrons had stopped talking. She looked around the room, utterly humiliated, as the townspeople stared. Everyone heard Natalie's crude revelation, including the Baptist minister's wife, who sat with her teenaged daughter in a quiet corner drinking tea.

"Not so tough now, are you?" Natalie hissed.

Before Julia could respond, Diane suddenly appeared at the counter. "Natalie, go on home. You can't come into my restaurant and talk like that."

Angrily, Natalie withdrew a few steps but not before muttering a few choice curse words. "This isn't over."

Julia lifted her chin. "Oh, yes, it is. You're too smart to jeopardize your future by doing something stupid. Go back to *him* and leave me alone."

Natalie stared daggers at her before turning on her heel and storming out.

"What's going on?" Tom suddenly appeared behind Julia. "Jules? What's wrong?"

Before she could respond, Diane told him an extremely sanitized account of what happened.

Tom cursed and put his hand on his daughter's shoulder. "Are you all right?"

She nodded reluctantly before running to the ladies' room. She wasn't sure how she'd ever be able to face the townspeople after what Natalie had shouted. Fighting nausea, she grabbed the top of the vanity for support.

Diane followed Julia into the washroom. She dampened some paper towels with cold water and handed them to her. "I'm sorry, Jules. I should have slapped her upside the head. I can't believe she'd talk that kind of trash in my place."

Julia was quiet as she slowly wiped her face.

"Honey, nobody heard a thing that girl had to say. It's noisy out there and everyone is talking about how the Santa Claus over at the mall got drunk on his lunch hour yesterday and tried to make out with one of the elves."

Julia cringed.

Diane smiled at her sympathetically. "You want me to make you a cup of tea or something?"

Julia shook her head and inhaled deeply as she tried to compose herself.

If any god is out there listening, please give all the people in Kinfolks restaurant amnesia, just concerning the past fifteen minutes.

A short time later she reassumed her place at the counter, next to her father. She kept her head down, refusing to make eye contact with anyone. It was too easy to imagine the entire restaurant whispering her sins and judging her.

"I'm sorry, Dad," she said in a small voice.

He frowned and asked Diane for a fresh cup of coffee and a jelly doughnut. "What are you sorry about?" His voice was gruff.

Diane served them, patting Julia's arm sympathetically, and moved to wait on some tables in order to give them some privacy.

"This is all my fault—Deb, Natalie, the house . . ." She didn't want to cry, but somehow the tears welled up and she couldn't stop them. "I've embarrassed you in front of the whole town."

Tom leaned toward her. "Hey, I don't want to hear that kind of garbage. You have never embarrassed me. I'm proud of you." His voice broke slightly and he began coughing. "It was my responsibility to protect you, and I didn't."

Julia wiped a tear away. "But now your life is ruined."

He snorted. "I wasn't that attached to my life anyway. I'd rather lose the house and Deb than lose you. There's no contest. None."

He pushed the jelly doughnut in front of her and waited until she took a bite. "When I met your mother, I was happy. We had a few good years together. But the best day of my life was the day you were born. I always wanted a family. I'm never going to let anything or anyone separate me from my family again. You've got my word on that."

Julia smiled up into her father's face, and he leaned over and ruffled her hair.

"I'd like to swing by Deb's place to talk to her about what just happened. She needs to explain to her daughter how to behave in public. Why don't you phone that boyfriend of yours and ask him to pick you up? I'll see you at Richard's house later on."

Julia agreed and wiped her tears away. She didn't want Gabriel to see her crying.

"I love you, Dad."

Tom cleared his throat roughly, without looking at her. "Me too. Now finish your doughnut before Diane starts charging us rent."

Chapter Eight

Gabriel was only too glad to cut his Christmas shopping short. When he and Richard arrived at the restaurant, they walked over to the counter to join the Mitchells.

Julia stood up and hugged Gabriel tightly.

"What happened?" He frowned. "You've been crying."

"It's just the Christmas blues." Julia noticed uncomfortably that some of the restaurant patrons were still staring.

"What Christmas blues?"

"I'll tell you later." She began to tug him toward the door.

Richard took a moment to greet Tom, and while the two old friends were talking, Gabriel gently swept Julia's hair behind her ear in order to whisper something sweet.

A sudden flash caught Richard's attention—Grace's earrings. Clearly, he'd underestimated his son's new relationship. He knew that Grace would be happy that their son gave her earrings to Julia. Grace loved Julia liked a daughter and always considered her part of their family. Perhaps someday Gabriel would make Julia part of their family officially . . .

Gabriel and Tom exchanged polite greetings, and Gabriel picked up Julia's Christmas gift from Paul. To his credit, he resisted the urge to say something snide and carried the box without comment.

As the trio approached the door, Officer Roberts walked in. She was wearing her uniform.

"Hello, Jamie." Gabriel smiled, but his body tensed.

"Hi, Gabriel. Home for Christmas?"

"That's right."

She greeted Julia and Richard, and turned back to Gabriel, noticing the way Julia's arm was tucked into his elbow.

"You look good. You look happy."

"Thank you. I am." He smiled genuinely.

Jamie nodded. "I'm happy for you. Merry Christmas."

Julia and Gabriel thanked her and quietly exited the restaurant, reflecting privately on the way forgiveness made certain burdens lighter.

As they walked through the front door of the Clark house, Gabriel was plotting with Richard to enjoy Scotch and cigars on the patio. Julia was still feeling a little shell-shocked from her confrontation with Natalie, but she was so relieved to be home that she pushed all thoughts of her afternoon aside. She disappeared into the living room while Gabriel and Richard hung up their coats.

"Sweetheart? Can I take your jacket?" Gabriel called. When she didn't answer, he followed her.

His next question died in his throat as he skidded to a stop. His beloved Julianne was frozen like a statue, staring at a woman who was sitting in the living room with Aaron and Rachel. Instinctively, Gabriel gripped Julia's waist and drew her backward to his chest.

He watched as the woman rose gracefully from her seat and floated over to them. She moved like a ballerina or a princess, a subtle air of old money clinging like perfume to her every movement.

She was tall, almost the same height as Gabriel, with long, straight blond hair and large, ice-blue eyes. Her skin was flawless, and she was model thin except for her generous and perfect breasts. She wore knee-high black suede stiletto boots, a black wool pencil skirt, and a pale blue cashmere sweater that hung provocatively off of her alabaster shoulders.

She was beautiful. And imperious. She took one look at the way Julia was tucked under Gabriel's arm and arched her back like a Russian blue cat.

"Gabriel, darling. I've missed you!" Her voice was rich and clear, with just a hint of a British accent. She embraced him tightly.

Julia wriggled away from them, none too keen to engage in a group hug.

"What are you doing here?" A myriad of emotions flashed across Gabriel's face as she pressed her full pink lips to both of his cheeks.

She kissed him slowly, oozing sensuality. To add insult to injury, she wiped her lipstick stain from his skin, chuckling softly as if it were a private joke.

His eyes fled to Julia's, and she returned his gaze, eyes tinged with disappointment.

Before he could say anything, Richard cleared his throat and stepped forward. She brushed his proffered hand aside and hugged him.

"Richard. A pleasure as always. I was so sorry to hear about Grace."

He graciously accepted her embrace and walked over to Julia to assist her with her coat. After he'd hung it up, he quietly persuaded Aaron and Rachel to join him in the kitchen, denying Paulina her audience.

"I didn't know you had two sisters." She acknowledged Julia's existence with a frosty smile. She towered over Julia, who was wearing plain flat shoes, jeans, and a black cardigan. Beside her, Julia felt dowdy and small.

"I have only one sister and you know it," Gabriel snapped. "Why are you here?"

Julia came to herself and bravely extended her hand, before Gabriel made a scene. "I'm Julia. We spoke on the phone."

Paulina kept a tight rein on her facial expression, but Julia saw what she was attempting to conceal—*the cold flames of resentment.*

"Really?" she laughed artfully. "Surely you can't expect me to keep track of all the girls who've answered Gabriel's phone over the years. Unless you were one of the girls I spoke with when I interrupted a *ménage?* Remember that night, Gabriel?"

Julia withdrew her hand as if she'd been smacked.

"I expect an answer to my question," Gabriel spoke, his voice stiff and cold as a frozen lake. "Why are you here?"

Julia tried to step away. The verbal picture Paulina had painted repulsed her, and she wasn't sure she could stomach the answer, whatever it might be. Gabriel caught Julia's arm, pleading with her with his eyes not to flee.

"I came to see you, of course. You wouldn't return my calls, and Carson said that you'd be with your family." Paulina sounded irritated.

"Are you on your way to Minnesota?"

"You know my parents don't speak to me. Anyway, Gabriel, I need to talk to you." She gave Julia a venomous look. *"Alone."*

Gabriel was conscious of the fact that the kitchen was still within hearing range of the living room. He took a step closer to Paulina, his voice hovering above a whisper.

"Allow me to remind you that you are a guest. I won't tolerate your disrespect for anyone, especially Julianne. Do you understand?"

"You never treated me like a guest when you were in my mouth," Paulina muttered, eyes flashing.

Julia inhaled sharply, her stomach rolling. If she'd met Paulina a few weeks ago, the encounter would have been awkward and uncomfortable. But meeting her now, after having spent hours in Gabriel's bed, was incredibly painful.

Paulina knew what it was like to be intimate with him. She knew his sounds, his smell, the look on his face when he climaxed. She was taller, more sophisticated, and far more beautiful. And it was clear that unlike Julia, she had no hesitation about performing oral sex. Furthermore, and far more damaging, she'd created a child with Gabriel, something he was now unable to do with anyone else.

Julia tore herself from Gabriel's grasp, turning her back on the former lovers. She knew it would be better if she and he maintained a united front. She also knew it would be better to stand her ground rather than retreat. But her spirit had taken a beating at Kinfolks restaurant, and she no longer had the energy to fight. Emotionally exhausted, she shuffled up the stairs without a backward glance.

Gabriel watched her walk away, and he felt his heart plummet to the soles of his feet. He wanted to go after her, but there was no way he was going to leave Paulina alone with his father and sister. He excused himself for a moment, disappearing into the kitchen to tell Rachel that Julia had fallen ill and to ask if she would check on her.

Rachel climbed the staircase and found Julia exiting the washroom on the second floor. "Are you all right?"

"No. I need to lie down."

When Rachel obligingly opened the door to Gabriel's old room, Julia disdained it and walked across the hall to enter the guest room. Rachel watched as her friend slowly removed her shoes, placing them on the rug next to the bed.

"Can I get you an aspirin or something?"

"No. I just need to rest."

"Who is that woman? And why is she here?"

Julia spoke through clenched teeth. "You need to ask your brother."

Rachel's hand tightened on the doorknob. "I will. But the fact that I don't know who she is tells me something. She can't have been very important if Gabriel never brought her home." She turned to leave. "That should tell you something too."

Julia reclined on the bed, hoping that sleep would take her quickly.

Gabriel walked into the kitchen three hours later and found Aaron and Rachel engaged in an argument over the correct way to make Grace's famous chicken Kiev.

"I'm telling you, you need to freeze the butter first. That's the way your mom used to do it." Aaron sounded exasperated.

"How do you know? She didn't say anything about freezing the butter." Rachel gestured to the recipe card.

"Grace always froze the butter," said Gabriel, frowning. "She probably assumed everyone would know that. Where's Julia?"

Rachel turned on him, wielding a very large wire whisk. "Where have you been?"

His jaw tightened. "Out. Where is she?"

"Upstairs. Unless she decided to go back to her father's house."

"Why would she do that?"

Rachel turned her back on her brother and resumed beating a few eggs. "Oh, I don't know. Maybe because you went out with one of your ex-girlfriends and left her for three hours. I hope Julia dumps your ass."

"Honey . . ." Aaron reproved her, touching her shoulder.

"Don't." She pushed his hand away angrily. "Gabriel, you're lucky Scott isn't here. Because he'd have dragged you outside by now."

Aaron frowned. "What about me? I could drag Gabriel outside, if I wanted to."

Rachel rolled her eyes. "No, you couldn't. And right now, I need you to freeze the goddamned butter."

Gabriel muttered something unintelligible and walked away. He took his time as he climbed the stairs, trying desperately to formulate an apology that would be worthy of her.

(Not that it was possible, even with his silver tongue.)

He stood outside the door while he gathered his bearings, inhaling deeply before entering. But the bed was empty.

Puzzled, he searched the room. No Julia.

Returning to the hall, he wondered if she'd sought refuge in Scott's room, but she hadn't. The bathroom, likewise, was unoccupied. His eyes alighted on the closed door of the guest room across the hall. He opened it.

Julia was lying in the center of the bed, sound asleep. He contemplated leaving her to her dreams but rejected the idea. They needed to talk, away from prying ears, and at least for the next little while his family was preoccupied.

Wordlessly, he removed his shoes and crawled into bed, spooning behind her. The surface of her skin was smooth but cool. He wrapped himself around her.

"Gabriel?" She blinked sleepily at him. "What time is it?"

"Six thirty."

She rubbed her eyes. "Why didn't anyone wake me up?"

"They were waiting for me."

"Waiting for you to do what?"

"I was out. When I came back, Richard wanted to speak with me."

"Where did you go?"

He looked away guiltily.

"Were you with *her*?"

"Her driver's license is suspended because of the DUI. I dropped her off at a hotel."

"Why were you gone so long?"

He paused, his expression conflicted. "We were talking."

"Talking? At a hotel?"

"She's upset about the turn her life has taken. Her appearance here was a desperate attempt to change direction."

Julia began curling in on herself, drawing her knees flush against her chest.

"No, no, no," he chanted, tugging her arms and knees away from her body, trying desperately to relax her defensive posture. "She's gone, and she won't be coming back. I told her again that I've fallen in love with you. She has my money and she has my lawyers, and that's it."

"That's never been enough for her. She wants you, and she doesn't care that you're with me."

He put his arms around Julia's unyielding body. "I don't care what she wants. I'm in love with you, and *you* are my future."

"She's beautiful. And sexy."

"She's malicious and petty. I saw nothing beautiful in her today."

"You made a child together."

He winced. "Not by choice."

"I hate sharing you."

Gabriel scowled. "You will *never* have to share me."

"I have to share you with your past—with Paulina, with Professor Singer, with Jamie Roberts—with countless other women I'm probably going to pass on the street in Toronto."

He set his teeth. "I'll do my best to protect you from such embarrassing encounters in the future."

"It still hurts."

"I'm sorry," he whispered. "If I could change the past, I would. But I can't, Julianne, no matter how badly I wish I could."

"She gave you what I can't."

He leaned over her body, his hand pressing down on the mattress next to her hip. "If you were thirsty and someone offered you water from the ocean, would you drink it?"

"Of course not."

"Why?"

She shuddered. "Because the water is salty and dirty."

"And if someone gave you the choice between that water and a glass of Perrier, which would you choose?"

"The Perrier, of course. But I don't see what this has to do with *her.*"

His eyes narrowed. "Don't you?"

He moved, bringing his chest to hers, kneeling in between her legs so he could press their hips together. "You don't see the comparison between you and her? *This* is my water." He pressed himself against her again. "*You* are my water. Making love with you is all I need to quench my thirst. Why would I throw this away for water from the ocean?"

He moved against her as a reminder. "She has nothing to offer me."

He lowered his face so their noses were inches apart. "And you are beautiful. Every part of you is a masterpiece, from the top of your head to the tip of your toes. You're Botticelli's Venus and Beatrice. Do you have any idea how much I adore you? You captured my heart when I first saw you, when you were seventeen."

Her body began to relax incrementally under his touch and his quiet words. "How was it left with her?"

"I told her that I didn't appreciate her dropping in on me and that she was never to do it again. She took it as well as could be expected."

Gabriel was interrupted by a loud knock at the door. "Come in!"

He rolled onto his side just as Rachel walked in.

"Dinner is on the table, and Tom and Scott are here. Are you two coming downstairs?" She looked from her best friend to her brother and back again. "Do I need to send Scott up here?"

Julia shook her head. "Did he bring his girlfriend?"

"No, she's spending Christmas with her parents. I asked him to invite her but he gave me a big song and dance." Rachel looked annoyed. "Do you think he's embarrassed by us?"

"More likely he's embarrassed by her," said Gabriel. "She's probably a stripper."

"Professors in glass houses shouldn't throw stones." Rachel glared at her brother and stormed out.

Julia looked puzzled. "What was that about?"

His expression tightened. "My dear sister is less than impressed with Paulina—and me."

Chapter Nine

It was a different Christmas Eve than any of them had ever experienced. Grace's absence was felt most keenly by her husband and children, Aaron wished that he was already married, and Rachel wished that her chicken Kiev was even half as good as her mother's, frozen butter or not.

After dinner, Gabriel, Tom, and Richard retreated to the back porch to smoke cigars and drink Scotch while the rest of the family enjoyed coffee in the kitchen.

"How was Italy?" Aaron asked Julia as the two of them refilled their mugs from the coffee maker.

"It was great. The weather was good, and we had a wonderful time. How are the wedding plans?"

"They're coming along. When Rachel tried to rent one hundred doves to be released after the ceremony, I put my foot down. I think some of my gun-toting relatives might be tempted to shoot the damn things." He winked.

"How are your parents?"

"They're good. Rachel has been including my mom in the wedding planning, so she's pretty excited. How are things with you and Gabriel?"

Julia hid her face as she opened the fridge to look for the cream. "Good."

"Except for his ex showing up."

She glanced over at him, and he gave her a sympathetic look.

"I don't want to talk about it."

Aaron toyed with a teaspoon. "Gabriel is different when you're around." He placed the spoon on the counter and rubbed his chin. "He seems happy."

"He makes me happy too."

"A happy Gabriel is about as rare as a hobbit. We're all glad to see it. As far as the ex is concerned, well, I doubt they were serious. Not like the way he is with you."

"Thanks, Aaron."

The two friends exchanged a quick hug.

Later that evening, Julia and Gabriel retired to their room at a bed and breakfast. She was washing her face in the bathroom when she heard the strains of "Lying in the Hands of God" wafting from the bedroom.

Gabriel came to stand behind her, wearing nothing but a pair of navy-blue silk boxer shorts and a smile.

"It isn't Barry White, but it's ours." He watched her for a moment or two, his expression becoming heated. He nuzzled her neck, pushing her hair aside as he fluttered his lips against her skin.

"I want you," he whispered. "Now."

He slid his hands underneath her T-shirt, exposing the flesh of her abdomen above the band of her yoga pants.

"Why don't you change into one of those pretty things you bought in Toronto? Or maybe the blue basque. You know it's my favorite." His voice was low as his mouth moved seductively to her shoulder.

"I can't."

He smirked. "Not here, love. I'm not sure you're ready to watch us in a mirror. Although I wouldn't mind."

When he began to remove her T-shirt, she pulled away. "Not tonight."

He dropped his arms to his sides, watching her.

She avoided his eyes as she went back to washing her face.

Gabriel frowned and walked away, silencing the stereo in a huff. Apart from their interlude in the Uffizi, she'd never turned him down. Of course, they'd only been together a little over two weeks. But still . . .

Professor Emerson was not used to being rejected by a lover. He was sure she had her reasons—or at least one reason beginning with *P* and ending with *A*. He flopped onto the bed, bringing his arm to rest across his face. Understandably, Julianne was still upset about Paulina's reappearance. Sex would be the last thing on her mind. Not to mention the fact that something troublesome had happened to her at Kinfolks restaurant that afternoon.

Being turned down made him crave her all the more. The scent of her hair, the feel of her satin skin under his fingertips, the way she closed her eyes tightly just before she came, the sensation of her moving underneath him, with him . . .

He needed to make love to her to know that it was all right—that they were all right.

Yes, sex was his apple a day, and he needed it. He needed to show her not with words but with actions that he loved her, worshipped her, would do anything for her. He needed to know that she still wanted him, to hear her whisper his name.

But she didn't seem to need him. Certainly, she didn't want him. Not tonight.

Gabriel's depressed musings continued until she joined him in bed. She rested on her side, watching him, but he didn't acknowledge her. He simply turned off the lamp on the bedside table.

In the darkness, they were both silent as a cold and invisible barrier sat between them.

"Gabriel?"

"Yes?"

"I need to explain something to you."

He exhaled slowly, expelling all the air from his lungs. "I understand, Julianne. Good night." He tried to keep the strain out of his voice but failed, miserably. He rolled away from her.

Julia winced. Now the invisible barrier seemed more like a high, impenetrable wall.

Men have such fragile, eggshell egos.

She wanted to explain things to him and bring everything out into the open, but if he was going to be so easily offended, then she would wait until morning. Or later. Julia rolled over and shut her eyes, determined to forget the whole miserable day. She tried to suppress her sniffles, hoping that she could hold the hormonal tears back. The last thing she wanted was for him to catch her crying.

Boys are dumb.

She sniffled for a few minutes, then Gabriel was spooning behind her, pressing his naked chest to her back.

"I'm sorry," he whispered.

She nodded, still sniffling.

"Please don't cry."

"I'm not crying."

"I didn't mean to be an ass." He propped himself up on his elbow. "Look at me."

He gave her a repentant smile. "I've been spoiled with all the times we've made love over the past two weeks. But I know that there will be days when you're tired or you don't feel like it. I promise not to sulk—too much."

She smiled wryly and reached up to kiss his pouty lower lip.

He wiped her eyes. "Will you tell me why you were crying this afternoon at the restaurant?"

Julia shook her head.

"Please?"

"I'm too tired."

He nuzzled her until her body relaxed in his arms. "What can I do?"

"I don't need anything."

"A hot bath? A massage?" The look on his face was one of a little boy, eager to please. "Let me touch you. I'll make you feel better."

"Gabriel, I can barely keep my eyes open."

"I wanted to do something for you."

"Just hug me."

"I'd gladly do that anyway." He kissed her once more before spooning behind her.

"Merry Christmas, Gabriel."

"Merry Christmas."

❋❋

A few hours earlier, a lone woman stepped into a taxi outside the Comfort Inn. She was crying.

The cabbie politely ignored her tears and turned the radio up, hoping to give her some privacy on their long drive to Harrisburg. The song that was playing was catchy, so catchy in fact that they both found themselves humming.

As she hummed she thought of the parcel she'd given to the hotel's night manager, Will. She'd given him five crisp twenty-dollar bills in exchange for his promise to deliver said package to a particular address in Selinsgrove by nine o'clock the following morning. Christmas morning.

When he'd revealed (in typical small-town fashion) that he was acquainted with that address, having been a high school classmate of Gabriel's brother, Scott, the woman casually pressed him for information about Gabriel's new girlfriend.

Will responded enthusiastically, since his family had known Tom Mitchell and his daughter for years. In fact, Will reported, Tom had recently bragged that Julia was excelling in her graduate studies at the University of Toronto.

As soon as the woman learned this surprising fact, she decided to check out of the hotel and leave Selinsgrove. As she watched the snow-tipped trees pass by the cab's windows, she wondered how she could discover if Julianne was a student of Gabriel's when they began their affair.

Chapter Ten

Very early Christmas morning, Gabriel sat in his boxer shorts and glasses, debating whether or not to wake Julianne. He could have returned to the light of the living room of their suite, where he'd played Santa Claus only an hour before. But he preferred to be near her, even in the dark.

Richard's conversation with him from the day before plagued his mind. His adoptive father had asked about Paulina, and he'd said about as much on the topic as he dared, emphasizing that Paulina was his past and Julia his future. Richard, who was a compassionate man, encouraged his son to make professional counseling a necessary condition for Paulina's continued access to her trust fund, pointing out that she clearly needed help.

Once Gabriel agreed, Richard smoothly changed the subject to Julia, asking if he was in love with her. Gabriel replied unequivocally in the affirmative, to which Richard responded by bringing up the R-word, *responsibility*.

"I am taking responsibility for her."

"She's still a student. What if she gets pregnant?"

Gabriel's expression hardened. "That won't happen."

Richard smiled. "I thought that once. Then we had Scott."

"I've already demonstrated that I more than take care of my responsibilities." Gabriel's voice was glacial.

His adoptive father sat back in his chair, tenting his fingers reflectively.

"Julia is like Grace in several ways—not least of which is her willingness to sacrifice herself for those she loves."

"I won't allow her to sacrifice her dreams for me, you can be assured of that."

Richard's eyes flickered over to the picture of his wife that he always kept on his desk, a laughing, smiling woman with kind eyes.

"How did Julia react to Paulina's visit?"

"I haven't discussed it with her."

"If you abandon Julia, you will have a serious problem with your siblings, as well as with me."

Gabriel's eyebrows knit together like thunderous clouds. "I would never abandon her. And I won't live without her."

"Then why don't you tell her that?"

"Because we've only been together for two weeks."

Richard raised his eyebrows in surprise, but elected not to interrogate his son over the semantic ambiguity of the phrase "being together."

"You know my views on this. You should marry her. At the moment, you appear to be with her under false pretenses; your actions indicate that she is only a partner in a sexual affair, when your intentions are serious."

Gabriel bristled at the characterization. "Julianne is not my mistress."

"You won't make a commitment to her."

"I am committed to her. There's no one else."

"But Paulina appears, looking for you and making a spectacle in front of Julia and your family."

"I can't help that," Gabriel snapped.

"Can't you?" Richard pursed his lips together. "It's difficult for me to believe that a woman as intelligent as Paulina would simply arrive without any hope that her overtures would be accepted."

Gabriel scowled, but didn't bother to argue.

"Why won't you make some promises to Julia? I'm sure she's anxious about what the future might hold. Marriage is a sacrament that exists partially to protect women from sexual exploitation. If you take that protection away from her, then she is little more than your mistress, no matter what you choose to call her. And she has seen what happened— what is happening—to Paulina."

"That isn't going to happen to Julianne."

"How does she know that?" Richard tapped his fingers on the top of his desk. "Marriage is more than a piece of paper. It's a mystery. In fact, there's a Midrash that suggests that marriage is made in heaven between soul mates. Don't you want to be with Julia forever?"

"What I want is immaterial. I won't rush her into making a life-changing decision in the middle of the academic year," Gabriel muttered, rubbing at his eyes. "It's too soon."

"Pray that you don't wait until it's too late," Richard countered, gazing sadly at Grace's photograph.

With these words, then, ringing in his ears, Gabriel sat watching his soul mate sleep on Christmas morning.

As if she could hear his thoughts, she stirred, a nameless anxiety wafting over her. A moment later she rolled toward him, her fingers making contact with the silk at his hip.

In the darkness of the room, Gabriel looked like a gargoyle—a gray, motionless figure that stared back at her from behind his glasses in stony silence. It took a moment for Julia to recognize him.

"What are you doing?"

"Nothing. Go back to sleep."

Her face creased in puzzlement. "But you're sitting half-naked in the dark."

He gave her a tentative smile. "I'm waiting for you to wake up."

"Why?"

"So we can open presents. But it's early. Go back to sleep."

She slid closer to him, searching for and finding his hand. She kissed the back of it and pulled it toward her heart.

He smiled and pressed his palm flat against her chest so he could feel her heart beat. His face grew serious.

"Forgive me for last night." He cleared his throat roughly. "I don't want you to think that sex is all I want. It isn't."

Her smile faded. "I know that."

He moved his hand to stroke her eyebrows with his fingers. "I desire you, obviously. It's difficult for me not to touch you, not to want to be with you that way."

His hand floated across her cheek, hesitantly. "But I love you, and I want you to be with me because you want to be. Not because you feel obligated."

She leaned into his hand. "I don't feel obligated. There were so many times when you could have pressured me, like the night we were in your old room and I—I took my top off. But you were patient. And when it was our first time, you were wonderful. I've been lucky to have you as my lover."

She gave him a sleepy smile. "Why don't you come over here? I think we could both use some rest."

Gabriel slid under the covers and cuddled close to his beloved. When her regular breathing indicated that she'd fallen asleep, he whispered a few promises to her in Italian.

When Julia awoke she was treated to breakfast in bed. Then she was nagged impatiently until she agreed to accompany Gabriel to the sitting room. He was so excited he was practically bouncing.

(In a very dignified and professorial way, of course, despite his lack of shirt.)

A small, *Charlie Brown* Christmas tree had been conveniently "borrowed" from the bed and breakfast's parlor and was placed in the center of the room. Several brightly colored parcels rested beneath it. Two large, red stockings embroidered with the names "Julianne" and "Gabriel" were each sitting in a corner of the loveseat.

"Merry Christmas." He kissed her forehead, feeling very proud of himself.

"I've never had a stocking."

He led her to the loveseat and placed the stocking in her lap. It was filled with candy and panties that had Yuletide images on them. And in the toe was a flash drive that contained video of a certain tango against the wall at the Royal Ontario Museum.

"Why haven't you had a stocking before?"

"Sharon didn't always remember Christmas and my dad didn't think of it." She shrugged.

He shook his head. He hadn't had stockings either, before he came to live with the Clarks.

Julia pointed to a couple of presents that were wrapped in red and green plaid and sitting on the coffee table. "Why don't you open your gifts first?"

Gabriel beamed and sat on the floor by the tree, cross-legged. He picked up a small box and tore at the paper with abandon.

Julia laughed at the sight of him, this very proper professor sitting in his spectacles and underwear, attacking his presents like a four-year-old.

Gabriel opened the box and was very surprised at what he saw inside. Nestled in cream-colored silk was a pair of silver cufflinks. But these were no ordinary cufflinks. These cufflinks bore the shield of the city of Florence. He gazed at them in wonder.

"Do you like them?"

"I love them, Julianne. I'm just surprised. How did you . . .?"

"While you were at one of your meetings, I walked over to the Ponte Vecchio and bought them. I thought they would look good with your fancy shirts." She looked at the floor. "I'm afraid I bought them using some of my scholarship money. So really, you bought them for yourself."

Gabriel rose to his knees and shuffled over to her, kissing her in gratitude. "That money is yours. You earned it. And the cufflinks are perfect. Thank you."

She smiled at the sight of him kneeling in front of her. "There's another gift for you."

He grinned as he found a second small, flat present. Underneath the wrapping paper he found a framed eight-by-ten inch reproduction of Marc Chagall's painting *Lovers in the Moonlight*.

Inside the enclosed card Julia had written a few sweet nothings, declaring her love and her gratitude at finding him again. She also added another, more important, gift.

I'd like to pose for your photographs.
All my love,
Your Julia.
XOXO

Gabriel was speechless. His eyes met hers with a questioning look.

"I think it's time you had some photographs of us to hang on the walls of your bedroom. And I would like to do this for you. If that's all right."

He moved to join her on the love seat and kissed her deeply. "Thank you. The painting is lovely, but what is far more lovely is you." He grinned. "Your fondness for Chagall will be our inspiration. But I think we'll have to practice our poses first."

He moved his eyebrows suggestively, before leaning forward to tug her lower lip into his mouth.

"You are the greatest gift," he murmured. He felt her lips move into a smile beneath his mouth, and he pulled back to retrieve one of her gifts from under the tree.

She rewarded him with shining, eager eyes. When she opened the small box, she found a compact disc that he'd recorded for her, entitled *Loving Julianne*.

"It's the playlist that we listened to in Florence," he explained.

"Thank you. I was going to ask you for a copy of those songs. They'll bring back happy memories."

Underneath the jewel case she found a series of gift certificates for various spa treatments at the Windsor Arms Hotel in Toronto, some of which had various exotic sounding names such as *Vichy shower* and *seaweed and salt body wrap*.

She thanked him, reading the titles aloud until she came to the last certificate.

> *Arrangements have been made for you to see a plastic surgeon in Toronto as soon as we return. Based upon the information I provided, he's confident that your scar can be removed completely. You don't need to worry about it anymore,*
> *Gabriel.*

He released the page from her tense fingers, smiling apologetically. "I probably shouldn't have included that in the box. Sorry."

Julia caught his hand. "Thank you. I thought I would have to wait. But this is the best gift you could have given me."

Gabriel exhaled deeply and leaned over to kiss the top of her head. "You are worth it," he declared, his eyes blazing.

She smiled a little and peered around him, gazing at a large box that was still underneath the Christmas tree.

"There's one more present. Is it for me?"

He nodded.

"Well, can I open it?"

"I'd rather you waited."

She frowned. "Why? Do you want me to take it to Richard's house? To open it in front of your family?"

"God, no!"

He ran his fingers through his hair and gave her a half-smile. "Sorry. It's just kind of—ah—*personal*. Would you wait and open it tonight? Please?"

She looked at the gift curiously. "Judging by the size of the box, it isn't a kitten."

"No, it isn't. Although if you wanted a pet, I'd buy one." He looked suspiciously at the open box that was sitting by the door.

"What was in your gift from Paul?"

Julia shrugged, pretending that she hadn't known that question was coming. "A bottle of maple syrup, which I gave to Dad, and a couple of toys."

"Toys? What kind of toys?"

She appeared indignant. "Children's toys, of course."

"Didn't he give you a toy bunny a couple of months ago? I think he has some kind of rabbit fetish."

Angelfucker.

"Gabriel, you have a fetish for women's shoes. Professor Pot, meet Mr. Kettle."

"I've never denied my *aesthetic appreciation* for women's footwear. They're works of art, after all," he said primly. "Especially when a woman as lovely as you is wearing them."

She couldn't help smiling. "He gave me a stuffed Holstein and a pair of Dante and Beatrice figurines."

Gabriel's face manifested a look of intense perplexity. "Figurines?" His mouth widened into a provocative smile. "Don't you mean *action figures?*"

"Figurines, action figures. Whatever."

"Are they anatomically correct?"

"Now who's being a child?"

He reached over to trace the curve of her cheek. "I was just wondering what kind of *action* they were capable of participating in—privately, of course."

"Dante would be rolling over in his grave."

"We could re-enact that event by taking Paul's action figure and burying it in the back yard. But I'd like to keep Beatrice."

"You're incorrigible." Julia couldn't help but laugh. "Thank you for my presents. And thank you for taking me to Italy, which was the best present of all."

"You're welcome." He cupped her face in his hands and searched her eyes for a moment before pressing their lips together.

What started as a shy, closed mouth kiss quickly escalated until feverish, needy hands pulled and grasped at one another. Julia stood on tiptoes, pressing against his naked chest. Gabriel groaned with frustration and gently pushed himself back. He moved his glasses so he could rub his eyes.

"I'd rather continue what we were just doing, but Richard wants us to go to church."

"Good."

Gabriel replaced his glasses. "Wouldn't a nice Catholic girl like you prefer to go to Mass?"

"It's the same God. I've gone to church with your family before." Julia searched his expression. "Don't you want to go?"

"Church is not the place for me."

"Why not?"

"I haven't gone in years. They'll . . . judge me."

She looked up at him in earnest. "We're all sinners. If only non-sinners went to church, the churches would be empty. And I doubt very much that the people in Richard's church will judge you. Episcopalians are very welcoming."

She gave him a quick peck on the cheek and disappeared into the bedroom to lay out her clothes. He followed her into the bedroom and collapsed on the bed, watching her rifle through the hangers in the closet.

"Why do you still believe in God? Aren't you angry with him for all of the things that happened to you?"

Julia paused what she was doing in order to regard him. He looked very unhappy.

"Bad things happen to everyone. Why should my life be any different?"

"Because you're good."

She looked at her hands. "The universe isn't based on magic—there isn't one set of circumstances for the good and one for the evil. Everyone suffers sometime. The question is what you do with your suffering, right?"

He gazed at her impassively.

She continued. "Maybe the world would be a lot worse if God didn't exist."

He cursed softly, but didn't argue.

She sat next to him on the bed. "Did you ever read *The Brothers Karamazov?*"

"It's one of my favorites."

"Then you know the conversation between Alyosha, the priest, and his brother Ivan."

Gabriel snickered, but not unkindly. "I suppose I'm the rebellious free thinker, and you're the religious boy?"

Julia ignored him. "Ivan gives Alyosha a list of reasons why either God doesn't exist or if he exists, that he's a monster. It's a very powerful discussion, and I've spent a lot of time thinking about it.

"But remember how Ivan ends his discussion. He says he rejects God's creation, this world, and yet, there's one aspect of the world that he finds surprisingly beautiful—the sticky little leaves he sees on the trees in the spring. He loves them even though he hates the world around them.

"The sticky little leaves aren't faith or salvation. They're the remnant of hope. They stave off his despair, demonstrating that despite the evil he has seen, there is at least one good and beautiful thing left."

She moved so she could see Gabriel's expression more clearly, and very tenderly, she placed a hand on either side of his face. "Gabriel, what are your sticky little leaves?"

Her question took him entirely by surprise. So much so he simply sat there, staring at the pretty brunette in front of him. It was in moments like this that he remembered why he'd initially thought she was an angel. She had a compassion about her that was rare in human beings. At least, in his experience.

"I don't know. I've never thought about it before."

"Mine was Grace. And you." She smiled at him shyly. "And even before that, there were the Salvation Army workers back in St. Louis who were kind to me when my mother wasn't. They gave me a reason to believe."

"But what about the suffering of the innocent? Of children?" Gabriel's voice was barely above a whisper. "What about the babies?"

"I don't know why babies die. I wish they didn't." Julia wore a grave expression.

"But what's wrong with the rest of us, Gabriel? Why do we allow people to abuse their children? Why don't we defend the sick and the weak? Why do we let soldiers round up our neighbors and make them wear a star on their clothing and cram them into boxcars? It isn't God who's evil—it's us.

"Everyone wants to know where evil comes from and why the world is riddled with it. Why doesn't anyone ask where goodness comes from? Human beings have a tremendous capacity for cruelty. Why is there any goodness at all? Why are people like Grace and Richard so kind? Because there's a God, and he hasn't allowed the earth to be entirely corrupted. There are sticky little leaves, if you look for them. And when you recognize them, you can feel his presence."

Gabriel closed his eyes, drinking in her words with her touch, knowing in his heart that she had spoken a very deep, very profound truth.

Try as he might, he could never stop believing; even in his darkest days the light had not gone out. He'd had the guidance of Grace, and providentially, when she died, he met his Beatrice again, and she'd shown him the rest of the way.

He kissed her chastely, and when she left him to shower, he marveled at her quiet brilliance. She was far more intelligent than he, since her intellect was marked with a true creative originality that he only dreamed of having. Despite everything that had happened to her, she had not lost faith or hope or charity.

She is not my equal; she is my better.

She is my sticky little leaf.

❊ ❊

An hour later Julia and Gabriel drove to All Saints Episcopal Church. Gabriel wore a black suit and white shirt, proudly displaying Julia's cufflinks, while she wore a plum-colored dress that skimmed the bottom of her knees, and tall black boots that he'd purchased for her in Florence.

A sea of awkwardness. That's how Gabriel would have described the atmosphere as he sat with Julianne at the end of the family pew.

He was grateful for the liturgy, the order, and the way in which Scripture and music were used in the service. He found himself contemplating his life and the steps that led him to the beautiful woman who held his hand throughout the service.

Christmas was a celebration of birth—one birth in particular. All around him he saw babies and children: the manger scene at the front of the church, the banners and stained glass windows, and the glowing skin of the pregnant woman who was seated across the aisle.

In one brief moment, Gabriel realized that he regretted his sterilization, not just for himself and the fact that he was no longer able to father a child, but also for Julianne. He imagined lying in bed with a very pregnant Julia and placing his hand on her stomach in order to feel their child kick. He thought about holding their infant son in his arms, shocked by the array of dark hair on his head.

His imaginings startled him. They marked a shift in character and priority, away from the guilt and selfishness that had marked his life up until the reappearance of his Beatrice. A shift toward the permanence of a commitment to a woman with whom he wanted to create a family, with whom he wanted to create a child. His love for Julianne had changed him in multiple ways. He hadn't been aware of how dramatic the changes were until he gazed at the pregnant stranger with a kind of wistful envy.

Those were the thoughts that occupied his mind as he held Julianne's hand until it was time to participate in the Eucharist. He was the only one in the family pew who didn't stand and file to the center aisle in order to walk to the communion rail.

There was something comforting about church, he thought. Although he found the overall experience, especially the homily, convicting. He had wasted a good deal of his life—years that he could never get back.

He hadn't told Grace the things he'd wanted to tell her before she died. He hadn't treated Paulina or Julianne with the dignity that they deserved. He hadn't treated any of the women with whom he'd been involved with respect.

In thinking of Paulina, Gabriel tore his eyes away from the dark haired woman in the pretty plum dress and hung his head, praying almost unconsciously for forgiveness and also for guidance. He was walking a tightrope, he knew, between taking responsibility for his past indiscretions and eliminating Paulina's dependence on him. He prayed that she would be able to find someone who would love her and help her put the past behind her.

Gabriel was so deep in prayer that he didn't notice his family squeeze past him to retake their seats, or Julia's warm hand snake through the crook at his elbow, pressing herself soothingly to his side. And he didn't notice the moment in the service, just before the benediction, when his father broke down into silent, shoulder-shaking tears, and Rachel placed her arm around him, leaning her blond head to his shoulder.

The Kingdom of Heaven is like a family, thought Julia, as she watched Rachel and Scott hug their father. *Where love and forgiveness replace tears and suffering.*

Chapter Eleven

After lunch, Rachel marshaled her family into helping her prepare the large turkey dinner. Julia spoke briefly to Tom on the phone, exacting his promise that he would arrive around three o'clock in order to participate in the gift exchange, then she and Rachel parked themselves in the kitchen to peel apples for a pair of pies.

Rachel had cheated and bought the pastry, but had removed it from its Pillsbury packaging and placed it in between layers of plastic wrap in the refrigerator so no one would know.

"Hey, pretty girls." Scott entered the kitchen, wearing an overly large grin, and began rummaging in the fridge.

"What has you so happy?" asked his sister, peeling an apple.

"The Christmas season." He chuckled as Rachel stuck her tongue out at him.

"I hear you met someone," prompted Julia.

Scott began assembling a plate of leftovers, ignoring her comment.

Rachel was about to reprove her brother for his bad manners when the telephone rang. She answered it, disappearing into the dining room when she discovered it was her future mother-in-law.

Scott turned around immediately and gave Julia an apologetic look. "Her name is Tammy. I'm not ready for everyone to give her the third degree."

"I understand." Julia gave him a small smile and returned to the apple she was peeling.

"She has a kid," he blurted. He leaned his large body back against the counter, crossing his arms in front of his chest.

Julia put her paring knife down. "Oh."

"He's three months old. They live with her parents. She couldn't come without him because she's breastfeeding." Scott's voice was low, just above a whisper, and his eyes kept traveling to the doorway that led to the living room.

"When you introduce her to your family, you should bring him too. They'll welcome both of them."

"I'm not so sure." Scott looked very uncomfortable.

"They'll be happy to have a baby around. Rachel and I will fight over him."

"What would you think if your son came home with a girlfriend who was a single mother? And the baby belonged to another guy?"

"Your parents adopted Gabriel. I don't think your dad would object." Julia exhaled slowly, giving Scott a searching look. "Unless your girlfriend is married."

"What? No! Her ex-boyfriend left her when she was pregnant. We've been friends for a while." He ran his fingers through his hair, pulling on it so it almost stood straight on end. "I'm worried my Dad will think it's weird for me to be dating a woman with a newborn."

Julia pointed in the direction of the manger scene that was displayed under the Christmas tree in the next room.

"Joseph and Mary had a similar story."

Scott looked at her as if she'd sprouted a second head.

Then he chuckled, turning back to his sandwich. "That's a good point, Jules. I'll have to remember that."

Later that afternoon, the family gathered around the Christmas tree to open gifts. The Clarks were a generous family, and there were lots of presents, some serious, some in jest. Julia and her father each received their fair share.

When everyone was admiring their gifts and drinking egg nog, Rachel plunked the last present on Gabriel's lap. "This arrived for you this morning."

"Who is it from?" He eyed it in confusion.

"I don't know."

Gabriel gave Julia a hopeful look, but she shook her head.

Eager to uncover the mystery, he began to rip off the wrapping paper. He slid his fingers in between the cover of the white box and its bottom, separating the two, lifted the lid of the box carefully, and peeled back the layers of white tissue paper.

Before anyone could see what he'd uncovered, he shoved the box aside, springing to his feet. Without a word, he strode quickly to the back door, slamming it behind him.

"What was it?" Scott's voice broke the silence.

Aaron, who witnessed what had just transpired from the hallway, entered the room. "I bet it's from his ex. I'd lay money on it."

Julia stumbled to the kitchen and across the back porch, following her lover's retreating form.

"Gabriel? Gabriel! Wait."

Large, fat snowflakes fell like feathers from the sky, blanketing the grass and trees in cold whiteness. She shivered.

"Gabriel!"

He disappeared into the woods without a backward glance.

She hastened her pace. If she lost sight of him she'd have to return to the house. She wouldn't risk being lost in the woods again without a coat. Or a map.

She began to panic, remembering her recurrent nightmare about being trapped in the woods, alone. "Gabriel! Slow down."

Pushing her way into the trees, she traveled a few feet before she saw him, pausing in front of a tall pine.

"Go back to the house." The arctic tone of his voice matched the falling snow.

"I'm not leaving you."

She walked a few more steps. At the sound of her approach, he turned around. He was clad in a suit and tie, wearing expensive Italian shoes that were now ruined.

One of her high heels caught on a branch, and she pitched forward, breaking her fall by clinging to the trunk of a tree.

Gabriel was at her side in an instant. "Go back to the house before you get hurt."

"No."

Her hair was long and curling over her shoulders, arms now crossed in front of her chest because of the cold. A light dusting of white covered her head and her plum dress.

She looked like a snow angel—a figure one might find in a fairy tale or a snow globe, the dancing flakes hovering around her like friends. He was reminded of the time he surprised her in his library carrel and a ream of paper had been tossed into the air, falling all around her.

"*Beautiful.*" He was momentarily distracted by the sight of her. The warmth of his mouth caused his words to form clouds in the air between them.

She held out her pink and naked hand. "Come back with me."

"She's never going to let me go."

"Who?"

"Paulina."

"She needs to start a new life. She needs your help."

"Help?" He glared at her. "You want me to *help* her? After she got on her knees and tried to take my pants down?"

"What?"

He clenched his teeth, cursing his own stupidity. "Nothing."

"Don't lie to me!"

"It was a desperate attempt by a desperate woman."

"Did you say no?"

"Of course! What do you take me for?" His eyes flamed a dangerous blue.

"Were you surprised?"

A muscle jumped in his jaw. "No."

Julia closed her hands so tightly her nails dug into her palms. "Why?"

Gabriel glanced at the trees behind her, unwilling to answer her question.

"Why weren't you surprised?" she repeated, her voice growing louder.

"Because this is what she does."

"Does or did?"

"What's the difference?" he snapped.

Julia's eyes narrowed. "If I have to explain it to you, then we are more damaged than I thought."

He didn't want to answer her. His recalcitrance was telegraphed by his eyes, his face, even his body.

She gave him a piercing stare.

Gabriel's eyes flickered over her shoulder, into the distance, almost as if he were looking for an escape. Then he looked at her again.

"She'd show up on occasion and we'd . . ." His voice trailed off.

Julia felt ill. She screwed her eyes shut. "When I asked if Paulina was your mistress, you said no."

"She was never my mistress."

Julia's eyes flew open. "Don't play word games with me! Especially about your fuck buddies."

He ground his teeth together. "That's beneath you, Julianne."

She laughed without amusement. "Oh, yes. It's beneath me to tell the truth. But you can lie through your teeth!"

"I never lied to you about Paulina."

"Yes, you did. No wonder you were so angry when I called her your fuck buddy in the Dante seminar. I was right." Julia gave him a shattered look. "Were you with her in your bed? In the bed we slept in together?"

Gabriel lowered his eyes.

She began to back away from him. "I am so angry with you right now, I don't know what to say."

"I'm sorry."

"That isn't good enough," she called, walking away from him. "When was the last time you slept with her?"

He followed her quickly, reaching out to grasp her arm.

"Don't touch me!" She pulled back, stumbling over a tree root.

Gabriel caught her before she fell. "Just wait a minute, okay? Give me a chance to explain." Satisfied that she was on surer footing, he released her.

"When I met you in September, things with Paulina had ended. I hadn't been with her since last December, when I told her that we needed to stop once and for all."

"You led me to believe that you ended things with her at Harvard. Do you have any idea how much this hurts? Do you have any idea how stupid this makes me feel? She traipses into your parents' house as if she belongs there—as if I'm the fuck buddy. And no wonder! You've been sleeping with her for *years*."

Gabriel shifted his shoes in the snow. "I was trying to protect you."

"Tread very carefully, Gabriel. Tread very, very carefully."

He froze. He'd never heard her use that tone before. All at once, he felt himself losing her. The mere idea was crippling.

He began speaking very quickly. "We only saw each other once or twice a year. As I said, I haven't been with her since last December." He ran his fingers through his hair. "Did you expect me to catalogue each and every sexual encounter I've ever had? I told you I had a past."

Gabriel's eyes met hers. He held her gaze, taking a tenuous step forward.

"Do you remember the night I told you about Maia?"

"Yes."

"You told me I could find forgiveness. I wanted to believe you. I thought if I told you how I gave in to Paulina again and again, I'd lose you." He cleared his throat. "I didn't mean to hurt you."

"Are you lying to me now?"

"No."

Her expression was skeptical. "Do you love her?"

"Of course not." He took another cautious step in her direction, but she held her hand up.

"So you slept with her for years—after you made a child with her and she had a nervous breakdown—but you didn't love her?"

His lips thinned. "No."

He saw tears shimmering in her big, dark eyes and watched as she fought them, her pretty face marred with sadness. He closed the distance between them, removing his suit jacket and tenderly placing it around her shoulders.

"You'll catch pneumonia. You should go back to the house."

She clutched his jacket, bringing the lapels up to her neck.

"She was Maia's mother," Julia whispered. "And look how you treated her."

Gabriel stiffened. *Maia's mother.*

Julia and Gabriel stood silently, noticing briefly that the snow had ceased falling.

"When were you going to tell me?"

Gabriel hesitated, his heart beating a furious tattoo in his chest. He wasn't entirely sure what he would say until the words escaped his lips.

"I wasn't."

She turned around and began to walk in the direction she thought would lead back to the house.

"Julia, wait!" He came after her, tugging at her arm.

"I told you not to touch me!" She pulled her arm back, glaring at him furiously.

"You made it clear that you didn't want to know the details of what I was like before we met. You said you forgave me."

"I did."

"You knew I was lustful," he reproved her, softly.

"Clearly, I thought there were limits."

Gabriel recoiled, for her remark had cut him. "I deserved that," he said, the temperature of his voice rivaling that of the snow on the ground. "I didn't tell you everything and I should have."

"Was the Christmas gift from her?"

"Yes."

"What was it?"

Gabriel's shoulders slumped. "An ultrasound picture."

Julia inhaled roughly, making a wheezing sound as the bracing winter air filled her lungs. "Why would she do such a thing?"

"Paulina assumes I've kept everything secret. She's right, of course, when it comes to my siblings. But she assumes I haven't told you. This was her way of ensuring I did."

"You used her." Julia's teeth began chattering. "No wonder she won't let you go. You fed her with scraps, like a dog. Would you treat me like that?"

"Never. I know that I treated Paulina abominably. But that doesn't give her the right to hurt you. You're innocent in all of this."

"You misled me."

"Yes. Yes, I did. Can you forgive me?"

Julia was quiet for a moment, rubbing her hands together against the cold. "Have you ever asked Paulina to forgive you?"

Gabriel shook his head.

"You toyed with her heart. I know what that's like. I can have compassion for her because of that."

"I met you first," he whispered.

"That doesn't give you license to be cruel." Julia coughed a little as the cold air burned her throat.

He pressed a light hand to her shoulder. "Please go back. You're cold."

She turned to leave and Gabriel reached out to catch her hand.

"I felt something for her, but it wasn't love. There was guilt and lust, and some affection, but never love."

"What will you do now?"

He wrapped his arm around her waist, drawing her into his side. "I'll resist the urge to react to the present she left and try my damnedest to make things up to you. You're who I want. I'm so sorry to have injured you."

"Maybe you'll change your mind."

He held her more tightly, his expression fierce. "You're the only one I have ever loved."

When Julia didn't respond, he began walking with her toward the house. "I would never be unfaithful, I swear it. As far as what Paulina tried to do yesterday . . ." He squeezed her waist. "There was a time when I could have been led astray. But that was before I found you. I would rather spend the rest of my life drinking your love, than emptying all the oceans of the world."

"Your promises are meaningless when they aren't accompanied by honesty. I asked if she was your mistress, and you played a word game with me."

He grimaced. "You're right. I'm sorry. It won't happen again."

"You'll tire of me eventually. And when you do, you'll go back to what's familiar."

Gabriel stopped. He turned to face her. "Paulina was never familiar. We have a history, but we were never compatible. And we were never good for each other."

Julia simply stared at him skeptically.

"I wandered in the darkness looking for something better, something real. I found you, and I'll be damned if I'm going to lose you."

She looked away, surveying the trees and the path she thought led to the orchard. "Men get bored."

"Only if they're stupid."

His eyes were dark, narrowed with concern and worry. He blinked a little under her gaze, before frowning. "Do you think that Richard would have cheated on Grace?"

"Of course not."

"Why?"

"Because he's a good man. Because he loved her."

"I make no claim to being a good man, Julia. But I love you. I'm not going to cheat."

She was quiet for a moment. "I'm not so wounded that I can't say no to you."

"I never said you weren't." Gabriel looked grim.

"I'm saying no to you now. If you lie to me again, it will be the last time." Her voice held a warning.

"I promise."

She exhaled slowly, unclenching her fists.

"I won't sleep with you in the bed you shared with her."

"I'll have everything redone before we return to Toronto. I'll sell the damn place, if you want."

She pursed her lips. "I'm not asking you to sell your apartment."

"Then forgive me," he whispered. "Give me a chance to show you that I am worthy of your trust."

She hesitated.

He stepped toward her and took her in his arms. She accepted him reluctantly, and they stood under the falling snow, in a darkening wood.

Chapter Twelve

Late that evening Gabriel and Julia sat together in their pajamas on the floor next to their *Charlie Brown* Christmas tree. Julia encouraged Gabriel to open Paulina's gift, so all the secrets could be revealed. He didn't want to do it, but for Julia's sake, he did.

He picked up the ultrasound picture in his hand and grimaced. Julia whispered a request to look at it, and he gave it to her with a sigh.

"This picture can't hurt you. Even if Rachel and Scott found out, they would be sympathetic." She traced a finger across the curve of the baby's little head. "You could keep this somewhere private, but she shouldn't be kept in a box. She had a name. She deserves to be remembered."

Gabriel placed his head in his hands. "You don't think it's morbid?"

"I don't think there's anything morbid about babies. Maia was your daughter. Paulina meant this picture to hurt you, but really, it's a gift. You *should* have this picture. You're her father."

Gabriel was too choked up to respond. To distract himself, he placed the rest of Paulina's gifts by the door. He was returning them to her as soon as possible.

Julia followed him. "I look forward to wearing your Christmas gift." She pointed toward the black corset and shoes that were still sitting in their box under the tree.

"You do?"

"I'll have to give myself a pep talk first, but I think it's feminine and very pretty. I love the shoes. Thank you."

Gabriel's shoulders relaxed. He wanted to ask her to try his gifts on. He wanted to see her in those shoes—perhaps perched atop the bathroom counter with him between her legs—but he kept his desires to himself.

"Um, I need to explain something." Julia took his hand, weaving their fingers together. "I can't wear it tonight."

"I'm sure that after the past two days wearing something like that would be the last thing you'd want to do." Gabriel stroked the back of her hand with his thumb. "Especially with me."

"It will be a little while before I can wear it."

"I understand." He began to extricate his fingers.

"I tried to explain this to you last night but, uh, I didn't quite finish."

He stilled.

"Um, I'm having my period."

Gabriel's mouth dropped open slightly. Then he closed it. He pulled her into his arms, embracing her warmly.

"That wasn't the reaction I was expecting." Julia's voice was muffled by his chest. "Maybe you didn't hear me?"

"So last night—it wasn't because you didn't want me?"

She pulled back in surprise. "I'm still upset about what happened with Paulina, but of course I want you. You always make me feel special when we make love. Right now, I'm not going to go there. Or actually, have you go there. Uh, you know what I mean." She grew flustered.

Heaving a sigh of relief, Gabriel kissed her forehead. "I have other plans for you."

He led her by the hand to the spacious washroom, pausing to press play on the stereo. The strains of Sting's "Until" began to fill the room as they disappeared through the door.

❊ ❊

Paulina sat up, wide-awake in a strange bed in Toronto, covered in a cold sweat. No amount of repetition made the dream vary in its events or its terror. No amount of vodka or pills could remove the ache in her chest or the tears from her eyes.

She reached for the bottle by the bed, knocking the hotel's alarm clock off the nightstand. A few shots and a few small, blue pills and she would fall asleep again, letting the darkness take her.

She could not be comforted. Other women could have a second child to assuage the loss of their first. But she would never bear a child. And the father of her lost baby no longer wanted her.

He was the only man she'd ever loved, and she'd loved him from afar and then she'd loved him close by, but he'd never loved her. Not really. But he was too noble to cast her off like the used piece of goods she was.

As she sobbed into her pillow, her head spinning, she mourned a double loss aloud—

Maia.

Gabriel . . .

Chapter Thirteen

Professor Giuseppe Pacciani wasn't virtuous, but he was clever. He didn't believe Christa Peterson when she declared that she was willing to meet him for a sexual rendezvous. In order to ensure that their liaison actually happened, he withheld the name of Professor Emerson's Canadian *fidanzata* on condition that Christa meet him in Madrid in February.

Christa was unwilling to wait that long or to sleep with him again in order to ferret out the information, so she didn't respond to his last email. She decided to regroup and find an alternative way of discovering the name of Professor Emerson's fiancée.

It could be said that she was jealous and that this was her primary reason for wondering who had successfully captured the Professor's attention when she had failed (inexplicably). It could be said that she'd begun to nurse a suspicion about a certain doe-eyed brunette, ever since Professor Emerson had almost come to blows with that student over a mistress called Paulina.

But perhaps the most accurate explanation was her new and rather prurient fascination with the rumors she'd heard about Professor Singer and her not-so-secret lifestyle. When Professor Emerson embraced her after his lecture at the University of Toronto, it set a good number of tongues wagging. Christa's tongue was among them.

Perhaps Giuseppe was wrong. Perhaps the Professor did not have a *fidanzata* after all. Perhaps he had a mistress.

In order to solve this very juicy mystery, Christa contacted an old flame from Florence who wrote for *La Nazione*, hoping that he would provide her with information about Professor Emerson's personal life.

While she waited for a response, she focused on an information source closer to home. In the *Vestibule,* all sins would be revealed.

Professor Emerson's marked absence from Lobby began the evening she tried to seduce him. So, she reasoned, his relationship with his fiancée must have begun around that time. Previously, he hadn't cared who he hooked up with or when. Or perhaps he and his fiancée had been involved only causally until that fateful night. It was possible that the Professor was far from monogamous in his relationship and that he'd had a fiancée all along, although such an attachment would have likely made the rounds of the rumor mill.

(Toronto is, after all, a small town.)

Christa's way forward was clear. It was likely that the Professor and his fiancée had visited Lobby sometime over the course of the winter semester, since it appeared to be his watering hole of choice. All she needed to do was to find someone who worked at the club and pump him for information.

Late on a Saturday night, Christa stalked the staff at Lobby, trying to discover the weakest link. She sat at the bar, absolutely ignoring the tall, blond American woman who was there for the same purpose, having just flown in from Harrisburg. Christa's full, red lips curled back in disgust when the woman pulled out her iPhone and spoke very loudly in Italian to a maître d' called Antonio.

As the night wore on, Christa soon realized her options were few. Ethan had a serious girlfriend, which meant that he wouldn't be ripe for the picking. More than one of the bartenders were gay, and all the servers were women. Which left Lucas.

Lucas was a computer geek (not that there's anything wrong with that) who assisted Ethan with security at the club, in a technical capacity. Lucas had access to the video recordings from the security cameras, and it was he who rather enthusiastically agreed to let Christa into the club after hours so they could sift through CD upon CD of footage, starting with September 2009.

And that was how Christa found herself sitting on the vanity in the women's washroom with Lucas pounding into her on a Sunday morning when she should have been in church.

❀ ❀

Gabriel and Julia arrived back in Toronto late in the evening on January first. They went to Julia's apartment so she could drop off some things and retrieve some clean clothes. Or so Gabriel thought. With the taxi waiting at the curb for them to return, he stood in the middle of her cold and shabby apartment expecting her to pack an overnight bag. She didn't.

"This is my home, Gabriel. I've been gone for three weeks. I need to do laundry, and I need to work on my thesis tomorrow. Classes start on Monday."

His expression grew very dark very quickly.

"Yes, I'm aware of when classes begin." His tone was clipped. "But it's freezing in here. You don't have any food, and I don't want to sleep without you. Come home with me, and you can return to-morrow."

"I don't want to go home with you."

"I told you I'd have the master bedroom redone, and it has been. The bed, the furniture, it's all new." He grimaced. "They even painted the walls."

"I'm still not ready." She turned her back on him and began unpacking her suitcase. He took one look at her activities and strode through the apartment door, closing it somewhat loudly behind him.

Julia sighed.

He was trying, she knew. But his revelations had scorched holes in her already fragile self-confidence, a self-confidence that had only begun to be rebuilt during their time in Italy. She knew herself well enough to know that her fear of losing him was grounded in her parents' divorce and in Simon's betrayal. Although she knew all these things, it was very difficult to will herself to disregard them and to believe that Gabriel's love would never wane.

She'd just walked to her door to bolt it when he walked in, suitcase in hand. "What are you doing?"

"Keeping you warm," he said stiffly.

Gabriel placed his suitcase down and disappeared into the bathroom, closing the door behind him. He emerged a few minutes later with his shirt untucked and unbuttoned, muttering something about having successfully turned on her damned electric heater.

"Why did you come back?"

"I am not accustomed to sleeping without you. In fact, I'm about ready to sell the damn condo and all my furniture and buy something else." He shook his head and proceeded to undress unashamedly without further conversation.

While Julia used the bathroom, Gabriel examined some of the items she'd displayed on her card table—the book containing the Botticelli reproductions he'd given her for her birthday, a pillar candle, a book of matches, and the photo album of pictures he'd taken of her.

As he leafed through the album, he found himself aroused. She'd promised to pose for him again. She *wanted* him to photograph her. A month earlier he never would have believed that such a thing could come to pass. She'd been so timid, so nervous.

He recalled the look she had in her eyes when he took her to his bed after their horrible argument in his seminar. Thinking of Julianne's eyes, large and terrified, and the way her body trembled under his hands, diminished his arousal. He didn't deserve her. He knew that. But her own perceived unworthiness prevented her from seeing the truth.

He flipped through the pictures before focusing on one—Julianne in profile with his hand on her shoulder, his other hand holding up her hair, while he pressed his lips to her shapely neck.

She was unaware of the fact that he had a copy of that picture hiding in his closet. He'd never displayed it, for he was worried about her reaction. When he returned to his newly redecorated bedroom, hanging that photograph would be his first task.

The thought alone was more than enough to fuel his desire, so he took the candle and struck a match to light it, placing it on the card table before turning out the lights. A romantic glow fell over the photographs and the bed just as Julia entered the darkened space.

He sat on the edge of her narrow bed, completely naked, while she stood clutching a pair of worn flannel pajamas. They had rubber duckies on them.

"What are you doing?" He glanced at her sleepwear with barely disguised distaste.

"I'm getting ready for bed."

Gabriel stared. *"Come here."*

She walked over to him slowly.

He took the fabric from her, tossing it aside. "You don't need pajamas. You don't need to wear anything."

Julia carefully proceeded to disrobe in front of him, placing her clothes on one of the folding chairs.

He paused her movement toward the bed and placed his hands on top of her head, almost as if he were blessing her. Then he began to touch her, passing his fingers through her long hair to her face, where he caressed her eyebrows and cheekbones. His eyes remained stubbornly fixed on hers, the heat of their intensity searing into Julia's consciousness.

Something of the old Professor Emerson was visible now, especially in his expression, which was sexual and raw. She closed her eyes briefly, and his hands moved from her neck to her face, pausing for a moment.

"Open your eyes."

She opened them and gasped at the hunger reflected back to her. He was like a lion, eager to feed but still stalking his prey. He didn't want to scare her off. But she was helpless in her own desire for him.

"Have you missed me touching you like this?" he asked, his voice a scorching whisper.

Julia's affirmation escaped her mouth as a strangled groan. Gabriel's chest swelled with pride.

It was a long journey from her face to her knees, and he seemed to enjoy it, pausing slowly at different parts, his touch light but heated. She felt warm beneath his gentle fingers, despite the coldness of the room. As soon as she thought of the cold, she flinched.

Gabriel stopped his explorations immediately, and moved aside to allow her to crawl into bed, closest to the wall. He pressed his chest to her back, pulling the purple duvet over their naked bodies.

"I've missed making love with you. It was as if one of my limbs was missing."

"I missed you too."

He smiled his relief. "I'm very glad to hear that. It was torturous to go a week without being able to touch you like this."

"It was torturous to go a week without being able to feel you touching me."

The stirrings of desire in her voice set fire to Gabriel's blood. He tightened his hold on her, squeezing gently. "Cuddling is a very important component to making love."

"I would never have pegged you as a cuddler, Professor Emerson."

He drew some skin from her neck into his mouth, sucking it lightly. "I have become a great many things since you made me your lover." He placed his face in her hair, inhaling her vanilla scent deeply. "Sometimes I wonder if you realize how much you've changed me. It's no less than miraculous."

"I'm no miracle worker. But I love you."

"And I love you." He was quiet for a moment or two, which surprised her. She had expected him to begin making love immediately.

"You never told me what happened at Kinfolks restaurant the day before Christmas." Gabriel tried to sound relaxed, for he didn't want her to think he was scolding her.

In the hope of ending the conversation quickly so they could move on to other activities, Julia described her altercation with Natalie. She left out the part where Natalie had mocked her sexual encounters with *him* in front of everyone. Gabriel rolled her onto her back so he could see her face.

"Why didn't you tell me?"

"It was too late for you to do anything."

"I love you, damn it! Why didn't you tell me?"

"Paulina was waiting for us when we returned to the house."

He scowled. "Right. So you threatened your former roommate with a newspaper article?"

"Yes."

"Do you think she believed you?"

"She wants out of Selinsgrove. She wants to be Simon's official girl-friend and hang on his arm at political events in Washington. She isn't going to do anything to jeopardize that."

"Doesn't she have all that now?"

"Natalie is Simon's dirty little secret. Which is why it took me so long to figure out he was fucking her."

Gabriel winced. Julia didn't use profanity often, and when she did, it was jarring.

"Look at me." He pressed his forearms into the mattress on either side of her shoulders.

She looked up into concerned blue eyes.

"I'm sorry he hurt you. I'm also sorry I didn't do more damage to his face when I had the chance. But I can't say I'm sorry he went after your roommate. Otherwise you wouldn't be here with me."

He kissed her, his hand tracing the curve of her neck until she sighed contentedly into his mouth.

"*You* are my sticky little leaf. My beautiful, sad, sticky little leaf, and I want to see you happy and whole. I'm sorry for every tear I've made you shed. I hope that someday you'll be able to forgive me."

She hid her face in the crook of his shoulder as she clutched him closer. Her hands explored his body until they were one. The silent air of her tiny studio was broken only by heavy breathing and muffled pants and her own voice moaning to a fevered pitch.

It was a subtle language—this shared language of lovers: the recip-rocation of sigh and groan, anticipation growing and feeding until groans became cries and cries became sighs once more. Gabriel's body covered hers completely, a delicious weight of man and sweat and naked skin upon naked skin.

This was the joy that the world sought—sacred and pagan all at once. A union between two dissimilars into a seamless one. A pic-ture of love and deep satisfaction. An ecstatic glimpse of the beatific vision.

Before Gabriel withdrew from her, he pressed one more kiss to her cheek. "Will you?"

"Will I what?"

"Forgive me for deceiving you about Paulina. For taking advantage of her."

"I can't forgive you on her behalf. Only she can do that." Julia chewed at her bottom lip. "Now, more than ever, you need to see that she gets help so she can move on with her life. You owe her that."

He wanted to say something, but somehow the strength of her goodness silenced him.

Chapter Fourteen

As the semester unfolded, Julia was under tremendous pressure to complete her thesis, and Katherine Picton was pushing her to submit chapters more quickly. Quicker chapters would make it easier to speak more specifically about Julia's abilities to Greg Matthews, the Chair of the Department of Romance Languages at Harvard, should he follow up on her reference letter.

Julia couldn't concentrate when Gabriel was around. Her voice grew soft when she told him why. Something about blue eyes and sexual pyrotechnics and a chemistry that vibrated in the air between them, all of which kept her from focusing on the tasks at hand. Gabriel was extremely flattered.

So the happy couple worked out a compromise. There would be telephone calls and texts and the occasional Gmail, but apart from a lunch or dinner during the week, Julia would stay at her apartment. On Friday afternoons she would arrive at Gabriel's in order to spend the weekend with him.

One Wednesday evening in mid-January, Julia called Gabriel after her homework was done.

"I had a rough day," she said, sounding tired.

"What happened?"

"Professor Picton is making me scrap about three-quarters of one of my chapters because she thinks I'm offering a Romanticized version of Dante."

"Ouch."

"She hates the Romantics, so you can imagine how annoyed she was. She went on and on about it. She makes me feel stupid."

"You aren't stupid." Gabriel chuckled into the phone. "Professor Picton makes me feel stupid sometimes."

"I find that hard to believe."

"You should have seen me the first time I was summoned to her house. I was more nervous than I was on the day I defended my dissertation. I almost forgot to wear pants."

Julia laughed. "I can only imagine that a pantless Professor Emerson would be very well received."

"Thankfully, I didn't have to find out."

"Professor Picton told me that 'my strong work ethic makes up for my occasional lapses in reasoning.'"

"That's high praise coming from her. She thinks most people fail to reason at all. The way she describes the world today, most people are monkeys who happen to wear clothes. On occasion."

Julia groaned, rolling onto her stomach. "Would it kill her to tell me that she likes my thesis? Or that I'm doing a good job?"

"Katherine will never tell you that she likes your thesis. She thinks positive feedback is patronizing. This is simply the way those old, pretentious Oxonians are."

"You aren't like that, Professor Emerson."

Gabriel found himself twitching at the mere change in her tone.

"Oh, yes I am, Miss Mitchell. You've simply forgotten."

"You're sweet with me now."

"I should hope so," he whispered, his voice almost breaking. "But remember, you're my lover, not my student." He grinned wickedly. "Except in the ways of love."

She laughed, and he found himself laughing with her.

"I finished the book you lent me, *A Severe Mercy*."

"That was quick. How did you manage that?"

"I'm loneliest at night. I've been reading to help me fall asleep."

"You have no reason to be lonely. Take a cab to my place. I'll keep you company."

Julia rolled her eyes. "Yes, Professor."

"Okay, *Miss Mitchell*. So how was the book?"

"I'm not sure why Grace liked it so much."

"Why?"

"Well, it's a romantic love story. But when they became Christians, they decided their love for each other was pagan—that they'd made idols of one another. That made me sad."

"I'm sorry it saddened you. I haven't read it, although Grace used to talk about it."

"How could love be pagan, Gabriel? I don't understand."

"You're asking me that question? I thought I was the pagan in this relationship."

"You aren't a pagan. You told me so yourself."

He sighed thoughtfully. "So I did. You know as well as I that Dante views God as the only thing in the universe who can satisfy the longings of the soul. This is Dante's implicit critique of Paolo and Francesca's sin. They forego a higher good—the love of God—for the love of a human being. Of course, that's a sin."

"Paolo and Francesca were adulterers. They shouldn't have fallen in love with each other in the first place."

"That's true. But even if they were unmarried lovers, Dante's criticism would be the same. If they love one another to the exclusion of everything and everyone else, then their love is pagan. They've made idols of one another and their love. And they're also very foolish, because no human being can ever make another human being completely happy. Human beings are far too imperfect for that."

Julia was stunned. Although there were aspects of Gabriel's explanation that she knew already, it truly surprised her to hear such words from his lips.

It appeared that she was a pagan about her love of Gabriel, and she hadn't even realized it. Moreover, if he actually believed what he was saying, then he had a much less exalted view of their attachment. She was shocked.

"Julianne? Are you still there?"

She cleared her throat. "Yes."

"It's just a theory. It has nothing to do with us."

He spoke the words, but the unease remained. He knew that he'd made an idol of Julianne, his Beatrice, and no denial or sophisticated rhetoric could make that truth false. Given all the time he'd spent in a twelve-step program that encouraged him to focus on a higher power and not himself, his lovers or his family, he knew better.

"So why did Grace like this book? I don't understand."

"I don't know," said Gabriel. "Maybe when Richard swept her off her feet she viewed him as a savior. He married her, and they rode off into the sunset of Selinsgrove."

"Richard is a good man," Julia murmured.

"He is. But Richard is not a god. If Grace married him thinking that all her troubles would disappear because of his perfection, their relationship would not have lasted. She would have become disillusioned eventually, and she would have left him in order to find someone else to make her happy.

"Perhaps the reason why Richard and Grace were so happily married was because they had realistic expectations; they didn't expect one another to meet all their needs. It would also explain why a spiritual dimension was so important to each of them."

"Maybe you're right. My book is a lot different from the Graham Greene novel you were reading."

"They aren't so different."

"Your novel is about an affair and a man who hates God. I Wikied it."

Gabriel resisted the urge to growl. "Don't Wiki things, Julianne. You know that website is unreliable."

"Yes, Professor Emerson," she purred.

He groaned.

"Why do you think Greene's protagonist hates God? Because his lover gave him up *for* God. We both read a novel about pagans, Julianne. It's just the endings that were different."

"I'm not sure they were so different."

Gabriel smiled in spite of himself. "I think it's a bit late for us to be having this conversation. I'm sure you're tired, and I have some paperwork I need to do."

"I love you. Madly."

Something about the way her voice sounded in his ear made his heart quicken.

"I love you too. I love you far too much, I'm sure. But I don't know how to love you any other way." His final words were a whisper, but they burned in the air.

"I don't know how to love you any other way, either," she whispered back.

"Then God have mercy on us both."

If you were to ask Gabriel if he wanted to be in therapy, he would have said *no*. He didn't relish the idea of talking about his feelings or his childhood, or being forced to relive what happened with Paulina. He didn't want to talk about his addictions or Professor Singer and the myriad other women he'd bedded.

But he wanted a future with Julia, and he wanted her to be healthy— to bloom fully and not just partially. He privately worried that he was somehow impairing her ability to blossom, just because he was, well, *Gabriel*.

So he vowed to do everything in his power to support her, including changing his behavior for the best and focusing more on her needs. In so doing, he recognized that he could do with an objective evaluation of his own selfishness and some practical advice as to how to overcome it. Consequently, he was determined to brave the discomfort and embarrassment of admitting he needed help and see a therapist on a weekly basis.

As the days of January slipped by, it became abundantly clear that both Gabriel and Julia were very fortunate in their choice of therapists. Drs. Nicole and Winston Nakamura were a married couple who sought to work with clients on their psychological and personal issues with a view to integrating those considerations with both existential and spiritual pursuits.

Nicole was concerned about the nature of Julia's relationship with her boyfriend. She worried that the power differential between Julia and Gabriel, coupled with his strong personality and Julia's diminished self-confidence, would make their romantic relationship more of a mental health hazard to Julia than a help.

But Julia claimed to be in love with Gabriel and to be very happy with him, and it was clear that she derived a lot of pleasure and no small amount of security from their relationship. However, the strange account of how they met and then met again, when added to certain facts about Gabriel's past and his addictive personality, raised all sorts of red flags in Nicole's mind. The fact that Julia did not recognize these red flags showed more about her own psychological state than she could reasonably realize.

Winston pulled no punches, informing Gabriel that he was placing his recovery in jeopardy by continuing to drink alcohol and by failing to go to Narcotics Anonymous meetings. What was supposed to be an introductory meeting exploded into an angry confrontation, which resulted in Gabriel storming out of the office.

Nevertheless, Gabriel returned to his next session, promising that he would attend Narcotics Anonymous meetings. He attended one or two and never returned.

Chapter Fifteen

Snowfall in the city is very different from snowfall in the country, thought Julia, as she and Gabriel walked through the cascading flakes to his building so he could pick up his car. Tonight would be an evening of celebration at a fancy French restaurant, *Auberge du Pommier*.

Gabriel tugged on Julia's arm and pulled her into the doorway of a shop, kissing her firmly as he backed her into a wall of glass. She giggled breathlessly when he finished, and in return, dragged him out to the sidewalk so they could admire the falling snow.

In the country, you can hear the snow whispering around you, the large, fat flakes unfettered by skyscrapers and office buildings. In the city, the wind drives the snow in between the tall buildings, but the snowfall is lessened considerably by the many obstacles. Or so Julia thought.

When they arrived at Gabriel's building, she paused in front of the large china shop that dominated the first floor. But Julia wasn't interested in the great window of china that gazed out at her matrimonially. She was only interested in the handsome man beside her.

Gabriel wore a long black wool coat that boasted a black velvet collar and a Burberry scarf wrapped like an ascot at his neck. The hand that clasped hers was clad in black leather gloves. But it was his hat that fascinated her.

Professor Emerson wore a beret.

She found his choice of haberdashery strangely appealing. Gabriel had refused to succumb to the local custom of wearing knit caps or toques. A black wool beret to match his overcoat did nicely enough. And he was very elegant in it.

"What?" His face crinkled as he watched her watching his reflection, a slow smile playing about his lips.

"You're handsome," she stammered, unable to take her eyes away from his striking figure.

"You're the attractive one, inside and out. A beautiful popsicle."

He kissed her long and good in front of a hundred bone china place settings, and gently pecked her ear. "Let's take a cab to dinner. Then I'll be able to devote my full attention to you. I'll run inside to take out some cash from the ATM and I'll be back in a minute. Unless you'd rather join me."

Julia shook her head. "I want to enjoy the snow while it lasts."

He snorted loudly. "This is a Canadian winter. Believe me, the snow will last." He moved her scarf aside to kiss her neck, and he chuckled to himself as he disappeared into the Manulife Building.

She peered through the window at the display of china and began to admire one place setting in particular, wondering how it would look in Gabriel's apartment.

"Julia?"

She turned around and came face to chest with Paul. He smiled at her and engulfed her in a warm hug. "How are you?"

"I'm fine," she responded somewhat nervously, worrying that Gabriel would surprise them.

"You look great. Did you have a good Christmas?"

"Very good. I brought you a souvenir from Pennsylvania. I'll put it in your mailbox in the department. How was your Christmas?"

"Fine. Busy, but fine. How are your classes?"

"They're good. Professor Picton is keeping me busy."

"I'll bet she is." Paul chuckled. "Maybe we can get coffee sometime next week and you can tell me all about it."

"Maybe." Julia smiled back, resisting the urge to turn around and look for Gabriel, when all of a sudden Paul's smile slid off his face.

His dark brows came together, and he took a step closer, a scowl clouding over his usually benign features. *"What happened to you?"*

Julia looked down at her winter coat but saw nothing that would alarm him. And then she wiped at her face, wondering if Gabriel had smeared her lip-gloss across her cheeks.

But Paul was looking elsewhere. He was looking at her neck.

He came closer still, so he was truly violating her personal space, and pulled the edge of her purple pashmina aside with his bear-like paw.

"Holy God, Julia, what the hell is that?"

She flinched as one of his work-roughened fingers tentatively skimmed the bite mark on her neck, cursing the fact that she'd apparently forgotten to use concealer that morning when she applied her makeup.

"It's nothing. I'm fine." She moved backward and wrapped her pashmina around her neck twice, fussing with the ends so she wouldn't have to look at him.

"I know what nothing looks like, and that ain't nothing. Did your boyfriend do that?"

"Of course not! He would never hurt me."

Paul cocked his head to one side. "You told me he hurt you before. I thought that was why you broke up the last time."

Julia found herself wrapped in the coiled python grip of her lies. She opened her mouth to protest and quickly closed it, trying to think of something to say.

"Did he bite you out of love? Or anger?" Paul tried to keep his voice calm. He was furious with whoever had treated Julia so violently and more than willing to track down the offender and kick his ass. Several times.

"Owen would never do something like that. He's never put a violent hand on me."

"Then damn it, Julia, what happened?"

She blinked at his anger and found herself looking down at her boots.

"And don't lie to me," he breathed.

"Someone broke into my father's house during Thanksgiving and attacked me. That's how I got the scar. I know it's hideous. I'm having it removed."

Paul was quiet for a moment as he considered what she said. "A bite mark seems awfully personal for a burglar, don't you think?"

Julia chewed at the inside of her mouth.

"And why should you be ashamed of being attacked? It wasn't your fault." Paul fumed. "You don't want to tell me. I get it." He reached out and took her hand in his, stroking the surface of her palm with his thumb. "If you need to get away from him, I can help."

"That's very kind, but the police caught him. He can't reach me here."

Paul's shoulders softened. "I'm your friend, Rabbit. I care about you. Let me help you before something worse happens."

She withdrew her hand. "I'm not a rabbit, and I don't need your help."

"I didn't mean anything by the nickname." Paul offered her a repentant look. "Why didn't Owen come to your rescue? I would have beaten the burglar to a pulp."

She began to tell him that Owen had, in fact, rescued her but swiftly thought better of it.

"He must not be a very good boyfriend if he allows you to be manhandled like that."

"I was home alone. No one could have known that someone would break in and attack me. I'm not a damsel in distress, Paul, despite what you might think." Her eyes flashed.

Paul gazed at her sharply. "I never said you were a damsel in distress. But that thing on your neck is not something a burglar would do. It's a fucking mark. And you have to admit that you've been knocked around by a couple of people, even in the short time I've known you. Christa, Professor Pain, *Emerson* . . ."

"This was different."

"You deserve better than to be someone's punching bag." His voice was soft and it made Julia shiver. "I'd never treat you like that."

She looked into his kind, brown eyes and stood mutely, hoping Gabriel would not appear.

Paul thrust his hands into the pockets of his coat and shifted his weight back and forth. "I'm heading over to Yonge Street to meet some friends for dinner. Would you like to join me?"

"I've been out most of the day. I'm going home."

He nodded. "I'm running late, or I'd walk you. Do you need money for a cab?"

"No, I've got it. Thanks." She fidgeted with her gloves, adjusting the fingers. "You're a good friend."

"I'll see you around." He gave her a pained smile and began walking away.

Julia turned to look through the glass doors of the building, but couldn't see Gabriel.

"Julia?" Paul called to her.

"Yes?"

"Be careful, okay?"

She nodded and waved, watching as he turned and walked away.

At two o'clock in the morning, Julia startled. She was in Gabriel's bed, and his room was dark. But she was alone.

After Paul disappeared, Gabriel returned to her side. If he'd seen her exchange with Paul, he gave no sign of it, although he was somewhat quiet during their celebratory dinner. Later, when she was ready for bed, he'd kissed her on the forehead and said he'd join her soon. Hours later, he still hadn't come to bed.

She tiptoed down the hall. The apartment was swathed in darkness. Only the light from underneath Gabriel's study door was visible. She stood in the hallway, listening. When she finally heard a few clicks of the computer keys, she turned the doorknob and walked in.

To say that Gabriel was surprised would have been an understatement. His eyes swung to hers, narrowed and uneasy, from behind his glasses.

"What are you doing?" He stood up immediately, placing a large Oxford dictionary on top of the papers that were scattered across his desk.

"I—nothing." She hesitated, looking down at her bare legs. She wiggled her toes on top of the Persian carpet.

He was at her side in an instant. "Is something wrong?"

"You didn't come to bed. I was worried."

Gabriel removed his glasses, rubbing his eyes. "I'll come to bed soon. I just have a few things to do that can't wait."

Julia reached up to kiss his cheek before turning to go.

"Wait. Let me tuck you in." He took her hand in his and led her down the dark hallway to their room.

Gone was the large medieval bed, the dark furniture, and ice blue silk fabrics from his bedroom. Gabriel had hired an interior designer to recreate the master bedroom he'd shared with Julia in Umbria. Now the walls were cream-colored, and a large canopy bed hung with gauzy curtains sat in the center of the room. Julia had approved of the transformation and the inspiration behind it. The room was no longer his, but theirs.

"Sweet dreams." He pressed an almost parental kiss to her forehead before closing the bedroom door behind him.

Julia lay awake for some time, wondering what he was hiding. She wrestled with the question of whether or not she should strive to find out or simply trust him. Without a satisfactory resolution, she fell into a troubled sleep.

Chapter Sixteen

Paul couldn't sleep. Had he been a melodramatic sort of person he would have described his restless evening as a *dark night of the soul*. But Paul was from Vermont and thus not melodramatic. Nonetheless, after a long evening over dinner and beer with players from his rugby team, Paul couldn't get the image of Julia's marked skin out of his mind.

He had well-defined views about how a man should treat a woman, views that had been shaped largely by his parents. His mother and father weren't overly demonstrative in their affection nor were they sentimental. But they always treated one another with respect. Paul's mother had encouraged him to treat girls like ladies, and his father had demanded the same, saying that if he ever heard of Paul treating a girl badly, he'd have to answer for his behavior.

Paul thought back to his first keg party, during his freshman year at St. Michael's College, and how he'd run into a girl in a torn shirt on his way to the bathroom. He'd calmed her down and demanded that she point out who had attacked her. Paul cornered her assailant and held him until the campus police showed up, but not before roughing him up a little.

When his younger sister Heather was being tormented by boys in junior high school, boys who made lewd comments and snapped her bra strap against her back, he waited for the little fuckers after school and threatened them. Heather continued her education bully-free after that.

In Paul's romantic economy, violence against women was absolutely unthinkable, and he would have used his savings to get on a plane to track down the person who had marked Julia, if he only knew the asshole's name and location.

It was his own fault she wouldn't talk to him, he reasoned, as he stared at the wall of his simple apartment. He had gone all knight in shining armor on her, and she'd retreated. If he'd been less angry and more supportive, then perhaps she would have revealed what actually happened. But he'd pushed her, and now it was unlikely that she'd ever tell him the truth.

Should I respect her by staying out of it? Or should I try to help her no matter what she says?

Paul didn't know which arm of the dilemma he was going to choose, but one thing he knew for sure—he was going to keep his eye on Julia, and he'd be damned if anyone would injure her when he was around.

❄ ❄

Shortly before eleven the next morning, Julia rolled out of bed from under Gabriel's arm. She pulled on one of his white Oxford button-down shirts and stood in front of the large black-and-white framed photograph of Gabriel kissing her neck.

She loved the photograph but had been surprised to see it so prominently displayed on his wall and in so large a size. It made her think back to her first visit, when she studied the black-and-white photographs that used to grace his walls. And he'd vomited all over her and his British-racing-green sweater.

Gabriel certainly had panache when it came to his clothing. He would have looked good wearing nothing but a brown paper bag. (Julia meditated on that thought for more than a few seconds.)

Leaving Gabriel to snore softly in peace, she walked to the kitchen. As she helped herself to breakfast, she thought back to his behavior the night before.

What had he been doing in his study on a Friday night?

Before she could consider the implications of her actions, she found herself wandering into his office. She walked over to his desk and saw that his laptop was switched off. All the papers from the night before had been cleared away, the gleaming oak of the desktop almost bare. There was no way she was going to open his files and desk drawers in search of his secrets.

However, she found something on his desk that she had not

expected—a small, sterling silver frame with a black-and-white picture in it.

Maia.

She picked up the photo and held it in her hand, marveling that Gabriel had progressed so far as to have the ultrasound picture framed. Lost in thought, she stood looking at it for what seemed like a long time.

"Did you find what you were looking for?"

She whirled around to find Gabriel leaning against the doorframe, arms across his chest, clad only in a T-shirt and a pair of striped boxer shorts.

He stared a little too long at the naked flesh that peeked out from between the top buttons and at her shapely legs. He glanced at the picture frame and his expression shifted.

Julia quickly replaced the frame on the desk. "I'm sorry."

Gabriel strode toward her. "I haven't decided where to put it." He looked at the picture. "But I don't want to keep it in a drawer."

"Of course. It's a beautiful frame," she offered.

"I found it at Tiffany."

Julia cocked her head to one side. "Only you would buy a frame at Tiffany's. I would have gone to Walmart."

"I went to Tiffany for quite a different purpose." He searched her face.

Her heart skipped a beat. "Did you find what you were looking for?"

Now his eyes burned into hers. "Absolutely. But I found it long ago."

Julia blinked as if she were in some sort of fog until he leaned down to kiss her. It was a remarkable kiss. He placed his hands gently on either side of her face and then brought his lips to hers, pressing firmly before beginning his joyous movement. Within a moment, she'd forgotten all about why she'd wandered into the study.

He stroked her tongue tenderly with his, sliding his hands through her hair to rest on the back of her head. And when he withdrew, he kissed her cheeks.

"I wish I'd known you my whole life. I wish everything had been different."

"We're together now."

"That we are, my lovely. You look beautiful in my shirt." His voice was gruff all of a sudden. "I was planning to take you out for breakfast. There's a small crêperie around the corner that I think you'd like."

She took his hand gladly as he led her back to the bedroom so they could shower together and begin their day.

Later that afternoon they worked in his study. Gabriel sat at his desk, reading an article, while Julia sat perched in his red velvet armchair, checking her email.

Dear Julia,

I owe you an apology. I'm really sorry I upset you when I ran into you yesterday. I didn't mean to. I was worried about you.

If you ever need someone to talk to, I'm just a phone call away.

Hoping we can still be friends,

Paul.

PS. Christa has been asking why Professor Picton is directing your thesis.

Julia looked over at Gabriel and found him lost in thought behind his eyeglasses. She quickly typed a response.

Hi Paul,

Of course we're still friends. The incident in Selinsgrove was traumatic, and I'm trying to forget about it.

I should mention that my boyfriend saved me—in more ways than one.

Someday I'd like to introduce you to him. He's wonderful.

Not sure why Christa cares who is directing my thesis. I'm only an MA student.

Thanks for the warning.

I'll put your Christmas present in your mailbox in the department on Monday.

It's small but I hope you like it.

And thanks,

Julia.

❀ ❀

Katherine Picton lived a reserved life. She owned a nice home in the Annex neighborhood of Toronto, which was within walking distance to the university. She spent her summers in Italy and Christmas holidays in England. And she spent most of her time publishing articles and monographs on Dante. In other words, she lived the life of the respectable academic spinster, except that she didn't garden or take lovers or own a bevy of cats. (Regrettably.)

Despite her age, she was very much in demand for public lectures and more than one university had attempted to lure her out of retirement with promises of extravagant salaries and modest teaching responsibilities. Katherine would rather have dug the Panama Canal with her fingernails while suffering from yellow fever than give up the time she could devote to research in order to maintain an office on campus and attend faculty meetings.

So when Greg Matthews of Harvard University telephoned her in January about an opening for an endowed chair in Dante studies, that's what she told him.

He reacted in stunned silence before fumbling over his next words. "But Professor Picton, we could arrange it so you wouldn't have to teach. All you would have to do would be to deliver a couple of lectures a semester, have a presence on campus, and supervise some doctoral students. That's it."

"I don't want to move all my books," said Katherine.

"We'll hire a moving company."

"They'll mix them up and it will take weeks to put them back in order."

"We'll hire special movers—movers accustomed to moving libraries. They'll take your books off the shelf, pack them in order, and replace them on your shelves here in Cambridge exactly the way they were in Toronto. You wouldn't have to do a thing."

"Moving companies don't know how to catalogue books," she scoffed. "What if they mis-shelve something? I have thousands of volumes in my library, and I might never be able to find what they misplace. And what if they lose something? Some of those books are irreplaceable!"

"Professor Picton, if you would accept the endowed chair, I'll come to Toronto and move your books personally."

Katherine paused for a moment until she realized that Greg was serious. Then she burst into peals of laughter.

"Harvard sounds very accommodating."

"You have no idea," he muttered, hoping that she would change her mind.

"I'm not interested. There are lots of younger persons you should be considering instead of a sixty-eight-year-old retiree. While we're on the subject of your department, I want to talk to you about my graduate student, Julianne Mitchell, and why I think you need to admit her to your doctoral program."

Katherine spent ten minutes telling Greg why it had been a mistake for him to fail to offer Julianne adequate funding the previous year. Then Professor Picton impressed upon him the need for Julianne to receive a lucrative fellowship beginning in September. Finally, when she finished scolding him and effectively telling him how to do the job of the Director of Graduate Studies (which was not, in fact, his job), she promptly hung up.

Greg stared at the phone in his hand with a look of incredulity.

During the last week of January, Julia was weightless, floating and happy, the skin on her neck now perfect through medical technology. Her scar removal was healed, and no one would ever know that she'd been marked. Therapy was going well and so was her relationship with Gabriel, although on occasion he seemed distracted and she would have to call his name to bring him back to her.

She'd just finished an amiable coffee with Paul, during which they discussed Christa's recent inexplicable good mood and was on her way to the library when she received a telephone call that would change her life. Greg Matthews offered her early acceptance into the doctoral program in Romance Languages and Literatures at Harvard, on a very generous fellowship, for the fall semester.

The acceptance was conditional on the satisfactory completion of her MA at the University of Toronto, but as Professor Matthews pointed out, given her letters of recommendation and the glowing endorsement offered by Professor Picton, Julia should have no problem completing her degree. Professor Matthews was eager to hear Julia's acquiescence to the offer, but he knew that most graduate students would need a little time to think about it, and so he asked her to telephone him with her decision in seven days.

Julia was surprised at how calm and professional she sounded on the phone. Of course, she wasn't doing much talking. After the call ended, she texted Gabriel with trembling, nervous fingers.

> Harvard just called—they want me.
> Conditional on my MA. Love, J.

A few minutes later, she received a reply.

> Congratulations, darling. In a meeting.
> My place—one hour? G.

Julia smiled at her iPhone and quickly completed her library errands before walking to the Manulife Building. She was excited but worried. On the one hand, her admission to Harvard was the culmination of her dreams and hard work. On the other, Harvard represented separation from Gabriel.

Bolstered by Doctor Nicole's encouragement to be kind to herself, Julia decided to have a hot shower in order to allow herself a few minutes to think. She left a note on the hall table where Gabriel always dropped his keys and proceeded to make herself at home in his spacious bathroom. Fifteen minutes later she was half-asleep under the tropical rain showerhead.

"This is a welcome sight," Gabriel whispered, opening the door to the shower. "A warm, wet, and naked Julianne."

"There's room for a warm, wet, and naked Gabriel too," she said, grasping his hand.

He smiled. "Not right now. We should celebrate. Where would you like to go to dinner?"

There was a time when Julia would simply have accepted Gabriel's suggestion because she wanted to make him happy. But on this occasion, she spoke up. "Can we just stay in? I don't want to be around a lot of people."

"Of course. Let me change and I'll be right back."

By the time Gabriel returned, Julia was standing in the center of the bathroom, wrapped in a towel.

He handed her a flute of champagne and they clinked their glasses together.

"I have something to give to you," he said, disappearing into the bedroom. He returned a moment later with something crimson in his hands. He held it up so she could read the lettering on the front.

"This was mine. I'd like you to have it." He took her glass and placed it next to his on the vanity, then tugged at her towel until it dropped to the floor.

Julia pulled the hooded Harvard sweatshirt over her head, standing like a nearly naked sorority girl who had just rolled out of bed with her boyfriend.

"Gorgeous," he whispered, wrapping her in his arms and kissing her enthusiastically. "This is quite an accomplishment, and I know that you've worked very hard for it. I'm proud of you."

Julia grew a little teary at his praise, for apart from Grace, no one had ever expressed pride in her or her accomplishments. "Thank you. Are you sure you want to part with your sweatshirt?"

"Of course, my smart, smart girl."

"I haven't decided if I'm accepting their offer or not."

"What?" He pulled away, and his expression morphed into a scowl.

"I just received the call today. I have a week to decide."

"What's to decide? You'd be crazy not to accept it!"

She fidgeted with her hands. She thought that Gabriel would be saddened at the idea of their separation. She hadn't thought that he would be so enthusiastic.

He paced back and forth. "Didn't they offer you enough money? Because you know I'll cover the cost. I'll buy you an apartment near Harvard Square, for God's sake."

"I don't want to be kept."

"What are you talking about?" He turned his head, peering over at her sharply.

Julia squared her shoulders and lifted her chin. "I want to pay my own way."

Gabriel groaned in frustration and cupped her face in his hands. "Julianne, we will never be equals. You are my better."

He stared at her, his sincerity bringing a particular light to his blue eyes, and he kissed her, before pulling her into his chest. "I have more vices and more money. I refuse to share my vices, but my money is yours. Take it."

"I don't want it."

"Then let me help you secure a loan. Please don't turn down this opportunity. Please. You've worked so hard for it."

"Money isn't the issue. Greg Matthews offered me a very generous fellowship, which will be more than enough to cover my expenses."

She grasped the hem of her sweatshirt, tugging it to cover more of her naked body. "I'm worried about what will happen to us if I go."

"Do you want to go?"

"Yes. But I don't want to lose you."

"Why would you lose me?"

She buried her face in his chest. "Long distance relationships are difficult. You're very handsome. Lots of women will try to take my place."

He scowled. "I'm not interested in lots of women. I'm interested in you. I've applied for a sabbatical. If that doesn't work, I could take a leave of absence. It wouldn't hurt for me to spend a year at Harvard finishing my book. We can go together, and that will buy me some time to figure out what I should do."

"I can't let you do that. Your career is here."

"Academics take sabbaticals all the time. Ask Katherine."

"What if you resent me?" she asked.

"It's far more likely that you'll resent me—being tied to an older man when you should be dating men your own age. And an older man who is a selfish know-it-all and can't stop bossing you around."

Julia rolled her eyes. "The man I love is not the person you described. Not anymore. Besides, there's only a ten-year age difference between us."

He grinned wryly. "Thank you. We don't have to live together if you don't want to. I'll be your neighbor. Of course, if you don't want me to go . . ." He swallowed and waited for her response.

Julia threw her arms around his neck. "Of course I want you to come with me."

"Good," he whispered, pulling her into the bedroom.

After Julia returned to her apartment the following day, Gabriel spent the afternoon working in his home office. He was about to telephone her to ask if she wanted to meet for dinner when his cell phone rang. Realizing that it was Paulina, he refused to answer it.

A few minutes later his home telephone rang, its unique ring indicating that the call was coming from the security guard downstairs. He picked up the phone.

"Yes?"

"Professor Emerson, there is a woman here who says that she needs to see you."

"Her name?"

"Paulina Gruscheva."

Gabriel cursed. "Tell her to go away."

The security guard lowered his voice. "Of course, Professor. But you should know that she seems upset. And she's using your name rather loudly."

"Fine," he spat. "Tell her I'll be right there."

Gabriel grabbed his keys and strode out of the apartment heading toward the elevator, cursing.

Chapter Seventeen

With the relief that an early acceptance to Harvard brought, Julia was able to redouble her efforts on her thesis. When she and Gabriel were apart, she worked tirelessly, spending hours upon hours in the library or at her apartment writing.

As a reward, Gabriel decided to whisk her away to Belize for Valentine's weekend. It was a celebration of love, Julia's acceptance to Harvard, and other things that Gabriel was not yet ready to share.

On the day of their departure, Julia stood on the front porch of her building, checking her mailbox. She found a letter from Harvard, which she opened immediately. It was a formal offer of admission to the doctoral program, and it included the terms of her conditional acceptance and her fellowship.

She also found a business sized envelope with the University of Toronto insignia on it. The words *Office of the Dean of Graduate Studies* were printed above the return address. She quickly ripped open the envelope and read its contents. Then she dragged her luggage to Bloor Street, flagging a cab to Gabriel's condominium.

She flew into the lobby, past the security guards, and into the elevator that would take her to his floor. Tripping down the hall, she let herself in with her key.

"Darling?" Gabriel walked to the front door with a smile. "You're early. I'm flattered that you couldn't stay away from me."

She batted away his outstretched arms and shoved one of the letters into his hand.

"What's this?"

He glanced down at the letter.

February 5, 2010
Office of the Dean of Graduate Studies
University of Toronto
Toronto, Canada

Dear Miss Julianne Mitchell,

*A complaint has been filed in our office alleging that you have
violated the University of Toronto's Code of Behaviour on Academic
Matters. In conjunction with this complaint, you are requested to
appear in person at the Dean's office on February 19, 2010, for a
preliminary interview. The Chair of Italian Studies, Professor
Jeremy Martin, will also be in attendance.*

*You may bring an individual with you to this meeting. This
individual may be a representative of the Graduate Student
Association, a family member or friend, or an attorney.*

*This meeting is for information purposes only and does not
constitute a hearing, nor has the Dean's office taken any position on
the legitimacy of the complaint.*

*Please confirm with this office that you have received this letter
and that you will be attending this meeting. If you do not attend,
an investigation into the complaint will begin automatically.*

Yours very truly,

David Aras, PhD

Dean of Graduate Studies

Gabriel looked down into Julia's panicked eyes and tried to find the
words to reassure her that she had nothing to worry about—but he
couldn't.

Chapter Eighteen

Julia saw fear flash across Gabriel's eyes, but only for an instant. There was nothing more terrifying to her than the sight of Gabriel's fear.

He helped her take off her coat and urged her to sit down in the red chair next to the fireplace. Flipping a switch, which caused the flames to ignite, he walked to the other room. Julia leaned back in the chair and covered her face with her hands.

"Drink this." He nudged her hand with a glass.

"What is it?"

"Laphroaig. Scotch."

"You know I don't like that stuff."

"One swallow, just to take the edge off."

She tipped the crystal glass to her lips and drank, feeling the burn of the alcohol in her mouth and throat. Coughing wildly, she handed the glass back. He downed the rest of the Scotch and sat on the sofa opposite her.

"What's the 'Code of Behaviour on Academic Matters'?" she asked.

"It's the policy that governs any kind of scholastic infraction—cheating, plagiarism, fraud, etc."

"Why would someone report me for academic fraud?"

Gabriel scrubbed at his face. "I have no idea."

"Are you sure?"

"Of course! You think I'd keep this from you?"

"You've been keeping something from me. That night you were working late in your office, you wouldn't tell me what you were—"

"I was working on a job application," he interrupted. "Greg Matthews called me the night that you and I went to *Auberge* for dinner. He invited me to apply for an endowed chair but told me they needed my portfolio right away. Preparing it took longer than I expected."

"Why didn't you tell me?"

He averted his eyes. "I didn't want you to get your hopes up. The chances of me getting that job are slim. I'm not a full professor and without a doubt they're recruiting senior people. But I had to try—for your sake."

"I wish you'd told me. I imagined all kinds of things."

His eyes flew to hers. "I thought you trusted me."

"Of course I trust you. It's the women around you I don't trust."

"I shouldn't have kept my application a secret." He shuffled his feet. "I didn't want to disappoint you when I don't get the position."

"You aren't going to disappoint me, Gabriel, unless you keep secrets from me."

He grimaced and disappeared into the dining room. When he returned, he was sipping another finger's worth of Scotch.

"I have a meeting with Jeremy this week. I could ask him about you."

She shook her head. "You should stay out of this."

"Do you have any idea what the complaint might be about?"

"I haven't done anything but go to school and do my work since I got here. Except for having some conflict with Christa and that run-in with Professor Pain—*Professor Singer*. Do you think that she . . .?"

Gabriel seemed to consider this possibility for a moment.

"I don't think so. She was hauled in front of a Judicial Committee last year when Paul Norris filed a complaint. I'm sure she wouldn't want to appear in front of them again. She isn't one of your instructors, so how would she know about your academic work?"

"She wouldn't." Julia paused and a look of horror came over her pretty face. "You don't think Katherine Picton reported me for something?"

"No. She wouldn't do that without confronting you first. And she'd call me, as a courtesy."

"What are the penalties for academic infractions?"

"It depends on the severity of the offense. They could reprimand you or give you a zero on an assignment or in a course. In extreme circumstances, they can expel you."

Julia inhaled shakily. If she were expelled, she wouldn't be completing her MA. And that would mean that Harvard . . .

Gabriel fixed his gaze on her. "Would Paul do this?"

"No. He wants to help me, not hurt me."

"*Angelfucker*," Gabriel muttered.

"What about Christa?"

He shifted against the leather of the sofa. "It's possible."

Julia's eyes narrowed. "What aren't you telling me?"

"You already know she's a troublemaker."

"What's going on with Christa, Gabriel? Tell me."

He stood up and began pacing in front of the fireplace. "I don't want to talk about it."

Julia grabbed the Dean's letter and walked to the front hall.

"Wait, what are you doing?" He jogged after her.

"I warned you not to lie to me. I guess I should have been more specific and told you not to be evasive, either." She retrieved her coat from the hall closet, pulling it on hastily.

"Don't leave."

She looked up at him, eyes blazing. "Then tell me about Christa."

He pressed the heels of his hands over his eyes. "Fine."

Gabriel helped her take off her coat and escorted her back to the living room. She refused to sit down, choosing rather to stand in front of the fire, arms crossed.

"Is Christa blackmailing you? Is that why you approved her thesis proposal?"

"Not exactly."

"Spit it out, Gabriel."

He turned away from her, looking out the window at the Toronto skyline. "Christa Peterson has accused me of sexual harassment."

Chapter Nineteen

Julia stared at Gabriel, wide-eyed. "What?"

"Christa filed a complaint with the sexual harassment officer, who referred the file to Jeremy. That's why I have to meet him this week."

Shakily, Julia lowered herself to sit in the red velvet chair. "When did you find out?"

A muscle jumped in Gabriel's angular jaw. "He called me a few days ago."

"A few days ago?" She clenched her teeth. "How long were you going to wait before you told me?"

"I didn't want to ruin our trip to Belize. I was going to tell you when we got back. I swear."

Julia glared at him angrily. "I thought we weren't keeping secrets from each other."

"It wasn't a secret—I just wanted you to have a few days to relax before I gave you the bad news." With a sigh, he turned to face her.

"Why would Christa accuse you of harassment? She's been harassing you!"

"I don't know the specifics of the allegations. I should have filed a complaint with the harassment officer, myself, but I didn't want to draw unwanted attention."

"What are we going to do?"

Gabriel stared determinedly into the fire. "I'm going to call my lawyer, and we're going to see that both of these accusations are dealt with. Swiftly."

Julia stood up and clasped her hands around his waist, burying her face in his sweater.

❦ ❦

"What is it now, Emerson? I'm in bed with a hot young law clerk from a competing firm." John Green answered his cell phone amidst the sounds of squealing and high-pitched giggles.

"Zip up your pants, John. This is going to take a while."

The lawyer cursed before covering his cell phone with one hand. "Don't go anywhere, sugar." He addressed his female pelvic affiliate before scuttling off in his red bikini briefs to the washroom.

"I'm already on top of your harassment complaint, Emerson. You don't need to pester me. I was about to have the best sex of my life."

"I need to speak to you about something else." Gabriel briefly summarized the contents of the Dean's letter to Julia.

"I can't help your girlfriend."

Gabriel began to sputter and protest, but John ignored him.

"Listen, if they're dragging you in for sexual harassment and your twink—ahem—*girlfriend* in for some kind of academic infraction, I'll bet my Porsche that the two complaints are connected. Have you told her not to mention you during her conversation with the Dean?"

Gabriel gritted his teeth. "No."

"Well, you should. You don't want to be drawn into anything through her. You have enough to worry about."

The Professor breathed in and out chillingly slowly.

"I'm not in the habit of cutting loose my friends, least of all Julianne. Is that clear? Or do I need to find myself another lawyer?"

"Fine. But she needs her own attorney. If these two matters are connected, it's likely to raise a conflict of interest for me. And I think the university might become suspicious if I represented both of you."

"Fine!" spat Gabriel. "Who do you recommend?"

John thought for a moment. "I'd recommend Soraya Harandi. She works for one of the Bay Street firms, and she has represented faculty against the university in the past. We had a thing a couple of years ago and she hates my guts. But she's good at what she does."

He grunted into the phone, apparently reaching for his BlackBerry. "I'll text you her contact information. Ask your girlfriend to call Soraya's office and explain the situation to her secretary. I'm sure she'll jump at the opportunity."

"What's the likelihood of either complaint resulting in—negative consequences?"

"I have no idea. It's possible the university will conduct an investigation and dismiss both complaints. But don't let her go in there without a lawyer, or this could turn around and bite both of you in the ass."

"Thanks, John." Gabriel's voice was laced with sarcasm.

"In the meantime, I'd like you to make a list of everything—and I mean everything—that is relevant to the harassment complaint. Any kind of evidence she might present, such as emails, texts, messages, and photographs. Send everything to me, and I'll start looking at it. And send me everything on your girlfriend too.

"I don't like having to say, 'I told you so,' Gabriel. But I did. The university has a zero-tolerance policy with respect to fraternization, which means they can expel your girlfriend and fire you. Let's hope the two complaints are not connected and that someone reported her for failing to return her library books."

"It's always a pleasure to speak with you," said Gabriel icily.

"If you didn't think with your dick, you wouldn't be speaking with me. I just hope your girlfriend was worth it, because if the shit hits the fan, she's going to turn out to be an extremely costly lay."

Before John could say good-bye, Gabriel hurled the handset against the wall, watching it smash into several large pieces and falling to the hardwood floor below. Then he took several deep breaths so he could convince Julia they should simply enjoy their vacation.

That same afternoon, Dean David Aras sat in his office on St. George Street and looked at his telephone with surprise. Usually, his administrative assistant was much better at screening his calls. But Professor Katherine Picton was nothing if not persistent, and she usually received whatever she wanted. In this case, that was a conversation with the Dean of Graduate Studies at the University of Toronto.

He lifted the handset and pressed the button. "Hello, Professor Picton. To what do I owe this pleasure?"

"There's no pleasure at all, David. I demand to know why I received a letter from your office requiring me to be interviewed at one of your Stalinist proceedings."

David pressed his lips together in order to avoid biting back. She was famous, she was old, and she was a woman. He wasn't about to curse her out.

(Except in Lithuanian. Perhaps.)

"I need to ask you a few questions. It will take ten minutes, tops, and you'll be on your way," he replied smoothly.

"Nonsense. It takes me ten minutes to walk down the front steps of my house in the winter. It will take forever to walk over to your office. I demand to know what I am being summoned to and why, or I'm not coming. We can't all spend our afternoons having assistants screen our calls and make us coffee so we can dream up ways of making other people's lives miserable."

The Dean cleared his throat.

"A complaint has been made against the graduate student you're supervising."

"Miss Mitchell? What sort of complaint?"

In a very understated way, he explained the nature of the complaint that he'd received.

"That's outrageous! Have you even met her?"

"No."

"This is a ridiculous complaint made against an innocent and hard-working *female* student. And need I remind you, David, that this is not the first time that a successful female graduate student has been slagged in a university proceeding."

"I am quite aware of that. But there are related matters that I am not at liberty to discuss with you. I wish to interview you about your dealings with Miss Mitchell. That's all."

"I am not going to lend any credence whatsoever to a witch hunt that is targeting *my* graduate student."

David frowned at her through the phone. "Without your testimony, it's quite possible a grave injustice might occur. You might be exactly what we need to clear Miss Mitchell's name."

"Codswallop! It's *your* responsibility to see that justice is served. I'm surprised that you have taken the complaint seriously. Quite surprised. And wipe that frown off your face, David. I can hear you sulking and I don't appreciate it."

The Dean suppressed a Lithuanian curse. "Professor Picton, are you refusing to answer my questions?"

"Are you hard of hearing? Or has your quest for administrative power made you intellectually lazy? I've said that I refuse to cooperate. I don't work for the university anymore. I am retired. Furthermore, I will be bringing this matter up over dinner tonight at the President's house. I'm sure he and his guests will be most interested in how the administration of his own university is operating.

"And by the way, the dinner party is being given in honor of Mary Asprey, the famous novelist. As an alumna, I know she takes an avid interest in the affairs of her *alma mater*, particularly the more patriarchal machinations. I wonder what she'll make of this?"

And with that, Professor Picton hung up.

When Gabriel and Julia finally arrived at the Turtle Inn resort in Belize, it was late in the evening and the stars were already out. Julia explored their accommodations—a private hut on a secluded beach—while Gabriel ordered room service.

The walls of their hut were white, with the exception of a row of tall, teak panels that accordioned to open out onto the covered porch. The ceilings were a mixture of bamboo and thatch, and a large bed was centered in the room, shrouded in mosquito netting. Julia was particularly taken with the open air shower and bathtub that were located on a side veranda.

While Gabriel wrestled with the kitchen staff over the telephone, Julia quickly slipped out of her clothes and took a shower. The space was not completely closed, affording the bather a view of the ocean. But since it was dark out and they were on a private beach, there was no possibility of being surprised by anyone, apart from one's lover.

"Dinner will arrive in about an hour. I'm sorry it's going to take so long." Gabriel licked his lips as he took in the sight of Julia in her bathrobe.

In contrast, he'd changed into a white linen shirt that was mostly unbuttoned with the sleeves rolled up to expose his forearms. He wore khaki pants with the hems rolled up, exposing his bare feet.

(Parenthetically, it should be noted that even his feet were attractive.)

"Would you like to take a walk with me on the beach?"

"I think I'd rather do something else." She tugged him, smiling, toward the bed, and gave him a gentle push so he was seated on its edge.

He caught her by the belt of her robe. "I'd be content just to relax. It was a long trip." His face showed that he was in earnest, which somewhat surprised her.

"I miss you." Her voice dropped to a throaty whisper.

He pulled her so she was standing in between his knees and slid his hands to rest on her backside. "We could nap before dinner. There's no rush."

She rolled her eyes. "Gabriel, I want you to make love to me. If you're saying no, just tell me."

He gave her a very wide, very delighted grin. "I'd never say no to you, Miss Mitchell."

"Good. Give me five minutes, *Professor Emerson.*"

He sank down on his back, his feet still on the floor. Julia's new-found confidence was absolutely enticing. In a single sentence, she'd aroused him so much that he was already suffering.

It seemed like forever, but it was really only a few minutes later when Julia emerged from the bathroom, wrapped in his Christmas gift. The black satin fabric accentuated the pink and cream of her skin, while the corset itself made her breasts look fuller and her waist smaller. Gabriel couldn't help but admire the exquisite hourglass that was Julia's now transformed figure.

His eyes hungrily regarded the merest glimpse of black lace panties, paired with black-silk stockings that were held up by a garter belt. Finally and gloriously, a pair of black pumps decorated her feet.

Gabriel nearly had a heart attack when he gazed at the shoes alone.

"*Bonsoir, Professeur. Vous allez bien?*" Julia purred.

It took a moment for him to figure out why she'd made this linguistic choice, so taken as he was by her figure and her footwear.

Julia was wearing his beret.

When his eyes finally met hers, she watched him swallow hard. She pouted at him provocatively and removed her hat, tossing it at him. After he threw it aside, she walked slowly, very slowly, to the bed.

"I really like my Christmas present, Professor."

Gabriel gulped, at a loss for words.

"Have you seen the back?" She pivoted her hips, watching him over her shoulder.

He reached out a finger to touch the laces that tied the corset, dragging his hand down to the panties that cut across her pert backside.

"Enough teasing, Miss Mitchell. *Come here.*" He pulled her to him, bringing their mouths together in a forceful kiss.

"I'm going to take my time unwrapping my gift—with the exception of the shoes. I hope for your sake they're comfortable."

After ten minutes of knocking on the door, the room service waiter had to take their dinner back to the kitchen and await further instructions.

The instructions never came.

Long after midnight, beautiful music hung in the air from Gabriel's new playlist, including songs by Sarah McLachlan, Sting, and Matthew Barber. Julia was lying on her stomach amidst a tangle of linen sheets, drowsy and satisfied. Her back was exposed down to the two dimples that rested above the curve of her backside.

Gabriel had artfully placed part of the sheet over her bottom and retrieved his camera. He stood by the bed, snapping picture after picture until she yawned and stretched, like a sleepy cat.

"You're exquisite," he said, placing the camera to one side so he could sit by her.

She looked up with wide, happy eyes as he began running his long fingers down her spine, then gave a rueful smile. "When you love something, you don't see its flaws."

"That's true, I suppose. But you're beautiful."

She shifted so she could see him better, hugging her arms around a pillow. "Love makes things beautiful."

A familiar tightness spread across Gabriel's lips. His hand stilled on her lower back, just over the dimples.

She read the unspoken question in his eyes. "Yes, Gabriel, you're beautiful to me. The more I know you, the more I see who you really are and the more beautiful you become."

He kissed her, the light, appreciative kiss of a teenage suitor, and ran his fingers through her long, brown hair. "Thank you. You're hungry, aren't you?"

"Yes."

He looked over at the door. "I think we missed our dinner because we were feasting on—ah—*other things.*"

"And what a feast it was, Professor. At least there's a fruit basket."

She sat up, wrapping the sheet around her torso, while he walked over to the large basket that was sitting on the coffee table. He found a Swiss army knife in the kitchenette, made an adjustment to the music, and brought a mango with him to bed.

"I needed to match the song to the fruit," he said, his blue eyes sparkling. "Now lie back."

She felt her heart rate begin to increase.

"You don't need this." Boldly, he pulled the sheet away. Now they were both naked.

"Who's singing?"

"Bruce Cockburn."

He began cutting the mango slowly, his eyes exploring Julia's body.

She gave him a quizzical look. "Naked lunch?"

"More like a naked midnight snack."

With deft fingers he cut a small slice of the fruit, juice dripping from his hands and onto her abdomen. She arched an eyebrow.

"Hmmm." He peered at the juice with an impish expression. "I'll have to take care of that."

She opened her mouth as he leaned forward to feed her. "You have a feeding fetish," she said, licking her lips and angling for more.

He bowed before her in obeisance, his tongue snaking out to capture the liquid from her stomach. "Pardon?" he asked.

Julia groaned incoherently.

"It isn't a fetish so much as an act that gives me joy. I like to care for you, and there's something sensual about sharing food with a lover." He eschewed her lips to kiss her shoulder, the tip of his tongue tasting her skin. Withdrawing, he cut another slice of fruit. A few droplets fell like liquid sunshine on her left breast.

"Damn. Forgive my mess."

He ran a sticky hand up and down her ribs, tantalizing one of his favorite erogenous zones, before placing his lips to her chest.

"You're killing me," she managed as his wet mouth found her nipple.

"I seem to recall saying that to you once. And you promised it would be a sweet death."

Julia opened her mouth to indicate her willingness to accept another piece. "I should have said *a sticky death*."

He placed a piece of mango on her tongue before stroking her lower lip with his thumb.

"I've thought of that. Don't worry."

Without warning, she moved so she was straddling his lap and placed her hands on either side of his face, pulling him toward her. They kissed passionately for a moment before she took the mango and knife from his hand and placed a piece temptingly in her mouth.

He gave her a heated look before he brought their lips together, tugging the piece of fruit away with his teeth.

"Mmmmm," she hummed. "By the way, I don't think I ever saw the security video from our date at the museum."

She gently squeezed a piece of mango over his chest and began kissing and sucking across the droplet trail.

"Ah—ah—" Gabriel had trouble finding his words. "I've seen it. It's pretty hot."

"Really?" She sat back and languidly ate a piece of fruit in front of him, licking her fingers slowly.

"I'll show it to you later." He pulled her into a tight embrace, his hands sliding up and down her back. Then, when he couldn't stand it any longer, he tossed everything aside so he could lift her into his arms.

"Where are we going?" she asked, slightly alarmed.

"To the beach."

"But we're naked."

"Our beach is private." He kissed the tip of her nose and carried her down to the water's edge.

"Someone will see us," she protested as he stepped into the sea.

"There's only a little sliver of a moon. Anyone who came by would only see you in silhouette. And what a view."

He kissed her long and good, adoring her face and neck with his lips as the gentle tide lapped against them. Then he placed her on her feet so he could press every inch of his body to hers.

"See how we fit together?" His voice was urgent. "We're a perfect match."

They cupped salt water in their hands, cleaning one another's flesh. Julia couldn't help but lean forward to kiss his tattoo, reveling in the way the taste of the sea mingled with the flavor of his skin.

He began kissing her neck and she could feel him smile against her. "Have you ever seen the film *From Here to Eternity*?"

"No."

"Then I need to introduce you to it." He took her hand and led her to the beach, where he lowered himself to the sand. "Please," he beckoned, motioning that she should lie atop him.

"Here?" Her heart thumped wildly in her chest.

"Yes, here. I want to be inside you, but I don't want the sand to scratch your skin." Gabriel pulled her down, and his mouth sought hers eagerly as the waves gently lapped at their legs. When they cried out their pleasure, the pale moon smiled.

A tropical rainstorm moved through the area the following morning. While the raindrops tapped against the roof of the hut, the couple made love slowly in a bed covered with mosquito netting. They found their rhythm in the steady dance of the rain.

When they were both blissful, he suggested that they rinse the sweat and humidity from their skin in the large bathtub on the veranda. Reclining in vanilla-scented bubbles, Julia leaned against his chest as he wound his arms around her middle. When she was in his arms she could almost forget the troubles that waited for them in Toronto.

She felt safe with Gabriel. It was not that he was a powerful man, although his wealth gave him some measure of strength. It was the way he'd confronted her bullies—first, Christa, then Simon. And the fact that he'd excoriated her father for a lifetime of neglect.

The vulnerability of the lovers' bed was well-known to Julia now. She knew nakedness and intimacy, desire and burning need, and deep, deep satisfaction. But she also knew that Gabriel loved her and wished to protect her. In his arms, she felt safe, for the first time in her life.

"Saturday mornings were my favorite when I was a child." Gabriel interrupted her musings with a wistful voice.

Julia traced his lifeline with a single finger. "Why?"

"My mother was passed out. I could watch cartoons. This was before we lost our cable." He gave her a half smile, and Julia tried not to cry, thinking of Gabriel as a sad little boy whose only happiness was a few hours of cartoons.

"I used to make my own breakfast. Cold cereal or peanut butter on toast." He shook his head. "When we ran out of milk, which we did frequently, I'd use orange juice."

"How was it?"

"Awful. It wasn't even real orange juice—it was Tang." He stroked her hair absentmindedly. "I'm sure a psychiatrist would have much to say about the connection between my childhood and my attachment to fine things."

Impulsively, Julia turned and threw her arms around his neck, causing a great tidal wave of water to slosh over the sides of the tub.

"Hey, what's all this?"

She buried her face into his shoulder. "Nothing. I just love you so much it hurts."

He hugged her gently. "Those things happened thirty years ago. Grace was more of a mother to me. I regret not being with her when she died. I didn't have the chance to say good-bye."

"She knew, Gabriel. She knew how much you loved her."

"I think your childhood was far more painful."

She sniffled against his shoulder but said nothing.

"If meanness makes people ugly, your mother must have been hideous. My mother was neglectful and indifferent, but never cruel."

He paused, wondering if he should broach the topic both of them had been avoiding since the advent of their vacation.

"Once I became acquainted with Christa Peterson, I thought that she was ugly. I owe you a debt for keeping me from sleeping with her. Although I'd like to think that even intoxicated I have better taste than that."

Julia withdrew, sitting back slightly and toying with the end of a lock of her hair.

He lifted her chin, forcing her to meet his gaze. "Talk to me."

"I don't like thinking about you and Christa together."

"Then it's a mercy you saved me from her."

"She's trying to end your career."

"The truth will out. You said yourself that Paul heard her aspirations with respect to me. I'm hoping she'll wash out of the program and we'll both be rid of her."

"I don't want her to flunk," Julia said quietly. "Then I'd be just as ugly as her, taking pleasure in her misfortune."

Gabriel's expression grew fierce. "She was mean to you on more than one occasion. You should have cursed her out when you had the chance."

"I'm too old to call people names, whether they deserve it or not. We don't live in a nursery school."

Gabriel tapped the end of her nose gently with his finger. "And where does that wisdom come from? *Sesame Street?*"

"The benefits of a Catholic education," she muttered. "Or maybe a little Lillian Hellman."

His eyebrows crinkled. "What do you mean?"

"Lillian Hellman wrote a play called *The Little Foxes.* In it a young girl tells her mother that some people eat the earth, like locusts, and others stand around and watch them do it. She promises her mother she isn't going to stand around and watch anymore. Instead of standing around and watching Christa's ugliness, we need to fight her with something stronger, like charity."

"People underestimate you, Julianne. Nevertheless, it pains me when people fail to give you the respect that you deserve."

Julia shrugged. "There will always be Christas in this world. And sometimes, we become the Christas."

He placed his chin on her shoulder. "I've changed my mind about you."

"You have?"

"You aren't a Dantean, you're a Franciscan."

She laughed. "I doubt the Franciscans would approve of me having sex, unmarried, outside, in a bathtub."

He brought his mouth to her ear. "Is that a promise?"

Julia shook her head and stroked his eyebrows, one at a time. "I like to think of you as a little boy, sweet and inquisitive."

He snorted. "I don't know how sweet I was, but I was definitely inquisitive. Especially about girls." He leaned over to kiss her, and when his lips left hers she smiled.

"See? Any boy who can kiss like that can't be all bad. St. Francis would approve."

"I hate to tell you, but your beloved Francis wasn't always right. There's a passage in the *Inferno* in which he argues with a demon over the soul of Guido da Montefeltro. Do you know it?"

Julia shook her head, so Gabriel recited the text for her in Italian.

"Francesco venne poi com'io fu' morto,
    (Francis came afterward, when I was dead,)
per me; ma un d'i neri cherubini
    (for me; but one of the black Cherubim)
li disse: 'Non portar: non mi far torto.
    (said to him: "Take him not; do me no wrong.)

Venir se ne dee giù tra ' miei meschini
    (He must come down among my servitors,)
perché diede 'l consiglio frodolente,
    (because he gave the fraudulent advice,)
dal quale in qua stato li sono a' crini;
    (from which time forth I have been at his hair;)

ch'assolver non si può chi non si pente,
    (For who repents not cannot be absolved,)

né pentere e volere insieme puossi
> (nor can one both repent and will at once,)

per la contradizion che nol consente'."
> (because of the contradiction which consents not".)

"So you see, Julia, even St. Francis was wrong about people on occasion. He thought Guido's soul belonged in Paradise."

"Yes, but it's like Francis to think the best of someone—to think that Guido's repentance was real and to fight for his soul," she protested. "Even if in the end he was wrong."

"St. Francis gave up too quickly."

"Do you think so?"

Gabriel gazed at her intently. "If it were your soul I was after, all the dark Cherubim in Hell couldn't keep me from you."

A shiver snaked up and down Julia's spine.

"I would have done whatever it took to save you." His voice and his expression were grave. "Even if that meant I had to spend eternity in Hell."

❊❊

Gabriel and Julia spent their last full day of vacation in and out of the ocean. They sunned themselves, then relaxed in the shade with a beer and an umbrella drink. Julia nodded off in her lounge chair, her large floppy hat discarded on the sand.

Gabriel loved to watch her sleep—the way her chest rose and fell with her gentle breathing. The way her lips curled back with the occasional sigh. She looked so peaceful. Gabriel was convinced that Grace would have been delighted that he and Julianne were a couple. No doubt she would already be pressuring him to put a ring on her finger and pick out china patterns.

There had been so many moments during their Valentine's weekend that he had wanted to bend his knee and ask her to marry him. But not only was he worried about enacting a cliché, he was worried about her future. It was likely they were about to be embroiled in a scandal that could jeopardize his career and her admission to Harvard.

Even if the complaint against her was investigated and dismissed, she would need to be able to complete her MA free of other distractions. He was sure that she'd want the full university experience at Harvard without the pressure of planning a wedding. And there was still the question of what he would do—whether he would be able to take a sabbatical. That is, if he survived Christa Peterson's harassment complaint.

Despite the fact that he found the words *marry me* on his tongue on more than one occasion, he bit them back. There would be a time and a place for a proposal. That time and place should be in their orchard, sacred as it was to both of them. Not to mention the fact that it would be a polite gesture to alert Tom to his intentions before broaching the topic with Julianne. Without doubt, he wanted her to be his wife. And no matter what the next few months brought, he would make her his.

Later that evening, Gabriel found himself brimming with emotion, the fruit of much contemplation and the pleasure he always found in Julianne's company. They'd just returned from the resort restaurant. Julia had planned on visiting the washroom to clean the makeup from her face, but he caught her wrist and wordlessly led her to the bed.

He kissed her softly and began to undress her, his eyes shining with worship and need. He took his time, adoring shoulders and arms and naked skin, his mouth beginning to make eager promises as she arched beneath his touch.

He pulled her astride him, gazing up with an expression of wonder mixed with desire. She moved her hips to taunt him a little, closing her eyes in order to let the feeling take center stage.

After a few minutes, Gabriel flipped her so she was on her back and he was kneeling between her legs. She let out a cry as he entered her.

He stilled. "Are you all right?"

"Mmhmmm," she hummed. "You just surprised me." She brought her hands to rest on his back, urging him forward.

Gabriel liked her on top, she knew it. He would gaze up at her adoringly and touch and tease. He would praise her sexiness, for he knew that even after these few months she was slightly self-conscious at being so exposed. Julia was surprised that he moved them so his body was covering hers, his lips at her neck, when they'd enjoyed that position several times already.

A few more kisses and he was pressing a hand to her face, his eyes dark and desperate.

"Gabriel?" She searched his expression.

He closed his eyes and shook his head before opening them again.

Julia gaped at what she saw—insecurity, passion, hope, want, and need. She threw back her head from time to time as groans of pleasure escaped her lips.

"I need you," he whispered against her throat as his movements increased to a fevered pitch. "I can't lose you."

Julia's response was lost in a series of pants as she grew closer and closer to her release.

"Ah—ah, hell." Gabriel cursed as he climaxed, knowing that Julia had yet to do so. He tried to keep moving, hoping that she would follow him, but it was not to be.

"Damn it. I'm sorry." He hid his face against her skin.

"It's all right. I enjoyed myself." She tangled her fingers in his hair, tugging playfully, before pressing a kiss to his face. "And I'm glad you came."

A self-deprecating mumble escaped him. He moved to lie beside her and began to pet between her legs, but she pressed her knees together. "You don't need to do that."

His eyes darkened with determination. "Yes, I do. Let me."

She stilled his hand. "You aren't going to lose me if you fail to give me an orgasm now and then."

Gabriel's expression tightened. "It's embarrassing."

"It's life." She kissed his nose. "I don't expect you to be perfect, in bed or out of it."

"Bless you for that." He kissed her slowly, sighing when she pulled away to nest in his arms. "But that doesn't mean I shouldn't try."

"Well, if you insist, there is something you could do for me . . ."

Gabriel moved so quickly Julia was torn between shock and the urge to laugh. But as soon as he touched her, she stopped laughing.

Later that evening Gabriel lay on his back in the center of the bed, underneath the mosquito netting. Julia rested her head just below his pectorals, her arm wrapped around his waist.

"Are you happy?" His voice came out of the candle-soaked darkness, as he ran his fingers over the top of her head and down to trace the curve of her neck.

"Yes. Are you?"

"More than I ever thought I could be."

Julia smiled against his chest and kissed the skin there.

"Things seem—different since we came back from Italy," he prompted, his hand still gliding across neck and shoulder.

"We have a lot to be grateful for. We have each other. I have Harvard. Doctor Nicole has been helping me. I feel like I'm finally putting the pieces back together."

"Good," he whispered. "And the way that we make love, in general, you're happy with that?"

Now Julia lifted her head so she could gaze up into his concerned blue eyes. "Of course." She laughed quietly. "You can't tell?"

"I can tell that I please your body. But your body is not your mind, or your heart."

He seemed embarrassed, and Julia repented of her decision to laugh.

"Tonight was an aberration. But even if it wasn't, I'm sure we'd work through it. Are you happy with the way that we make love?" She sounded shy.

"Yes, very much. I feel it changing—I feel the connection deepening." He shrugged. "I just wondered if you felt it too."

"Sometimes I think this is a dream. Believe me, I'm happy." She leaned up to kiss him and then rested her head on his chest again. "Why are you asking me these things?"

"Where do you see yourself in the future?"

"I want to be a professor. I want to be with you." Julia's voice was on the quiet side, but remarkably assertive.

He began threading the sheet in between his fingers. "Wouldn't you rather find a nice man who could give you children?"

"You can't ask me if I'm happy with one breath, and push me away with the next."

When he didn't respond, she gently took hold of his chin, forcing his eyes to hers.

"No, I don't want to find a nice man to have a child with. I want a child with you."

Gabriel stared at her incredulously, his blue eyes widening.

"Truthfully, I don't know if we'll ever get to the point where we're healthy enough to open our home to a child. But if we do, I'm sure we'll find a little boy or girl who is supposed to be our child. Grace and Richard adopted you; we can do the same."

Her face grew pained. "Unless you decide you don't want that. Or you don't want that with me."

"Of course I want you." The intensity of his voice matched his eyes. "I'd like to make promises to you. But I want us to wait a little before we have that conversation. Does that trouble you?" He reached out a finger to toy with the diamond in her ear.

Julia didn't need a narrator to understand what his physical gesture meant. "No."

"I don't want you to think that any hesitation on my part is due to lack of feeling." Gabriel gave voice to her unspoken fear.

"I'm yours. All of me. And I'm so glad we won't be apart next year. The thought of losing you was torturous."

He nodded as if he understood.

"Now come here, Julia, so I can worship you."

Chapter Twenty

"Miss Mitchell." The tall, dark-haired woman in the power suit strolled into the corner office, shook Julia's hand, and sat behind her large desk.

Miss Soraya Harandi was of Iranian descent, with light, unfreckled skin and cascades of blue-black hair. Her mouth was wide and full, and her dark eyes sparkled. She was not necessarily beautiful, but she was striking, and Julia could not help but stare.

Soraya chuckled.

Julia immediately looked down at her book bag and began to fidget with it.

"Now that's something you cannot do in front of the Dean. No matter what he says or does, you cannot look away. It makes you look guilty and weak." Soraya softened her criticism with a smile. "Law is as much about psychology as it is about precedent. Now, why don't you tell me what led up to the Dean's letter?"

Julia took a deep breath and told her story, beginning when she was seventeen and ending with the letter from the Dean's office. She only left out a few details.

Soraya listened carefully, jotting down notes on her laptop and nodding on occasion. When Julia finished, Soraya was quiet for a moment.

"That's quite a story. Since the Dean hasn't disclosed what the complaint is about, let's not assume it's about your boyfriend. Although we should prepare for that scenario. Was your relationship with Professor Emerson absolutely consensual?"

"Of course."

"Have you ever had a sexual relationship with one of your professors or teaching assistants before?"

"No."

"Is it possible he seduced you solely for his own amusement?"

"Of course not. Gabriel loves me."

Soraya appeared relieved. "Good. Well, good for you personally, not so good depending on the complaint."

"What do you mean?"

"If your relationship was consensual, then the university can pursue disciplinary action against both of you. If you were a victim, then they'll only pursue him."

"*I am not a victim.* We are in a relationship, and we waited until after the semester was over before we became involved."

"No, you didn't."

Julia was incredulous. "Excuse me?"

"According to your story, you had an amorous relationship with him beginning around the end of October. You waited until after the semester was over to sleep with him. But given the way the non-fraternization policy is written, you violated it. Who knows about your relationship?"

"His family. My father. That's it."

"What about the student who accused your boyfriend of sexual harassment?"

Julia gritted her teeth. "I don't know what she knows. But she hates me."

Soraya tapped her chin with her pen. "If you were accused of violating the non-fraternization policy, what kind of evidence, other than your testimony, could you offer for the fact that you weren't having a sexual relationship with him while you were his student?"

"Why would you think the complaint has to do with Gabriel? The academic conduct policy covers things like plagiarism."

"I've met Dean Aras. He doesn't waste his precious time with plagiarism cases."

Julia sat back in her chair. *"Oh my God."*

"Let's hope someone is accusing you of a minor academic offense and that Dean Aras is simply taking a personal interest in your case. But just in case, what kind of evidence can you offer to prove you weren't trading sex for grades?"

Julia flushed deeply. "Um, there is something."

"What is it?"

"I was a virgin before we went to Italy."

Soraya stared at her as if she was a mythical creature, such as, say, a heterosexual man who knew the difference between Manolo Blahniks and Christian Louboutins.

"Do you have medical proof of that? Such as a doctor's note?"

Julia squirmed. "No."

"Then there's no point in bringing it up. Did anyone from the university see you and Gabriel together during the semester?"

"Not as far as I know. Although we went to a dance club with his sister back in September."

Soraya pursed her lips. "Bringing up the fact that you are a friend of his family is not a good idea. It establishes a possible conflict of interest. And being seen in his company in a public venue was not an intelligent choice, Miss Mitchell. But frankly, he bears more blame than you because he should have known better.

"Since we don't know the nature of the complaint, our strategy should be to gather as much information as possible from the meeting while giving nothing away. That will buy us time to prepare for any disciplinary proceedings, should they arise. Hopefully, they won't.

"At the meeting with the Dean, I will speak for you. Since they haven't disclosed the nature of the complaint, it's possible that the complaint is specious and that they know this. We won't add fuel to their funeral pyre."

Soraya looked at Julia's downcast face and frowned. "You have to have confidence. You have to believe that the complaint is frivolous and that you've done nothing wrong. I've had dealings with the university's judiciary before, and I was fairly successful. I will be successful with your case too."

Julia took small comfort in Soraya's confidence, but some comfort was better than nothing.

"In the meantime, I would like a list of anyone who might have filed a complaint against you and why, and a detailed account of all your interactions with Miss Peterson. I'll have one of my assistants perform some background checks. I'll also place a call to a contact of mine at the university and see what I can find out.

"Until this matter is settled, you and Professor Emerson need to cool it. Don't be seen in public together. Don't talk to him about what you and I discuss. If the complaint is about fraternization, he will have his own counsel, who will look after his interests. I don't want my defense of you compromised by your pillow talk."

Julia's eyes flashed with a momentary heat. "Gabriel is much more than just a boyfriend. If I'm in danger so is he. Our relationship was consensual, and I have no interest in being defended at his expense. Any blame we have is equal between us."

Soraya gazed at Julia curiously.

"Are you sure that's his position? You told my secretary that John Green is Gabriel's attorney. Why isn't John representing you, if you and Gabriel are determined to show a united front?"

Julia opened her mouth to form an answer, but none occurred to her.

Soraya smiled sympathetically. "Listen, you aren't the first student to find herself in this situation. I'm sure it's upsetting and confusing. But you need to realize that if the complaint against you and your boyfriend escalates, it's quite possible he will break things off with you in order to protect his job. You need to prepare yourself in case he decides to throw you to the wolves."

"He would never do that. He loves me. We're talking about moving in together. And—other things."

Soraya gave her a condescending look. "Love can be easily killed, especially by unemployment. But let's take things one step at a time.

"Gabriel has sent over a retainer, which I will return. I think it's best for me to represent you *pro bono*."

Julia nodded uncomfortably. She had forgotten about the legal fees. "I will pay you, but it might take some time . . ."

"The point of taking a case *for the good* is so one can further the good. I don't see much good coming out of taking your money. You should be spending it on text books and moving expenses to Massachusetts."

Soraya's smile tightened. "I am not a fan of the university's sexual inquisitions. Anything I can do to embarrass or humiliate Dean Aras is definitely for the good. Believe me, representing your interests will be one of the few pleasures I've had recently. I should be paying you for the privilege."

Later that evening Julia was curled up into a ball, trying to sleep in Gabriel's bed. He was in his study, furiously researching all the university policies that applied to graduate students, trying to figure out what had possibly come to the attention of the Dean.

The thought of Gabriel having to do that for her—the thought of his career possibly being threatened because of her, combined with the possibility of losing Harvard, made the tears come. It was all so overwhelming. And the worst part was not knowing what the specific danger was.

She wiped the tears away, willing herself to be strong. Gabriel walked into the bedroom to check on her, and upon seeing her face, slipped into bed behind her.

"Don't cry, sweetheart. Please don't cry." He paused. "I wouldn't have continued working if I'd known you were so upset. We've hired the best lawyer and we're going to fight this complaint. It's quite possible it's simply a misunderstanding and by Friday evening, it will all be over."

"What if this is about us?"

Gabriel clenched his teeth. "Then we'll deal with it together."

"What about the harassment complaint?"

"Don't worry about that. You focus on your thesis and your studies, and you let me worry about myself. I'm not going to let anyone hurt you. I promise."

He rolled her onto her back and began sweeping soft kisses across her face.

"I'm afraid," she whispered.

Gabriel stroked her hair and pressed a kiss to the tip of her nose. "I know. But no matter what, I won't let them keep you from Harvard. It's going to be fine." He gave her a pained look. "What can I do, Julia? I don't know how to—comfort you."

"*Kiss me.*"

Gabriel kissed her mouth—the hesitant, light kiss of a boy who was unsure how the girl next door would react. He needn't have worried.

Julia responded by wrapping his hair around her fingers and pulling his lips to hers, kissing him fiercely and coaxing his tongue into her mouth.

He kissed her back but with restraint, then pulled away before pressing their foreheads together. "I can't," he said.

"Please." She tugged at him, running her hands across his broad shoulders and down the sinews of his back, pulling him toward her.

"I can't make love to you while you're sad. I would feel like I was hurting you."

"But I need you."

"Wouldn't you rather I ran a hot bath or something?"

"Making love with you makes me happy because it reminds me how much you love me. Please. I need to feel like you want me."

His eyebrows knitted together. "Of course I want you, Julia. I just don't want to take advantage."

She was not the sort of woman who made many demands, and what demands she made were almost always good. And almost always about what was good for him.

Gabriel knew this, and it pained him to deny her and those large, sad brown eyes. But the trails of her tears had dampened his libido. He would far rather have held her tightly and tried to soothe her by being close, than to attempt an act he would not be able to perform.

Her face told him that she needed him, that she needed *this* and *them* and the conjunction of body and soul. While he stroked her hair, deciding what to do, he realized something about himself. No matter what his therapist had intimated, he was not a sex addict. He was not a wanton hedonist with a massive hunger who was willing to, as Scott had put it, screw anything female and attractive.

Julianne had changed him. He loved her. And even if she begged him, he couldn't become aroused while seeing her in pain.

She was still staring up at him, her fingers tracing up and down his naked back. He decided to give her part of what she wanted, to touch and caress her, focusing on distracting her with pleasurable feelings and sensations, hoping that it would be enough. He kissed her, slowing their pace to a gentle exploration. She ran her fingers through his hair, anchoring him to her as she softly scratched his scalp. Even in the midst of her sorrow and need, she was kind.

He feathered his lips to her neck and her ear where he whispered about how much she'd changed him. How much happier he was now that she was his.

She began to sigh as he adored her neck, dipping a playful tongue into the hollow at the base of her throat before kissing it chastely. He nipped at her collarbones, gently pulling aside the thin strap of her tank top so the white slope of her shoulder was bare to his mouth.

She would have removed her tank top for him, exposing her breasts, but he stopped her.

"Patience," he whispered.

He wound their fingers together and kissed the back of her hand, extending her arm so he could draw the flesh of her inner elbow into his mouth, pausing when she began to moan. He kissed every inch of her, gliding strong hands across soft skin, taking his cue from the heat that shot across her flesh and the sounds that escaped her lips.

When he was satisfied that her tears had stopped and she was asking him for more, he cast their clothes aside and knelt between her legs.

Soon she was shaking and crying out his name. In itself, this was the moment he craved most, even beyond his own climax—the sound of his name tripping from her lips amidst the waves of her satisfaction. She'd been so shy the first few times they made love. Every time she said *Gabriel* in that ecstatic, breathy whisper, a precious warmth overtook him.

This is what love is, he thought. *Being naked and bare before one's lover and unashamedly calling her name in need.*

In his own orgasm, he reciprocated, telling her that he loved her. It was inextricably linked in his mind and experience—sex and love and Julianne. The holy three.

He held her tightly while they caught their breath, smiling to himself. He was so proud of her, so happy she could give voice to her desires, even when she was sad. He kissed her softly and was grateful to see that her smile had returned.

"Thank you," she whispered.

"Thank you, Julianne, for teaching me how to love."

❋❋

Paul walked into the departmental office on Wednesday and was shocked by what he saw.

Julia was standing in front of the mailboxes, her skin pale and dull, with dark circles under her eyes. As he made his way over to her, she lifted her head and smiled at him thinly. Her smile alone pained him.

Before he could ask her what was wrong, Christa Peterson breezed in, her large Michael Kors bag dangling from her wrist. She looked remarkably well rested, and her eyes were bright. She was wearing red. Not cherry red or blood red, but scarlet. The color of triumph and power.

She saw Paul and Julia together and cackled quietly.

Paul's dark eyes shifted from Julia to Christa and back again. He watched as Julia hid her face while she checked her mailbox.

"What's wrong?" he whispered.

"Nothing. I think I'm coming down with a cold."

Paul shook his head. He would have pressed her, gently this time, but Professor Martin entered the office at that moment.

Julia took one look at him and quickly picked up her messenger bag and her coat, hoping to make a break for the door.

Paul stopped her. "Would you like a cup of coffee? I was going to walk over to Starbucks."

Julia shook her head. "I'm pretty tired. I think I need to go home."

Paul's eyes glanced down at her bare neck, her bare *unmarked* neck, and moved back to her face.

"Is there anything I can do?" he asked.

"No. Thanks, Paul. I'm fine, really."

He nodded and watched her turn to leave, but before she could enter the hallway, he followed her. "On second thought, I should head home now too. I can walk with you, if you want."

Julia bit her lip but nodded, and the two friends exited the building into the bone chilling winter air. She wrapped her Magdalen College scarf around her neck, shivering against the wind.

"That's an Oxford scarf," Paul observed.

"Yes."

"Did you buy it in Oxford?"

"Um, no. It was a gift."

Owen, he thought. *I guess he can't be a complete bonehead if he went to Oxford. Then again, Emerson went to Oxford . . .*

"I really like the Phillies cap you gave me. I'm a Red Sox fan, but I'll wear it with pride, except when I'm in Vermont. My dad would burn it if I wore it on the farm."

Julia couldn't help but smile, and Paul mirrored her expression.

"How long have you been sick?"

"Um, a few days." She shrugged uncomfortably.

"Have you been to the doctor?"

"It's just a cold. They wouldn't be able to do anything for me."

Paul stole glances at her while they walked past the Royal Ontario Museum, snowflakes swirling around them and the crystal monstrosity that was the north wall.

"Has Christa been hassling you? You seemed upset when she walked into the office."

Julia stumbled in the ankle-deep snow, and Paul quickly reached out one of his large paws to steady her.

"Careful. There could be black ice under there."

She thanked him and began to walk a little more slowly after he released her.

"If you slip again, grab hold of me. I don't go down. Ever."

She glanced at him sideways, completely innocently, only to see him blush. Julia had never seen a rugby player blush before.

(It was rumored to be impossible.)

"Um, what I meant is that I'm too heavy. You wouldn't be able to pull me over."

She shook her head. "You aren't that heavy."

Paul smiled to himself at the perceived compliment.

"Has Christa been rude to you?"

Julia looked down at the snow-covered sidewalk in front of them. "I've been staying up late every night working on my thesis. Professor Picton is very demanding. Last week she rejected several pages of my *Purgatorio* translation. I've been redoing it, and it just takes so long."

"I could help you. I mean, you could email your translations to me before you give them to her so I could check them."

"Thanks, but you're busy with your own stuff. You don't have time for my problems."

He stopped walking and placed a light hand on her arm. "Of course I have time for you. You're working on love and lust, and I'm working on pleasure. Some of our translations will overlap. It would be good practice for me."

"I'm not working on love and lust anymore. Professor Picton made me change my topic to a comparison between courtly love and the friendship between Virgil and Dante."

Paul shrugged. "Some of the translations will still overlap."

"If we're working on the same passage we could compare translations. I don't want to bother you with stuff that's unrelated to your project." She looked over at him tentatively.

"Send me what you have and what your deadlines are, and I'll look at it. No problem."

"Thank you." She appeared relieved.

He withdrew his hand, and they began walking again. "Did you know that the Chair of Italian Studies sent out an email announcement about your admission to Harvard? He said that you won a pretty big fellowship."

Julia's eyes went wide. "Um, no. I didn't know that. I didn't get that email."

"Well, it was sent to everyone else. Emerson made me print out the email and post it on the bulletin board next to his office, *after* he insisted that I highlight all the important information, including your name, with a bright yellow marker. Figures. He was nothing but rude to you while you were in his seminar, and now he's probably going to take credit for your admission to Harvard. Asshole."

Julia's eyebrows furrowed, but she didn't comment.

"What?"

She flushed slightly under his scrutiny. "Nothing."

"Julia, spit it out. What were you thinking just now?"

"Um, I was just wondering if you'd seen Christa hovering around the department? Or Professor Emerson's office?"

"No, thank God. It looks as if she's moved on to someone else. She knows better than to talk to me. I'm just waiting for her to give me a chance to tell her off." Paul winked and patted her shoulder fraternally. "She better not give you a hard time. Or I have a few stories I could tell."

On Thursday, Julia met with her therapist in preparation for her meeting with the Dean, which was scheduled for Friday morning.

Recognizing that Julia needed to discuss what was happening, Nicole set aside her goals for that session and listened patiently before offering her opinion. "Stress can be very destructive to our health, so it's important to deal with it adequately. Some people prefer to talk about their problems, while others prefer to think about them. How have you dealt with stress in the past?"

Julia fidgeted with her hands. "I've kept quiet."

"Can you share your concerns with your boyfriend?"

"I can. But I don't want to upset him. He's worried about me as it is."

Nicole nodded sagely. "When you care about someone, it's understandable that you would want to protect them from pain. And that's perfectly appropriate on some occasions. But on others, you run the risk of shouldering more than your fair share of stress or responsibility. Can you see why that might be a problem?"

"Well, I don't like it when Gabriel keeps things from me. I feel like a child. I'd rather have him share things than shut me out."

"It's possible that Gabriel feels the same way, that he worries about you shutting him out. Have you discussed this with him?"

"I've tried to. I've told him I want to be equals, that I don't want to keep secrets."

"Good. And what was his response?"

"He either wants to take care of me or he's worried about disappointing me."

"And how does that make you feel?"

Julia gestured with her hands as she tried to find the words. "I don't want his money. It makes me feel poor and dependent and—and helpless."

"And why is that?"

"He gives me so much already, and I can't reciprocate."

"Is it important to you that your relationship be reciprocal?"

"Yes."

Nicole smiled kindly. "No relationship is absolutely reciprocal. Sometimes, when couples try to split everything in half, they discover that the relationship is not a partnership but a bean counting exercise. Striving for reciprocity in a relationship can be unhealthy.

"On the other hand, striving to have a partnership in which each partner is valued equally and shares both burdens and responsibilities can be healthy. In other words, it isn't a problem if he makes more money than you. But he needs to understand that you want to contribute to the relationship, perhaps not financially but in other ways, and that those ways should be respected just as much as the money. Does that make sense?"

"Yes. I like that idea. A lot."

"As for protecting one another . . ." She smiled.

"You could make a biological argument as to why men feel the need to protect their women and children. Whatever the reason, it's a fact. Men tend to find their self-worth in actions and accomplishments. If you refuse to let him do things for you, he'll feel useless and superfluous. He wants to know that he can take care of you and protect you, and that's not necessarily a bad thing. Partners should want to protect one another. But like any view, it has its extremes and it has its middle.

"What you and your boyfriend should do is to strive for the middle. Allow him to take care of you in some ways, while exerting your independence in others. And you should impress upon him the need for you to take care of him too."

Julia nodded. The concept of moderation appealed to her. She wanted to care for Gabriel, and she wanted him to care for her, but she didn't want to be a burden, and she didn't want him to look at her as if she was broken. But sorting all of that out practically was a different matter.

"Some men have what I call *chivalry syndrome*—they want to protect their women as if they were absolutely helpless. And this might be romantic and exciting for a time, but eventually reality will set in and it will become stifling and patronizing. When one partner does all the protecting and the other does all the receiving, it's unhealthy.

"Of course, some women have the feminine equivalent of chivalry syndrome—*wounded duck attachment*. They seek out men who are bad boys or broken and afflicted and attempt to fix them. But we'll table that discussion for another day.

"At his extreme, a chivalrous male can do all kinds of rash things to protect his woman, including riding into battle on his horse, or taking up arms against thousands of Persians, when he should be running in the opposite direction. *Discretion is the better part of valor*." She chuckled slightly. "Did you see the film *300?*"

Julia shook her head.

"It's about the Battle of Thermopylae, when three hundred Spartans held off two hundred and fifty thousand Persians before being defeated. Herodotus writes about it."

Julia regarded Nicole with no little interest. How many psychologists could cite Herodotus?

"King Leonidas was an extreme case. One could argue that his last stand was precipitated by political concerns rather than chivalry. But my point is that sometimes the chivalrous man ends up doing more damage through his protection than can be done by the force threatening his partner. Spartan women used to tell their husbands and sons to come home carrying their shields on them. If you found yourself in that situation, you'd probably prefer that Gabriel didn't die holding the line against thousands of Persians and came home to you, instead."

Julia nodded in absolute agreement.

"In your conversations with Gabriel, you might want to talk about that—how you feel about being protected to his own detriment, how you should share your risks and responsibilities, why you want to be a partner rather than a child or a helpless female.

"Perhaps Gabriel would be willing to attend joint sessions with us even though he isn't coming in privately."

Julia wasn't quite sure that she'd heard Nicole correctly. "Pardon?"

Nicole smiled. "I said that in your conversations with Gabriel, you might want to talk about how you feel protected—"

"No," Julia interrupted. "I meant the last part. You said that Gabriel isn't coming in anymore?"

Nicole froze. "Um, that was very unprofessional of me. I shouldn't speak to you about another client and his counselor."

"When did he stop seeing Winston?"

"I really can't say." Nicole shifted in her seat. "Now, we should probably discuss some ways in which you can deal with stress before your meeting tomorrow . . ."

❧❧

The Dean of Graduate Studies favored formality and refinement. For these reasons, he always conducted meetings in a large, wood-paneled conference room adjacent to his office on St. George Street. Professor Jeremy Martin, the Chair of Italian Studies, sat at his right in a large, high-backed chair that was vaguely medieval in style, behind an imposing, dark wood table that ran almost the width of the room.

Two small folding chairs were centered before the table, and that is where Soraya and her client sat most uncomfortably at the beginning of their meeting.

"A moment for introductions." The Dean's rich, baritone voice rang out in the room.

"Miss Julianne Mitchell?"

Julia nodded, but said nothing.

"And who is your representative?" His pale, cold blue eyes gave away nothing, but it was clear that he recognized the dark haired woman at Julia's left.

"Soraya Harandi, Dr. Aras. I will be representing Miss Mitchell."

"Is there a reason why Miss Mitchell has elected to bring an attorney to this informal meeting?" It was clear that he was already irritated.

"Why, Dr. Aras, my client was simply following your instructions. You suggested she retain a lawyer in your letter." Soraya's voice was deceptively sweet.

David resisted the urge to growl at her, for he did not like being made a fool. He gestured to the man beside him. "This is Professor Martin."

Julia took a moment to appraise the Chair's appearance. She knew that he would be meeting with Gabriel to discuss Christa's harassment complaint after this meeting concluded. She tried very hard to discern his disposition but found herself puzzled. His demeanor was decidedly neutral, at least toward her.

The Dean cleared his throat. "We have received a very serious complaint about you, Miss Mitchell. Our purpose in inviting you to speak to us today is solely for information purposes as we begin our investigation. We will ask a few questions, then you will have the opportunity to ask questions of us. I hope the meeting will terminate in about thirty minutes."

Julia inhaled slowly, watching him and waiting.

"Are you having a romantic relationship with Professor Gabriel Emerson?"

Julia's eyes bugged out of her head, and her jaw dropped open. Before she could speak, Soraya jumped in.

"My client will not answer any questions until the substance of the complaint is revealed. The letter was understandably vague, given the policies of the university, but you have passed the point of vagueness with that question. Exactly what is the complaint against my client, what is the evidence for the complaint, and who is the complainant?"

David tapped a finger at the glass water pitcher in front of him, making the slices of lemon dance to his drumming.

"That is not how these meetings work. I am the Dean. I ask the questions."

"Dr. Aras . . ." Soraya's voice took on an almost patronizing tone. "We both know that the policies and procedures assumed by the university are governed by the principles of natural justice. My client deserves to know the specifics of the complaint, the nature and scope of the evidence against her, if any, and the identity of the complainant *before* she answers any questions. Otherwise, this is an unjust proceeding and I will have no choice but to file a complaint to that effect. Immediately."

"I have to agree with Miss Harandi," said Professor Martin quietly.

David gave Jeremy an annoyed look out of the corner of his eye. "Very well. An allegation of graduate student misconduct reached our office concerning your client. It was alleged that she entered into a sexual relationship with one of her professors for the purpose of procuring academic favors."

Julia's eyes grew wide and round.

Soraya laughed. Loudly. "This is a farce. My client is an extremely talented student who was recently offered an early acceptance to Harvard, as you well know." She nodded in Professor Martin's direction. "My client doesn't need to prostitute herself."

"The allegation is not without precedent at this institution, Miss Harandi. And we take all complaints seriously, as dictated by our policies."

"Then why isn't the complaint being processed as a sexual harassment case? Surely, if a student initiates a transaction in which favors are exchanged for sex it would count as sexual harassment?"

"That avenue of inquiry is also being explored," David snapped.

Soraya chuckled. "Fine, fine. What are the alleged favors?"

"A high mark in a seminar in which the professor was the instructor, financial payments in the form of a bursary, and the procurement of an established, retired scholar to direct Miss Mitchell's thesis."

Soraya waved a dismissive hand, almost yawning in boredom. "I reiterate the fact that my client's academic merits speak for themselves. And who, pray tell, is the unfortunate professor?"

David watched Julia closely. "Gabriel Emerson."

Soraya smiled widely. "Your complainant has a wild imagination. He or she must be majoring in fiction. Did Professor Emerson file the complaint?"

Julia held her breath, horrified, as she waited for David's answer.

He tapped the papers in front of him with the end of his pen. "No, he did not."

"Well, what was his testimony when you spoke with him?"

"We intend to speak with Professor Emerson once we have gathered more information. Our protocols dictate that faculty members who are a party to a complaint are brought in last, not first." Professor Martin spoke for the first time, his voice firm but calm.

Soraya fixed him with a stern eye. "So in the hierarchy of the university, female graduate students are preyed upon first? And only afterward the professor, whose testimony could exonerate her, is approached? I'm shocked that you would drag my client in here without the courtesy of even attempting to speak to the other person involved. This entire matter could have been put to rest with two telephone calls. This is a disgrace."

David began to protest but Soraya interrupted him again. "Before we end this meeting, who is the complainant?"

"The complainant is a person who I believe is known to Miss Mitchell. Her name is Christa Peterson."

Soraya received the news impassively, but Julia's eyes flew to Professor Martin's. It was one quick movement, but he noticed it and stared straight back at her with knitted brows.

Blushing, she looked down at her hands.

David held up two pieces of paper.

"Based upon our preliminary investigation, it seems that Professor Emerson awarded a very high mark to Miss Mitchell in his graduate seminar. She was awarded the M. P. Emerson bursary, which was mysteriously donated by an American foundation after Miss Mitchell began the program. And Professor Martin has provided me with Miss Mitchell's academic file, in which it shows that Katherine Picton was approached by Professor Emerson last semester to replace him as Miss Mitchell's thesis supervisor."

He passed a file over to Soraya.

"As you will see, Miss Harandi, that file contains additional evidence provided by Miss Peterson. It includes a series of photographs and news clippings from a Florentine newspaper showing Miss Mitchell and Professor Emerson at a public event in Italy, where Professor Emerson is quoted as saying that Miss Mitchell is his fiancée.

"And there is a sworn statement by an employee of a local club who claims to possess security videos that show personal interactions between Miss Mitchell and Professor Emerson at that club during the time that she was his student. These interactions appear to be of an intimate nature and certainly go well beyond the appropriate boundaries of a professional relationship."

He paused for effect. "It's possible that the evidence provided by the complainant could be proof of more than one infraction. So for this reason, we are eager to hear Miss Mitchell's side of the story. So I ask you again, did you receive special academic favors from your professor because of your personal relationship with him?"

"Dr. Aras, I am astonished that a man of your stature would be persuaded to give credence to a complaint that not only strains credulity but is supported by the very flimsiest of evidence. Newspaper clippings from an Italian tabloid? Videos that cannot be authenticated? There is no *prima facie* case. None whatsoever."

"Don't question my competency, Miss Harandi." The Dean's swift temper got the best of him. "I've been working in higher education since you were in kindergarten."

Soraya raised her eyebrows at him and closed the file ceremoniously, tossing it onto his desk.

"What kind of interest does the complainant have in making such an allegation?"

David glared.

Soraya looked from the Dean to the chair and back again. "Perhaps the complainant's true target is Professor Emerson. Why am I suddenly getting the impression that my client is collateral damage?"

"Any other matters are outside your purview, Miss Harandi." The Dean's chin began to wobble. "Even if this office would prefer to ignore the supporting information filed with the complaint, we can't. The newspaper article demonstrates that Miss Mitchell and Professor Emerson were romantically linked only days after the end of the semester. It appears to demonstrate the existence of a prior inappropriate relationship, if nothing else."

"I can't believe you summoned my client to listen to these bizarre accusations. The complainant is clearly unstable and living in a fantasy world. If she has an issue with Professor Emerson, she needs to pursue a complaint against him, not my client. Given what I have seen here today, I will advise my client that she is well within her rights to file a harassment complaint against Miss Peterson and to see that she is investigated for making a fraudulent and defamatory charge."

The Dean cleared his throat noisily. "If your position is such that Miss Mitchell and Professor Emerson engaged in a consensual relationship, I will gladly make note of such a declaration and we can dispense with the charade. When did this consensual relationship begin?"

"The only charade is the one your office is performing, in which you attempt to appear to be investigating an academic infraction but rather are engaging in some kind of prurient sexual McCarthyism. This meeting is over." Soraya closed her briefcase dramatically and stood to her feet.

"Just a minute, Miss Harandi. If you had troubled yourself to take a closer look at Miss Mitchell's academic file, you'd have seen a form signed by Professor Picton and dated in October, declaring that she would be supervising Miss Mitchell's thesis because Professor Emerson had a conflict of interest. What reason would he have to approach Professor Picton other than giving Miss Mitchell what she wanted? What kind of conflict of interest could there be, other than an inappropriate relationship?"

Julia opened her mouth to answer him, to reveal the fact that she had known Gabriel since she was a teenager, but Soraya grabbed her forearm in a death grip.

"You sound as if you have already taken a position on the complaint, Dr. Aras. Perhaps your letter would have been less disingenuous if you had stated that your true purpose in this meeting was to *poison the well* against my client so you could punish her."

The Dean appeared to swallow his growing anger. He gestured to the paperwork in front of him. "The complaint alleges that academic favors were granted to Miss Mitchell for reasons other than academic performance.

"The complainant testifies that Professor Emerson and Miss Mitchell engaged in a lover's quarrel in front of a room full of witnesses during one of his seminars. Shortly after that embarrassing public display, Professor Picton signed the paperwork that allowed her to become Miss Mitchell's thesis advisor. *Quid pro quo. Quod erat demonstrandum.*"

"*Nemo me impune lacessit,* Dr. Aras." Soraya smiled at Professor Martin, before turning a stony gaze in David's direction. "I started studying Latin when I was in kindergarten.

"The complaint is malicious and false. If the Provost decides to lay charges on the basis of this complaint, I will pursue other avenues of remedy against the complainant and this office."

Julia watched as the Dean gripped his pen rather tightly. "Are you sure this is the position you wish to take, Miss Mitchell? An argument for leniency can be made if you cooperate."

"You've basically called my client a whore and accused her of sleeping with a professor to gain a preferment. I don't need to remind you of the laws regarding defamation of character. I believe we found ourselves in a similar situation last year. We don't give in to threats."

"We do not threaten, we adjudicate. We will be interviewing witnesses and other relevant parties and then we will repeat this conversation. Jeremy, have you any further comments or questions?"

Professor Martin measured Julianne with his gaze, then shook his head dispassionately.

The Dean closed his file. "Since you refuse to answer my questions, Miss Mitchell, you are dismissed."

Soraya nodded at the two men and escorted Julia out of the room.

Chapter Twenty-one

"That meeting was a confederacy of dunces," announced Soraya, leaning against the banquette in the bar of the Windsor Arms Hotel.

Julia nodded, wondering if she was Ignatius Reilly, the protagonist of that book, or whether Gabriel was Ignatius and she was Myrna Minkoff.

The bartender delivered their martinis with a smile and a few dishes of tapas, "on the house." He winked at Soraya, who was a regular, and returned to the bar.

She took a long sip of her drink and settled herself in her seat. "My advice is to file a harassment complaint against Christa Peterson, citing malicious intent, as soon as possible. There are provisions in the university's academic policies that are supposed to protect students from fraudulent accusations."

"I'm not sure I want to antagonize her."

Soraya laughed darkly. "What more could she do to you? Boil your bunny?"

Julia cringed.

"Listen, a complaint against her would be a shot across the bow. We don't have to follow through on it, but it would give her and the Dean something to think about. You told me that she accused Gabriel of sexual harassment. Don't you want to strike back?"

"I want all of this to end. I don't understand how she can file a complaint against me when my situation has nothing to do with her."

"Based upon what we learned today, I think it's pretty clear what she's doing. She accused you of sleeping your way to the top, and she accused your boyfriend of trying to make the same arrangement with her. It's clever, really, because she doesn't need her complaints to be successful in order to take both of you out at the same time."

Julia blanched. "What do you mean?"

"She's forcing you into admitting that you had a relationship with your professor. Then the university can hit you and him with a fraternization charge. She's either brilliant or she's had some coaching."

Julia traced a finger up and down the side of her martini glass, fighting the urge to be sick.

Soraya sipped her cocktail once more. "I need you to make a list of people the Dean might interview and anything they might say that would be damaging. The evidence he has is slight, but if you put it all together, it could be enough to convince a tribunal that Gabriel gifted you with favors because of your relationship."

Julia began sawing on her lower lip with her teeth.

"Don't worry, yet. Let's focus on beating this complaint and worry about everything else later. The administration is very cautious when it comes to matters involving faculty members because of their union. The university will continue the investigation until they're sure, and then they'll pounce.

"In the meantime, let me file a complaint against this Christa Peterson character. From now on, you and Gabriel need to stay out of the public eye. David will be investigating both of you this week, and we should assume he'll interview everyone who has come in contact with both of you."

Julia shook her head, a wave of nausea crashing over her as she thought of other faculty and students from the department being asked to give testimony in front of the Dean.

"All right, Soraya. File the complaint. I don't think it will accomplish anything other than to antagonize her, but you're the lawyer."

"Excellent." Soraya smiled widely and downed the rest of her dirty martini.

Later that afternoon Julia was exiting the elevator on Gabriel's floor. She passed his French Canadian neighbor as she walked down the long hallway, and they exchanged a brief but friendly nod. Then she let herself in with her key.

"Julianne? Is that you?"

"Yes. How was your meeting with the Chair?" She quickly removed her coat and boots and was ready to walk into the living room when Gabriel met her in the front hall.

"I want to hear about your meeting first." He placed his hands on her shoulders and kissed her forehead. "Are you all right? What happened?"

"They asked me a few questions and let me go."

He let out an expletive and pulled her into his arms. "If anything ever happened to you . . ."

She returned his embrace, exhaling slowly against his dress shirt. "It was Christa Peterson."

"What?" He pulled back so he could see her face.

"Christa accused me of exchanging sexual favors with you for academic benefits."

"*What?*"

While Julia hurriedly described the nature of the complaint and David and Soraya's exchanges, Gabriel's expression grew darker and more dangerous. When she quoted David's final words, he took a large step away from her.

He reared back and thrust his fist through the wall. Then, for good measure, he withdrew, dragging fragments of plaster and dust with him, before punching through the wall twice more in rapid succession.

Julia stood, open-mouthed, as Gabriel trembled before her, eyes closed and chest heaving. Part of her wanted to run, but she found herself rooted to the spot.

No matter how much she wanted to run at that moment, the sight of a few drops of blood dripping from his knuckles and onto the hardwood floor captured her attention.

"What have you done to yourself?" She looked up into his blazing eyes and pulled him toward the guest washroom. "Sit down." Once he was situated, she examined his knuckles and found the skin had split in more than one place.

"You might need stitches," she said. "I'm worried you've broken something."

Gabriel opened and closed his hand several times, wordlessly demonstrating that his hand wasn't broken.

"I think you should have an x-ray, just in case."

His only response was to rub at his eyes with his uninjured hand and heave a deep, shuddering sigh.

She opened the medicine cabinet and removed a few first aid items. "I'll try to clean this, but you should go to the hospital."

"I'll be fine." His voice was tight.

Using tweezers, she removed the bits of plaster from his wounds and cleaned them with iodine. Gabriel barely flinched as she bathed his knuckles, and she noticed that he was shaking, possibly from residual anger.

"I'm sorry I upset you," Julia whispered.

"I nearly brought a wall down, and *you're* apologizing to *me?*"

"I should have told you when you were sitting down. Or after you'd had a drink."

He shook his head. "Then I really would have knocked the wall down. I'm too angry to drink."

Julia continued her first aid until the wound was completely clean. When she was finished, she ghosted her lips over his bandaged knuckles. "I'm so sorry."

Gabriel caught her hand in his. "Stop it. I seem to remember another time in this washroom when I was the one playing doctor."

"I was mortified. I wanted to make a good impression and then I smashed your crystal and sprayed your nice shirt with Chianti."

"It was an accident. I had to work up the courage to put iodine on your cuts. I was afraid of hurting you. And that was before I . . ."

He closed his eyes and rubbed at them again. "What happened to you today is my fault. I should have protected you."

"Gabriel," Julia said, her voice a warning. She leaned over and took his face between her hands, forcing him to look at her. *"Don't.* We knew the risks when we got involved. I don't care what they do to me." Her voice broke on the words, but she spoke them anyway. "I don't care about Harvard or my PhD. I don't want to lose you."

A strange fire illuminated Gabriel's eyes. "Not even Hell could keep me from you," he whispered.

The lovers embraced desperately, drawing comfort from each other's very skin.

"Are you going to tell me what happened with Professor Martin?"

Gabriel took Julia's hand and led her into the master bathroom where he began drawing a bath. "You relax, I'll talk."

"I'm not in the mood for a bubble bath. I kind of feel like taking a crow bar to something."

(Something appalling and poorly made. Like domestic beer.)

"That's why you need a bubble bath. I have to preserve the walls of my apartment."

Julia undressed and settled herself amongst the suds. He regarded her intensely—the way her long hair was pinned up haphazardly on top of her head, the gentle contours of her breasts floating amidst the water like two white, pink-tipped lilies, the way she bit at her lip until she realized he was staring at it.

"Do you remember the first time we bathed together?" she asked as she watched him settle his tall form on a low stool.

"I'm not likely to forget it."

"You were worried I was hurting, and you carried me to the tub." She smiled shyly. "That was one of the kindest things you've ever done for me."

"Thank you." He gave her a peck on a cheek. "But I can't reminisce about happy things with you. I'm far too angry for that. I'd like to rip out David Aras's tongue and strangle him with it."

"What about Professor Martin?"

Gabriel paused, clearing his throat. "If Christa's complaint had stood alone, he would have interviewed me, perhaps spoken to a few others around the department, and concluded that her charge was fabricated. Her complaint against you, however, complicates things."

"What did your lawyer say?"

"I decided to meet with Jeremy alone."

Julia sat bolt upright, the water sloshing around her. "What? I thought you told your lawyer about the complaint so he would accompany you."

Gabriel leaned forward, resting his forearms on his knees.

"Jeremy hired me. I consider him a friend. I thought it was more likely that we could cut through the bullshit and deal with the issue if I didn't bring my lawyer."

Julia's eyes widened in disbelief. "What did he say?"

"Christa claims that I tried to initiate a sexual relationship with her on a number of different occasions, including meetings that we had on and off campus. She mentioned our interactions at Starbucks and at Lobby." His eyes shifted to Julia's.

"She's also accusing me of punishing her by rejecting her thesis proposal and threatening to have her dismissed from the PhD program. She claims that after she spurned me, I made her life hell."

"But it's all lies. She was the one harassing you."

"Exactly, and I said as much. Jeremy was quite cross. He told me that I should have come to him immediately and filed a complaint. Obviously, my claim is not very credible at this point, but there are a couple of things that Christa did not take into consideration."

"Such as?"

"Her academic file. Jeremy and I had at least two discussions about her poor progress over the course of last semester. He was well aware of the fact that she was struggling. Notes from those discussions, along with copies of her work, are in her file. Also, Paul was present during some of my interactions with Christa. I suggested that Jeremy speak with him, along with Mrs. Jenkins."

"Paul was with me in Starbucks the day you met with Christa. She told us she was planning on persuading you to take her to Lobby—that she was going to be exchanging more than names with you that evening."

Gabriel's eyebrows furrowed. "What?"

"I forgot about that conversation, or I would have mentioned it earlier. Paul and I were having coffee and Christa came in before you arrived. She was bragging about how she was going to seduce you."

Gabriel stroked his chin, deep in thought. "And Paul heard her say this?"

"Yes," said Julia, fighting a smile. "I guess the *Angelfucker* might turn out to be a guardian angel."

Gabriel scowled. "Let's not get ahead of ourselves. What else did she say?"

"Not much. We saw you meet with Christa, but we were too far away to hear what you were saying. Her body language seemed pretty obvious. She was trying to flirt with you, and you scolded her. I could tell Professor Martin that."

"Absolutely not. You're too involved as it is." He scratched at his chin once again. "Jeremy asked that I not speak to Paul about Christa. The situation is a bit touchy because Paul is working for me, but Jeremy agreed to talk to him. It would be best if you didn't speak to Paul about this, either. The less said on the topic the better."

"He doesn't like Christa. One of the first things he ever said to me was that she wanted to become Mrs. Emerson. He knows she was after you."

Gabriel grimaced. "I reminded Jeremy that I approved Christa's dissertation proposal back in December, after giving her numerous chances to fix it. Let's hope that when he talks to Paul, he's able to grasp a clear picture of what actually happened."

Julia closed her eyes, resting her head back in the bathtub. She knew that they could rely on Paul to tell the truth. Despite his antipathy to Professor Emerson, he wouldn't give credence to Christa's false allegations.

Gabriel stood up. "There's one other thing I need to tell you."

"What's that?" Julia asked, eyes still closed.

"Jeremy asked if we were involved. And I said—yes."

She opened her eyes, staring up at him. "What?"

"I told him that we didn't get involved until the Christmas break." Gabriel's expression grew tense.

"Did he believe you?"

"He seemed to, but he was angry. He told me I should have come to him immediately. He said that he was obligated to report me to the Dean for failing to follow university policy."

"Oh, no." Julia reached for Gabriel's hand. "What are we going to do?"

"He said that because of our other troubles, he isn't going to muddy the waters—for now. But he was adamant in telling me that he wasn't going to cover things up."

Gabriel leaned over to kiss her forehead. "Don't worry about Jeremy. I'll handle him. While you're finishing your bath, I'll update my lawyer so we can plan our next move." He smiled and turned to leave.

"Gabriel, there is one more thing. Well, two more things, actually.

"Soraya is filing a complaint against Christa, on my behalf, arguing that she targeted me maliciously."

"Good. Maybe that will cause her to rethink her actions."

"And in my meeting with Nicole yesterday she mentioned that you weren't in therapy anymore."

Gabriel saw Julia's expression, one of irritation mixed with sadness, and his shoulders slumped.

Chapter Twenty-two

In the grand scheme of things, Gabriel's failure to mention the fact that he'd stopped going to therapy was unimportant. Or so Julia believed. They argued about it briefly, but both of them were too worried about their troubles with the university to do more than that.

Gabriel received a terse note from Jeremy the following week, indicating that he'd interviewed both Mrs. Jenkins and Paul. Other than that, he and Julia didn't receive any communication from the university.

David Aras spent his Friday night alone in the office of his house with a bottle of Jameson whiskey. It was not unusual for him to do so. In his position as Dean of Graduate Studies he often brought work home. On this particular evening he found himself mired in a very tricky, very sensitive situation.

Miss Peterson's harassment complaint had been challenged by the testimony of more than one witness. However, the academic fraud complaint against Miss Mitchell had alerted him to a possible case of fraternization between Julia and Professor Emerson. The problem was that the evidence was contradictory.

According to the information passed on by Professor Martin, Paul Norris had painted a glowing picture of Miss Mitchell and her character. As the whiskey burned his throat, David wondered if all women Mr. Norris came in contact with had mysteriously sprouted wings or if he simply had a weakness for young women from Selinsgrove, Pennsylvania.

(Wherever the hell that was.)

According to Mr. Norris and Mrs. Jenkins, Miss Mitchell was a timid young woman who was disliked by Professor Emerson. Mr. Norris went further to claim that the professor had fought openly with her in his seminar.

Subsequent to the confrontation in class, Emerson had approached Professor Picton to supervise Miss Mitchell's thesis, citing the fact that she was a friend of his family as the reason why he could no longer continue to supervise her. Here is where David was puzzled.

Professor Emerson hadn't objected to Miss Mitchell's admission to the program, knowing that he was the only professor who directed theses on Dante. If there was such an obvious conflict of interest, why hadn't he objected? Or declared the conflict of interest to Professor Martin at the beginning of the semester?

The files on Professor Emerson and Miss Mitchell did not make sense. And David did not like it when things did not make sense. (For his universe was nothing if not sensical.)

As he pondered the evidence, he inserted a flash drive into his computer. He opened the single folder on the drive and began scanning through the emails that had been culled obligingly from Professor Emerson's account by someone in the Information Technology office. He adjusted the parameters to include only those messages that had been sent to or received from Miss Mitchell, Miss Peterson, Mr. Norris, and Professor Picton.

In a few minutes, David found something that surprised him. On his screen, were emails that had been sent before the end of October 2009. The first email had been written by Professor Emerson to Miss Mitchell:

> Dear Miss Mitchell,
> I need to speak to you concerning a matter of some urgency.
> Please contact me as soon as possible. You may telephone
> me at the following number: 416-555-0739 (cell).
> Regards,
> Prof. Gabriel O. Emerson,
> Associate Professor
> Department of Italian Studies/
> Centre for Medieval Studies
> University of Toronto

The second email was sent by Miss Mitchell to Professor Emerson in response to his message:

Dr. Emerson,

Stop harassing me.

I don't want you anymore. I don't even want to know you. If you don't leave me alone, I will be forced to file a harassment complaint against you. And if you call my father, I will do just that. Immediately.

If you think I'm going to let an insignificant thing like this drive me from the program, then you are very much mistaken. I need a new thesis director, not a bus ticket home.

Regards,

Miss J. H. Mitchell,

Lowly Graduate Student,

On-Knees-More-Than-The-Average-Whore.

P.S. I will be returning the M. P. Emerson bursary next week. Congratulations, Professor Abelard. No one has ever made me feel as cheap as you did Sunday morning.

The Dean straightened in his chair. He read the two emails once again, examining every word.

Although he had a vague memory of who Peter Abelard was, he indulged his curiosity and Googled him. He clicked on a reputable biography and began reading.

Quod erat demonstrandum, he thought.

Chapter Twenty-three

Downtown, Jeremy Martin was reclining on his leather sofa, eyes closed, listening to Beethoven while his wife got ready for bed. As the Chair of Italian Studies, he was responsible for a number of people, including faculty and students. Gabriel's revelation that he was dating a former student troubled him.

He knew that Christa Peterson's complaint was malicious, but like any other complainant, she should be taken seriously. Given the fact that she was correct in surmising that Gabriel and Julianne were involved, it was quite possible that her allegation that Julianne had received special favors was also correct. Gabriel, his friend and colleague, had tried to keep the relationship secret. Now the Dean was asking questions, placing Jeremy in a hell of a bind.

Over the course of his career in the United States and now in Toronto, he'd seen too many bright and promising graduate students become the playthings of their professors. His wife, for example, had been a graduate student in linguistics at Columbia University, only to have her career ruined by her professor/lover after she tired of his alcoholism. It had taken years for Danielle's wounds to heal, and even now she would have nothing to do with academia. Jeremy didn't want to see Julianne's career come to a similar end.

On the other hand, he would not allow the rising star of his faculty to be slandered and vilified for an infraction he hadn't committed. If the Dean investigated Professor Emerson and Miss Mitchell further, Jeremy would do his damnedest to ensure that justice was served. Failing that, he was determined to ensure that his department was protected. Which is why he was horrified to find copies of letters addressed to Professor Emerson and Miss Mitchell with his daily mail on the first Thursday in March.

Muttering expletives, he glanced at the contents quickly before making a discreet call to one of his contacts in the Dean's office. Half an hour later, he was placing a call to Professor Emerson's home.

"Have you checked your snail mail today?"

Gabriel frowned. "No. Why?"

"Because I have a letter from the Dean indicating that you and Julianne are being investigated for engaging in an inappropriate relationship while she was your student."

"Fuck," said Gabriel.

"Exactly. Are you sitting down?"

"No."

"Well, take a seat. I just got off the phone with a friend who works in the Dean's office. Julianne has filed a harassment complaint against Christa Peterson, pursuant to the allegations against her. In retaliation, Christa has threatened the university with a lawsuit over the fact that Julianne received preferential treatment because she slept with you. Christa's allegations are now part of the investigation into you and Julianne."

"That's preposterous!"

"Is it?"

"Of course it is. It's ridiculous."

"I'm glad to hear that, Gabriel, because the university takes complaints like this very seriously. The Provost's office has ordered the Dean and two others to form a committee and investigate the allegations. You and Julianne are being summoned to appear before them, together."

Gabriel cursed. "Who else is on the committee?"

"My contact wouldn't tell me. The good news is that the meeting is only an investigatory hearing. Depending upon how the hearing officers decide the matter, it could be referred to the Provost's Office for charges to be laid, and then the two of you would have to appear before a disciplinary tribunal. I don't need to explain to you how deep the shit would be at that point."

"Why doesn't the Dean simply meet with me? All of this could be laid to rest in a few minutes."

"I doubt that. Allegations and complaints are piling up and you're at the center of all of them."

Gabriel's heart almost stopped. "You think there are more allegations forthcoming?"

"I have my suspicions. But nothing has been confirmed."

"Shit," said Gabriel, rubbing his eyes roughly. "Just how much trouble are we in?"

"If I were you, I'd stop thinking as a *we* and focus on *I*. That's what got you into this mess in the first place."

"Just answer the question, please."

Jeremy paused, flipping through the letters on his desk. "Since there is some question about the integrity of your marking scheme with respect to Julianne, the Dean has suspended her grade in your seminar. That means that her transcript will be incomplete until the matter is resolved either with a dismissal or a tribunal and its outcome."

"She won't graduate," Gabriel whispered.

"It's University policy to withhold a final grade until all academic infractions are dealt with."

"So depending on how long this takes, she won't be able to go to Harvard."

"If the matter is settled in her favor, they'll let the grade stand and backdate her graduation. But by that time, I would assume she'd lose her place at Harvard. Unless she can persuade them to defer her admission."

"Her admission was conditional on the satisfactory completion of her MA. She can ask, but I don't think she's in a position to ask for a deferral. And if Harvard catches wind of this, they might withdraw their offer."

"Then she'd better pray this matter is settled in time for her to apply to graduate. And frankly, so should you. If you're found guilty of academic fraud, the Provost can strip you of your tenure."

"Fuck." Gabriel slammed his hand down on his desk. "When will we have to appear before the committee?"

"Thursday, March twenty-fifth."

"That leaves them less than a month to sort everything out before she needs to apply for graduation."

"Academic procedures move at a glacial pace. You know that." He cleared his throat. "Aren't you the slightest bit worried about your predicament?"

"Not particularly," Gabriel growled.

"Well, you should be. And what's more, my primary concern is you, although I would be sorry to see Julianne's academic future threatened."

"I won't let that happen."

"And I'm not about to let one of my star professors be hung out to dry." Jeremy heaved a deep breath. "Under the policy you're suspected of violating, you bear more responsibility than her. You're under suspicion of evaluating a student with reference to a criterion that has nothing to do with academic merit."

"That's preposterous and you have the paper trail to prove it."

"No, I don't." Jeremy began tapping his finger against the pages in front of him. "I have a paper trail, but it's incomplete. You didn't notify me until recently that you were involved with her. Now my boss is starting to ask questions. Do you have any idea how embarrassing this is for me? I look like I just fell off the turnip truck and have no idea what the hell is going on in my own department!"

Gabriel inhaled and exhaled slowly.

"What are you saying?"

"I'm saying that you fucked up, Gabriel, no matter how you look at it. And I'm not about to jeopardize everything I've worked for to cover your ass."

Professor Emerson was stunned into silence.

"Why didn't you tell me you were dating her? I hired you, for God's sake."

"Because I didn't think it was anyone's business who I was sleeping with."

"You can't be serious." Jeremy muttered a curse. "You know the rules governing relationships with students. Since you kept your relationship secret from me and everyone else, you look guilty."

Gabriel gritted his teeth. "Jeremy, can I count on your support or not?"

"I'll do what I can, but that might not be much. If I were you, I'd notify the Faculty Association and make sure you bring your union representative to the hearing."

"This is a witch hunt that was started by a disgruntled graduate student. Christa Peterson is trying to have me fired."

"You might be right. But before you get on your soapbox, realize that you violated university policy. That makes it much easier for the administration to infer that you're guilty of other infractions. And by the way, I received an email from the Dean asking me about the M. P. Emerson bursary. For your sake, I hope your fingerprints aren't on it."

Gabriel let loose with a string of curses. Jeremy interrupted him.

"If you don't have a lawyer, my friend, now would be the time to hire one."

Gabriel muttered something and hung up the phone, walking swiftly to his dining room to pour himself a drink.

Although Gabriel notified the Faculty Association of his situation, he declined their offer to accompany him to the hearing. John was of the opinion that his legal acumen was far more threatening than that of the union, but he was willing to admit that should the matter result in charges, it would be appropriate at that point to involve them.

John's advice was to stonewall, although he urged Gabriel to coach Julianne on what *not* to say. Failing that, he had every intention of arguing that she was an unstable, impressionable student who had become fixated on Gabriel at a young age and had seduced him.

Hoping that his client would follow instructions, John didn't bother to explain this strategy.

Soraya's advice paralleled that of John. She told Julia to say nothing and if pressed, to blame Gabriel for everything. Soraya almost cackled with glee at the prospect of arguing that he was the older, rakish professor who had seduced an innocent young woman with promises of a long and happy future. When Julia declared that she wanted to tell the truth, Soraya told her that that was a very bad idea. She planned to bring up Gabriel's promiscuous reputation and brushes with law enforcement.

Like John, she anticipated a cooperative client and thus didn't bother articulating the details of her strategy.

The night before the hearing, Julia was awakened mid-dream by the sound of something tapping against her apartment window. At first, she thought she was still dreaming. When the sound repeated, this time more loudly, she exited her bed and pulled aside the curtain. There, standing with his nose almost pressed against the glass, was Gabriel. He looked slightly wild, eyes frantic, wearing his beret and his winter coat, standing knee-deep in a snowdrift.

She quickly unlocked the window and stood aside as a gust of frozen air whooshed past him with his entrance into the room. He closed the window soundly, locked it, and drew the curtain.

"Gabriel, what are you—"

She wasn't given the chance to finish her question as he wrapped her in his arms. She smelled the Scotch before she tasted it, as he pressed his lips to hers. His lips were freezing, it was true, but his mouth and tongue were warm and inviting. And the heat of his kiss, which was deep and sensual, began to blossom across her skin.

"Are you drunk? What happened?"

He pulled away, but only for a moment, so he could divest himself of his hat and coat. Then he was embracing her once again, tracing icy fingers up and down her arms, unbuttoning her pajama top and slipping a hand inside to cradle her breast.

He moved her to the bed as he pulled his shirt out of his trousers, watching her slip off her pajamas as he carelessly dropped everything to the floor. Within an eye blink they were naked and he was pulling her into his arms, tugging her legs around his hips. They'd never been this quick to undress and to love.

As he walked her to the closed door and pressed her back against it, his movements grew frantic and desperate. His cold fingers teased her while his mouth trapped her breast, sucking and nipping.

She was crying out already, still shocked at his speechless fervor.

A few moments later she was distracted by the difference in temperature between their bodies: the taut, hard coldness of his chest pressing against her soft, warm curves. When he felt with thawing fingertips that she was ready, he thrust up into her, grunting into the crook of her neck in preliminary satisfaction, his upper body relaxing slightly at the feel of her. There was no space between their bodies or air between their skin.

Julia moaned appreciatively at the sensation of being one with her beloved. Her hands immediately slid from his shoulders to his hips, and she pulled at his lower back to encourage him forward. It was a cacophony of unembarrassed sounds and noises, made far more animalistic by its lack of language and of course, the rhythmic bumping of Julia's back against the heavy wooden door.

Their coupling was loud and fast, perhaps the most intense physical connection they'd ever had, topping even their sex against the wall in Florence. Soon they were exploding jointly into bliss, hearts racing and blood pumping, clutching one another and crying out. Then finally, finally, they collapsed into a tangle of flesh and limb in limpid satisfaction on Julia's narrow bed.

Gabriel was on top of her, but she would not let him move. He shifted slightly to distribute his weight to the mattress, but he too was unwilling to break the contact of skin against skin.

She petted his hair and told him how much she loved him as he buried his nose in the hollow of her throat, inhaling her scent. She told him that he didn't need to drink, that he could talk to her, instead.

Gabriel sighed against her neck. "I am talking to you," he whispered, pressing insistent kisses across her shoulder. "You aren't listening."

Before Julia could argue, he began exploring her mouth. Further discussion was silenced as he enticed her to join with his body once more.

When she awoke the next morning the apartment was quiet. In fact, there was no sign of her evening visitor apart from an unlocked window and the scent of Gabriel and sex that clung to her body and the bed.

She searched the studio expecting a note, a message, *something*. But there was nothing, not even an email. A creeping sense of dread spread over her.

Julia wore her hair long the next morning, following Soraya's instructions, for it made her look sweet and innocent. At eleven o' clock sharp she met her lawyer in the hallway outside the boardroom.

Gabriel and John were already there, huddled next to the wall and talking in low, hurried tones. They were both dressed in dark suits and white shirts. But the similarity ended there. Gabriel wore a bow tie. The green of his tie contrasted sharply with the blue of his eyes.

He made eye contact with her briefly, enough for her to notice that he looked worried. He didn't smile or beckon to her. He seemed content to keep his distance.

She wanted to go to him, but Soraya pulled her to sit on a low bench just outside the door. Suddenly, the door swung open and a large, angry looking rugby player strode into the hallway.

"Paul?" Julia stood up.

He stopped, surprised.

"Julia? Are you all right? Tell me it isn't—"

Mid-sentence and mid-stride Paul stopped as he saw the face of Soraya, who was now standing behind her. He stared at the two women, eyes wide and questioning at first, then narrowing. Muttering curses, he scowled and strode past both of them.

"Paul?" Julia called to him, but he disappeared down the stairs.

"Do you know him?" asked Soraya.

"He's a friend."

"Really?" Soraya seemed incredulous.

Julia turned to face her. "Why? Do you know him?"

"He filed a complaint last year against one of my clients. That's when I made an enemy of the Dean."

It took a moment for the import of Soraya's revelation to sink into Julia's brain. But when it did, she sat down slowly.

Soraya was Professor Singer's attorney? What have I gotten myself into?

Her answer to that question was interrupted by the Dean's assistant, Meagan, who announced that the hearing officers would prefer to interview Miss Mitchell and Professor Emerson, together.

After a quick consultation with their lawyers, Gabriel and Julia entered the boardroom, followed by John and Soraya. As soon as they arranged themselves on opposite sides of the aisle, Dr. Aras spoke. As was his practice, he introduced himself and the other members of the committee, Professors Tara Chakravartty and Robert Mwangi.

"Dr. Tara Chakravartty, Vice-President of Diversity." Professor Chakravartty was a beautiful and petite woman of Indian descent, with dark eyes and long, straight black hair. She was dressed in a black suit with a large persimmon-colored scarf swathed like a sari around her torso. She too, smiled at Julia, in between withering glances and the occasional scowl in David's direction.

"Dr. Robert Mwangi, Vice-President of Student Affairs." Professor Mwangi was a Kenyan Canadian who wore wire-rimmed spectacles and a button down shirt with no jacket and no tie. He was the most casually dressed of the four of them and the most obviously friendly. He smiled at Julia, and she smiled back.

The Dean proceeded with his opening remarks.

"Miss Mitchell, Professor Emerson, you have been notified by letter as to why your presence was required. Pursuant to our investigation of the allegation of academic misconduct against you, Miss Mitchell, we have talked to Professor Picton, Miss Peterson, Mrs. Jenkins, Professor Jeremy Martin, and Mr. Paul Norris.

"During the course of our investigation, several facts emerged, facts that have been corroborated by more than one witness." The Dean stared at Gabriel, pursing his lips. "For this reason, the Provost's office ordered this committee be formed to investigate matters further.

"The facts that have come to light so far are as follows: first, that a public argument with possible personal overtones took place between Miss Mitchell and Professor Emerson during his graduate seminar on or about October twenty-eighth, two thousand and nine.

"Second, that on or about October thirty-first, Professor Picton agreed to supervise Miss Mitchell's MA thesis at the urging of Professor Emerson, who later notified Professor Martin about the change. Professor Emerson claimed that the switch was necessary due to a conflict of interest, namely, that Miss Mitchell was a *friend of his family*. Paperwork was filed in the School of Graduate Studies in November to effect this change.

"Third, on December tenth, Professor Emerson gave a public lecture in Florence, Italy, to which he was accompanied by Miss Mitchell. Over the course of the evening, he introduced Miss Mitchell as his fiancée. These facts are substantiated in print and in photographs, and they have also been corroborated by a Professor Pacciani who was present at the event." The Dean held up a piece of paper that appeared to be a hard copy of an email.

Gabriel glared darkly at the mention of Pacciani, mumbling an expletive under his breath.

The Dean fixed his gaze on Gabriel. "Did Miss Mitchell harass you into participating in an amorous relationship with her?"

Julia nearly fell off her chair.

All eyes in the room focused on Gabriel, whose color deepened. His lawyer began whispering furiously in his ear but Gabriel waved him aside.

"Absolutely not."

"Very well. Are you currently engaged in an amorous relationship with Miss Mitchell?"

"Dr. Aras, you've offered no evidence of any policy infractions here. All you've offered is a sketchy timeline that is open to interpretation and tabloid journalism from Italy. I will not allow you to railroad my client," John complained.

"If your client has nothing to hide, then he should answer our questions. When did the relationship between you, Professor Emerson, and your student begin?"

Before John could open his mouth to protest, Professor Chakravartty interrupted. "I object to this line of questioning on the grounds that relationships between professors and students in the same department cannot be consensual. And I'd like my objection minuted."

The Dean nodded at his assistant, Meagan, who was typing notes furiously on her laptop. "Duly noted," he huffed. "We'll discuss that issue shortly. Professor Emerson?"

"With respect, Dr. Aras, my client is not obligated to respond to supposition and speculation. Perhaps Miss Mitchell might take a different view." John cast a snide look at Soraya, then smiled innocently at the hearing officers.

"Very well. Miss Mitchell?"

Soraya glared at John before turning to face the committee.

"My client has already been subjected to a harassing experience by the Dean's office when she was forced to defend herself against a serious but entirely malicious complaint by another student. In view of the stress and emotional trauma that has already been inflicted on her, I ask you to direct your questions to Professor Emerson. He instigated the transfer of my client's thesis supervision to Professor Picton, it's his signature on the forms, and we have nothing to say on the matter."

Julia leaned over to protest in Soraya's ear, but Soraya waved her off.

Julia gritted her teeth.

"Ah. A classic prisoner's dilemma emerges. I wonder if either of you realize the outcome you are headed toward if you continue in this manner." Dr. Aras cleared this throat. "I can allow you a short recess in order for you to confer with your attorneys, Miss Mitchell and Professor Emerson, but I expect you to answer our questions expeditiously and truthfully.

"In the absence of any testimony at all, we reserve the right to decide the matter for ourselves, based upon the evidence we have been able to gather. And to refer the matter to the Provost's office so he can lay charges, if that is our recommendation. You have five minutes." The Dean's voice was cold and dispassionate.

"Since relationships between professors and students in the same department cannot be consensual, I move that we excuse Professor Emerson so we can interview Miss Mitchell." Professor Chakravartty gave Julia a sympathetic look. "Let me assure you that this is a safe space. There will be no reprisals from the Department of Italian Studies because of anything you disclose to us. If you've been a victim of sexual harassment, we can help you."

Tara's sympathy immediately morphed into disgust when she glanced in Gabriel's direction.

Julia quickly rose to her feet. "I wasn't harassed by Professor Emerson."

Soraya clutched her arm, but Julia ignored her. So Soraya stood beside her, waiting for the appropriate moment to interrupt and to object.

Gabriel began shaking his head in agitation, but Julia couldn't see him, fixated as she was on the hearing officers.

"We weren't involved while I was his student. And our current relationship is consensual."

The room was silent for a moment, before the silence was broken by the sounds of the hearing officers' pens scratching against paper.

The Dean sat back in his chair, looking remarkably unsurprised.

This was Julia's first indication that something had just gone very, very wrong. She sat down slowly, ignoring the hiss of Soraya's voice in her ear and turned to look at Gabriel. He stared straight ahead, but she knew he could feel her looking at him, she could tell by the set of his jaw. He crossed his arms angrily over his chest, his eyes fixed on the Dean's like a cobra waiting to strike.

"Thank you, Miss Mitchell. So the relationship is amorous." Dr. Aras glanced in Gabriel's direction before looking at Julia again.

"Since you've been so forthcoming, allow me a follow-up question. When did you purchase the airline ticket to Italy, knowing that you would be traveling with Professor Emerson?"

Julia gazed at the Dean blankly.

"Surely the tickets would have been reserved before December eighth, which would place the purchase date squarely within the semester. So prior to his submission of your grade, you must have had a conversation about your intention to accompany him to Italy as his guest. That seems problematic for the professor-student relationship, does it not?"

Julia opened her mouth to speak, but Soraya interrupted her.

"With respect, Dr. Aras, you're speculating."

"Actually, Miss Harandi, I'm making a reasonable inference of a *quid pro quo*." The Dean's lips visibly thinned. "Moreover, I'm suggesting your client just perjured herself. She said she wasn't involved with Professor Emerson last semester. Are we to believe that they magically became involved the moment the semester ended?"

Julia inhaled loudly, the sound echoing off the walls. Across the aisle, Gabriel's anxiety was telegraphed by the way he clenched and unclenched his fists, trying to hide them at his sides.

The Dean began to speak but he was interrupted by Professor Mwangi. "Miss Mitchell, at this point I need to remind you of the penalties for perjury and also for the violation of the non-fraternization policy of this University." His calm and kind voice was a studied contrast to the Dean's impatient directness.

"Perjury can result in expulsion or serious sanctions. A violation of the non-fraternization policy can jeopardize your academic standing in last semester's seminars." He shuffled a few papers on the table in front of him.

"You were writing your thesis with Professor Emerson until the beginning of November, about a month prior to your trip to Italy. You were registered in his Dante seminar for the entire fall semester, and awarded a mark of *A*.

"The non-fraternization policy exists to protect students from being preyed upon by their professors and to prevent any possibility of unfair preferments being dispersed. If you'd dropped Professor Emerson's class, we would not be here today. But since you remained in his class, we have a problem."

Professor Mwangi handed some papers to Meagan, who walked them obediently to Julia and Soraya. While Soraya glanced at the documents, Julia gaped in horror. She looked over at Gabriel once again, but he wouldn't return her gaze.

"Professor Martin testified before this committee that he has no recollection of any conversation with Professor Emerson about having Professor Picton grade your work in the Dante seminar. The Registrar's Office reports that it was Professor Emerson who submitted your grade via the online grading system. We have dated copies of those electronic documents, which you've just received."

"Dr. Mwangi, since we are just receiving these documents now I'd like a short recess in order to speak to my client." Soraya's voice broke through Julia's shock.

"Those moments are past, Miss Harandi, since your client has already perjured herself." The Dean's voice was harsh.

"I disagree," Professor Chakravartty interjected. "Miss Mitchell might not be in the best position to judge whether or not she was the victim of coercion. Certainly, any perjury on her part would be excused if she's the victim of harassment."

"Professor Picton graded my work in the Dante seminar. I'm sure she could clear up this misunderstanding." Julia's voice took on a stubborn tone that contrasted sharply with the tremor in her voice.

"Dean Aras, forgive me for interrupting, but I've just received an email from Professor Picton." Meagan's voice broke in hesitantly. She walked over to the Dean and presented him with her laptop.

He scanned the screen quickly before waving her aside.

"It would seem that Professor Picton confirms your story, Miss Mitchell."

Soraya leaned forward in her chair. "Then that should clear up any problems. Respectfully, we ask this committee to conclude the investigation and end this matter."

"Not so fast, Miss Harandi." Professor Mwangi looked between Gabriel and Julia curiously. "If the relationship truly is consensual, then why is Professor Emerson hiding behind his lawyer?"

"All you've done is present us with speculation and fantasy. Why should my client respond?" John's tone was contemptuous.

"We're entitled to come to our own conclusions with respect to evidence. I can't speak for my learned colleagues, but I'll state that in my opinion, your client and Miss Mitchell were involved last semester. Which means they violated the non-fraternization policy, and Miss Mitchell perjured herself."

John stood to his feet. "If this body intends to continue in this way, then we will be invoking the assistance of the University of Toronto's Faculty Association and the Canadian Association of University Teachers, as well as pursuing all legal means. I would caution the hearing officers against slandering my client."

The Dean waved a dismissive hand in the air. "Sit down. We don't respond to threats."

He waited until John took his seat before he tossed his pen on the table in front of him. He removed his glasses and placed them next to the pen.

"Since we seem to have hit upon an iceberg here, perhaps it would be best if I suspend this hearing, pending further investigation."

Gabriel gritted his teeth, knowing that any delay would further jeopardize Julia's admission to Harvard.

"Before we suspend the hearing, I think that Miss Mitchell should be given the opportunity to have her story heard without having to be in the same room as Professor Emerson." Professor Chakravartty nodded in Julia's direction.

"Professor Emerson is a powerful man. Perhaps, Miss Mitchell, you were worried about your status and he took advantage of that. Maybe you believe that the relationship is consensual now, but did you always feel that way? More than one witness has reported that he was very harsh with you last semester."

"This is outrageous! Dr. Aras, are you just going to sit there while my client is slandered by one of the hearing officers? I want my objection minuted, and I want it noted that I intend to file a complaint with the Provost about Dr. Chakravartty's unprofessional behavior." John was nearly apoplectic as he jumped to his feet.

"I want the professor to stay," said Julia, quietly.

"Very well." Professor Chakravartty's voice softened. "I'm sure this situation is stressful and confusing. But you should know that the committee is already aware of the email you sent to Professor Emerson, in which you pleaded with him to stop harassing you. Once again, I want to reiterate that we are here to discover the truth."

Julia blinked as the room around her grew fuzzy. Muffled sounds assaulted her eyes, almost as if she were sinking in water. Everything slowed down, especially her mind, as the enormity of Dr. Chakravartty's revelation crept over her skin like a frozen finger.

Meagan passed a few sheets of paper to John and Soraya.

John glanced at them quickly, before tossing them aside. "It's completely out of order for you surprise us with documents that were not mentioned in the letter you sent to my client."

"This is not a trial; it's merely an investigatory hearing. We aren't bound by the rules of discovery, Mr. Green. Professor Chakravartty, you may proceed." The Dean leaned back in his chair, giving Tara his full attention.

"I know that you didn't file a sexual harassment complaint against Professor Emerson. But it isn't too late to do so. If you wish, we can have him dismissed from the room so we can discuss this."

John shook his head. "My client unequivocally denies any harassment, sexual or otherwise, against Miss Mitchell. If anyone should be investigated for harassment, it should be Christa Peterson, who maliciously instigated this mess in the first place."

"Miss Peterson will be held accountable for her actions, don't worry about that." Professor Mwangi's voice was smooth and direct. "Miss Mitchell, I'm also interested in the email exchange we have here, in which you direct Professor Emerson to stop harassing you. Can you give us the context in which you made that statement?"

"It was a mistake." Julia's voice was low, yet it echoed loudly in the room.

"A mistake?" Professor Chakravartty repeated.

"We had a—misunderstanding. I should never have used the word harassment. I was angry. I didn't mean it."

Soraya began whispering in Julia's ear but she pulled away, wringing her hands.

"There was no harassment. That's why I didn't file a complaint."

Professor Chakravartty stared at Julia skeptically before addressing the Dean. "I'd like to move that we suspend this hearing. I have a lot of unanswered questions that I'd like to pose to the other witnesses. And I'd like to interview Miss Mitchell in a less hostile environment." She glared in Gabriel's direction.

"Miss Mitchell denied the allegation. She hasn't filed a complaint against my client, and under paragraph ten of the university's policy on sexual harassment, she can't be compelled to do so. Can we move on?" John objected.

"I don't need you to tell me how to run this proceeding, Mr. Green," the Dean snapped. "We can take all the time we need to investigate any matter pursuant to the matters before us."

The Dean gestured to the other hearing officers to move closer to his chair so they could whisper among themselves. The mere mention of a delay caused Julia's heart to pound, and she fixed frightened eyes on Gabriel, whose face had turned very red.

A few minutes later, the Dean put on his glasses and looked around the room.

"As Professor Chakravartty has suggested, I'm going to suspend this hearing. You've been forthcoming, Miss Mitchell, and for that I thank you. But you, Professor Emerson, have told us nothing. Your lack of cooperation has left us with no choice but to go back and speak to all the other witnesses. In particular, I have a few questions I'd like to put to the chair of your department, Professor Martin.

"If the relationship between the two of you was consensual, you're both at risk of having violated the non-fraternization policy. And you, Miss Mitchell, have possibly perjured yourself about when the relationship truly began. On the other hand, the email that you sent to the professor is inconsistent with your other statements. There's also the issue of the M.P. Emerson bursary, which you mention in your email.

"I'm not about to allow this proceeding to rush to judgment. So a delay is in order for us to complete our investigation. This delay could take several weeks, depending upon the level of cooperation we receive. Of course, if you'd rather not have a delay, you could simply answer our questions." At this, the Dean gave Gabriel and John a stern look.

Julia watched as Gabriel closed his eyes, his lips moving as if he were whispering something to himself. Then his eyes snapped open and he stood to his feet.

"*Enough,*" he said.

Six pairs of eyes swung to stare at the angry looking professor as he glared defiantly at the hearing officers.

"There's no need for a delay. I'll cooperate." Gabriel's jaw was set, his blue eyes flashing.

Julia's heart sank.

"It appears we've finally captured your attention, Professor Emerson, and persuaded you to come out from behind your lawyer," said Professor Mwangi sarcastically.

"Such a remark is beneath you." Gabriel waved a dismissive hand in the air.

"Are you willing to answer the committee's questions?" The Dean interrupted the staring match between the two men.

"Yes."

Once John got over his surprise, he stood at Gabriel's side. "Dr. Aras, my client has retained counsel. Can you give me a moment to consult with him?"

The Dean nodded, and John began whispering hastily in Gabriel's ear.

Julia could see that he did not like what John was saying, and she watched him mouth the words "*No, no, no.*"

Eventually, Gabriel dismissed John with a murderous look. "I am willing to answer any and all questions, but not while Miss Mitchell is in the room. Some of the answers I wish to give are of a personal nature and for various—ah—reasons I prefer to keep those answers confidential."

The Dean measured Gabriel intently and nodded. "Very well. Miss Mitchell, you are dismissed for the moment, but please don't leave the building. We might have need of you shortly."

"If Professor Emerson is intending to malign my client, he can do so in front of us," Soraya protested.

"The collective agreement with the faculty union ensures confidentiality in all judicial proceedings." The Dean's voice grew very cold. He took a moment to consult with his colleagues, then nodded in Julia's direction.

"If Professor Emerson offers testimony that implicates your client, you will be given the opportunity for rebuttal. Any matters not bearing on your case, Miss Mitchell, will be kept confidential. Miss Harandi, Miss Mitchell, you are both dismissed for the present. My assistant will notify you when your presence is required."

Soraya shook her head but took Julia's arm and tried to pull her toward the door at the back of the room.

Julia planted her feet. "Our relationship was consensual. I knew what I was doing and I don't regret it. *At all.* This is not a tawdry affair. There was no harassment."

The Dean couldn't help but notice as Professor Emerson began to rub his eyes and mouth, cursing silently.

"Miss Mitchell, you will have your chance for a rebuttal. Now if you please . . ."

Soraya quickly pulled Julia out of the room. She tried in vain to catch Gabriel's eye before she exited, but he hung his head, eyes shut.

Chapter Twenty-four

W hat?" Professor Jeremy Martin almost shouted into his office telephone.

Across campus, Meagan, the Dean's assistant, turned her back on the hearing officers as she prepared to speak more loudly.

"I said that the Dean would like to ask you a few questions about Professor Emerson and Julianne Mitchell. Professor Emerson just confessed to having broken several university policies with respect to her. Can you hold the line, please, while I put you on speaker phone?"

"Holy God," breathed Jeremy, blinking and gaping like a fish.

"Professor Martin? The hearing officers would like to speak to you now." Meagan turned and locked eyes with the Dean.

"I'll be right there. Ask the Dean not to do anything until I arrive!" Jeremy slammed the telephone down on his desk and quickly exited his office, forgetting to close and lock the door behind him. He jogged out of the building and across Queen's Park, pausing only to avoid being run over by downtown traffic. By the time he'd traversed the few blocks to where the hearing committee sat, he was winded, disheveled, and incredibly annoyed at how out of shape he was.

"Stop," he panted, bursting through the doors. He placed his hands on his knees so he could attempt to catch his breath.

"Thank you for joining us, Professor Martin." The Dean's tone was sarcastic.

"I came—as fast—as I could. What's—going on?"

The Dean gestured to his assistant to fetch the ailing professor a glass of water, which he drank gratefully. The beverage gave him a moment to find Gabriel, who was sitting stoically next to his lawyer.

The Dean frowned. "It appears that things are amiss in your department. Professor Emerson has just confessed to pursuing Miss Mitchell and engaging in an amorous relationship with her while she was his student. I'd like to know how long you've known about this."

"Excuse me?" Jeremy grabbed a chair and sat on it heavily.

"You told us Professor Emerson disclosed his relationship with Miss Mitchell to you this semester, but that you couldn't recall when. I'm wondering if you had any inkling that they were involved last semester?"

Jeremy's eyebrows knitted together in confusion. "I—what?"

"Gabriel Emerson tried to cover up his affair with his student by transferring her thesis supervision and seminar work to Katherine Picton," Professor Mwangi explained. "What did you know about this and when?"

Jeremy's expression grew grim. "With respect, am I on trial here or is Gabriel? I was told that you wanted to ask me questions about a matter arising between Gabriel and Miss Mitchell. I was offered no indication that I was under suspicion, otherwise I would have informed the Faculty Association and brought my union representative."

Professor Mwangi abruptly closed his mouth.

"Jeremy, there's no need to be defensive. We're simply interested in whether or not you can shed any light on the account Professor Emerson has offered us. That's all." The Dean offered a withering look in Robert's direction.

"We can return to the question of the timeline in a moment. I'm interested in an email that Miss Mitchell sent to Professor Emerson in which she accused him of harassment and told him that she would be returning the M. P. Emerson bursary. What can you tell us about that?"

Jeremy's eyes slid over to Gabriel's.

He had no idea why Gabriel had confessed; it didn't make sense. He was far more likely to avoid any kind of discipline if he said nothing. Having confessed, he'd handed his career to the Dean in an act that could only be described as academic *hara-kiri*. Moreover, he'd implicated Jeremy with his confession, and that was something he did not appreciate, not one bit.

"I know of no such harassment. In my position as Chair of Italian Studies, I have a spotless record of upholding university policies." He glanced in Meagan's direction. "And I'd like my administrative record to be included as part of this proceeding."

The Dean waved a hand at his assistant, acquiescing to Jeremy's demand.

He looked at the hearing officers. "Has Miss Mitchell filed a harassment complaint?"

The hearing officers shook their heads.

"May I see the email?"

The Dean nodded to Meagan, and she quickly passed a piece of paper to Jeremy.

He used this opportunity to buy some time for his over-wrought brain, hoping to get some clue from Gabriel's body language as to what the devil he'd been thinking. But still, Gabriel would not look at him, simply sitting stone-faced, clenching his fists.

"Since Miss Mitchell never reported the harassment, I can only infer that she changed her mind. Perhaps she sent the email in haste and repented at leisure. It sounds as if she didn't hold his behavior against him." Jeremy handed the paper back to Meagan.

"What do you know about the bursary?" asked Professor Chakra-vartty.

Jeremy's eyes flitted to the Dean's. "I advised the Dean in an email that donor services was approached by a philanthropic organization from the United States, whose name escapes me. The charity wished to bestow a bursary on the top MA student in my department. That's all I know."

"What's the connection between Professor Emerson and the bursary?" asked the Dean.

Jeremy shrugged. "None."

Professor Mwangi clasped his fingers together on the table in front of him. "I find that difficult to believe. There is a coincidence of name, department, and student. Miss Mitchell seems to have associated the bursary with Professor Emerson—why else would she threaten to return it?"

Jeremy smiled wryly. "Do you remember what life was like when you were a grad student? Living on coffee and ramen noodles and going without sleep? Students engage in all kinds of erratic behavior under those conditions. I'm sure we've all seen worse.

"I assure you—" At this, he nodded in Gabriel's direction. "Professor Emerson had nothing to do with the bursary. I'm the one who awarded it, and I did so based on the fact that Miss Mitchell was the top master's student admitted into our program. You can speak to Tracy in donor services about the charity that made the donation and you can view her paperwork."

Gabriel tried very hard to hide his surprise at the fact that his chair was defending him. He fidgeted in his seat, swiping a hand through his hair as he waited to see how the Dean would respond.

"That won't be necessary." The Dean took off his glasses and nibbled at one of the ends of the arms thoughtfully. "As you've heard, Professor Emerson has confessed, taking upon himself full responsibility for his involvement with Miss Mitchell. By his own admission, he played on her vulnerability, promising her that 'he would take care' of their situation. His use of Professor Picton seems to bear that out, as does Miss Mitchell's nervous behavior during these proceedings.

"Since Professor Emerson was in a position of power over Miss Mitchell, and since more than one witness has testified that he was initially very harsh with her, we don't believe that their relationship was consensual." At this, his eyes met Professor Chakravartty's, who nodded triumphantly. "Consequently, we are inclined to excuse her perjury, since it was clearly under duress, and we will dismiss any allegations against her. Unless you can suggest a reason why we shouldn't."

Gabriel caught Jeremy's eye with a stare so sharp, Jeremy almost winced.

"I see no reason why Miss Mitchell should be punished, no." Jeremy tugged at his shirt collar uncomfortably.

"We will be encouraging Miss Mitchell to consider the possibility of filing a harassment complaint. Having said that, and given the fact that Professor Emerson has been forthcoming, I'm not inclined to drag this matter out. However, I wonder if I should recommend to the Provost that your department be placed under scrutiny. We're facing a lawsuit from another of your students, Miss Peterson. And Miss Mitchell has filed a harassment complaint against her. That's several unfortunate events in one semester, Professor Martin. What is going on in your department?" The Dean gave Jeremy a stern look.

He straightened his spine. "I am as surprised and distressed as you are. But surely you can't blame me for failing to have a prurient interest in the personal lives of those in my department."

"No, but we expect you to maintain a safe environment for students, especially females." Professor Chakravartty's tone was firm and disapproving.

The Dean nodded in her direction. "Nevertheless, I am cognizant of your spotless record and the reputation of your department. So I'd like to ask for your input on what we should do in terms of consequences for these policy violations, and I invite you to meet with us while we discuss it." The Dean waved Jeremy over.

Jeremy cleared his throat. "Thank you. I'd like a word with Professor Emerson first."

"His testimony has been minuted. Meagan will provide you with a transcript."

"Since I am his supervisor, I'd prefer to ask my own questions. I doubt you'd deny me that right, as his Chair."

The Dean frowned. "Very well. You have five minutes."

With a nod of his head, Jeremy walked to the door, waiting for Gabriel to join him.

Gabriel waved aside John's attempt at accompanying him and walked slowly toward his old friend, his shoulders sagging.

"What the fuck have you done?" Jeremy hissed, turning his back on the hearing officers.

Gabriel mirrored his position. "They were going to suspend the meeting and launch an extended investigation. Julianne would have lost her spot at Harvard, not to mention the fact that she was in danger of being punished for academic fraud and perjury."

"What the hell do you think is going to happen now? The Dean could dismiss you!"

"Before I made my statement, my lawyer asked for leniency. The Dean agreed, provided I wasn't involved in any criminal activity."

Jeremy scrubbed at his face with his hands. "So you went ahead and admitted everything? Are you crazy? You should have kept your mouth shut."

"And ruin Julianne's life? Never!"

Jeremy gave his colleague a long, cold look. "They could revoke your tenure. If you're dismissed, no university will touch you. Your career will be over."

Gabriel's expression hardened. "I don't care."

"Well, I do!" Jeremy fumed. "I'm not about to lose one of my best professors over some grad student. With all the funding cuts being made in our division, I might not be able to replace you. It's bad enough we have only one Dante specialist. How am I supposed to run a decent department without one?"

"That isn't my problem."

"The hell it isn't." Jeremy glared. "You and Julianne and—and that Christa are crippling my department in one fell swoop. Even if I could get permission to replace you, who is going to want to work for me when news of Christa's lawsuit gets out? Not to mention your affair with Julianne!"

"It wasn't an affair," Gabriel whispered, stubbornly. "The Dean promised complete confidentiality. That's why I agreed to speak on the record."

Jeremy shook his head in disbelief. "You just don't get it, do you? I'm your friend. And you made me look like an imbecile in front of my boss. It's quite possible they're going to investigate me in order to discover what I knew and when. I'll have to appear before God knows how many committees and possibly in court!"

"I'm sorry," said Gabriel stiffly.

"You should be. I look like an idiot who allowed a predatory professor to wreak havoc on two female grad students. You're lucky Tara is on the committee and not the Chair of Women's Studies. She would have strung you up by your balls in the middle of campus."

Gabriel straightened his shoulders. "I'll tell them you knew nothing and take the consequences."

Jeremy took a step closer, staring his younger colleague straight in the eye. "Don't give me that martyrdom bullshit. You're hurting a lot of people in your quest to protect your conquest. Now my ass is on the line. What do you think is going to happen to her if they fire you?"

"If they try to fire me, I'll sue them."

Jeremy put his hands on his waist. "It will be too late. As soon as you're dismissed, the people at Harvard will hear about it and Julianne's MA will be tainted. You'll ruin her and my reputation and the reputation of all the other professors and students in my department. We'll all be tarred with your brush." Jeremy shook his head. "How could you do this to us?"

Gabriel was silent, slowly clenching and unclenching his fists.

Jeremy swore loudly and was about to turn away when Gabriel caught his arm. "I'm sorry."

"It's too late for apologies."

"I didn't realize this would have implications for you and everyone else. I wasn't thinking." Gabriel paused, a tortured look on his face. "Help us. Please."

Jeremy stared in disbelief. Professor Emerson looked panicked and desperate, which was an expression he'd never seen before. "You've done a tremendous amount of damage trying to protect her. You should have denied everything."

"Then the Dean would have punished her or dragged the investigation out."

"She could have re-applied next year."

"And been turned down outright. The longer the investigation continued, the more likely that details would be leaked. It's a small academic community and you know it."

"Of course I know it." Jeremy shook his head. "And you knew better than to fuck a student."

Gabriel's face reddened and he took a menacing step forward. "I didn't fuck her."

"The hell you didn't. Now we're all fucked," Jeremy snapped.

Gabriel's nostrils flared as he held back an angry retort.

Jeremy gave his friend a long, searching look. "My first priority is to my department. But I don't want to see you or Julianne ruined. Enough young women have suffered at the hands of their professors, don't you agree?"

Gabriel was silent, his lips pressed together.

"I'll help you, but we're doing this my way. Do you understand? I'm not risking everything so you can turn around and fuck it up again."

Gabriel paused. Then he nodded his agreement.

"Now all I have to do is convince the Dean to be satisfied with an ounce of your flesh rather than a pound."

With barely an acknowledgement, Jeremy walked to the front of the room and joined the hearing officers in their deliberations.

Gabriel hung his head, breathing a restrained sigh of relief.

Chapter Twenty-five

By the time Meagan ushered the ladies back into the room, Julia's fingernails had been chewed to the quick and Soraya's adrenaline was at an all-time high.

Julia's eyes were drawn immediately to Gabriel, and what she saw upset her. His shoulders were hunched, and he was leaning forward in his chair, hands clasped between his knees tensely, head lowered.

She stared at him, willing him to look at her.

But he wouldn't.

Professor Martin sat next to Gabriel, arms crossed against his chest. He didn't appear happy.

"Miss Mitchell, allow me to come straight to the point. In light of Professor Emerson's testimony, you are excused. We will be informing the Registrar's Office that the grade assigned to you in Professor Emerson's seminar should be allowed to stand."

Julia's mouth opened in shock at the Dean's pronouncement.

"We will do our utmost to ensure that you are not victimized further." The Dean glared in Gabriel's direction. "If Professor Emerson troubles you in any way, or if you have concerns about the repercussions of your former involvement with him, please inform Professor Martin immediately.

"You are free to pursue a harassment complaint against Professor Emerson, but you must do so within sixty days of the submission of your final academic work in your program."

The Dean nodded at Soraya. "I'm sure your lawyer will explain the particulars of the harassment policy to you. I know you've filed a complaint against Miss Peterson, but we're hopeful that you and she can drop your complaints against each other, given the outcome of this hearing. You're free to go."

He began shuffling his paperwork.

"Thank you, Dr. Aras." Soraya smiled widely and exchanged a nod and a meaningful look with Tara.

"I'm not a victim," said Julia, stubbornly.

"Pardon?" said the Dean, peering over the rims of his glasses.

"I said, *I'm not a victim*. Our relationship is consensual." She turned to look at Gabriel. "What's going on?"

Gabriel kept his eyes fixed on the floor.

"Miss Mitchell, the committee has ensured that Professor Emerson was given due consideration." Professor Mwangi spoke to her gently. "But in light of his confession, we are holding him accountable for his actions. And that includes seeing to your welfare."

"My welfare is tied to him. If he's going to be punished, then punish me too." She took a step closer to the table behind which the committee sat.

Gabriel's head shot up, and he gave Julia a furious look.

"Miss Mitchell, the university has a duty to protect students from being preyed upon by their supervisors. Please, let us do our job." Professor Chakravartty's tone was not unsympathetic.

"We did this together. If he's guilty, so am I."

"Not necessarily."

"Then tell me what he said! Give me a chance to respond." Julia looked desperately at the faces of the hearing officers, one after the other, hoping that someone, *anyone* would relent.

"Professor Emerson has admitted to engaging in an inappropriate relationship with you while you were his student. Professor Picton has confirmed that she marked your work in his seminar and supervised your thesis. So we are inclined to be lenient with him. Unless you insist otherwise."

"Of course I insist otherwise! I want you to let him go."

The hearing officers shook their heads.

"Why do you believe him instead of me? I'm the student. You should weigh my testimony more heavily. He didn't hurt me. You have to believe me!" Julia grew desperate, on the verge of tears.

"Miss Harandi, control your client." The Dean's voice rose with irritation.

"Please," said Julia, taking a step closer to the hearing officers. "You have to believe me. Let him go!"

"We will ask you and all other parties to sign a confidentiality agreement that is as much for your protection as for the integrity of these proceedings. Once again, if you have further difficulties, you are to inform Professor Martin." The Dean nodded at Soraya.

"Come on, Julia." Soraya tugged on her arm, in vain. "Let's go before they change their mind."

"Gabriel, what happened?"

Julia took a step in his direction, but the pointed toe of her boot got caught in the carpet and she tumbled to her knees.

Finally her eyes connected with Gabriel's as he looked down on her. She inhaled slowly as she realized that his dark blue eyes were cold and empty. He lowered his head.

In an instant, the fire in her veins turned to ice.

Chapter Twenty-six

"*Something is rotten in the state of Denmark.*" Soraya leaned back against the vanity in the ladies' washroom while her client sat crying softly in a chair. She pulled her BlackBerry out of her briefcase, scrolling through her emails before returning the cursed device to its former resting place.

"I know John. His plan would have been to say nothing, then file a lawsuit. He would have tried to show that everything was *your fault*, setting the groundwork for Gabriel's defense. He never would have agreed to this kind of outcome."

Soraya fixed her client with a stern eye. "Do you know something? Some secret that Gabriel might worry would come out? Something extremely damaging?"

Julia shook her head vehemently. Gabriel's drug use was in the past as was his rampant promiscuity, including his encounter with Professor Singer. Of course, there was the small matter of the black market Botticelli prints, but she would never reveal their existence to anyone, least of all to Soraya.

"Are you sure?" The attorney's eyes narrowed.

"There's nothing." Julia sniffled, wiping her nose with a tissue.

Soraya tossed her long, dark hair. "Then he must be keeping secrets from you too. I can't imagine what would be more damaging to him than confessing to having an inappropriate relationship with you. I thought you told me you didn't sleep with him until December?"

"That's right."

"Then why would he tell them you were together while you were still his student?"

"Do you think they fired him?" Julia changed the subject.

"No." Soraya exhaled loudly. "Emerson is tenured and from the body language in the room, he has the support of his Chair. But who knows? David is a self-righteous bastard."

"You don't think Gabriel was lying to protect me?"

Soraya smothered a patronizing smile, for really, it would have been inappropriate to smile at that moment. "Human beings are selfish. He was protecting himself—hiding some secret that he didn't want to come out or trading a confession for leniency. Gabriel went rogue and re-fused to let John fight the charges. Otherwise, we'd still be sitting in the hall, waiting."

Julia stood at the sink and washed her face and hands, trying to make herself appear presentable.

Soraya shook her head. "I don't mean to be callous, but I really don't think you should be wasting your tears on him."

"What do you mean?"

"I'm sure you were an intriguing diversion, in comparison to his other women. He probably said pretty things so you'd screw him and keep your mouth shut. But men like him can't be trusted. And they never change." She continued hurriedly as she saw the horrified expression on Julia's face.

"I wasn't going to mention this, but a friend of mine hooked up with him a couple of times. They met at a club about a year ago and ended up fucking in the washroom.

"One day last fall, he called her out of the blue. One more hook up and she never saw or heard from him again. It was as if he'd vanished." Soraya measured Julia's reaction. "Why would you want to be with someone like that? He was probably screwing other women the entire time he was with you."

"You don't know him. Don't judge him." Julia's voice was quietly ag-gressive.

Soraya simply shrugged and dug around in her briefcase for her lipstick.

Julia closed her eyes and took a deep breath, trying to process these new revelations.

Gabriel and I started getting close last fall—was he sleeping with someone else when he was sending me flowers and emails? Was he lying to me about Paulina?

Julia didn't know what to believe. Her heart told her to believe Gabriel, but she couldn't deny the fact that Soraya had planted a seed of doubt.

They walked into the hallway and headed for the stairs, hoping to make their escape.

John and Gabriel were doing the same thing. Neither of the men looked happy.

"Gabriel!" Julia called.

John glared in her direction. "Let's go, Gabriel. You can't be seen with her."

Julia looked over into conflicted blue eyes. He didn't look disgusted anymore; he looked sober and anxious.

"Haven't you done enough damage for one day?" spat his attorney as Julia took a hesitant step in their direction.

"Don't speak to her like that." Gabriel moved to stand in between them, shielding Julia with his body. He still wouldn't look at her.

"Listen, you two, David and his minions are about to come through that door, and I'd prefer to be gone before that happens. So whatever conversation you need to have, make it quick," Soraya snapped.

"Over my dead body." John glowered. "We're in enough trouble as it is. Come on."

Gabriel shot his lawyer a look of warning and gritted his teeth, turning around to face Julia.

"What's going on? Why did you tell them our relationship was inappropriate?" Julia looked up into dark, tormented eyes.

"You were not sensible of your own distress." Gabriel leaned forward to whisper in an urgent tone.

"What's that supposed to mean?"

"It means that he just saved your ass, that's what it means!" John interrupted, pointing at Julia contemptuously. "What, exactly, were you trying to accomplish by emotionally vomiting all over the proceedings? I knew you were naïve, but just how stupid are you?"

"John, take your finger out of Miss Mitchell's face or I will separate it from your body." Gabriel's voice dropped, his tone quiet but chilling. "You do not speak to her like that. *Ever*. Do I make myself clear?"

John closed his mouth.

Soraya used this as an opportunity to put him on the defensive. "My client is better off without the *theatrics* of either one of you. Don't pretend you weren't going to blame her for everything to save your client. Bloody coward."

John muttered an oblique curse in response, but said nothing.

Julia turned to search Gabriel's eyes. But his mask was firmly in place.

"Why did the Dean say that they were going to protect me from you?"

"We need to go. Now." John tried to separate the couple as a noise inside the meeting room alerted them to the fact that the hearing officers were about to recess.

"Did they fire you?" Julia asked tremulously.

Gabriel gave her a pained look, then shook his head.

"Well done, John. I'm sure you're proud of yourself," Soraya hissed. "Did you have to sell your soul to David? Or maybe your body?"

"Blow me, Soraya," said John.

"So you kept your job, but you can't talk to me? What about last night, Gabriel?" Julia reached out a trembling finger toward his hand.

He pulled out of her reach and glanced sideways at John and Soraya, shaking his head.

"You promised you'd never fuck me. But what about last night? No words, no *I love you*, not even a note or a text this morning. Is that all it was to you? *A good-bye fuck?*" Julia's whisper caught on an involuntary sob, and she raised her voice. "Who's the *Angelfucker* now?"

Gabriel flinched.

It was more than a flinch; actually, it was more like a reel backward from a punch. He closed his eyes and groaned softly, shifting his weight to his heels as his fists clenched at his sides.

Everyone watched as his skin took on a ghostlike pallor.

"*You wound me, Julianne,*" he whispered.

"You keep your job, but you won't talk to me? How could you do this?" she cried.

His eyes flew open, and they were a brilliant, livid sapphire.

"You think that I'd just show up, *fuck you,* and that would be how I would say good-bye?"

Julia watched his fists shake as he fought to maintain control.

"That *was* good-bye?" Her voice caught on the last word.

Gabriel's eyes lasered into hers as if he were trying to communicate something wordlessly. He leaned forward so his nose was only inches from hers and dropped his voice so it was almost inaudible. "I did *not* fuck you. I've *never* fucked you."

He pulled back slightly so there was some distance between them. He drew a long, unhurried breath. "You were throwing your life away for *nothing*—all those years of hard work, everything you dreamed of and ever wanted was going to be taken from you and you would *never* be able to get it back.

"There was no way I could watch you commit academic suicide. I told you that I would go to Hell to rescue you and that's just what I did." He lifted his chin. "And I'd do it again."

Julia leapt forward, jabbing a finger into Gabriel's chest.

"You don't get to make decisions for me! This is my life and my dreams. If I want to give them up, who the hell are you to take that decision away from me?

"You're supposed to love me, Gabriel. You're supposed to support me when I decide to stand up for myself. Isn't that what you wanted me to do? And instead, you cut a deal with them and dump me?"

"Would you two shut the hell up?" Soraya hissed. "The Dean will be walking through the door any minute. Come on, Julia. Right now."

She tugged on her client's elbow while John tried to step in between the two quarreling lovers.

"So that's it? They say it's over and it's over? When have you ever followed the rules, Gabriel? Now you decide to follow them?" Julia asked, still furious.

Gabriel's expression changed immediately. "I had no choice, *Héloise*," he whispered. "Circumstances were beyond—"

"I thought my name was *Beatrice*. Of course, Abelard abandoned Héloise to keep his job. So I guess the name is more than apt," she spat, stepping away from him.

At that moment, Professor Martin entered the hallway. He scowled and began walking toward them.

Gabriel turned away from Jeremy, lowering his voice further. "Read my sixth letter. Paragraph four."

Julia shook her head.

"I'm not your student, Professor. I won't be doing any reading assignments."

Soraya pulled Julia away, and the two women hurried down the stairs just as the hearing officers came through the door.

Chapter Twenty-seven

Gabriel ducked into the men's room as soon as Julia left. He couldn't risk calling her, since Jeremy might enter at any moment, but he was far from satisfied that she understood what was happening. Turning on a faucet in order to make noise, he quickly tapped out a short but explanatory email on his iPhone.

Having sent it, he turned off the faucet and exited, tucking his phone into his jacket pocket. He tried very hard to look grim and defeated.

As he walked over to the two men, Jeremy's cell phone chirped.

When Julia awoke the next morning the numbness had worn off. Sleep would have been a welcome respite from reality, except for the nightmares. She'd been haunted by various dreams, all involving the morning she woke up alone in the orchard. She was frightened and lost and Gabriel was nowhere to be found.

It was almost noon when she crawled out of bed to check her messages. She'd expected at least a text or a one line email, offering some kind of explanation. But there was nothing.

He'd acted so strangely the day before. On the one hand he'd told her he hadn't fucked her; on the other, he'd called her *Héloise*. She didn't want to believe that he was so cruel as to flaunt the fact that he was ending things with a play on words, but he'd used the word *good-bye*.

Her feelings of betrayal ran deep, for Gabriel had promised that he would never leave her. He was far too eager to go back on his promise, she thought, despite the fact that the university had no jurisdiction over his personal life, so long as she was no longer his student.

A dark thought occurred to her. Perhaps Gabriel had tired of her and decided to put an end to their union. The university had simply handed him an opportunity to do so.

If her falling-out with Gabriel had occurred a few months earlier, she would have stayed in bed for three days. As it was, she dialed his cell phone with the intention of demanding an explanation. He didn't answer. She left a terse and impatient voice mail, asking him to call her.

Frustrated, she took a shower, hoping that the time to herself would afford her the opportunity to see her situation with clarity. Unfortunately, all she could think about was the evening in Italy when Gabriel showered her and washed her hair.

After she dressed, she decided to search for Gabriel's sixth letter, so she could read paragraph four. He'd given her a clue, she thought, as to what was really happening. All she needed to do was find his words.

She wasn't sure what he meant by *letter*. Did he mean emails or texts? Or both? If Gabriel was counting the emails, cards, and notes that he'd written to her from the very beginning of their relationship, then by her calculation the sixth letter was a note he'd left her the morning after their horrendous fight in the Dante seminar. Luckily, she kept it.

She pulled out the paper and read it eagerly.

> Julianne,
> I hope you'll find everything you need here.
> If not, Rachel stocked the vanity in the guest washroom with a number of different items. Please help yourself.
> My clothes are at your disposal.
> Please choose a sweater as the weather has turned cold today.
> Yours,
> Gabriel.

Julia wasn't exactly in the best frame of mind to embark on a detective mission or to engage in any elaborate decoding of messages. Nevertheless, she turned her attention to the fourth paragraph and tried to figure out what Gabriel had been trying to communicate to her.

He'd lent her the British-racing-green sweater, but she'd returned it. Was he trying to tell her to look at one of the clothing items he'd bought her? Julia pulled out everything he'd ever bought her or that she'd borrowed and placed them all on her bed. She forced herself to take her time examining each item. But there didn't appear to be anything unusual about any of them.

Was he trying to tell her to *weather* the storm? Or was he simply saying that his affection for her had turned cold and this was good-bye?

Her anger burned blue. She stomped to the bathroom to wash her hands, catching sight of her image in the mirror. The wide-eyed nervous girl who had started at the University of Toronto in September was gone. Instead, Julia saw a pale and upset young woman, with pinched lips and flashing eyes. She was no longer the timid Rabbit or the seventeen-year-old Beatrice. She was Julianne Mitchell, almost-MA, and she would be damned if she'd spend the rest of her life simply taking the scraps that others deigned to throw at her.

If he has a message for me, he can damn well say it in person, she thought. *I'm not going on a scavenger hunt just so he can assuage his conscience.*

Yes, she loved him. Looking at the photograph album he made for her birthday, she knew that she would love him forever. But love was not an excuse for cruelty. She was not a plaything, an Héloise, to be dropped like a pair of dirty socks. If he was breaking things off with her, she'd make him say so to her face. She was simply going to give him until after dinner to do so.

In early evening, she walked to the Manulife Building, the key to Gabriel's apartment in her pocket. With every step she imagined what she would say. She wouldn't cry, she promised herself. She would be strong. And she would demand answers.

As she turned the corner and approached the front door, she saw a tall, impeccably dressed blonde exit the building. The woman looked at her watch and tapped her foot impatiently as the doorman waved over a waiting taxi.

Julia hid behind a tree. She peeked around the trunk in order to take another look.

At first glance, she'd thought the woman in question was Paulina;

upon inspection she realized her mistake. Julia breathed a sigh of relief as she approached the building. Seeing Paulina with Gabriel on this day of all days would have been devastating. Surely, he wouldn't do that to her. Gabriel was supposed to be her Dante. He was supposed to love her enough to travel through Hell to protect her, not take Paulina back the moment their relationship was threatened.

With some trepidation, Julia entered the lobby and waved to the security guard, who recognized her. She decided against announcing her presence to Gabriel and took the elevator to his floor. She shivered as she contemplated what she might find in his apartment.

She didn't bother to knock but simply let herself in, fearing that she'd find Gabriel compromised. But something strange caught her attention as soon as she'd closed the door. All the lights in the apartment were off and the hall closet was open and half-empty, hangers and shoes haphazardly thrown on the floor. It was very unlike Gabriel to leave things in such a mess.

She switched on several lights and placed her key on the table where he always kept his keys. His keys were not to be found.

"Gabriel? Hello?"

She ventured into the kitchen and was shocked by what she found. An empty bottle of Scotch lay on the counter, next to a broken glass. Dirty plates and cutlery were dumped in the sink.

Steeling herself for what she might find, she walked to the fireplace, only to discover a mark on the wall and scattered glass shards on the floor. She could see Gabriel flinging his Scotch in anger, but she had a hard time imagining him leaving broken pieces for someone to step on.

Desperately worried, she crept down the darkened hall and into the master bedroom. Clothes were strewn across the bed, the drawers to Gabriel's dresser half-opened. His closet was similarly disarrayed, and Julia noticed that many of his clothes were gone as was his large suitcase.

But what caused her to inhale sharply were the walls. All the framed photographs of her, and of Gabriel and her together, had been removed and piled face down on the bed, leaving the walls bare except for the hooks on which the photographs had been hung.

Julia gasped in horror as she saw that the reproduction of Holiday's painting of Dante and Beatrice had been taken down and was now leaning against the credenza, its back on display.

Shocked, she sank down on a chair. *He's gone*, she thought.

Julia burst into tears, wondering how he could have so easily broken his promises. She searched the apartment in vain for a note or some indication of where he'd gone. When she came across the telephone she contemplated calling Rachel. But the thought of having to explain that she and Gabriel were over was too much to bear.

With one last look she turned out all the lights and was about to walk through the door when she stopped. Something niggled at the back of her mind. Closing the door, she returned to Gabriel's bedroom. Searching with her fingers, she fumbled about, looking for something. When she didn't find it, she turned on the light.

The photograph that Rachel had taken at Lobby several months earlier was missing. Gabriel always kept it on top of his dresser. In the picture, he and Julia were dancing, and he was looking at her with no little heat.

Julia stood for a moment, looking at the empty space. It was possible, she thought, that he'd destroyed the picture. But a quick inspection of the wastepaper baskets in the bedroom and bathroom suggested he hadn't thrown it away.

She didn't understand why he'd left or why he'd left without offering her an explanation, but she began to suspect that all was not as it seemed.

As she took one last look at the empty hangers in the closet, she contemplated taking her clothes with her but only for an instant. Strangely enough, they no longer felt as if they were hers.

A few minutes later, she was waiting for the elevator, feeling battered and bruised. Her nose began to run as she wiped away a few tears. A hasty search of her pockets yielded no Kleenex, only lint. This made her tears fall faster.

"Here," a voice at her elbow said, holding out a man's handkerchief.

Julia took it gratefully, noticing the embroidered initials *S.I.R.* on it. She wiped her eyes and attempted to return it, but a pair of hands made a motion of refusal.

"My mother is always giving me handkerchiefs. I have dozens."

She looked up into kind brown eyes that were partially hidden behind a pair of rimless spectacles and recognized one of Gabriel's neighbors. He was wearing a heavy wool coat and a navy beret.

(Which, because of his age and heterosexuality could only be explained by the fact that he was French Canadian.)

When the elevator arrived, he politely held the door open for her before following her inside.

"Is something wrong? Can I help?" His lightly accented voice cut through her haze.

"Gabriel is gone."

"Yes, I ran into him while he was on his way out." The neighbor frowned at the tears that were still welling up in Julia's eyes. "Didn't he tell you? I thought you were his—" He looked at her expectantly.

Julia shook her head. "Not anymore."

"I'm sorry to hear that."

They were both silent as the elevator continued its descent to the ground floor. Once again, when the door opened, he held it for her.

She turned to him. "Do you know where he went?"

The neighbor accompanied her to the lobby. "No. I'm afraid I didn't ask. He was in quite a state, you see." The neighbor leaned closer and dropped his voice. "He reeked of Scotch and was extremely cross. Not in the mood to chat."

Julia smiled a watery smile. "Thanks. I'm sorry to bother you."

"It isn't a bother. I'm guessing he didn't tell you he was leaving."

"No." She wiped her face with his handkerchief once again.

The neighbor began muttering something about Gabriel in French. Something that sounded a good deal like *cochon*.

"I could deliver a message for you, when he returns," the neighbor offered. "He tends to drop by my apartment when he runs out of milk."

Julia was quiet for a moment, then she swallowed hard. "Just tell him that he broke my heart."

The neighbor gave her a reluctant, pained nod before taking his leave of her.

Julia walked outside into the bracing wind and began her long walk home, alone.

Chapter Twenty-eight

Several hours after the hearing, Gabriel sat in his apartment shrouded in darkness. The only light visible came from the blue and orange flames that flickered in his fireplace. He was surrounded by *her*. Completely surrounded by her memory and her ghost.

Closing his eyes, he swore he could smell her scent or hear her laughter echoing down the hall. His bedroom had become like a shrine, which was why he was sitting in front of the fire.

He couldn't bear to look at the large black-and-white photographs of the two of them. Especially the one that hung over his bed—*Julianne in all of her magnificence, lying on her stomach with her naked back exposed, partially wrapped in a sheet, gazing up at him in adoration with sex-mussed hair and a sweet, sated smile . . .*

In every room he had a memory of her—some of them joyous and others bittersweet, like dark, dark chocolate. He stalked to the dining room and poured himself two fingers' worth of his very best Scotch and downed it quickly, relishing the burning sensation as it stung his throat. He tried desperately not to think about Julia standing in front of him, jabbing an angry finger into his chest.

"You're supposed to love me, Gabriel. You're supposed to support me when I decide to stand up for myself. Isn't that what you wanted me to do? And instead, you cut a deal with them and dump me?"

At the memory of the look of betrayal in her eyes, Gabriel threw his empty glass at the wall, watching it shatter and fall to the floor. Shards of crystal like jagged icicles scattered over the hardwood, glimmering in the firelight.

He knew what he had to do; he simply needed the courage in order to do it. Grabbing the bottle, he walked reluctantly to the bedroom. Two more swallows and he was able to throw his suitcase on the bed. He didn't bother to fold his clothes. He barely cared about taking the essentials.

He thought about what it was like to be banished. About Odysseus's tears at being so far away from home, from his wife, from his people. Now Gabriel understood exile.

When he was finished, he placed the framed photograph from atop his dresser in his briefcase. Stroking a tender finger over the face of his beloved, he downed more Scotch before staggering to the study.

He ignored the red velvet wing chair, for if he turned to look at it, he would see her, curled up like a cat, reading a book. She'd worry her lower lip between her teeth, her adorable eyebrows scrunched in thought. Had any man ever loved, adored, worshipped a woman more?

None but Dante, he thought. And he was seized by a sudden inspiration.

He unlocked one of the drawers of his desk. This was the memory drawer. Maia's picture was there, along with the scant remnants of his childhood—his grandfather's pocket watch, some jewelry that belonged to his mother, her diary, and a few old photographs. He removed a photograph and an illustration before locking the drawer again, placing the items in his pocket. Pausing only to open a black velvet box and withdraw a ring, he headed for the door.

The chill in the Toronto air sobered Gabriel as he walked determinedly to his office. He only hoped he would be able to find what he needed.

The building in which the Department of Italian Studies was housed was dark. As he switched on the light in his office, he was assaulted by memories. Memories of the first time Julia visited his office and he'd been unspeakably rude. Memories when Julia stood by the door after that disastrous seminar, telling him she wasn't happy. Telling him she didn't want Paul. He rubbed his eyes with the heels of his hands, as if he could block out the visions.

He packed his fancy leather briefcase with only the files he needed and a few books, before searching the shelves. Moments later, he found the simple textbook and breathed a sigh of relief. He penned a few words, added his bookmarks, then switched off the light and locked the door.

All faculty in the department held keys to the departmental office, where Mrs. Jenkins's desk and the mailboxes were located. Gabriel used the light from his iPhone to find the box he wanted. He deposited the book, stroking his fingers lovingly across the name labeling the mailbox. He noted with satisfaction that other textbooks were in other boxes, then with a heavy heart, he exited the office.

Paul Norris was angry. His anger was directed at the most evil man on the planet, Gabriel Emerson, who had verbally abused and seduced his friend before dumping her.

If Paul had been a fan of Jane Austen, he would have likened Professor Emerson to Mr. Wickham. Or perhaps, to Willoughby. But he wasn't.

Nevertheless, it was all he could do not to pummel Emerson senseless and give him the ass whipping he'd been in desperate need of all year. Additionally, Paul felt betrayed. For God knows how long, Julia had been involved with a man she called *Owen*.

Gabriel Owen Emerson.

Perhaps she wanted Paul to figure it out. But it had never crossed his mind that Owen was, in fact, Professor Emerson. He'd cursed the man and told her secrets about him, for God's sake. Secrets about Professor Singer. And while she was accepting his sympathy, she was sleeping with *him*. No wonder she'd sworn up and down that *Owen* hadn't bitten her neck, that it was some other asshole.

Paul thought of Professor Emerson doing depraved things to Julia, and her small, small hands. Julia, who was sweet and kind, with blushing pink cheeks. Julia, who never passed a homeless man on the street without giving him something. Perhaps the true pain of betrayal was the realization that sweet Miss Mitchell had shared a bed with a monster who got off on pain, who had been a plaything of Professor Singer. Perhaps Julia *wanted* that lifestyle. Perhaps she and Gabriel invited Ann into their bed, as well. After all, Julia had picked Soraya Harandi to be her attorney. Didn't that mean she was *familiar* with Professor Pain?

Clearly, Julia was not who he thought she was. But his suspicions morphed into something else when, on the Monday after the hearing, he ran into Christa Peterson as she exited Professor Martin's Office.

"Paul." She nodded at him smugly, adjusting the expensive watch on her wrist.

He jerked his chin in the direction of Professor Martin's door. "Having some trouble?"

"Oh, no," she said quickly, smiling altogether too widely. "In fact, I think the only person who's having trouble is Emerson. You'd better start looking for a new dissertation director."

Paul narrowed his eyes. "What are you talking about?"

"You'll find out soon enough."

"If Emerson drops me, he'll drop you too. If he hasn't already."

"I'm dropping him." She tossed her hair behind her shoulder. "I'm transferring to Columbia in the fall."

"Isn't that where Martin came from?"

"Give my best to Julia, would you?" Laughing, Christa brushed past him.

Paul jogged after her, catching her elbow with his hand. "What are you talking about? What did you do to Julia?"

She wrenched her arm free, her eyes narrowing. "Tell her she fucked with the wrong woman."

Christa walked away as a stunned Paul stood, wondering what she had done.

❄ ❄

Julia didn't respond to Paul's worried messages or emails. So on the Wednesday after the hearing, he stood on the front porch of her building, buzzing her apartment.

She didn't answer.

Undeterred, Paul waited, and when a neighbor exited the building, he went inside and knocked on her door. He rapped several times until a hesitant voice called to him. "Who is it?"

"It's Paul."

He heard what sounded like the thud of Julia's forehead against the door.

"I wanted to check on you since you aren't answering your phone." He paused. "I have your mail."

"Paul—I don't know what to say."

"You don't have to say anything. Let me see that you're all right and I'll go."

He heard the shuffling of feet. "Julia," he called to her softly. "It's just me."

A scraping sound echoed in the hallway, and the door slowly creaked open.

"Hi," he said, looking down into the face of a woman he did not recognize.

She looked like a girl really, white skin against dark hair that was messily pulled up into a ponytail. Purple circles rimmed her eyes, which were bloodshot and glassy. She looked as if she hadn't slept since the hearing.

"Can I come in?"

She opened the door more widely, and Paul walked into her apartment. He'd never seen it so disordered. Dishes were abandoned on every surface, her bed was unmade, and the card table was straining under the weight of papers and books. Her laptop was open as if she'd been interrupted while working on it.

"If you came to tell me how stupid I am, I don't think I can handle that right now." She tried to sound defiant.

"I was upset when I found out you'd been lying to me." Paul shuffled her mail from one arm to the other and scratched at his sideburns. "But I'm not here to make you feel badly." His expression softened. "I don't like to see you hurting."

She looked down at her purple woolly socks and wiggled her toes. "I'm sorry for lying."

He cleared his throat. "Um, I brought your mail. You had some stuff in the mailbox outside, and I also brought your mail from the department."

Julia looked at him with a worried expression.

He held up a hand as if to reassure her. "It's only a couple of flyers and a textbook."

"Why would someone send me a textbook? I'm not teaching."

"The textbook reps put exam copies in the professors' mailboxes. Sometimes they give books to the grad students too. I got one on Renaissance politics. Where should I put everything?"

"On the table. Thanks."

Paul did as he was bidden while Julia busied herself by retrieving the cups and bowls from around the apartment and stacking them neatly on top of the microwave.

"What kind of textbook?" she asked, over her shoulder. "It isn't about Dante, is it?"

"No. It's *Marriage in the Middle Ages: Love, Sex, and the Sacred.*" Paul read the title aloud.

She shrugged, for the title didn't interest her.

"You look tired." He gazed at her sympathetically.

"Professor Picton asked me to make a lot of changes to my thesis. I've been working around the clock."

"You need some fresh air. Why don't you let me take you to lunch? My treat."

"I have so much work to do."

He brushed at his mouth with the back of his hand. "You need to get out of here. This place is depressing. It's like Miss Havisham's house."

"Does that make you Pip?"

Paul shook his head. "No, it makes me a nosy jerk who interferes in someone else's life."

"That sounds like Pip."

"Is your thesis due tomorrow?"

"No. Professor Picton gave me a week's extension. She knew I wouldn't be ready to turn it in April first because of—everything." She winced.

"It's just lunch. We'll take the subway and head to Queen Street and be back before you know it."

Julia looked up at Paul, into concerned dark eyes. "Why are you being so nice to me?"

"Because I'm from Vermont. We're friendly." He grinned. "And because you need a friend right now."

Julia smiled in gratitude.

"I never stopped caring for you," he admitted, his eyes unexpectedly gentle.

She pretended she didn't hear his declaration.

"I need a minute to get dressed."

They both looked at her flannel pajamas.

Paul smirked. "Nice rubber duckies."

Embarrassed, she disappeared into her closet to find some clean clothes. Not having done laundry in a week, her choices were limited, but at least she had something halfway presentable for a casual meal.

While she was in the bathroom, Paul took it upon himself to clean up her apartment, or at least, to tidy it. He knew better than to touch her thesis materials, choosing rather to straighten her bed and pick up things from the floor. When he was finished, he shelved the textbook and sat down in a folding chair to look over her mail. He quickly disposed of the flyers and junk and stacked what looked like bills into a neat pile. He noticed there weren't any letters of a personal nature.

"Thank God," he muttered.

After she dressed, she covered the circles under her eyes with concealer, and pinked up her pale cheeks with blush. When she was satisfied that she no longer looked like a youngish version of Miss Havisham, Julia joined Paul at the card table.

He greeted her with a smile. "Ready to go?"

"Yes." She wrapped her arms around her chest. "I'm sure you have things you want to say. You might as well get it over with."

Paul frowned and gestured to the door. "We can talk over lunch."

"He left me," she blurted, looking pained.

"Don't you think that's a good thing?"

"No."

"Jeez, Julia, the guy seduced you for kicks, then dumped you. How much abuse do you want?"

Her head snapped up. "That's not how it was!"

Paul looked at her, at her sudden show of anger, and was impressed. He'd rather have her angry than sad.

"You should probably wear a hat. It's cold out."

A few minutes later they were outside, walking toward the Spadina subway station.

"Have you seen him?" she asked.

"Who?"

"You know who. Don't make me say his name."

Paul huffed. "Wouldn't you rather forget about him?"

"Please."

He glanced over to see a pinched look on Julia's pretty face. He stopped her gently. "I ran into him a few hours after the hearing. He was coming out of Professor Martin's office. Since then, I've been trying to finish my dissertation. If Emerson dumps me, I'm screwed."

"Do you know where he is?"

"In Hell, I hope." Paul's voice was cheerful. "Martin sent an email to the department saying that Emerson was on a leave of absence for the rest of the semester. You probably saw that email."

Julia shook her head.

Paul looked at her closely. "I guess he didn't say good-bye."

"I left a few messages for him. He finally emailed me yesterday."

"What did he say?"

"He told me to stop contacting him and that it was over. He didn't even call me by name—just sent me a two line email from his university account, and signed it 'Regards, Prof. Gabriel O. Emerson.'"

"Asshole."

Julia winced, but didn't disagree. "After the hearing, he told me I wasn't sensible of my own distress."

"*Pretentious fucker.*"

"What?"

"He stomps on your heart and then he has the balls to quote *Hamlet*? Unbelievable. And he misquoted it, the jackass."

She blinked in surprise. "I didn't recognize the line. I thought it was just—him."

"Shakespeare was a pretentious fucker too. That's probably why you couldn't tell the difference. The line is from Gertrude's speech about the death of Ophelia. Listen:

"When down her weedy trophies and herself
Fell in the weeping brook. Her clothes spread wide;
And, mermaid-like, awhile they bore her up:

Which time she chanted snatches of old tunes;
As one incapable of her own distress,
Or like a creature native and indued
Unto that element: but long it could not be
Till that her garments, heavy with their drink,
Pull'd the poor wretch from her melodious lay
To muddy death."

Julia's face grew pale. "Why would he say that to me?"

"You are nothing like her." Paul reiterated his list of favored profane adjectives with respect to the Professor. "Was Emerson worried you'd do something—to hurt yourself?" Paul was growing progressively more agitated as his undergraduate knowledge of Shakespeare came flooding back to him.

(The benefit of a liberal arts education.)

Julia feigned surprise at his question. "I don't know what he thought. He just mumbled something about me trying to commit academic suicide."

Paul seemed relieved. Marginally.

"There's something else I need to mention. I talked to Christa."

Julia chewed at the inside of her mouth before indicating that he should continue.

"Christa was happy that Emerson was leaving. And she referred to you."

"She's always hated me," said Julia.

"I don't know what she's up to, but I'd watch your back."

Julia looked off into the distance. "She can't hurt me. I've already lost what mattered most."

Chapter Twenty-nine

Paul and Julia sat across from one another at a hip but retro café on Queen Street. They engaged in small talk before they ordered their meals, falling into an uneasy silence as Julia pondered her situation.

"So how have you been?" Paul's voice broke into her internal musings.

She wouldn't say it aloud, because she wouldn't mention such a thing to Paul. But one of the reasons she had been so upset, apart from the loss of Gabriel, was the loss of what he represented—the attainment of her high school crush, the loss of her virginity, the discovery of what she thought had been a deep and reciprocated love . . .

When she thought of the first time he made love to her, she wanted to cry. No one had ever treated her with such rapt attention and gentleness. He was so worried about hurting her and making sure that she was relaxed. He was insistent on telling her that he loved her, over and over again as he moved toward his orgasm. The first one that he would have with her, *because* of her . . .

Gabriel staring into my very soul, moving inside me, telling me that he loved me while showing me with his body exactly that. He must have loved me. I'm just not sure when he stopped. Or rather, when he chose to love his job more than me.

Paul cleared his throat good-naturedly, and Julia smiled her apology.

"Um, I'm upset and angry, but I try not to think about what happened. I've been working on my thesis, but it's difficult to write about love and friendship when you've just lost both." She blew a breath of air out. "Everyone at the university must think I'm a whore."

Paul leaned over the table. "Hey, you are not a whore. I'd punch someone's lights out if they ever said anything like that about you."

She said nothing, fidgeting in her lap with an embroidered hand-kerchief.

"You fell in love with the wrong person, that's all. He took advantage of you."

Julie protested, but he continued.

"The Dean's office asked me to sign a confidentiality agreement. They're keeping everything having to do with you and Emerson quiet. So don't worry about what people think. No one knows anything."

"Christa knows," she muttered.

"I'm sure she had to sign the same confidentiality agreement. If she starts spreading rumors about you, you should go to the Dean."

"What good would that do? The gossip would follow me to Harvard."

"Professors aren't supposed to take advantage of students. If you'd said no to him, he would have fucked with your career. He's the villain." Paul fumed. "You have a lot of good things to look forward to, like graduation and going to Harvard. And someday, when you're ready, you'll find someone who will treat you properly. Someone worthy of you." He squeezed her fingers. "You're kind and gentle. You're funny and bright. And when you're pissed off, you're sexy as hell."

She gave him a half-smile.

"That day you took Emerson on in the seminar room—it was a total train wreck, but I would pay money to see it again. You are the only person I've ever seen stand up to him, other than Christa, who is crazy, and Professor Pain, who is twisted. As much as I was afraid of what he'd do in retaliation, your spunkiness was impressive."

"I lost my temper. It wasn't my finest moment."

"Perhaps not. But it showed me something. It showed Emerson something. *You're a bad ass.* You need to let the bad ass come out every once in a while. Within reason, of course."

He was grinning now and slightly teasing.

"I try not to give in to the anger, but trust me, it's there." Julia's voice was quiet but steely.

As they finished their meals and savored their coffee, Julia told Paul an extremely edited account of her affair with Gabriel, beginning with his invitation to accompany him to Italy. She described how Ga-briel saved her from Simon when she was home for Thanksgiving and that he paid to have the bite mark removed from her neck. Paul was surprised.

Julia had always felt comfortable talking to Paul. He wasn't as intense as Gabriel, of course, and far less mercurial. He was a good listener and a good friend. Even when he was scolding her for choosing Soraya Harandi as her attorney.

Of course, when she revealed that Soraya had been chosen by Gabriel, his ire shifted.

"I'm going to ask you something personal. If you don't want to answer, just say so." Paul looked around to ensure that no one was eavesdropping.

"What do you want to know?"

"Is Gabriel still involved with Professor Singer? Did you see her—socially while you were with him?"

"Of course not! He tried to keep me away from her, even when we went to dinner at Segovia."

"I can't believe I never realized you two were together." Paul shook his head.

"I know you don't think very highly of him. But that's because you don't know him. He told me his involvement with Singer was temporary and that it ended a long time ago. And so we're clear, Paul, I believed him." Julia said those last few words with no little intensity.

Paul rubbed at his chin. "I told you that I filed a complaint against Professor Pain last year. Soraya Harandi was her attorney. I sat in on Singer's Medieval Torture seminar because I hoped she would cover material relating to my dissertation. Then she hit on me. At first, I brushed it off. Then I received a strange email from her. She was careful to make her language ambiguous, but anyone from her seminar would have understood that she was propositioning me. So I filed a complaint.

"Unfortunately, Soraya Harandi did a hell of a job convincing the university that I'd misunderstood the email and that I was embellishing my reports of what she said to me in person. It was my word against Singer's.

"The only person on my side at the hearing was Dr. Chakravartty. She brought up emails that Singer had sent to other people and argued that there was a pattern. But Dr. Aras excused me as soon as she mentioned them. So I have no idea who they were to or what was in them. Professor Pain was given a warning and told to stay away from me. I never heard from her again. But I always wondered who else she went after. I was hoping that Emerson protected you from her."

"He did. I haven't had any contact with her, and he hasn't either. I'm really sorry that happened to you."

He shrugged. "It still pisses me off that she got away with it. That she's still getting away with it. That's why non-fraternization policies are in place—to protect students and their academic careers."

They were both quiet for a moment, sipping their coffees.

"I'm sorry I lied to you." She gazed at him with watery eyes.

He held her gaze, then looked down and sighed. "I'd probably have done the same."

Then he moved to hold her hand again.

By the time Julia returned home, her mood had improved considerably. She didn't feel well, mind you, or whole. For how could she be whole when her other half had rejected her?

After a productive weekend, Julia was heartened enough by the progress she made on her schoolwork to return one of Nicole's telephone calls. Nicole wondered why Julia stopped coming to her weekly therapy sessions. Julia shyly explained that she and Gabriel were no longer together and that he'd been paying for her therapy, to which her therapist responded that Gabriel was continuing to pay for her therapy—indefinitely.

Luckily, both women agreed that it would be inappropriate to allow him to continue footing the bill, especially since he had effectively created the new, pressing reason for Julia to continue with therapy. So Gabriel's money was unceremoniously returned to him and new fees were assessed on a sliding scale, geared to Julia's income.

In other words, Nicole would charge Julia a ridiculously low fee in keeping with her fixed income as a student and be perfectly happy to do so. In their appointment on Wednesday, roughly two weeks after Gabriel's departure, they discussed Julia's heartbreak and the way in which she'd chosen to deal with it. Nicole challenged her to focus on the positive aspects of her life and also, to finish her thesis. Both aspects of her advice resonated with Julia.

That evening, after having made progress on her writing, Julia fell asleep. She felt the bed shift and a warm body curled around her like a cocoon, drawing her close. An all too familiar nose nuzzled her neck, and the softest whisper of breath blew across her shoulder.

"Gabriel?"

He hummed into her skin but didn't answer.

"I missed you so much," she whispered, tears suddenly streaming down her face.

Gabriel was silent as he reached up to wipe away her tears, then he pressed his lips to her cheeks over and over again.

"I know you loved me." Julia relaxed into their spooned position and closed her eyes. "I just don't understand why you didn't love me enough to stay."

The hands that held her tightly relaxed minutely until they finally disappeared altogether, leaving Julia alone and cold in her single bed.

Julia spent part of the next morning staring out the window, contemplating the very strange dream she'd had the night before. Gabriel had returned to her, but he was still silent. He hadn't offered an explanation or begged for forgiveness. He'd simply rejoined her in bed.

She'd nestled into him, his body familiar and comforting. She'd sighed in relief at his return, her subconscious unwilling or unable to reject him.

It wasn't really a dream—just a different kind of nightmare.

After a modest breakfast, she checked her emails and text messages. As she scrolled through the incoming texts on her iPhone, she received the following from Rachel:

Hey Julia! What's up with Gabriel not answering his phone? I tried the landline too, but he wouldn't pick up. I guess things must still be hot and heavy, otherwise he'd answer his phone once in a while.

> I've picked out the bridesmaid's dresses—a dark red that will look
> great on you. I'll send the link thru email and you can tell me what
> you think. You'll have to email me your measurements so I can
> order the dress.
>
> By the way, I finally met Scott's girlfriend! Her son, Quinn, is
> adorable.
> Love you, Rachel.

Julia's first instinct was to close the text and ignore it. That's what she did to Rachel after Simon and Natalie humiliated her. But as her therapist had impressed upon her, this time she needed to do something different. Something braver.

She took a deep breath and typed out a response:

> Rachel, The bridesmaid dresses sound beautiful. I'll make sure to
> send you my measurements. I'm glad you met Scott's girlfriend.
> I'm looking forward to meeting her and her little boy.
>
> I haven't spoken to Gabriel in days. I don't know where he is. He
> left. It's over. J.

It took exactly one minute and forty-five seconds for Julia's iPhone to ring, indicating a call from Rachel. Unfortunately, Julia's courage gave out at that moment, and she didn't answer. The following text arrived shortly thereafter:

> I'm going to kill him. —R

Chapter Thirty

Gabriel strode through the misty blackness into the woods behind what had been the Clarks' house. He brought a flashlight, but he almost didn't need it. He knew the woods so well that even if he'd been drunk or coked out of his mind he could find his way to the orchard and back again. He was good at navigating the dark.

He stood at the orchard's periphery, eyes closed, as the chilled rain washed down. If he opened his eyes and squinted, he could almost see her—the outline of a teenage girl resting on a man's chest, the couple nestled on an old, wool blanket. Her hair floated across her shoulders, her arm rested on his waist. He could barely see the man's face, but he could tell that the man was besotted with the brown-eyed angel in his arms.

Gabriel stood very still, listening to the echoes of memories that were half-dreams . . .

"Do you have to leave?"

"Yes, but not tonight."

"Will you come back?"

"I'm going to be thrown out of Paradise tomorrow, Beatrice. Our only hope is that you find me afterward. Look for me in Hell."

He hadn't planned to return to the orchard without her. He hadn't planned to leave her. He'd broken her heart. Although he was oppressed by guilt and regret, he knew he'd make the same decision again.

Julianne had already given up so much to be with him. He'd be damned if she gave up her future too.

Gabriel stood shirtless in his old bedroom, drying his hair with a towel and fumbling with the stereo. He was in the mood for painful music.

Which meant, at that moment, that he was listening to "Blood of Eden" by Peter Gabriel. Midway through the chorus, the telephone began to ring. He'd forgotten to ask Richard to cancel the telephone service when he moved to Philadelphia, after Gabriel bought the house.

Leaving the call unanswered, Gabriel paced like a restless ghost. He reclined on the bed, staring up at the ceiling. It was a passing fancy, he knew, but he swore he could smell Julia's scent on his pillow and that he could hear the gentle tide of her breathing. He toyed with the platinum band on his finger, twisting it over and over again. Lines from Dante's *La Vita Nuova* crowded his mind, describing Beatrice's rejection:

> *"By this false and evil rumour*
> *which seemed to misfame me of vice . . .*
> *she who was the destroyer of all evil*
> *and the queen of all good, coming where I was,*
> *denied me her most sweet salutation,*
> *in the which alone was my blessedness."*

Gabriel had no right to compare his situation to Dante's, since his misfortune was the result of his own choice. Nevertheless, as the darkness closed in around him, he was stricken by the possibility that he'd lost his blessedness. Forever.

Chapter Thirty-one

That son of a bitch!" Tom Mitchell swore loudly into his daughter's ear. She had to hold her iPhone at arm's length in order to protect her eardrums. "When did this happen?"

"Um, in March." Julia sniffled. "He confirmed it via email."

"Son of a bitch. What was his reason?"

"He didn't give me one." She didn't have the energy to describe the events leading up to her separation from Gabriel, and anything having to do with the academic fraud allegations would just make Tom angrier.

"I'll shoot him."

"Dad, please." The conversation was difficult enough without having to worry about shotguns being loaded and Gabriel's lily-white tail being hunted through the woods of Selinsgrove.

Tom breathed heavily into the phone. "Where is he now?"

"I don't know."

"I hate to say this, Jules, because I know you—cared for him, but Gabriel is a cokehead. *Once an addict, always an addict.* Maybe he's using again. Maybe he ran into trouble with his dealer. Drugs are a messy business, and I'm glad he's gone. The farther away from you he is the better."

Julia didn't cry at her father's words, but her heart clenched. "Please don't say things like that, Dad. For all we know, he's in Italy working on his book."

"In a crack house."

"Dad, *please.*"

"I'm sorry. I really am. I want my little girl to find someone good and be happy."

"I want that for you too," she said.

"Well, we're quite a pair." He cleared his throat and decided to change the subject. "Tell me about graduation. I made some money from the sale of the house, and I'd like to come to graduation. We should also talk about what you want to do this summer. Your room in the new house is waiting for you. You can paint it any color you want. Hell, paint it pink."

She couldn't help but smile. "I haven't wanted a pink room in a long time, but thanks, Dad."

Although Selinsgrove was the last place Julia wanted to go at that moment, at least she had a parent and a home, a home that didn't have bad associations with either Simon or Sharon. Or him.

Chapter Thirty-two

On April ninth, Julia walked through the melting snow to Professor Picton's house, clutching her printed thesis in one hand and a bottle of Chianti in the other.

She was nervous. Although her relationship with Professor Picton had always been cordial, it was never warm. Katherine wasn't the kind of person to dote or fawn over her students. She was professional and demanding and decidedly unsentimental. So Julia was quite concerned when Katherine invited her to submit her thesis in person and to stay for dinner. Of course, there was no possibility of a refusal.

Julia stood on the front porch of Katherine's three-story brick home and rang the doorbell. She wiped her palms on the front of her pea coat, trying to eliminate the clamminess.

"Julianne, welcome." Katherine opened the door and ushered her student inside.

If Julia's small studio was a hobbit hole, then Professor Picton's house was the abode of a wood elf. A wood elf with a taste for fine, old furnishings. Everything was elegant and antique; the walls were paneled in dark wood with expensive carpets blanketing the floors. The decorating was aristocratic but spare, and everything was extremely ordered and tidy.

After taking Julia's coat, Katherine graciously accepted the Chianti and the thesis, and directed her to a small parlor off the front hall. Julia promptly sat herself in a leather club chair in front of the hearth and accepted a small glass of sherry.

"Dinner is almost ready," Katherine said and vanished like a Greek goddess.

Julia examined the large books about English architecture and gardens gracing the low coffee table. The walls were lined with pastoral scenes interspersed with the occasional severe black-and-white portrait of the ancestral Pictons. She sipped her sherry slowly, savoring the warmth as it slid down her throat to her stomach. Before she could finish, Katherine was escorting her to the dining room.

"This is lovely." Julia smiled, in an effort to mask her nervousness. She was intimidated by the fine bone china, crystal, and silver candlesticks that Katherine had set atop a white damask tablecloth that looked as if it had been ironed.

(Not even the linens would dare to wrinkle without Professor Picton's permission.)

"I like to entertain," said Katherine. "But truthfully, there are few dining companions that I can stand for an entire evening."

Julia felt a sinking feeling in her middle. With as little noise as possible, she took her place next to Katherine, who sat at the head of the long, oak table.

"It smells delicious," said Julia, trying not to ravenously inhale the scent of cooked meat and vegetables that wafted from her plate. She hadn't been eating much in the previous days but Professor Picton's offerings seemed to have stimulated her appetite.

"I tend toward vegetarianism, but in my experience graduate students never eat enough meat. So I've prepared an old recipe of my mother's. Normandy hotpot, she used to call it. I hope you don't mind pork."

"Not at all." Julia smiled. But when she saw the lemon zest atop the plate of steamed broccoli, her smile narrowed.

Gabriel had a thing for garnishes.

"A toast perhaps?" Katherine poured Julia's wine gift into their glasses and held hers aloft.

Julia raised her glass obligingly.

"To your success at Harvard."

"Thank you." Julia hid her mixed emotions behind the act of drinking.

Once a polite space of time had elapsed, Katherine spoke. "I brought you here to discuss a number of different things. First, your thesis. Are you satisfied with it?"

Julia swallowed a piece of parsnip hastily. "No."

Katherine frowned.

"What I mean is, there's room for improvement. If I had another year, it would be so much better. Um . . ." Julia wished a hole would open up under the floorboards and swallow her.

Inexplicably, Katherine smiled and sat back in her chair. "That's the correct answer. Good for you."

"Pardon?"

"Students these days think they're far more talented than they actually are. I'm glad, with all your success, you've maintained some academic humility.

"Of course another year would improve your thesis. You'll be a better student and a better scholar next year, if you continue to work hard. I'm pleased you realize you have room for improvement. Now, we can move on to something else."

Julia tore her eyes from Katherine and focused on her knife and fork. She had no idea what was coming next.

Katherine tapped an impatient finger on top of the table. "I don't like it when people pry into my private life, so I leave others' private lives alone. In your case, I was dragged into something by David Aras." Katherine grimaced. "I'm not privy to everything that went on at that McCarthyite hearing, and I don't want to be." She glanced at Julia meaningfully.

"Greg Matthews at Harvard is looking to hire an endowed chair in Dante studies. I'd hoped that Gabriel would be offered that job." Katherine saw Julia move out of the corner of her eye, but quickly continued. "Unfortunately, the chair has been offered to someone else. They foolishly tried to lure me out of retirement, but I declined.

"How that dreadful Pacciani man ended up on their short list, I'll never know. At any rate, Cecilia Marinelli will be the new endowed chair. They stole her from Oxford. It would be good if you could work with her. Provided all goes well with your thesis, I'd be happy to telephone Cecilia and let her know of your arrival."

"Thank you, Professor. That's very kind."

Katherine waved a casual hand. "Not at all."

The two women spent the next few minutes finishing their dinner in relative silence. While Katherine cleared the table, after refusing her student's repeated offers to help, Julia finished her wine.

Although she felt badly that Gabriel did not get his dream job, she was relieved that he would not be following her to Harvard. His presence in the department would have caused all kinds of problems. She could never work with him now. And it would have been extremely painful to have to try to maintain a professional and detached relationship with him. No, it was much better that Gabriel would stay in Toronto, while she moved to Boston. It was a mercy, albeit a severe one, that Harvard had hired Professor Marinelli.

After dessert and coffee, Katherine suggested they retire to the parlor. Once again, Julia sat in the comfortable club chair next to the fire and gratefully received the small glass of port that Katherine pressed into her hand. Although Katherine's decorating style was quite different from Gabriel's, it seemed as if Dante specialists enjoyed drinking by the fireplace.

"You will have a fresh start at Harvard, and no one will have an inkling of what transpired here. Until then, it would be wise not to draw any more attention to yourself." Katherine gave Julia a look that was piercing, if not severe.

"Graduate students, especially female graduate students, are vulnerable with respect to their reputation. There are still those in the Academy who would choose to mislabel the fruits of talent and hard work as the results of preferment and prostitution. It's best if you never give anyone the slightest suspicion that you haven't earned your accomplishments through hard work."

"Professor Picton, I swear that I worked very hard in the Dante seminar. He didn't help me with my essay or give me any special treatment. That's why he asked you to grade it."

"I'm sure that's true. But you deceived me, and quite frankly, I'm a bit put out."

Julia gazed at her advisor with undisguised horror.

"Nevertheless, I understand why I wasn't taken into your confidence. I'm sure Gabriel forbade it. I'm annoyed with him as well, but for reasons I won't divulge, I owe him a debt."

Professor Picton sipped her port thoughtfully, staring off into space.

"When I was a student at Oxford, it was shamefully common for dons to develop romantic relationships with their students. Sometimes the relationships were what we would now consider harassment cases. Other times true love was involved. I saw both."

Katherine fixed Julia with an unblinking eye. "I know the difference between a Willoughby and a Colonel Brandon. I hope that you do too."

The following evening, Julia walked to Paul's apartment. They'd agreed to meet for coffee so they could debrief after Julia's dinner with Professor Picton.

Paul turned to face Julia on the couch. "Now that the semester is over for you, when are you moving?"

Julia sipped her coffee. "My lease is up the end of July, but I was hoping to persuade my landlord to let me leave mid-June."

"After graduation?"

"Yes. My dad is going to help me move."

Paul placed his mug on the coffee table.

"I'm heading back to Vermont in June. You could drive with me, and I could help you move."

"My dad is coming for graduation."

"We can drive together. You two could stay with me at the farm for a day or so, then we could drive down to Boston to get you settled. Are you going to live in residence?"

"I don't know. They sent me something saying I couldn't get into the residence halls until August. But I'd need somewhere to live before that."

"My friend's younger brother goes to Boston College. Let me talk to him and see if he knows of a place you could sublet. Half the population of Boston is under twenty-five. There are a lot of students."

"You'd do that? Help me move and find an apartment?"

"I'd expect to be paid, in beer. I like *Krombacher*, by the way."

"I think I can do that."

Julia smiled and they clinked their coffee mugs together.

"Who are they?" She pointed to a photograph of four people, two men and two women, that Paul had partially hidden behind a penguin on top of his television.

"The girl on the far left is Heather, my little sister, and her husband, Chris. That's me on the right."

"And the other girl?" Julia gazed at the face of the pretty young woman who was clutching Paul's waist and laughing.

"Uh, that's Allison."

Julia waited politely for Paul to elaborate.

"My ex-girlfriend."

"Oh," said Julia.

"We're still friends. But she's working in Vermont and couldn't handle the long-distance thing. We broke up a while ago," Paul explained quickly.

"You're a good person." Julia shifted uncomfortably. "Maybe I shouldn't have said that."

Paul pulled her hand to his lips, kissing her knuckles chastely. "I think you should say whatever is on your mind. For the record, I've always thought you were a good person too."

She smiled but withdrew her hand delicately, so as not to give offense.

Shortly before midnight, she was asleep on his shoulder, their bodies close together on the futon. Paul's mind was drifting, imagining the feel of her lips against his, her skin beneath his hands. He turned his face into her hair, tightening his arms around her. She stirred, mumbling Emerson's name before burrowing her head in his chest.

He realized that he had a decision to make. If he was going to be Julia's friend, then he would have to suppress his romantic feelings for her. He couldn't kiss her or try to move things forward. It was far too soon. And it was quite possible she'd never want him, even when her broken heart was mended. But Julia needed a friend; she needed him. He wasn't going to abandon her in her time of need, even if it was going to be painful to set aside his true feelings.

So instead of falling asleep with her in his arms, he carried her to his room and placed her on the bed. He covered her with the sheet and blankets, making sure that she was comfortable, then he picked up an extra pillow and a quilt and retreated to the living room.

He spent much of the evening frustrated and staring at the ceiling, while Julia slept soundly in his bed.

✿ ✿

While Julia was spending the night at Paul's apartment, Gabriel sat in his hotel room, glaring at his laptop. He'd received another terse email from his Chair, Jeremy Martin, reminding him of how much personal and political capital Jeremy had expended to "save his ass." As if Gabriel needed a reminder.

His gaze drifted to the ring on his finger, resisting the urge to reexamine the words he'd had engraved on the inside. He spun the platinum band around and around as he cursed his most recent failure.

Harvard had kindly informed him that his candidacy was unsuccessful and that they'd hired Professor Marinelli, instead. Gabriel's lack of success was one more way in which he'd failed Julianne. But it mattered little, now. What use would it be to be at Harvard, if she wouldn't forgive him?

He cursed bitterly. What use was it to be anywhere, if she wouldn't forgive him? Even in the hotel, she was with him. On his computer, on his cell phone, in his iPod, *in his head.*

Oh, yes, in his head. He was correct when he said that he would never forget what it felt like to gaze upon her naked body for the first time, the way her eyes were fixed on the floor shyly, the way her face flushed under his heated touch.

He remembered looking down into her deep, dark eyes as she trembled beneath him, ruby lips parted, breathing heavily, and the way her eyes widened as he entered her.

She'd flinched. Somehow he could remember every time he'd made her flinch. And there had been many—when he shamed her for being poor, when he first carried her to bed, when he wove his fingers through her hair and she begged him not to hold her head down, when he admitted that he'd agreed to separate himself from her . . .

How many times could he hurt her in one short life?

He'd tortured himself by listening to the voicemail messages she'd left for him—messages he hadn't returned. They'd grown progressively more despondent until they'd ceased altogether. He couldn't blame her. It was clear that his messages had not gotten through, with the exception of a single email. He opened it again, imagining her reaction.

Stop contacting me.

It's over.

Regards,

Prof. Gabriel O. Emerson,

Associate Professor

Department of Italian Studies/

Centre for Medieval Studies

University of Toronto

A bitter laugh that he recognized as coming from his own throat echoed in the room. Of course, that would be the message she believed—not the others. He'd lost her now. What hope was there without her?

Gabriel thought back to a conversation he'd had with her about Grace's favorite book, *A Severe Mercy*. It was clear in the story that the main characters thought that they'd made an idol of their love—worshipping it and each other to their own detriment. He'd done the same with Julianne, he knew. He'd worshipped her very being, convinced that she was the light that would shine in his darkness.

He'd loved her enough to leave her in order to protect her future. And having left her, he was in peril of never possessing her love again. It was the bitterest twist of fate, that his love for his Beatrice would be precisely what separated him from her.

And what of Paul? Surely he'd use this as an opportunity to comfort Julia. And where would that comfort lead . . . Gabriel couldn't entertain the idea that she would be unfaithful. But he knew through her messages that she thought it was over. Paul would simply have to provide a shoulder for her to lean on and he'd be back in her life, in her apartment, in her thoughts.

Angelfucker.

The only relief he could find, if relief it was, would be to torture himself with music and poetry. He clicked a button, and Sting's retelling of the story of David and Bathsheba filled the room. As the song swirled in the air, he gazed at Dante's poetic reflection on the death of Beatrice and found his heart echoing the words from *La Vita Nuova*.

"An abject wretch like this
May not imagine anything of her,—
He needs no bitter tears for his relief.
But sighing comes, and grief,
And the desire to find no comforter,
(Save only Death, who makes all sorrow brief,)
To him who for a while turns in his thought
How she hath been among us, and is not.
With sighs my bosom always laboureth
On thinking, as I do continually.
Of her for whom my heart now breaks apace;
And very often when I think of death,
Such a great inward longing comes to me
That it will change the colour of my face;
And, if the idea settles in its place.
All my limbs shake as with an ague-fit;
Till, starting up in wild bewilderment,
I do become so shent
That I go forth, lest folk misdoubt of it.
Afterward, calling with a sore lament
On Beatrice, I ask, 'Canst thou be dead?'
And calling on her, I am comforted."

Gabriel closed the document on his computer and traced a light finger over the photograph of the lovely woman who graced his computer screen. He would discharge his duty over the next few days, but he would do so without his Beatrice to comfort him. In her absence, perhaps he would succumb to his old temptations to deaden the pain.

Chapter Thirty-three

On a Friday afternoon in mid-April, Julia arrived at Rachel and Aaron's apartment in Philadelphia. Rachel had planned on visiting her in Toronto and bringing the bridesmaid dress with her, but she had trouble getting the time off work. Since she was trying to save her vacation days for the honeymoon, Julia agreed to leave the comfortable confines of her hobbit hole, instead.

Rachel welcomed her friend with a hug, escorting her to the living room. Julia eyed the binders of samples and swatches that covered the coffee table.

"So the wedding planning is finished?"

Rachel shook her head. "Not quite. But I don't want to talk about the wedding; I want to talk about you." She eyed her friend with a concerned look. "This thing with you and Gabriel was a complete shock."

Julia winced. "To me too."

"He won't return our calls or answer our emails, and believe me, we've tried. Scott copied me on the email he sent, and it was scathing.

"Did you know that Gabriel was in Selinsgrove a couple of weeks ago?"

"Selinsgrove?" Julia was dumbfounded. "I thought he was in Italy."

"Why would he go there?"

"To finish his book. To get away from me."

"The jackass," Rachel cursed. "Have you heard from him?"

"Yes. He emailed to notify me that it was over." Julia retrieved her purse. She pulled out two keys and a security pass and handed them to her friend. "These are his."

Rachel gazed at the objects with confusion. "What am I supposed to do with them?"

"Keep them. Or give them to your father. I would have mailed them to Gabriel, but since he doesn't want contact . . ."

Rachel placed the offending items on one of her wedding binders. Then, thinking better of it, she dumped his things into a drawer in one of the end tables, closing it with an oath.

"I know he went to my parents' old house because one of the neighbors called my dad. Apparently, Gabriel was up at all hours playing loud music and prowling around outside."

Julia's mind instantly went to the orchard. It seemed reasonable, she thought, for him to take solace in the one place he'd always been at peace—his Paradise. But since she was tangled up in his memories of that space, she wondered at him going there. Shaking her head, she put the thought from her mind.

Rachel faced her friend. "I don't understand why he would do this. Gabriel loves you. He isn't the kind of person to love easily, or to say those words without meaning them. That kind of love doesn't disappear overnight."

"Maybe he loved his job more. Or maybe he decided to go back to her."

"Paulina? Is that what this is about? You didn't tell me that." Rachel's eyes flashed.

"Up until a year and a half ago, they were still—involved."

"What?"

"At Christmas, we were fighting about her and, uh, other things. He told me their history was more recent than I thought."

"I never so much as heard her name until the day she showed up at my parents' house."

"I knew about her. But when he and I first started dating, he made it sound as if he ended things with her back at Harvard. In reality, he'd been carrying on with her for years."

"You can't believe that he'd leave you for her, after Florence, after everything."

"I can believe anything now," Julia said coolly.

Rachel groaned, placing her hands over her eyes. "What a mess. My dad is really upset and so is Scott. When he found out that Gabriel was in Selinsgrove, he decided to drive out there so he could knock some sense into him."

"And did he?"

"Tammy needed him to babysit her little boy. So Scott decided that he could kick Gabriel's ass another time."

Julia smiled wryly. "I can imagine that conversation."

"Scott is head over heels for Tammy. It's pretty sickening."

"I'm glad they're coming for dinner."

Rachel looked at her watch. "I should probably start cooking. They'll arrive early so they can feed Quinn first. Scott's life has completely changed. Everything revolves around the baby's schedule."

Julia followed her host into the kitchen. "What does your dad think of her?"

Rachel began rummaging in the fridge. "He likes her. He adores the baby. You'd think Quinn was his grandson."

She placed the ingredients for a salad on the counter. "Do you really think Gabriel would go back to Paulina?"

Julia couldn't bring herself to say the word aloud, but yes, she thought it was possible. He'd changed a great deal of his life and his coping mechanisms for her. Now that their relationship was over, it was possible he'd return to his old life.

"She's familiar territory," Julia said.

"You make it sound as if she's western Europe." Rachel leaned against the counter. "Do you think the university demanded that he break things off with you?"

"Yes, but how is something like that enforceable? Can they make him leave the city? Can they tell him what to do in his personal life, when he's on a leave of absence? If Gabriel wanted to talk to me, he could have called. He didn't. The university handed him a convenient way to break up with me. He was probably planning it for a while." Julia crossed her arms around her chest. It was easier to give voice to her deepest fears with Rachel than to dwell on them when she was alone.

"What a mess," Rachel repeated, turning to wash her hands.

Chapter Thirty-four

In the wee hours of the morning, Rachel and Julia were sprawled across the sofa in their bathrobes, drinking wine and giggling. Scott, Tammy, and Quinn had long since left, and Aaron had been asleep for hours. They could hear reverberations of his snoring echo down the hall.

Bolstered by a very good Pinot noir, Julia described what had happened at the hearing, and Rachel, to her credit, resisted interrupting her.

"I don't think Gabriel would give you up just to keep his job. He doesn't need the money, and he can always work somewhere else. What I don't understand is why he wasn't more explicit about what he was doing. Why didn't he grab you afterward and say *I love you but we need to wait.*" Rachel giggled drunkenly. "Knowing Gabriel, he would have recited something in iambic pentameter just because he could."

"He mentioned something about Peter Abelard, but it wasn't comforting. Abelard kept his relationship with Héloise secret so he wouldn't lose his teaching position. Then he sent her to a convent."

Rachel reached over to pick up a pillow and threw it at her friend's head. "He isn't going to send you to a convent. He loves you. And I refuse to believe otherwise."

Julia clutched the pillow to her chest as she reclined on her side. "If he loved me, he wouldn't leave me. He wouldn't have broken up with me via email."

"Do you really think that Gabriel was stringing you along for fun?"

"No. But that doesn't matter now."

Rachel yawned loudly. "Whatever he did, he screwed up. I'm wondering if he isn't trying to protect you in some way."

"He could have texted me and said just that."

Rachel threw an arm over her eyes. "That's the part I don't understand. He could have asked us to give you a message. He could have written you a letter. Why didn't Gabriel tell the university to shove it?"

Julia rolled onto her back, asking herself a similar question.

Rachel retrieved her cell phone from the coffee table. "Do you want to call him?"

"No."

"Why not? Maybe he'll answer, thinking it's me."

"It's the middle of the night and I'm drunk. It's not exactly the best time to have a conversation. Plus, he told me not to contact him."

Rachel shook the phone in front of her. "If you're hurting, so is he."

"I left him a message saying that if he ever wants to talk to me, he needs to do it face to face. I'm not calling him again." Julia downed the last of her wine in one swallow.

"Maybe he'll be at graduation." Julia sighed, a wistful look on her face. All her anger and frustration hadn't eliminated her longing for him. At least, not all of it.

"When's graduation?"

"June eleventh."

Rachel swore obliquely at the lateness of the date.

After a few minutes of shared silence, Julia decided to voice one of her other, greater fears.

"Rachel?"

"Uh huh?"

"What if he sleeps with her?"

Rachel was quiet for a moment. So quiet, Julia began to repeat the question, but her friend interrupted. "If Gabriel were cruel, then maybe he'd screw someone else. But I can't imagine him doing that and thinking that you'd forgive him."

"If he's with someone else and you find out about it, tell me." Julia gave her friend a pleading look. "It would be better to hear it from you."

※ ※

"Darling, open your eyes."

His voice was warm and thick as he moved inside her, distributing his weight to his forearms. He leaned down to draw the delicate skin from the inside of her bicep into his mouth, kissing and sucking on it. It was just enough to tease her and perhaps to leave a gentle mark. He knew this drove her mad.

"I can't," she gasped, in between moans. Every time he moved it sent the most wonderful sensations coursing through her body.

Until he stopped.

Suddenly, her eyelids fluttered open.

He rubbed his nose against hers and smiled. "I need to see you." His gaze was gentle but intense, as if he were holding back the flame of desire momentarily.

"It's hard for me to keep my eyes open." She groaned a little as he moved inside her once again.

"Try for me." He kissed her softly. "I love you so much."

"Then why did you leave me?"

Gabriel looked down on her with dismay, his blue eyes narrowing. "I didn't . . ."

❋ ❋

That same evening Gabriel was lying in the center of the bed, eyes closed, while she trailed leisurely open-mouthed kisses across his pectorals, pausing reverently to kiss his tattoo, before extending her attentions to his abdominals. An oath left his mouth as she ran her fingers lightly up and down the well-defined muscles before swirling a tongue around his navel.

It has been so long . . .

That was the thought that came to mind as she gently traced the skin and strands of hair before reaching a hand down to grasp him firmly. He shifted his hips. She was stroking him now, and he was panting, begging. She teased him unhurriedly as her long, silky hair caressed the tops of his thighs, before taking him into the warm wetness of her mouth.

Gabriel muttered a surprised expletive as he gave himself over to the sensations, before weaving his fingers into her hair.

He froze.

A sick feeling bubbled up in his stomach as he remembered what happened the last time he'd done this. He withdrew his hand immediately, worried that he'd frightened her.

"I'm sorry." He extended a single finger to trace her cheek. "I forgot."

A cold hand caught him by the wrist before forcing him to grasp her head roughly.

"What did you forget?" she taunted. "How to enjoy a blow job?"

Gabriel's eyes flew open. In absolute horror he looked down into a pair of laughing blue eyes.

Paulina was naked and crouched over him, smiling triumphantly as she held him close to her mouth. Gabriel recoiled, cursing and crowding backward against the headboard while she sat on her heels, watching him.

She laughed and pointed to his nose, indicating that he should wipe the traces of cocaine from his nostrils.

What have I done?

He scrubbed his face roughly with both hands. As the enormity of his depravity sunk in, he retched, dry heaving over the side of the bed. When he came to himself, he held out his left hand to show her his ring—but there was none.

The wedding ring was gone.

Paulina laughed again and began crawling toward him, eyes feral, her naked body brushing against his own.

Chapter Thirty-five

Gabriel struggled and flailed before jolting awake. He tore at the bedclothes, earnestly looking for any sign of her. But there was none.

He was alone in a dark hotel room. He'd extinguished the lights before retiring, which was his first mistake. Neglecting to place the framed photograph on his nightstand was his second, for it served as a talisman against the darkness.

He swung his legs over the side of the bed and placed his face in his hands. Enduring rehab all those years ago had been excruciating but nothing compared with losing Julianne. He would have suffered the nightmares and haunting memories of old sins gladly if he could hold her in his arms every night.

As he gazed with contempt at the half-empty bottle of Scotch, he felt the darkness closing in. His desperate pursuit had placed a great deal of pressure on him. When that pressure was coupled with a striking sense of loss, it made it almost impossible for him to function at a high level without some kind of crutch.

Every day the drinks grew larger. Every day he realized that he needed to do something before he became trapped by his old coping mechanisms and ruined his future. He knew that if he didn't do something, quickly, he'd relapse.

Impulsively, he made two telephone calls before gathering his belongings and shoving them into his suitcase. Then he directed the concierge to secure him a cab that would take him to the airport. He didn't bother to ensure that his appearance was neat and professional. In fact, he didn't bother looking into the mirror at all, for he knew that what he saw would disgust him.

Many hours later, he arrived in Florence and checked into the Gallery Hotel Art. It had been short notice, but he'd persuaded the manager to give him the same suite in which he and Julia had consummated their relationship. It was either that or a rehabilitation program, and he was convinced his connection to her would prove far more redemptive.

As he walked into the room, he half-expected to see her, or at least, signs of her. A pair of tangerine stilettos carelessly kicked off under a coffee table. A taffeta dress pooled on the floor next to a blank wall. A pair of seamed black stockings strewn across an unmade bed.

But of course, he saw none of those things.

After a relatively restful sleep and a shower, Gabriel contacted his old friend *Dottore* Vitali at the Uffizi Gallery and met him for dinner. They spoke of Harvard's new chair of Dante Studies. They spoke of Giuseppe Pacciani and Gabriel was marginally gratified to learn that although Giuseppe had been offered a campus interview while Gabriel had not, Giuseppe's lecture had been regarded as poor by the Harvard faculty. It was cold comfort, but a comfort nonetheless.

The next day Gabriel sought to distract himself from his troubles by engaging in pleasurable activities—breakfast on a piazza, a walk along the Arno, a lengthy afternoon at his tailor's in which he ordered a handmade black wool suit, and an hour or so spent looking for the perfect pair of shoes to match his finery. His tailor joked that the suit was so fine Gabriel could be married in it. The tailor had laughed, until Gabriel held up his left hand and showed him his ring.

"I'm newly married," he explained, much to the tailor's surprise.

No matter where Gabriel walked in the city of Florence, he was assaulted with memories of her. He would stand on the Ponte Santa Trinita, hugging the sweet and sour feelings tightly to his chest, knowing that they were preferable to chemical alternatives.

Late one evening, slightly drunk, he wandered by the Duomo, retracing the path he'd taken with Julianne months earlier. Tortured by his memory of her face when she accused him of fucking her, he stumbled across a familiar looking beggar, who sat in the shade of Brunelleschi's dome.

Gabriel approached him.

"Just a few coins for an old man," the beggar cried in Italian.

Gabriel grew closer, eying the man suspiciously. The scent of un-washed flesh and alcohol assailed him, but he grew closer still. Recog-nizing the beggar as the same man who'd inspired Julia's charity back in December, Gabriel stopped, swaying on his feet.

He felt for his wallet. Without bothering to look at the denomina-tions, he withdrew several bills and held them in front of the man.

"I saw you last December. Yet, you're still here." Gabriel's Italian was only slightly accusatory.

The man eyed the money hungrily. "I'm here every day. Even Christmas."

Gabriel dangled the Euros closer to the man. "My *fidanzata* gave you money. You called her an angel. Do you remember?"

The man smiled toothlessly and shook his head, never allowing his eyes to leave the cash.

"There are many angels in Firenze, but more in Assisi. I think God favors the beggars there. But this is my home." The man hesitantly held out his hand, uncertain that Gabriel would actually give him the money.

In his imagination, Gabriel could see Julia's face as she compassion-ately argued the beggar's case. She wanted to give him money even if there was a strong possibility that he'd waste the money on drink.

As Gabriel regarded the beggar, no better off than he'd been before Julia's generosity, he was struck by the fact that she wouldn't have hesi-tated to donate again and again. She would have given the man coins every day, because she thought the act of charity was never wasted. She would have lived in hope that one day the man would realize that some-one cares for him and try to get help. Julia knew her kindness made her vulnerable, but she was kind anyway.

Gabriel placed the bills in the man's hand and turned sharply on his heel, the echoes of the beggar's joy and blessings ringing in his ears.

He wasn't deserving of a blessing. He hadn't committed an act of charity the way Julianne would have done it, out of compassion and kindness. He was simply doing justice to her memory, or purchasing an indulgence.

As he tripped over a cobblestone, he realized what he had to do.

❄ ❄

The next day he tried to secure the house in Umbria that he'd shared with her, but it was already occupied. So he traveled to Assisi where he checked into a small, private hotel that was simple in its furnishings and populated with pilgrims.

Gabriel had never styled himself as a pilgrim. He was far too proud for that. Nevertheless, there was something in the air in Assisi that allowed him to sleep peacefully. In fact, it had been the best sleep he'd had since leaving Julia's arms.

He rose early the next morning and made his way to the Basilica of St. Francis. It was a place of pilgrimage for persons of all faiths, if only for its medieval frescoes and the peaceful atmosphere that pervaded it. It was no little coincidence that he found himself retracing the steps he'd taken with Julianne prior to Christmas. He'd taken her to Mass in the *Basilica superiore* or upper part of the church, and had even waited patiently while she went to confession before the Mass began.

As he wandered through the upper Basilica, admiring the images and drinking in the comforting quiet of the sanctuary, he caught a glimpse of a woman with long, brown hair disappear through a doorway. Intrigued, he decided to follow her. Despite the crowd of tourists and pilgrims, it was easy to pick her out, and so he found himself descending to the *Basilica inferiore*.

Then she vanished.

Distressed, he searched the lower church. Only when his search proved fruitless did it occur to him to descend deeper into the bowels of the Basilica toward the tomb of St. Francis. There she was, kneeling in front of the crypt. He slipped into the last row of pews and out of respect, knelt. But he couldn't take his eyes off her.

It wasn't Julianne. The young woman in front of him was a little fuller in the hips and wider in the shoulders and her hair was darker. But she was beautiful, and her beauty reminded him of how much he'd lost.

The room was small and primitive, a studied contrast to the wide-open and elaborately frescoed upper Basilica. Gabriel was not alone in finding that the simplicity that was St. Francis's life and mission was more accurately reflected in the unassuming tomb. It was with such thoughts in mind that Gabriel found himself leaning against the pew in front of him and bowing his head. Before he could form the intention to do so, he began praying.

At first they were just words—desperate utterances and whispered confessions. As time wore on, his prayers took on a more repentant shape, while unbeknownst to him, the young woman lit a candle and departed.

If Gabriel's life had been a major motion picture, an old, weathered Franciscan brother would have stumbled across him as he knelt in prayer, and seeing his distress, would show him compassion, offering spiritual guidance. But Gabriel's life was not a motion picture. So he prayed alone.

If you had asked Gabriel afterward about what occurred in the tomb, he would have shrugged and evaded the question. Some things cannot be put into words. Some things defy language itself.

But there was a moment in his prayers in which Gabriel was confronted with the magnitude of all his failings, both moral and spiritual, while at the same time feeling the presence of One who knew the state of his soul and embraced him anyway. He was suddenly aware of what the writer Annie Dillard once referred to as the *extravagance* of grace. He thought of the love and forgiveness that had been lavished on the world and more specifically, on him, through the lives of Grace and Richard.

And Julianne, my sticky little leaf.

The magnet for sin found something very unexpected underneath the floors of the upper Basilica. When he left the church, he was more determined than ever not to return to his old ways.

Chapter Thirty-six

For Julia, the rest of April was a vortex of activity. There were final revisions to be made to her thesis, meetings with Katherine Picton and Nicole, and Friday nights to be spent with Paul.

Katherine ensured that Julia's final draft was error free and something that she could be proud of. Then she telephoned Cecilia Marinelli in Oxford to ask her to look for Julia at Harvard in the fall.

Paul secured a studio apartment in Cambridge for her to sublet. She began working through a list of texts Katherine had suggested she read in preparation for Professor Marinelli's seminar.

At the end of April, Julia received a very official looking letter from the Office of the Dean of Graduate Studies. Dr. Aras requested her attendance at his office in a week's time. He assured her that their appointment had nothing to do with a disciplinary matter, and he stated that Professor Martin would also be in attendance.

With great trepidation, she trudged across campus on a Monday afternoon, clutching her L.L. Bean knapsack. She took comfort in it, in the fact that it had been her companion for almost a year. Paul had offered to accompany her, but she'd declined, arguing that she needed to face the Dean alone. Still, he'd hugged her and promised to wait for her at their favorite Starbucks.

"Thank you for coming, Miss Mitchell. How was your semester?"

Julia gazed across the desk at Dean Aras in surprise. "It was—interesting."

The Dean nodded, his eyes shifting to meet Professor Martin's. "I know this academic year has been challenging for you. I asked to speak with you simply to find out if you have had any other problems since the hearing."

Julia looked between the two academics, measuring them. "What kind of problems?"

"Dean Aras is wondering if Professor Emerson bothered you at all after the hearing. Did he call or email you? Did he try to meet with you?" Professor Martin appeared friendly, but there was an undertone to his demeanor that made Julia suspicious.

"Why do you care? You got what you wanted. He left the city."

The Dean's expression tightened. "I'm not about to retry the case with you, Miss Mitchell. This meeting is a courtesy, an attempt to ensure that you have been able to proceed with your education free of interference. We're trying to determine if Professor Emerson kept his word and left you alone."

"I received an email from him a few days after the hearing. He told me to stop contacting him and that we were over. That's what you want to hear, right?" She couldn't keep the bitterness out of her voice.

Professor Martin exchanged a meaningful look with the Dean. "I'm sure you're glad to put this matter behind you."

Julia sat silently, not bothering to answer.

"You're free to go. Congratulations on a successful year and congratulations on being admitted to Harvard. We'll see you at graduation." The Dean nodded at her dismissively.

She picked up her knapsack and walked to the door. Just as her hand reached for the doorknob she stopped, turning to face the two professors.

How strange it is, she thought, that these two men, armed only with massive intellects and closets full of tweed, could wield so much power over her heart and her happiness.

"I don't regret my relationship with Professor Emerson, even though it ended badly. Both of you were incredibly dismissive and patronizing to me throughout this entire process. I understand the importance of protecting someone who needs protection, but the only people I needed protection from was you."

Julia gave them a withering look and exited the office.

Chapter Thirty-seven

Gabriel stayed so long in Assisi, he became a fixture at the Basilica. Every day he spent a long hour sitting by St. Francis's crypt, thinking. Sometimes he prayed. Sometimes God seemed near and other times he seemed far away. At all times, Gabriel wished he was with Julia, although he began to realize how flawed their relationship had been—how he'd wanted to change his ways to be worthy of her when really, he should have changed because he was an insufferable ass.

He was enjoying lunch one day at the hotel when a fellow American struck up a conversation with him. The man was a physician from California, who was visiting Assisi with his wife and teenaged son.

"We're going to Florence tomorrow, and we'll be there for two months."

"Doing what?" Gabriel asked, eying the gray-haired man curiously.

"We'll be staying with the Franciscans. My wife, who is a nurse, and I will be working in a medical clinic. My son is going to be helping the homeless."

Gabriel frowned. "You're doing this as volunteers?"

"Yes. We wanted to do this as a family." The man paused and looked at Gabriel intently.

"Would you consider coming with us? The Franciscans can always use more help."

"No," said Gabriel, stabbing a piece of beef determinedly. "I'm not Catholic."

"Neither are we. We're Lutherans."

Gabriel gazed at the doctor with interest. His knowledge of Lutherans was limited almost exclusively to the writings of Garrison Keillor. (Not that he was willing to admit it.)

The doctor smiled. "We wanted to lend a hand to a good work. I wanted to encourage my son to think beyond beach vacations and video games."

"Thank you for the invitation, but I must decline." Gabriel was firm in his response, and so the doctor changed the subject.

Later that evening, Gabriel stared out the window of his simple hotel room, thinking as he always did about Julia.

She wouldn't have said no. She would have gone.

As ever, he was reminded of the divide between her generosity and his selfishness. A divide that, even after spending so many months with her, was yet to be breached.

Two weeks later, Gabriel stood in front of the monument to Dante in Santa Croce. He'd joined the Lutherans in their trip to Florence and become one of the Franciscans' most troublesome volunteers. He served meals to the poor but was horrified by the quality of food on offer, so he wrote a check to hire a caterer to make the meals. He went with the other volunteers as they gave toiletries and clean clothing to homeless people, but he was so troubled by the lack of cleanliness of the men and women that he wrote a check to construct washrooms and shower facilities for the homeless at the Franciscan mission.

In short, by the time Gabriel had seen every aspect of the Franciscans' work with the poor, he'd endeavored to change everything and agreed to finance the changes himself. Then he paid a few visits to some wealthy Florentine families, who he knew through his academic life, asking them to support the Franciscans as they helped the poor of Florence. Their donations would ensure a steady stream of revenue for years to come.

As he stood in front of the Dante memorial, he was struck by a sudden kinship with his favorite poet. Dante had been exiled from Florence. Even though the city eventually forgave him and allowed a memorial to be placed in his honor in the Basilica, he was buried in Ravenna. In a strange twist of fate, Gabriel now knew what it was like to be exiled from his job, his city, and his home, for Julianne's arms would always be his home. Even though he was forced into exile.

The memorials around him reminded him of his own mortality. If he was lucky, he'd have a long life, but many people such as Grace had their lives cut short. He could be hit by a car, or contract cancer, or have a heart attack. Suddenly, his time on earth seemed very short and very precious.

Since he'd left Assisi, he'd tried to assuage his guilt and loneliness by doing good works. Volunteering with the Franciscans was certainly a step in that direction. But what about making amends with Paulina? It was far too late to make his peace with Grace, or Maia, or his biological mother and father.

What about Julianne?

Gabriel stared at the figure of a despairing woman who leaned on what looked like Dante's casket. He'd accepted his exile, but that didn't mean he'd refrained from writing letter after letter to her, letters that were never sent.

❊ ❊

Cemeteries had a stillness all their own. Even cemeteries located in busy urban centers possessed this stillness—an unearthly quiet that clings to the air.

Walking through the cemetery, Gabriel couldn't pretend that he was strolling in a park. The sparse trees that peppered the landscape were not teeming with singing birds. The grass, though green and very well kept, was not alive with squirrels or the occasional urban rabbit, playing with his brothers or looking for food.

He saw the stone angels in the distance, their twin forms standing like tall sentries among the other monuments. They were made of marble, not granite, their skin white and pale and perfect. The angels faced away from him, their wings spread wide. It was easier for him to stand behind the monument. He couldn't see the name etched in stone. He could stay there forever, a few feet away, and never approach. But that would be cowardly.

He inhaled deeply, his sapphire eyes shut tightly, as he said a silent prayer. Then he walked a half circuit around the monument, stopping in front of the marker.

He removed a pristine handkerchief from his trouser pocket. An onlooker might have guessed that he had need of it for sweat or tears, but he didn't. He leaned forward and with a gentle hand swept the white linen over the black stone. The dirt came away easily. He would need to tend the rose bushes that had begun to encroach upon the letters. He made a mental note to hire a gardener.

He placed flowers in front of the stone, his mouth moving as if he were whispering. But he wasn't. The grave, of course, was empty.

A tear or two clouded his vision, followed by their brothers, and soon his face was wet with their rain. He didn't bother to wipe them away as he lifted his face to gaze upon the angels, the souls of silent, marble compassion.

He asked for forgiveness. He expressed his guilt, a guilt he knew would ache for the rest of his life. He didn't ask for his burden to be removed, for it seemed to him to be part of the consequences of his actions. Or rather, the consequences of what he failed to do for a mother and their child.

He reached into his pocket to retrieve his cell phone and dialed a number from the iPhone's memory.

"Hello?"

"Paulina. I need to see you."

Chapter Thirty-eight

Julia's father insisted on attending her graduation and refused to allow Paul to move her to Cambridge alone. Tom paid the security deposit and rent on her summer sublet. And it was Tom who flew to Toronto so he could watch his only daughter graduate with her MA on June eleventh.

Dressed in simple black with artful shoes, Julia left Paul and Tom on the steps of Convocation Hall while she went to line up with all the other graduating students.

Tom liked Paul. A lot.

Paul was forthright and had a firm handshake. He looked Tom directly in the eye when they spoke to one another. Paul offered his assistance in helping move Julia to Cambridge, including accommodations on his family's farm in Burlington, even after Tom had insisted that he could move Julia by himself. Tom dropped a hint to his daughter over dinner the evening before graduation, suggesting that Paul was an obvious choice for a new love interest, but Julia pretended she hadn't heard him.

As the graduates filed into the hall, Julia couldn't help but scan the audience, looking for Gabriel. With so many people it was unlikely that she would see him, even if he were present. However, when she gazed over at the faculty section she easily located Katherine Picton, dressed in her Oxonian robes. If the faculty were arranged alphabetically, and it certainly seemed as if they were, then Julia should have been able to guess where Gabriel would be seated, dressed in Harvard's crimson. But he wasn't.

When they called Julia's name, it was Katherine who ascended the stage in slow but certain steps to hood Julia with the vestment of a *ma-*

gister. It was Katherine who shook her hand professionally, wished her well at Harvard, and handed her the diploma.

Later that evening, after a celebratory dinner with Paul and Tom at a local steakhouse, Julia checked her voice mail and found a new message. It was from Rachel.

"Congratulations, Julia! We all send our love and we have presents for you. Thanks for sending me your new address in Cambridge. I'll mail everything and make sure it arrives after you do. I'm also sending your bridesmaid's dress.

"Dad booked your flight from Boston to Philadelphia for August twenty-first. I hope that's okay. He wanted to pay for it, and I know that you were planning on coming a week early.

"I still haven't heard from Gabriel. I'm hoping he was at your graduation. But if he wasn't, maybe you two will be able to sort everything out at the wedding. I can't imagine that he'd miss it. He's supposed to be a groomsman, and I don't even have his measurements for his tux!"

Chapter Thirty-nine

A certain blue-eyed Dante specialist read T.S. Eliot's poem *Ash Wednesday* before offering his nighttime prayers. He was alone, and yet not alone.

Looking at the photograph on his bedside table he thought about her graduation. How beautiful and proud she would have looked in her robes. With a sigh, he closed his book of poetry and turned out the light.

In the darkness of his old bedroom in the Clarks' former house, he reflected on the past weeks. He'd left Italy and traveled to Boston and Minnesota. He'd promised the Franciscans he'd return, for they'd said (wisely) that they prized his presence more than his donations. With that thought in mind, he closed his eyes.

"Gabriel, it's time to get up."

Groaning, he kept his eyes shut, hoping the voice would go away. Sleep was peaceful and he needed it.

"Come on. I know you're awake." The voice laughed softly, and he felt the mattress dip next to his legs.

He opened his eyes and saw his adoptive mother sitting on the edge of his bed. "Is it time for school?" he asked, rubbing the sleep from his eyes.

Grace laughed again, the sound light and airy like music. "You're a bit old to be going to school, at least as a student."

He looked around, confused. Then he sat up.

She smiled warmly and held out her hand. He relished the feel of her soft hand in his before squeezing it.

"What's the matter?" She gave him a puzzled look that was not un-kind, as he held her hand in both of his.

"I never said good-bye. I wasn't able to tell you—" He paused and inhaled quickly. "That I love you."

"A mother knows these things, Gabriel. I've always known."

He was momentarily overcome with a wave of emotion as he reached over and pulled her into a hug. "I didn't know you were sick. Rachel told me you were getting better. I should have been there."

Grace patted him on the back. "I want you to stop blaming yourself for everything. You made the best decision you could given the infor-mation you had at the time. No one expects you to be omniscient—or perfect."

She pulled away so she could see his face. "You shouldn't expect it of yourself, either. I love all my children, but you were my gift from God. You've always been special."

Mother and son spent a moment or two in quiet communion before she stood up, smoothing her dress.

"There's someone I'd like you to meet."

Gabriel wiped his eyes, pulling back the blankets and swinging his flannel covered legs to the floor. He stood up, trying to comb his hair, momentarily forgetting that he was shirtless. Grace went into the hall-way then came back, with her arm around a young woman.

Gabriel stared.

The woman was young, although she seemed ageless. Her hair was long and blond, her face a flawless white, and she was slender and tall. Her eyes were familiar. Striking sapphire blue eyes greeted his, accom-panied by a wide, pink smile.

Gabriel gave Grace a questioning look.

"I'll let you two talk," she said, and disappeared.

"I'm Gabriel." He smiled politely and extended his hand.

She shook it, grinning happily in return. "I know." Her voice was soft and very sweet. It reminded Gabriel of a little bell.

"And you are?"

"I wanted to meet you. Grace told me what you were like as a child, about your work as a professor. I like Dante too. He's very funny."

Gabriel nodded, not quite understanding.

The young woman looked up at him wistfully. "Will you tell me about her?"

"Who?"

"Paulina?"

Gabriel stiffened, and his eyes narrowed suspiciously. "Why?"

"I never knew her."

He rubbed at his eyes with the heels of his hands. "She went to see her family in Minnesota, to try to reconcile with them."

"I know. She's happy."

"Then why do you ask?"

"I want to know what she's like."

He took a moment to carefully construct what to say. "She's attractive and smart. She's stubborn. She speaks several languages and she cooks well." He chuckled. "But she's not especially musical. She can't carry a tune in a basket."

The young woman giggled. "So I've heard." She eyed Gabriel curiously. "Did you love her?"

He looked away. "I think I love her now, in a way. We were friends in the beginning, when I met her at Oxford."

The young woman nodded and turned her head as if someone was calling her from the hallway. She quickly shifted her gaze back to Gabriel.

"I'm glad I met you. It wasn't possible before. But I'll see you again." She smiled and turned toward the door.

Gabriel followed her. "I didn't catch your name."

She looked up at him expectantly. "Don't you recognize me?"

"I don't. I'm sorry. Although there's something familiar about your eyes . . ."

She laughed and Gabriel smiled in spite of himself, for her laughter was infectious. "Of course my eyes are familiar; they're *yours*."

Gabriel's smile slid off his face.

"Don't you know me?" She seemed puzzled.

He shook his head.

"I'm Maia."

His expression froze. Then, as the moments passed, it ranged through several different emotions, like clouds floating across the sky on a summer's day.

She pointed to the tattoo he wore on his left pectoral. "You didn't have to do that." She leaned forward, whispering conspiratorially. "I know that you loved me.

"I'm happy here. It's filled with light and hope and love. And it's so beautiful."

She reached up and kissed him on the cheek, her touch lingering for only a second, before she left him to walk to the hallway.

Chapter Forty

Tom stood at Julia's front door the day after her graduation, wearing a gray T-shirt with the word *Harvard* emblazoned across the chest.

"Dad?" Julia's tone was a question.

"I'm so proud of you," he said gruffly, pulling her into a hug.

Father and daughter shared a quiet moment on the porch of Julia's building before they heard someone coming up the steps behind them.

"Uh, good morning. I brought breakfast." Paul held a tray containing three coffees and some doughnuts from Tim Horton's. He seemed somewhat embarrassed at having intruded on the Mitchells, but he was greeted with a handshake from Tom and a hug from Julia.

The trio shared breakfast at Julia's card table, then the two men began planning how best to pack up all of her things and move them. Luckily, Paul had persuaded Sarah, who was subletting to Julia, to allow her to move into the Cambridge apartment on June fifteenth.

"Um, Katherine Picton invited me to lunch today. But I don't have to go." Julia spoke quickly. She didn't want to leave Tom and Paul working while she went on a social call.

"You don't have a lot of stuff, Jules." Tom quickly appraised her studio's contents. "We'll let you pack your clothes while we start on the books. I'm sure we'll be close to finished by the time you have to see your professor." He smiled and tousled her hair with his hand before disappearing into the washroom, leaving Paul and Julia alone.

"You don't have to do this. Dad and I will be fine."

Paul frowned. "When are you going to accept the fact that I'm here because I want to be? *I don't leave,* Julia, not when I have a reason to stay."

Julia stiffened uncomfortably, and her eyes quickly fixated on the half-finished coffee in front of her.

"If Professor Picton summoned you, it's because she wants to talk to you. You'd better go." Paul squeezed Julia's hand lightly. "Your old man and I can handle things around here."

Julia exhaled slowly and smiled.

There were a few intimate things that Julia did not want her father or Paul to see so she hid them in her L. L. Bean knapsack. The items were not what one might expect a young woman to hide from her father—a journal, diamond earrings, and a few items related to her counseling sessions.

Nicole had been pleased by Julia's progress, and when they concluded their final session, gave her the name and contact information of a counselor near Harvard. Nicole had not only helped Julia cope, she was passing her into another set of capable hands that would help her take the next steps in her journey.

Julia wore a dress and modest sandals to Professor Picton's house, thinking that an invitation to lunch warranted attractive garb. She carried her knapsack on one of her shoulders and clutched a tin of what she was told was a very fine loose Darjeeling tea, which she'd purchased as a hostess gift. She and her Darjeeling were received with typical Pictonian restraint and immediately ushered into the dining room where they enjoyed a very pleasant lunch of prawn salad, cold cucumber soup, and a fine Sauvignon blanc.

"How is your reading list coming along?" Katherine asked, eying Julia over her soup.

"Slowly but surely. I'm reading the texts you've suggested, but I've only started."

"Professor Marinelli is looking forward to meeting you. It would be good for you to introduce yourself to her when she arrives in Cambridge."

"I'll do that. And thank you."

"It would be beneficial for you to meet the other Dante specialists in the area, especially at Boston University." Katherine smiled sagely. "Although I'm sure circumstances will arrange themselves so you end up being introduced to them eventually. But if they don't, promise me that you will you drop by the Department of Romance Studies at BU before September."

"I will. Thank you. I don't know what I would have done . . ." Julia's voice trailed off as she warred with her emotions.

Surprisingly, Katherine reached across the table and patted Julia's hand. She touched her awkwardly, as a distinguished bachelor professor might pat the head of a crying child, but not without feeling.

"You've graduated with honors. Your thesis is solid and could form the basis of what will hopefully be a fine dissertation. I look forward to watching your career with interest. And I think you will be very happy in Cambridge."

"Thank you."

When it was time for her to leave, Julia intended to shake Katherine's hand but was surprised when she was pulled into a restrained but warm hug.

"You've been a good student. Now go to Harvard and make me proud. And drop me an email now and then to let me know how you are." Katherine pulled back and looked at Julia fixedly. "It's quite possible I'll be giving a lecture in Boston in the fall. I hope we'll run into one another."

Julia nodded her agreement.

As she walked to her small studio on Madison Avenue, she stared in wonder at the gift Professor Picton had placed in her hands. It was a worn and rare early edition of Dante's *La Vita Nuova* that had belonged to Dorothy L. Sayers, who had been a friend of Katherine's dissertation director at Oxford. In it was Sayers's marginalia, written in her own hand. Julia would treasure it always.

No matter what Gabriel had done, persuading Katherine Picton to be her thesis advisor was a gift so great she would be forever in his debt.

Love is doing a kindness for someone else, not expecting to receive anything in return, she thought.

Early the next morning, Julia, Tom, and Paul loaded everything into the back of a U-Haul and drove eight hours to the Norris farm, which was located just outside of Burlington, Vermont. The Mitchells were warmly welcomed and were persuaded to stay a few extra days so Ted Norris, Paul's father, could take Tom fishing.

Julia silently doubted that any other inducement would have delayed his rigorous schedule, but that was before either of them had tried Louise Norris's cooking. Paul's mother was an excellent cook who made everything, including doughnuts, from scratch. Tom's stomach was in love.

On June fifteenth, the night before the Mitchells and Paul were supposed to leave for Cambridge, Paul couldn't sleep. His father had called him out of bed well after midnight because of a bovine emergency. By the time the crisis was averted, he was far too agitated to go back to bed.

He had two women on his mind. Allison, his former girlfriend, had been visiting when he arrived with Julia two days earlier. They were still friends, so the gesture was well meant, but Paul knew that part of her reason for being there was to size Julia up. He'd told Allison about Julia at Christmas, so she was more than aware of Julia's presence in his life and his attachment to her. An attachment that he had to admit was unrequited, at least, at that time.

Still, Allison was friendly to Julia, and of course, Julia was her own shy but charming self. It was awkward for Paul as he watched his past and his potential future make small talk while he fumbled for something to say.

When Allison called his cell phone before bed that evening and said that Julia was lovely, he didn't know how to respond. Of course he had feelings for Allison. They had a long and good history as friends before they began dating. He loved her still. But she'd broken things off with him. He'd moved on and met Julia. Why should he feel guilty?

While Paul was contemplating his very complex (yet simultaneously non-existent) love life, Julia was wrestling with insomnia. When she finally grew weary of tossing and turning she decided to creep from the third floor garret she was occupying to the kitchen to get a glass of milk.

She found Paul sitting alone at the large, harvest table, eating a rather expansive dish of ice cream.

"Hi." He took in her appearance with a swift but appreciative look.

Julia walked over to him wearing an old Selinsgrove High School T-shirt and a pair of running shorts that had *St. Joe's* cheekily sewn onto the seat.

(To Paul's eyes, she was Helen of Troy in leisurewear.)

"You can't sleep, either?" She pulled out a chair to sit next to him.

"Dad had a problem with one of the cows. Heath Bar Crunch?" He dished up a large spoonful of Ben and Jerry's ice cream and held it out to her.

It was her favorite flavor. She gently took the spoon out of his hand.

"Mmmmm," she groaned, eyes closed. She opened her eyes and handed back the spoon, resisting the urge to lick it clean.

Paul put the spoon in the bowl and stood up. She blinked at him and instinctively moved back in her chair.

"Julia," he whispered, pulling her to her feet. He pushed her hair behind her shoulders, noting that she didn't flinch when he did so. Their upper bodies grazed one another. He looked into her eyes with an expression of heated intensity. "I don't want to say good-bye."

Her face crinkled up into a smile. "We won't be saying good-bye. We'll email and talk on the phone. If you come to Boston, we'll see each other."

"I don't think you understand."

Julia freed her wrist from Paul's hand, stepping back. "It's because of Allison, isn't it? I don't want to create trouble for you. Dad and I can make the trip by ourselves."

She waited patiently for his response, but instead of looking relieved, he looked conflicted.

"This isn't about Allison."

"It isn't?"

"Do you really have to ask me that?" He took another step toward her. "Don't you know?"

Leery of rejection, he raised his hands slowly and cupped her face. Her fine features were engulfed by his large hands. He held her tenderly, worried about such fragility underneath his grasp, and slowly began to stroke her face with his thumbs.

Julia tore her eyes away from his. "Paul, I—"

"Let me say this," he interrupted forcefully. "Just once, let me tell you how I feel." He inhaled and waited until she met his gaze again before he spoke.

"*I'm in love with you*. I don't want to be apart from you because I love you. The thought of having to leave you in Cambridge is tearing me up."

Julia inhaled slowly and began to shake her head.

"Just hear me out. I know that you aren't in love with me. I know it's too soon. But do you think that you could be—in time?"

She closed her eyes. Her mind raced ahead to envision a future she hadn't previously considered—a crossroads of possibilities. She thought of what it would be like to love Paul, to be held and kissed by him, to have him take her to his bed upstairs and make love to her, gently and sweetly. For she knew above all things that Paul would be sweet.

He would want marriage, of course, and children. But he would be proud of her academic career and support her in it.

She found herself unrepulsed by these images, for they were good. She could have a contented life with a decent man who had never done her ill and who, she knew, would probably never so much as hurt her feelings as long as he lived. She could have a good life with him.

He lifted her chin and she opened her eyes.

"There won't be drama and fights and exes like Professor Pain. I will treat you respectfully, and I will never, *ever* leave you.

"*Choose me*," he whispered, his eyes deep and intense. "Choose me and I will give you a happy life. You'll never have to cry yourself to sleep again."

Tears began to stream down her face. She knew that what he was saying was true. But knowing the truth and wanting the truth are two very different things.

"I'm not like him. I'm not an inferno that blazes and dies out. I'm constant. I've held back because I knew that you only wanted to be friends. But just once, I'd like to be able to show you what I feel without holding back."

He took her silence as acquiescence and wrapped his arms around her. He bent down so their lips could meet and poured all his passion and love for her into a single kiss. Paul's mouth was warm and inviting. What began as a gentle contact quickly became urgent with desire.

With a split-second decision, she opened to him, tentatively, and his tongue quickly entered and met hers, his hands ending up in her hair. There was no domination, no pressing of boundaries, nothing overwhelming or crass.

Paul kissed her for as long as he could without becoming obscene, then slowly lessened the pressure of his lips on hers, pecking her briefly before moving his lips to her ear. "I love you, Julia. Say that you'll be mine. You won't regret it."

Julia tightened her arms around him as the tears fell.

Chapter Forty-one

Over breakfast the next morning, Louise Norris looked with concern between her son and the young woman he loved. Her husband, Ted, tried to keep the conversation moving by talking about the ill cow he'd tended to the night before. Tom tried to cram a homemade doughnut into his mouth without appearing like a barbarian, and failed.

After breakfast, the kitchen emptied like a galleon full of rats docking in a new port, leaving Paul and Julia sitting across from one another, each fidgeting with their coffee mugs and avoiding one another's eyes.

Julia broke the silence. "I'm so sorry."

"Me too."

She chewed on her lip as her eyes darted to meet his, wondering if he was angry or bitter. Or both.

But he wasn't. His dark eyes were still kind, but he appeared defeated. "I had to try, you know? I didn't want to wait until you'd found someone else. But I won't bring it up again." He pursed his lips, and a resigned expression passed over his face. "You don't need to worry about me embarrassing you."

Julia leaned over the table and took his hand in hers. "I wasn't embarrassed. I know that we would have had a good life together. I care for you too. But you deserve more. You deserve to have a life with someone who will love you the same way that you love her."

Paul released her hand and walked away.

❊ ❊

"Care to explain why he's so quiet?" Tom turned to Julia as they waited for Paul to come out of the men's room at a gas station in New Hampshire.

"He wants more than I can give him."

Tom squinted at something in the distance. "He seems like a good man. He comes from a good family. What's the problem? Got a thing against cows?"

He was trying to make her laugh, but it had the opposite effect. He quickly held his hands up in surrender. "What do I know? I thought the senator's son was a good match for you. So I guess I'm a horse's ass."

Before Julia could disagree, Paul returned to the U-Haul, ending the heart to heart conversation between father and daughter.

❅ ❅

Two days later Julia stood on the front steps of her new building, saying good-bye to Paul, feeling worse than she had when she rejected him in his parents' kitchen. He hadn't been cold, or rude, or resentful. He hadn't shirked any responsibilities in terms of driving from Vermont to Cambridge, or unloading Julia's things.

He'd even gone out of his way to set up a job interview for her at the trendy coffee shop across the street. The former occupant of the apartment had just quit her job there. Paul hoped that Julia could replace her, knowing that she needed the money.

He'd slept on the floor in Julia's small apartment and never complained. He'd been perfect, actually. And that made Julia almost feel as if she should change her mind.

It would be safer, easier, to choose Paul. Her heart would heal with him. But in choosing Paul, she would be settling for the good and not the exceptional. And even if the exceptional eluded her for the rest of her life, it would be better, she thought, to live the life of a Katherine Picton, than to be like her mother. In marrying a good man without loving him passionately and completely, she would only serve to short-change him and herself. And she was not that selfish.

"Good-bye." He hugged her tightly and released her, watching her expression carefully. Perhaps he was looking to see if she'd changed her mind.

"Good-bye. Thanks for everything. I don't know what I would have done without you, all these months—"

He shrugged. "This is what friends do."

Paul saw her eyes fill with tears and gave her a very worried expression. "We're still friends, aren't we?"

"Of course we are." Julia sniffled. "You've been a great friend to me, and I hope that we can still be friends, even though . . ." She didn't finish her sentence, and Paul nodded as if he was grateful she hadn't.

With much hesitation he reached out to stroke her cheek one last time. Then he walked toward the car where his friend Patrick was waiting. Patrick was going to drive him back to Vermont.

Suddenly, Paul stopped. He turned around and walked back to Julia, nervously.

"I didn't want to mention this in front of your father, so I was waiting until after he left. Then I thought maybe I shouldn't say anything at all." Paul looked away, up Mount Auburn Street, seemingly struggling with something.

"What is it?"

He shook his head, turning to look at her. "I got an email yesterday from Professor Martin."

Julia looked up at him in surprise.

"Emerson quit."

"What?" She placed a hand on either side of her temple as she tried to focus on the enormity of what Paul was saying. "When?"

"I don't know. He agreed to continue supervising my dissertation, even though he's leaving. At least, that's what Martin said. I haven't heard from Emerson at all."

Paul caught sight of Julia's agitated pose and quickly put an arm around her shoulders.

"I didn't want to upset you, but I thought you should know. The department is starting a search for his replacement, and I'm sure they'll be recruiting at Harvard. I knew you'd hear about it. I thought it would be better coming from me."

Julia nodded woodenly. "Where's he going?"

"I have no idea. Martin was tight-lipped about the entire thing. I think he's pissed. After all the shit Emerson put the department through, he up and quit."

Julia numbly hugged Paul good-bye and returned to her new apartment so she could think. That evening, she called Rachel. When she received a voice mail message she contemplated telephoning Richard, but she didn't want to bother him. She knew that Scott wouldn't have any inside information as to Gabriel's whereabouts.

So she left a couple of messages on Rachel's cell phone over the course of the next few days, then she waited. Rachel never responded.

As the days of June passed, Julia started a part-time job as a sales clerk at Peet's coffee shop, which was located in a remodeled three-story house across the street. Since Tom covered her rent and her moving expenses, and since he had demanded that she take some of the proceeds from the sale of his house back in Selinsgrove, she was able to live simply but comfortably on her part-time job and her savings until her fellowship began in late August.

She quickly arranged an appointment with the therapist that Nicole had recommended and began meeting with Dr. Margaret Walters on a weekly basis. When she wasn't learning the ropes of the retail coffee market and charming the citizens of Harvard Square, she followed Katherine Picton's instructions and introduced herself to Greg Matthews, the Chair of her new department.

Professor Matthews received her warmly, and they spent the better part of an hour discussing their common interest in Dante. He mentioned that Cecilia Marinelli was arriving from Oxford the following week and suggested that Julia drop by in order to attend a reception that was being held in Professor Marinelli's honor. Julia accepted the invitation gladly. Then he walked her to the graduate student lounge and introduced her to a group of students before politely taking his leave.

Two of the students were cordial but not particularly friendly. The third student, Zsuzsa, who was from Hungary, welcomed Julia immediately. She told Julia that a group of them met for drinks every Wednesday at Grendel's Den, a local pub overlooking Winthrop Park. Apparently, Grendel's had a lovely patio and an exceptional beer list. Julia promised to meet Zsuzsa there the following Wednesday night, and the two women exchanged email addresses.

Despite Julia's overall shyness, a character trait that she would never lose completely, she fit into the Harvard landscape like a hand into a glove. She found an undergraduate tour guide called Ari who gave her an orientation to the campus, the library, and the graduate school. She secured a library card in advance of registration, which would be held in August.

Julia dropped into the graduate student lounge on occasion to see Zsuzsa and to learn more about the atmosphere of the department. And she spent long hours in the library, hunting down books that she would need to read that summer. Exploring the neighborhood, she found a grocery store and a bank and claimed a particular Thai restaurant, which was just down the street from her apartment, as her new favorite place to eat.

So by the time Rachel called her on June twenty-sixth, Julia was completely at home in her new life and happy. Almost.

Julia was in between customers when Rachel called her cell phone, so she asked one of her co-workers to cover for her and walked out to the front lawn so as not to disturb anyone.

"Rachel, how are you?"

"We're fine! I'm sorry it took me so long to get back to you. Some bastard stole my phone and I had to get a new one. Then I had to go back through all the messages, starting with the ones about the wedding and—"

Julia gritted her teeth only slightly as she waited for Rachel to draw breath so she could steer the conversation in a completely different direction. In two or three paragraphs, her patience was rewarded.

"Gabriel quit his job."

"What?" Rachel almost shouted. "How do you know?"

"A friend of mine was his research assistant in Toronto."

"That explains it," Rachel said.

"Explains what?"

"Gabriel sold his condo. He sent Dad an email saying that he was moving and that he has been staying in hotels while he looks for a house."

Julia leaned her back up against the old, gnarled oak tree that stood in front of Peet's.

"Did he mention where he was looking?"

"No. Just that he'd hired a company to pack up his things and put them in storage. But if he quit his job—"

"He's in the process of quitting."

"Then you should call him! Julia, it's the perfect time. You have to call him."

Julia gritted her teeth. "No."

"Why not?"

"*He* broke up with *me*, remember? I'm not going to be the one to fix this—assuming it can be fixed."

Rachel grew very quiet for a moment. "I'm not suggesting you sweep whatever happened under the carpet. But I hope that you two could talk about what happened. He needs to hear how you feel about all of this and what happened to you after he left. And frankly, he needs to offer some kind of explanation. He owes you that. Then you can tell him to get lost, if that's what you really want."

Julia squeezed her eyes shut as a wave of pain washed over her. The thought of seeing Gabriel—and listening to his explanation—physically hurt.

"I'm not sure my heart can survive his explanation."

Chapter Forty-two

Julia buried herself in busyness for the next few days, studying in preparation for her introduction to Professor Marinelli. Since the Professor was the guest of honor at the lavish reception where they met, their conversation was short, but a success. Professor Marinelli was still settling into her new home, but recognized Julia's name thanks to Professor Picton's recommendation and suggested that they meet for coffee in July.

Julia wafted home on a breeze of optimism. She was so happy, she decided it was finally time to begin the project she'd been avoiding—unpacking her books and arranging them on shelves in her small apartment. Until that evening, she'd availed herself of Harvard's libraries. But every day the collection of boxes nagged at her, and so she finally decided it was time to organize them. The process took longer than she anticipated. She finished about a third of the boxes that evening before walking to the Thai restaurant and ordering take out.

Two days later, Julia was down to the final box. After a very enjoyable evening with Zsuzsa and a few other graduate students at Grendel's Den on June thirtieth, Julia came home determined to finish unpacking.

As had been her practice, she shelved the volumes in alphabetical order almost mindlessly. Until she came to the last book in the bottom of the last cardboard box, *Marriage in the Middle Ages: Love, Sex, and the Sacred*, published by Oxford University Press. Frowning, she turned the volume over in her hands. It took a few minutes for a distant memory to creep back to her—Paul, standing in her studio apartment, saying that he'd retrieved her mail from the department.

"*A medieval history textbook,*" he'd said.

Out of curiosity, Julia leafed through the volume and found a business card wedged in the Table of Contents. The card was for Alan Mackenzie, the Oxford University Press textbook representative in Toronto. On the back of his card was a handwritten note that stated he'd be happy to help her with her textbook needs.

Julia was about to close the book and shelve it when her eyes alighted on one of the readings.

The Letters of Abelard and Héloise, Letter Six.

It only took an instant for Julia to recall her last conversation with Gabriel.

Gabriel turned away from Jeremy, lowering his voice to a whisper. "Read my sixth letter. Paragraph four."

Her heart racing, she turned the pages, shocked to find an illustration and a photograph marking the place where Abelard's sixth letter was found:

> *But whither does my vain imagination carry me! Ah, Héloise, how far are we from such a happy temper? Your heart still burns with that fatal fire you cannot extinguish, and mine is full of trouble and unrest. Think not, Héloise, that I here enjoy a perfect peace; I will for the last time open my heart to you;—I am not yet disengaged from you, and though I fight against my excessive tenderness for you, in spite of all my endeavours I remain but too sensible of your sorrows and long to share in them. Your letters have indeed moved me; I could not read with indifference characters written by that dear hand! I sigh and weep, and all my reason is scarce sufficient to conceal my weakness from my pupils. This, unhappy Héloise, is the miserable condition of Abelard. The world, which is generally wrong in its notions, thinks I am at peace, and imagining that I loved you only for the gratification of the senses, have now forgot you. What a mistake is this!*

She must have read the passage five times before its message began to sink into her agitated mind.

Julia looked at the illustration closely. The title read *The Contention for Guido de Montefeltro.* The name was familiar, but she couldn't quite remember its significance. She grabbed her latptop, intent on looking the image up on the internet but quickly remembered that she didn't have internet access in her apartment.

She located her phone, but the battery was dead and she had no idea where the cord was to recharge it. Undeterred, she returned to the book and picked up the photograph that had been placed next to the illustration. It was a picture of the apple orchard behind the Clarks' house. Gabriel's handwriting was on the back:

> To my Beloved,
> My heart is yours and my body.
> My soul, likewise.
> I will be true to you, Beatrice.
> I want to be your last.
> Wait for me . . .

When she'd overcome her shock, she was desperate to speak to him. She didn't care that it was close to midnight and Mount Auburn Street was dark. She didn't care that Peet's had closed hours ago. She grabbed her laptop and fled her apartment, knowing that if she could stand just outside the door to Peet's, she'd be able to pick up a wireless signal and email Gabriel. Julia had no idea what she would say. All she could do was run.

The neighborhood was almost silent. Despite the gentle drizzle and mist of warm vespertine rain, a small group of what looked like frat boys were about a half a block away, talking and laughing. Julia stepped from the curb and began to cross the street, her flip-flops squishing against the wet asphalt. She ignored the droplets that fell from the sky, soaking through her T-shirt. She ignored the thunder that began to roll and the flash of lightning that illuminated the eastern sky.

In the very center of the road, she stopped because straight ahead of her, she glimpsed a shadowy figure lurking in the darkness behind the oak tree in front of Peet's. Another flash of lightning revealed that the figure was a man.

He was half-hidden by the tree and in the absence of light, she couldn't make out his features. She knew better than to approach a stranger in the shadows, so she stayed where she was, craning her neck to see him.

As if in response to her movements, he came around the edge of the tree and slowly walked into the pool of light that cascaded onto the sidewalk from the street lamp. Another bolt of lightning shimmered overhead, and for one brief instant Julia thought he looked like an angel.

Gabriel.

Chapter Forty-three

Gabriel saw the pain in her eyes. That was the first thing he noticed. Somehow, she looked older. But her beauty, her goodness made visible, was even more breathtaking than it had been before.

Standing in front of her, he was overwhelmed by how much he loved her. All his trials fell away. He'd been working up the nerve to go to her, to ring the doorbell and beg entrance. When he thought he couldn't wait a minute more, the door to her apartment building opened and she scampered like a deer into the road.

He'd fantasized about their reunion. On some days, it was the only thought that sustained him. But the longer she stood, statue still, making no move to come to him, the more a feeling of despair grew. Several different scenarios coursed through his consciousness, few of them ending happily.

Don't send me away, he begged her silently. Running an uneasy hand through his hair, he tried to smooth the rain dampened strands.

"Julianne." He couldn't disguise the tremor in his voice. She was staring through him as if he were a ghost.

Before Gabriel could give voice to that idea, he heard something approach. He turned in the direction of an approaching vehicle. Julia was still standing in the road.

He shouted to her wildly, "Julia, move!"

Frozen, she ignored his warning, and the car whipped past, narrowly missing her. Gabriel began walking toward her, arms and hands waving.

"Julia, get out of the road. Now!"

Chapter Forty-four

Julia's eyes were shut tightly. She could hear noises and the distant hum of his voice, but she couldn't make out any words. Droplets of rain fell on her bare arms and legs, and a solid chest pressed against her face as a warm, masculine body wrapped around her like a blanket.

She opened her eyes.

Gabriel's handsome face was lined with worry, his eyes shimmering with hope. He placed a hesitant hand against the curve of her cheek, brushing under her eye with the pad of his thumb.

For a few moments, at least, they said nothing.

"Are you all right?" he breathed.

She stared up at him, speechless.

"I didn't mean to shock you. I came as soon as I could."

His words broke through the haze that froze her. Julia wriggled out of his grasp. "What are you doing here?"

He frowned. "I would have thought it was obvious."

"Not to me."

Gabriel huffed in frustration. "It's July first. I came as soon as I could."

Julia shook her head, taking a cautious step back. "What?"

His voice took on a conciliatory tone. "I wish I could have returned earlier."

Her expression said it all—the narrowed, suspicious eyes, the ruby lips pressed tightly together, the clenched jaw.

"You knew I resigned. Surely you must have known I'd come back."

Julia clutched her laptop to her chest. "Why would I think that?"

His eyes widened. For a moment, he was too stunned to speak.

"Did you think that I wouldn't come back, even after I'd resigned?"

"That's what a person tends to think when her lover flees the city without so much as a phone call. And sends her an impersonal email saying that it's over."

Gabriel's expression hardened. "Sarcasm does not become you, Julianne."

"Lying does not become you, *Professor*." Her eyes flashed.

He took a step toward her, then stopped. "So we're back to that, are we? Julianne and the Professor?"

"According to what you told the hearing officers, we never got past it. You're the professor, I'm the student. You seduced and dumped me. The hearing officers didn't tell me if you said that you enjoyed it."

He swore under his breath. "I sent you messages. You simply chose not to believe them."

"What messages? The telephone calls you never made? The letters you never wrote? Apart from that email, I've heard nothing from you since you called me Héloise. Absolutely nothing.

"And what about the messages I left you? Maybe you deleted them without bothering to listen—just like you left without bothering to tell me. Do you know how humiliating that was? That the man who was supposed to love me fled the city in order to break up with me?"

Gabriel pressed a hand to his forehead, as if to help his mind focus. "What about the letter from Abelard to Héloise and the photograph of our orchard? I put the book in your mailbox myself."

"I didn't know the textbook was from you. I only looked at it a few minutes ago."

"But I told you to read Abelard's letter! I told you myself," he sputtered, a horrified expression on his face.

Julia clutched her laptop more tightly. "No, you said read *my* sixth letter. I did. You told me to choose a sweater because the weather had turned cold." She eyed him furiously. "You were right."

"I called you *Héloise*. Wasn't it obvious?"

"It was crushingly obvious," she snapped. "Héloise was seduced and abandoned by her professor. Your message was crystal clear!"

"But the textbook . . ." he began. He searched her eyes. "The photograph."

"I found it tonight when I was unpacking my books." Her expression softened. "Before this, I thought you were telling me that you'd tired of me."

"Forgive me," he managed. His words were woefully inadequate, but they came from the heart. "I . . . Julianne, I need to expl—"

"We should go inside," she interrupted, peering up at the windows of her apartment.

He reached out to take her hand but thought better of it, letting his arm drop to his side.

The thunder and lightning continued as they climbed the stairs. By the time they entered the studio apartment, the lights had flickered and gone out.

"I wonder if it's just this building," Julia mused. "Or if it's the whole street."

Gabriel murmured his response, watching impotently as she felt her way across the room. She pulled back the blinds to let in as much light as possible. Mount Auburn Street was dark.

"We could go somewhere with electricity." His voice sounded at her elbow, and she jumped.

"Sorry." He placed a hand on her arm.

"I'd rather stay here."

Gabriel resisted the urge to insist, realizing that he was in no position to demand that Julia do anything. He looked around the room.

"Do you have a flashlight or some candles?"

"Both, I think." She found a flashlight and handed Gabriel a towel while she retreated to the bathroom to change into dry clothes. By the time she'd returned, he was seated on the futon, surrounded by a half-dozen tea lights, which were spread artfully on the furniture and across the floor.

Julia watched the shadows flicker on the wall behind him. Unearthly shapes seemed to hover around him, as if he were trapped in Dante's Inferno. The lines on his forehead had deepened, it seemed, and his eyes appeared larger. He hadn't shaved recently, the scruff of his beard covering the planes of his face. He'd smoothed his damp hair back with his fingers, but a single curl had rebelled, clinging stubbornly to his forehead.

Julia had forgotten how attractive he was. How, with just a glance or a word he could make her blood heat. He was as dangerous as he was beautiful.

Gabriel reached out to pull her to sit next to him, but she curled into the opposite corner.

"I found a corkscrew and a bottle of wine. I hope you don't mind." He handed her a glass that was half-full of an inexpensive Shiraz. She was surprised he'd bothered, for it was the kind of wine he would have disdained in the past.

She took several long sips, savoring the wine on her tongue. She waited for him to cough, sputter, and complain about the *appalling bathwater*. But he didn't. In fact, he didn't drink at all. Instead, he stared at her, his eyes coming to rest unapologetically on the swell of her breasts.

"Are you changing schools?" His voice sounded husky.

"What?"

He gestured to her sweatshirt.

She looked down. *Boston College.*

"No, Paul gave this to me. He went there for his master's, remember?"

Gabriel stiffened. "I gave you a sweatshirt once," he observed, more to himself than to her.

Julia took another long sip of wine, wishing there was more of it.

He watched her drink, his eyes resting on her mouth and throat. "Do you still have my Harvard sweatshirt?"

"Let's talk about something else."

He shifted uncomfortably but couldn't drag his gaze away from her. He longed to run his hands up and down her body and press their mouths together. "What do you think about Boston University?"

She looked over at him warily. In response to her suspicion, the bravado seemed to leak out of his gaze and he chewed at the edge of his mouth.

"Katherine Picton told me to introduce myself to the Dante specialist in the Department of Romance Studies. But I haven't gotten around to it. I've been busy."

"Then I need to thank her."

"Why?"

He hesitated.

"I'm the new Dante specialist at Boston University."

He searched her eyes for a reaction. But there wasn't one. She sat very still, the candlelight flickering over her fine features.

He chuckled mirthlessly, pouring more wine into her glass. "That isn't the response I was hoping for."

She muttered her annoyance, tasting the wine again. "So you're—here to stay?"

"That depends." He looked at her sweatshirt significantly.

The heat of his gaze seemed to scorch her. She resisted the urge to hide her breasts from him, keeping her arms at her sides.

"I'm a full professor now. Romance Studies doesn't have a graduate program in Italian. The university wanted to be able to attract graduate students in Dante studies, so they cross-appointed me with Religion. They have a graduate program."

He gazed at the shadows that surrounded them, shaking his head. "Surprising, isn't it? That a man who spent his life running from God should become a professor of Religion."

"I've seen stranger things."

"Yes," Gabriel whispered, "I think you have. I would have resigned from Toronto sooner, but it would have caused a scandal. Once you'd graduated, I was free to accept the job here."

Julia turned away, and Gabriel noticed the nakedness of her ear lobes. She wasn't wearing Grace's earrings anymore. The thought gutted him.

Her brow wrinkled as she contemplated what he'd just said.

"What's so significant about July first?"

"Today is the day my contract in Toronto ends. It's the day my resignation takes effect." He cleared his throat. "I read your emails and listened to your voice mails—all of them. But I hoped you'd seen the book. I placed it in your mailbox myself."

Julia was still processing his words. She wasn't accepting his excuses; she simply wasn't arguing with him. At least, not yet.

"I'm sorry I missed your graduation." He sipped a glass of water. "Katherine sent me a few photographs." He cleared his throat, hesitating. "You looked beautiful. You *are* beautiful."

He dug into his trouser pocket and produced his iPhone. Curious, she took it, setting her wine aside. As his wallpaper, Gabriel had a photograph of Julia in her graduation gown, shaking Katherine Picton's hand.

"From Katherine," he explained, noting her confusion.

She scrolled through his photo album determinedly, her stomach queasy. There were pictures from their trip to Italy and photos from Christmas, but Paulina was not to be found. There were no compromising pictures of Gabriel, no images of other women. In fact, almost all the pictures were of her, including a series of very provocative shots that he'd taken in Belize.

She was surprised. After being so convinced he wanted nothing to do with her, the sight of his apparent regard was disorienting.

She returned his phone. "The picture that you used to keep on your dresser, the one of us at Lobby, did you take it with you?"

His eyebrows lifted in surprise. "Yes. How did you know?"

Julia paused for a moment as the revelation sunk in. "I noticed it was missing when I went looking for you."

He reached out to take her hand but once again, she withdrew.

"When I went back to my condo, I saw your clothes. Why you didn't take them?"

"They weren't really mine."

Gabriel's eyebrows knitted together. "Of course they were yours. They still are, if you want them."

She shook her head.

"Believe me, Julianne, I wanted you with me. The photograph was a poor substitute."

"You wanted me?"

Gabriel couldn't help himself. He gently stroked the curve of her cheek with his thumb, inwardly relieved that she didn't flinch. "I never stopped wanting you."

She moved away, leaving his hand to touch only air. Her tone grew harsh. "Do you have any idea what it's like to be left by the person you love, not once, but twice?"

Gabriel pressed his lips together. "No, I don't. Forgive me."

He waited to see if she would answer him, but she didn't.

"So Paul gave you that sweatshirt." He toyed with his glass. "How is he?"

"He's fine. Why do you care?"

"He's my student." Professor Emerson sounded prim.

"So was I, once," she said bitterly. "You should email him. He said he hasn't heard from you."

"So you've spoken with him?"

"Yes, Gabriel. I've spoken with him."

Julia pulled her wet hair out of its ponytail, running her fingers delicately through the tangles.

Gabriel watched, entranced, as a cascade of dark, shiny strands fell across her thin shoulders.

"My hair hurts," she explained.

The corners of his mouth turned up in amusement. "I didn't know hair could hurt."

He ran his fingers through her hair, and his expression changed instantly to one of concern. "You could have been seriously injured, standing in the middle of the street."

"I'm lucky I didn't drop my laptop. It has all my research on it."

"It's my fault for surprising you. I'm sure I looked like a ghost, skulking about behind that tree."

"I don't think you've ever skulked a day in your life. And you didn't look like a ghost. You looked like something else."

"Like what?"

Suddenly, Julia felt her skin flame.

He watched her cheeks take on the shade of pink he was most familiar with. He ached to feel her blush beneath his fingers. But he was wary of pushing her.

She gestured vaguely. "Paul suggested I back up my files on a flash drive, so if something happened to my computer I'd still have everything. But I haven't updated it recently."

At the second mention of his former research assistant, Gabriel suppressed a growl and the urge to mutter a favored expletive that involved copulating carnally with celestial creatures.

He turned to her. "I thought you'd expect me to get in touch with you once you graduated."

"What if I did, Gabriel? Graduation came and went with no word from you."

"As I said, I had to wait until my resignation took effect. My contract didn't end until July first."

"I don't want to talk about that right now."

"Why not?"

"Because I can't say the things I need to say while you're sitting on my futon."

"I see," he said slowly.

She shifted her feet, actively resisting the overwhelming urge to throw herself into his arms and tell him that everything was fine. Things between them weren't fine. And she owed it to herself, if not to him, to be honest.

"I've taken up enough of your evening." He sounded defeated.

He stood, glancing at the door, then back at Julia. "I understand if you don't want to talk to me. But I hope you'll give me one more conversation before you say good-bye."

Julia straightened her shoulders. "You didn't say good-bye with a conversation. You said it by fucking me against a door."

He strode toward her quickly.

"*Stop it*. You know my opinion of that word. Never use it in reference to us again."

Here was the old Professor Emerson, simmering beneath Gabriel's chastened exterior. He'd been soft with her, so she found his change in tone jarring. But she'd been exposed to his ill temper before and discovered, at that moment, that it didn't really trouble her. So she ignored him and stood up, prepared to escort him out.

"Don't forget this." She picked up his cell phone.

"Thank you. Julianne, please—"

"How's Paulina?"

Her question hung in the air like an arrow, poised in flight.

"Why do you ask?"

"I'm wondering how often you saw her while you were gone."

Gabriel placed his phone in his pocket. "I saw her once. I asked for her forgiveness and wished her well." His tone had the air of finality.

"Is that all?"

"Why don't you just come out and ask the question, Julianne?" His lips pressed into a thin, angry line. "Why don't you ask me if I slept with her?"

"Did you?" She crossed her arms over her chest.

"Of course not!"

Gabriel's answer was so swift, so vehement, Julia retreated slightly. He was righteously indignant, his fists clenched.

"Maybe I should have been more specific. There are a lot of things a man and woman can do short of sleeping together." She raised her chin defiantly.

Gabriel glared, forcing himself to count to ten. It would not do for him to lose his temper now. Not when he had so far to go.

"I realize that you and I have very different views of my departure, but I assure you, I didn't seek out other women." His expression grew gentle. "I was alone with your pictures and my memories, Julianne. They were poor companions, but the only other companion I wanted was you."

"So there wasn't anyone else?"

"I was faithful the entire time. I swear it, on Grace's memory."

His oath stunned them both, and as their eyes met she saw his sincerity. She closed her eyes. Relief began to well up inside her.

He took her hand, cradling it gently in his. "There are a lot of things I should have told you. I'll tell you now. Come with me."

"I'd rather stay here," she whispered, her voice taking on an eerie sound in the flickering darkness.

"The Julianne I remembered hated the dark." He released her hand. "Paulina is in Minnesota. She reconciled with her family and met someone. We agreed that I would no longer be supporting her, and she wished us well."

"She wished you well," Julia muttered.

"No, she wished *us* well. Don't you see? She assumed we were still together and I didn't tell her otherwise. In my mind, you and I were still together."

This was Gabriel's own arrow, pointed back at her. He hadn't told Paulina that he was single, because in his mind, he wasn't. The realization washed over her.

"There's no one else." His voice was the soul of sincerity.

She averted her eyes. "What were you doing in front of a closed coffee shop in the middle of the night?"

"I was working up the courage to ring your doorbell." Gabriel began twisting the platinum band on his left hand. "I had to convince Rachel to give me your address. She was understandably hesitant."

Julia's eyes dropped to his left hand. "Why are you wearing a wedding ring?"

"Why do you think?" He pulled off the ring and held it out to her.

She recoiled.

"Read the inscription," he urged.

Hesitantly, she took the ring and held it up to one of the candles. *Julianne—my Beloved is mine and I am hers.*

A sick feeling entered her stomach, and she quickly returned it to him. He replaced it on his left hand without a word.

"Why are you wearing a ring with my name on it?"

"You said that you didn't want to talk." His voice was gently reproving. "If you're allowed to ask me questions, can I ask about Paul?"

She blushed and looked away. "He was there to pick up the pieces."

Gabriel closed his eyes. He was perilously close to giving in to his temper and saying something cutting, but that would only succeed in pushing her further away.

He opened his eyes. "Forgive me. This ring has a mate, smaller in size. I purchased them at Tiffany in Toronto on the day I bought the silver frame for Maia's picture.

"I still think of you as my other half. My *bashert*. Despite what happened, there was never any question of me pursuing someone else. I have been faithful to you since you told me who you were, back in October."

Julia suddenly found it very difficult to speak. "Gabriel—these past few months, without a word, then tonight . . ."

He looked at her with compassion, his arms aching to hold her. But she was too far away. "We don't have to have this conversation now.

Just—if you can stand it, please let me see you tomorrow." He gave her a look filled with longing.

She met his gaze briefly. "Okay."

He exhaled loudly. "Good. I'll speak to you tomorrow, then. Rest well."

She nodded, opening the door.

"Julianne?"

He stood in front of her, far too close. She looked up at him.

"Will you—let me kiss your hand?" His voice was wistful and small, like a young boy.

She waited for him to kiss the back of her hand, then without thinking she reached up and pressed her lips to his forehead. Suddenly, his arms were around her back, pulling her flush against him.

Although he had trouble thinking of anything other than Julianne when he was kissing her, Gabriel focused his attention on trying to communicate with lips and mouth that he hadn't betrayed her. That he loved her.

When she kissed him back with equal passion, he moaned.

He made sure to be gentle, if not intense, and as her own movements slowed, he began to nibble slightly at the fullness of her lower lip, before pressing closed mouthed kisses to both cheeks and finally, the end of her nose.

When he opened his eyes he saw a flood of emotions pass over Julia's pretty face.

He ran his fingers through her damp hair, once, twice, and gazed down at her longingly. "I love you."

She was silent as he walked through the door.

❋ ❋

Gabriel's kiss did nothing to strengthen Julia's resolve, but she would not consider it a mistake. She'd been curious about what it would be like to kiss him again and was surprised at how familiar it was. In mere seconds he succeeded in causing her pulse to race and her throat to constrict.

She couldn't deny that he loved her. She'd felt it. Even Gabriel, with his polished manners and charm, couldn't lie with his kiss.

There was something different about him. He seemed softer, somehow, more vulnerable. Yes, there was the occasional show of temper and the old Professor Emerson, but she knew that Gabriel had changed. She just didn't know why.

By the following morning the power had been restored and Julia was able to recharge her phone. She called the manager at Peet's and explained that she was under the weather and would be taking the weekend off. He wasn't happy about it since it was the fourth of July weekend, but there was little he could do.

After a long hot shower, (a shower spent dreaming about Gabriel's lips and old, suppressed memories of the two of them together), Julia felt much, much better. And only a little worse. She sent a quick email to Rachel, explaining that Gabriel had returned and declared his love for her. An hour later, her phone rang. She expected that it would be Rachel. Surprisingly, it was Dante Alighieri.

"How did you sleep?" Gabriel sounded cheerful.

"Well. And you?"

He paused. "Not as well as I used to—tolerably, I suppose."

Julia laughed. This was the Professor Emerson she remembered.

"I want to show you my house," he said.

"What, now?"

"Today, if you're willing." He sounded worried she might refuse.

"Where is it?"

"It's on Foster Place, near Longfellow's house. Ideal for a commute to Harvard. Not so convenient for BU."

Julia was puzzled. "If it's inconvenient for BU, then why did you buy it?"

Gabriel cleared his throat. "I was thinking that—I was *hoping* that . . ." He struggled to find the right words. "It's small but it has a beautiful garden. I'd like to know what you think of it." He cleared his throat again, and she swore she could hear him tugging at his shirt collar. "Of course, I could always move."

She hummed in response, not sure what to say.

"Now that you've had a good night's sleep, will you talk to me a little?"

Julia had never heard Gabriel sound so nervous. "Of course. But it isn't something we can do over the phone."

"I need to pay a visit to campus to see my new office. It won't take long."

"There's no rush."

"Yes, there is." Now Gabriel's voice was heated.

She sighed heavily. "I could come over later."

"Come for dinner. I'll pick you up at six thirty."

"I'll take a cab."

Julia broke the awkward pause that followed with an explanation that she needed to go.

"Fine," said Gabriel stiffly. "If you wish to take a cab, that's your prerogative."

"I'm going to keep an open mind until we talk, and I'd like to ask you to do that too." Her tone was conciliatory.

Gabriel felt as if he were hanging on to his hopes by a very thin thread. He was far from certain that she would take him back. And even if she did, the old specter of jealously taunted him. He didn't know how he would react if she revealed that she'd turned to Paul in her grief and shared his bed.

God damned Angelfucker.

"Of course," Gabriel said, his voice strained.

"I'm surprised you called me. Why didn't you call me while you were away?"

He was silent for a moment. "That's a long story."

"I'm sure it is. I'll see you tonight."

She hung up the phone, wondering what his story would include.

When Julia arrived at Gabriel's new home, she surveyed it with no little puzzlement. It was a two-story frame house with a simple, unadorned front, and it was painted a charcoal gray with darker trim. There was almost no front yard to speak of and a small, paved car pad to the house's right.

In an email that included directions, Gabriel had sent Julia a link to the original real estate listing for the property. The asking price had been over a million dollars. The house had been built prior to World War II. In fact, the entire street had been a neighborhood of Italian immigrants who built the small, two bedroom houses in the nineteen twenties. Now the street was populated with old-moneyed yuppies, Harvard professors, and Gabriel.

As she took in the tidy simplicity of the building, Julia shook her head. *So this is what a million dollars can buy you in Harvard Square.*

As she prepared to knock on the front door, she was surprised to find a note on it in Gabriel's hand.

> Julianne,
> Please meet me in the garden.
> G.

She sighed, and just like that she knew that tonight was going to be very, very difficult. She walked around the side of the house and down the little paved driveway, gasping when she rounded the corner.

There were flowers and greenery, wisps of sea grass and elegantly trimmed boxwood, and in the very center of the garden stood what looked like a Sultan's tent. A fountain sat on the right side of the green space, featuring a marble statue of Venus. Underneath the fountain was a small pond filled with white and red Koi.

Julia walked toward the tent so she could peer inside. And what she saw pained her.

In the tent was a low, square bed, exactly like the futon that graced the terrace of the suite she'd shared with Gabriel in Florence. In the suite where they'd made love for the first time. On the terrace where he fed her chocolates and strawberries and danced with her to Diana Krall under the Tuscan sky. The futon where he made love to her the following morning. Gabriel had tried to reproduce the ambience of that terrace down to the very color scheme of the bedclothes.

The voice of Frank Sinatra seemed to float from somewhere closer to the house, while almost every flat, fireproof surface held a tall, pillar candle. Ornate Moroccan lanterns were suspended from crisscrossed wires overhead.

It was a fairy tale. It was Florence, and their apple orchard, and the wonders of an Arabian night. Unfortunately for Gabriel, the extravagant gesture begged the question: if he was resourceful enough to construct a Moroccan caravan in his garden, why couldn't he have told her he planned to return?

Gabriel saw her standing in his garden, and his heart leapt. He wanted to pull her into his arms and press their lips together. But he could see from the set of her shoulders and the stiffness of her spine that such an act would be unwelcome. So he approached her carefully.

"Good evening, Julianne." A silky voice caressed her ear as Gabriel leaned in from behind her.

She hadn't heard him approach, so she shivered slightly. He rubbed one arm and then the other, up and down, in an act that was supposed to be comforting but in reality caused a deep erotic flush to dance across the surface of her skin.

"I like the music," she said, pulling away from him.

He extended his palm as an invitation. Cautiously, she placed her hand in his. He pressed an unhurried kiss to her knuckles before releasing her.

"You're stunning, as always."

Gabriel's eyes slowly drank in the sight of Julia in her plain black dress, her pale, shapely legs in a pair of black ballet flats, and the way the gentle whisper of wind blew a few strands of hair across her glossy, reddish lips as she turned to face him.

"Thank you." She waited for him to comment on her shoes, for his eyes rested on them a little longer than was polite. She'd worn the flats because they were comfortable and because she wished to assert her independence. She knew he wouldn't like them. Surprisingly, however, he smiled.

Gabriel was a little more casually dressed in a white linen shirt and khaki pants, with a navy linen jacket. His smile was perhaps his most decorative asset.

"The tent is beautiful."

"*Does it please you?*" he whispered.

"You always ask me that."

Gabriel's smile faded slightly, but he resisted the urge to frown. "You used to like the fact that I am a considerate lover."

Their eyes met and Julia looked away. "It's a lovely gesture, but I would rather have had a letter from you or a telephone call three months ago."

It appeared as if he wanted to argue with her, but in an instant his expression changed.

"Where are my manners," he muttered. He offered his elbow, escorting her to a small bistro table that was set up in a corner of the stone patio.

Small white lights shone down on the patio from the branches of an obliging maple. Julia wondered if Gabriel had hired an exterior decorator just for the occasion. He pulled out her chair, and when she was seated, gently eased it closer to the table. She noticed that the centerpiece on the table was filled with orange and red gerbera daisies.

"How did you manage all of this?" Julia unfolded her napkin and placed it in her lap.

"Rebecca is a wonder of New England industriousness."

Julia gave him a questioning look, but her question was soon answered when Gabriel's housekeeper served dinner. Rebecca was tall and plain and wore her salt and pepper hair in a short bob. Her eyes, which were large and dark, sparkled with amusement. Julia divined quickly that Gabriel had taken Rebecca into part of his confidence, at least as far as this evening was concerned.

Despite the elaborate décor and the perfect music, dinner was a simple affair by Gabriel's standards: lobster bisque; a pear, walnut, and Gorgonzola salad; steamed mussels with *frites;* and then finally and most gloriously, a blueberry tart with sour lemon ice cream. Gabriel served her champagne, the same *Veuve Clicquot* he'd served the first time she dined at his apartment. That evening seemed so long ago, even though it was less than a year.

They made small talk during their meal, discussing Rachel's wedding and Scott's girlfriend and her son. Gabriel described the things he liked about his house and those he didn't, promising Julia a tour. Neither of them were in a hurry to begin discussing the events leading up to their separation.

"You aren't drinking?" She noticed that he'd imbibed only Perrier with his meal.

"I quit."

Her eyebrows shot up. "Why?"

"Because I was drinking too much."

"Not when you were with me. You pledged not to get drunk anymore."

"Precisely," he said.

She looked at him carefully, at the way his eyes indicated there was a very unpleasant experience behind his words. "But you enjoyed drinking."

"I have an addictive personality, Julianne. You know this." He smoothly changed the subject to something more pleasant.

When Rebecca served dessert, he and Julia exchanged a look.

"No chocolate cake tonight?"

"Non, mon ange," Gabriel breathed. "Although I'd love nothing more than to feed you again."

Julia felt her cheeks grow red, and she knew it would be a poor decision to go down that road with him before they had their conversation, but as he gazed at her with undisguised passion, she couldn't bring herself to care.

"I'd like that," she said, quietly.

Gabriel smiled as if the sun had just returned to the sky after a protracted absence and quickly shifted his chair so he was seated next to her. Close. *Very* close. So close that she could feel his warm breath on her neck, which goose pimpled in anticipation.

Gabriel picked up Julia's dessert fork and placed some pie and ice cream on it and turned to face her.

As she gazed at him with longing, his breath caught in his throat.

"What is it?" She looked at him in alarm.

"I'd almost forgotten how lovely you are." He traced the curve of her cheekbone with his unencumbered hand and brought the fork to her lips.

She closed her eyes and opened her mouth, and at that moment, Gabriel's heart soared. Yes, it was a little thing—almost inconsequential if one were to consider what tales to tell a confidante. But Julia didn't trust quickly or easily. The ease with which she made herself vulnerable to him made his heart beat quick and his blood pump fast.

She hummed at the mixture of flavors, opening her eyes.

He couldn't help himself. He leaned closer so their mouths were parted by mere inches and whispered, "May I?"

She nodded, and he pressed his lips to hers. She was sweetness and light, gentleness and goodness, and the burning and searing goal of all of his earthly hunts and fascinations. But she didn't belong to him. So he kissed her gently, like he first kissed her in the orchard, with both hands tangling in her long, curled hair. Then he pulled back to watch her face.

A contented sigh escaped her ruby lips as she sat with eyes closed, floating.

"*I love you,*" he said.

Now her eyes were open. Her expression reflected an unnamed emotion, but she didn't say it back.

When dessert was well and truly over, Gabriel suggested they take their espressos to the tent, dismissing Rebecca for the evening. Night had fallen on this little patch of Eden, and like Adam himself, Gabriel led a blushing Eve to his bower.

She kicked off her shoes and curled up on the futon against the cushions, nervously chewing her fingernails while Gabriel lit the candles in the Moroccan lanterns. He took his time, adjusting them so their light flickered over the futon seductively. Then he lit the other candles that were scattered throughout the tent. Finally, he lay on his back next to her, hands behind his head, angled so he could see her face.

"I'd like to talk about what happened," she initiated.

Gabriel gave her his full attention.

"When you showed up outside my apartment I didn't know whether to hit you or kiss you." Her voice was low.

"Didn't you?" he whispered.

"I didn't do either."

"It was never your nature to be vindictive. Or cruel."

She took a deep breath and began. She told him how it broke her heart to have left message after message with him, only to have them unacknowledged. She told him about her surprise at finding his apartment abandoned. She told him about the kindness of his neighbor, and Paul, and Katherine Picton. She spoke of her continued sessions with Nicole.

Julia was too busy fussing with her espresso to notice how unsettled he'd become. When she mentioned how the textbook he'd passed to her had ended up on her shelf unopened, Gabriel cursed Paul.

"You aren't allowed to curse him." Her tone was sharp. "It wasn't his fault that you put your message in a textbook. Why didn't you choose a volume out of your personal library? I might have recognized it."

"I'd been ordered to stay away from you. If I'd put a volume from my library in your mailbox, Jeremy would have noticed it. As it was, I chose a textbook and I placed it in your mailbox after hours." He huffed in frustration. "Didn't the title mean anything to you?"

"What title?"

"The title of the textbook: *Marriage in the Middle Ages: Love, Sex, and the Sacred.*"

"What should it have meant, Gabriel? For all I knew, you'd labeled me as your *Héloise* and left me. I didn't have any reason to think otherwise and you didn't leave me with one."

He leaned forward, eyes flashing. "The textbook was the reason. The title, the photo from the orchard, the image of St. Francis trying to save Guido da Montefeltro . . ." His voice cracked, and he paused, in agony. "Didn't you remember our conversation in Belize? I told you I'd go to Hell to save you. And believe me, I did."

"I didn't know you'd sent me messages. I overlooked the textbook because I didn't know it was from you. Why didn't you call me?"

"I couldn't talk to you," he whispered. "I was told that the Dean would interview you prior to your graduation and that he would ask if you'd heard from me. You're a lovely woman, Julianne, but a terrible liar. I had to send messages in code."

Julia's surprise registered immediately on her face. "You knew about the interview?"

"I knew about a great many things," he said stoically. "But I couldn't tell. That's the point."

"Rachel told me not to despair." She captured his gaze for a moment. "But I needed to hear those words from *you.* Our last night together, you had sex with me, but you wouldn't talk to me. What was I supposed to think?"

Tears overflowed her eyes. But before she could wipe them away with her hand, Gabriel's tugged her from her safe corner into his outstretched arms. He pressed her to his chest and kissed her head, before wrapping his arms around her back.

Somehow, the feel of his arms around her made her cry harder. He squeezed her gently.

"My pride was my downfall. I thought I could court you while you were my student and get away with it. I was wrong."

"I thought you chose your job instead of me." Julia's voice was filled with hurt. "When I discovered you'd moved out of your apartment . . . Why didn't you tell me you were leaving?"

"I couldn't."

"Why not?"

"Forgive me, Julianne. My goal was not to hurt you, I promise. I regret everything that you described." He kissed her forehead once again. "I need to tell you what happened. It's a long story. And only you can tell me how it ends . . ."

Chapter Forty-five

Julia pulled away so she could see his face better, bracing herself for what was to come. Her sudden movement seemed to cause the scent of her hair to waft over to him.

"Your hair is different," he murmured.

"A little longer, perhaps."

"It doesn't smell of vanilla anymore."

"I changed my shampoo." She sounded curt.

"Why?" Gabriel shifted his body to eliminate the gap between them.

"Because it reminded me of you."

"Is that why you aren't wearing your earrings?" he asked, fingering her earlobe.

"Yes."

He paused and gazed at her, his hurt evident.

She looked away.

"I love you, Julianne. No matter what you think of me or what I did, I promise that I was only trying to protect you."

She moved to lie on her side, careful not to touch him.

"*I am your faithful one, Beatrice,*" Gabriel quoted, his eyes brimming with emotion. "Please remember that when I tell you what happened."

He took a deep breath and said a silent prayer before beginning his story.

"When you and I appeared before the hearing officers, my hope was that we would say very little and force them to show what evidence they had. But it became clear that they weren't going to rest until they'd laid charges and punished us.

"I screwed up when I submitted Katherine's grade for your work to the Registrar. Since the administration was worried you'd been awarded the grade because you were sleeping with me, they were going to suspend your grade while they investigated further."

"Could they do that?"

"It's a provision listed in the policies governing academic behavior. As long as the grade was incomplete, you wouldn't be able to graduate."

Julia blinked at Gabriel as understanding washed over her. "No Harvard," she whispered.

"No Harvard this year and probably no Harvard ever, since they would have been suspicious as to why the University of Toronto was suspending your grade. Even if Harvard never learned the reason, they have so many applications. Why should they give you a second thought when they could admit someone with a spotless record?"

Julia sat very still, the weight of his words pressing down on her.

Gabriel scratched at his chin in agitation. "I was afraid the hearing officers were going to ruin your future. But it was my fault. I'm the one who persuaded you that it was safe to get involved with me; I'm the one who invited you to Italy. I should have waited. My selfishness is what led to all this."

He gazed into her eyes and lowered his voice. "I'm sorry I ruined our last night together. I should have talked to you. But all I could think about was how worried I was. I never should have treated you the way I did."

"I felt so alone the next morning."

"It was the worst way for me to deal with my anxiety. But I hope that you believe me when I tell you that it wasn't just a . . ." He paused, stumbling. "A fuck to me. Every time we were together it was always, *always* done with love. I swear."

Julia dropped her gaze to the futon. "For me too. There's never been anyone else, before or since."

He closed his eyes for an instant, relief coursing through him. Even though she'd felt angry and betrayed, she hadn't followed her anger to another man's arms. She hadn't given up on him completely.

"Thank you," he whispered.

He took a deep breath before continuing. "When you confessed to our relationship and I saw the Dean's reaction, I knew we were caught. My lawyer was prepared to stonewall, hoping that the committee would excuse me or hand down a ruling that I could challenge in court. But when you confessed, you provided the corroboration the committee needed."

"We had an agreement to show a united front. An *agreement*, Gabriel." Julia's voice grew heated.

"I acquiesced to you in good faith, Julianne. But I also promised that I wouldn't allow anyone to hurt you or to end your career. That promise takes precedence."

"An agreement is a promise."

Gabriel leaned forward. "They were threatening your future. Did you really expect me to sit there and watch it happen?"

When she didn't respond, he challenged her. "Did you sit there and say nothing when they told you they were pursuing charges against me?"

Her eyes flew to his. "You know I didn't. I pleaded with them. They wouldn't listen."

"Exactly." His blue eyes bored into hers. "From whom do you think I learned about self-sacrifice?"

She shook her head, not bothering to contradict him. "If we broke the rules, then why didn't the Dean try to punish both of us?"

"I'm the professor; I should have known better. And Professor Chakravartty was on your side from the very beginning. She doesn't think professor-student relationships can be consensual. And sadly for us, they found that old email of yours."

"So it was my fault."

Gabriel gently leaned over and brushed the back of his hand against her cheek. "No. I persuaded you that we could break the rules and get away with it. And then, instead of taking responsibility for my actions, I sat there behind my lawyer. You were the only one brave enough to tell the truth. And once you did, I had to confess.

"I agreed to accept their sanctions if they brought the investigation to a speedy conclusion. The hearing officers were only too glad to dispose of the matter without a lawsuit and they agreed, promising leniency."

Julia wore a pained expression.

"Unfortunately, their definition of lenience and mine were two different things. I expected to be censured, not forced to take a leave of absence."

He scrubbed at his face with his hands. "Jeremy was furious at the prospect of losing me, even for a semester. I'd caused a scandal that would embarrass not only him but my colleagues and the other students in the department. Christa was filing a lawsuit against the university too. It was a huge mess, and I was at the root of it."

"We were at the root of it, Gabriel. I knew the rules, and I broke them too."

He gave her a half-smile. "The rules are written in such a way as to excuse the student because the professor is the one with the power."

"The only power you had over me was love."

He kissed her softly. "Thank you."

Gabriel's heart was full, almost to the brim. She hadn't looked back at their time together and viewed him the way the hearing officers did. She hadn't recoiled when he kissed her. In fact, her lips had welcomed him. She gave him hope that by the end of his story, she'd still be at his side.

"When they brought Jeremy in, I begged him to help us. I promised I'd do anything."

"Anything?" Julia asked.

He shifted again. "I had no idea he was going to side with the hearing officers and demand that I cease all contact with you. It was a rash promise made in a fit of desperation."

Julia moved away from him. "What did he say?"

"He persuaded the committee to place me on administrative leave. It was effectively a suspension, but they didn't call it that in order to avoid tainting the department. I was also prohibited from supervising female graduate students for a term of three years."

"I'm so sorry. I had no idea."

He pressed his lips together. "I was told to end things with you immediately and cease all contact. They said if I violated this condition, the agreement would be void and they would re-open the investigation, into both of us." He paused, seemingly struggling for words.

"If they thought I was a victim, why would they threaten to investigate me again?"

Gabriel's blue eyes cooled. "The Dean suspected you were telling the truth—that our relationship was consensual and that I was trying to save your reputation. He wasn't about to let us go off into the sunset together. That's why I sent you the email."

"That email was cruel."

Gabriel's eyebrows knitted together. "I know. But since I was sending it from my university account to your university account, I assumed you'd realize it was all for show. Have I ever spoken to you like that before?"

She gave him a challenging look.

He winced. "I mean, have I spoken to you like that since I realized who you were?"

"Could the university really demand that you stop talking to me?"

Gabriel shrugged. "They did. The threat of Christa's lawsuit was hanging over all of us. Jeremy seemed to think that if I took a leave of absence that he could convince Christa to drop the lawsuit. And he did. But once again, he said that if he found out I was still seeing you, he wouldn't lift a finger to help me."

"That's blackmail."

"That's academia. Christa's lawsuit would have damaged the department, possibly irreparably. Jeremy would have lost the ability to recruit top faculty and students because people would hear that it wasn't a safe place to be. I didn't want to be embroiled in a scandal any more than he did, and I certainly didn't want you hauled into a courtroom as a witness."

Gabriel cleared his throat, clearly struggling. "I agreed. Jeremy and the Dean made it clear that they would interview you at the end of the semester to see if I'd kept my promise. I had no choice."

Julia toyed with the folds of her dress. "Why didn't you tell me? Why didn't you demand a recess so you could explain what was happening? We were a couple, Gabriel. We were supposed to work together."

He swallowed thickly. "What would have happened if I'd taken you aside and explained what I was about to do?"

"I wouldn't have let you go through with it."

"Exactly. I wasn't going to allow you to lose everything because of my failures. I couldn't live with that. I only hoped that you would for-give me—someday."

Julia was stunned.

"You were willing to risk everything to save me, thinking that I might not forgive you?"

"Yes."

Julia felt her eyes grow teary, and she swiped at them blindly. "I wish you could have told me."

"So do I, but I promised Jeremy that I'd stay away. Before he entered the hallway, I tried to speak to you, but John and Soraya kept inter-rupting."

"I know, but—"

He interrupted her. "If I'd told you it was only temporary, they would have realized from your expression. They would have known I had no intention of following through on my promise. I'd given my word."

"But you planned to break it."

"Yes. Yes, I did." He was quiet again for a moment, looking off into the distance.

"That doesn't make sense, Gabriel. You made all kinds of promises to them, but you broke them. You put the textbook in my box, you wrote me a message . . ."

"I planned to do more. I was going to email you, saying that it was only until the end of the semester. Once you'd graduated and I'd re-signed, we would renew our relationship. That is, if you still wanted me."

Gabriel's voice dropped. "I knew would be watched. And that the Dean would interview you to find out if I'd kept my promise. I wor-ried about your ability to lie."

"That's bullshit," said Julia fiercely. "You could have sent me an email and explained that I needed to pretend to be heartbroken. I'm not a great actress, but I can act a little."

"There were other—factors."

She closed her eyes. "When I fell, you looked at me as if you hated me. You looked disgusted."

"Julia, please." He grabbed her hand and pulled her to his chest.

"That look was not meant for you. Any disgust I felt was directed at the hearing and myself. That look was not meant for you, I swear."

Julia shed more than a few tears at that moment, the consequence of shock and anxiety and a measure of relief at having her questions answered. But some of the most important questions remained.

"I hate that I've made you cry again," Gabriel said ruefully, running a hand up and down her back to comfort her.

Julia wiped her eyes. "I need to go home."

"You can stay with me tonight." He glanced down at her cautiously.

She was conflicted. Staying with him could possibly undercut all the things she had yet to say, but running back to her cold, dark apartment seemed cowardly. As always, she knew that once she allowed herself to curl into his side, her body and heart would drag her mind along with them.

"I should go." She sighed in defeat. "But I can't bring myself to leave right now."

"Then stay—in my arms." He kissed her forehead, murmuring his love against her skin.

Slowly, he extricated himself from her embrace and retrieved a couple of blankets, pausing to blow out the candles as he did so. He left the tea lights lit in the Moroccan lamps overhead, admiring the play of light and color against the walls of the tent. The very air shimmered.

They made a nest together in the center of the futon. Gabriel lay on his back with his beloved at his side. He did nothing to stifle the deep sigh of contentment that escaped his lips as he wrapped his arm about her shoulders.

"Gabriel?"

"Yes?" He stroked her hair slowly, reveling in the feel of the silkiness of the strands as they slipped through his fingers. He tried to savor her new, unfamiliar scent but found himself mourning the loss of the old one.

"I—missed you."

"Thank you." He squeezed her tightly as a feeling of cautious relief coursed through him.

"I used to lie awake at night, wishing you were with me."

Gabriel's eyes watered at the sound of her vulnerability and her courage. If he ever had a moment's doubt that he would love and admire her forever, no matter whether she chose him or not, that doubt faded away like a wisp of smoke.

"Me too."

She hummed to herself and within minutes, the two weary, former lovers were sound asleep.

Chapter Forty-six

Julia opened her eyes and saw bright July sunlight streaming in through the open door of the tent. She was curled up under two cashmere blankets that had been lovingly tucked around her. She was alone. Were it not for the fact that she knew that the tent belonged to Gabriel, she would have thought that she'd dreamed the previous evening. Or that she'd woken up to a new dream.

As she got out of bed, she found a note next to her pillow.

> Darling,
> You were sleeping so peacefully that I didn't want to disturb you. I'll ask Rebecca to make waffles for breakfast because I know you like them. Falling asleep in your arms again reminded me that I was only half a person in your absence.
> You make me whole.
> With love,
> Gabriel.

Julia couldn't deny the fact that a variety of emotions came upon her as she read the note, like a symphony of different instruments. Perhaps the most dominant feeling was that of relief.

Gabriel loved her. Gabriel had returned.

But forgiveness and reconciliation were two different things, and she knew that although other forces had been at work to effect their separation, she and Gabriel each bore responsibility for the situation in which they currently found themselves. Julia didn't want to run back into his arms only to escape the pain of their separation; that would be like taking a pill to kill a pain without investigating its root causes.

She found her shoes and slowly walked across the garden, retrieving her purse before entering the back door. Rebecca was already at work in the small kitchen, preparing breakfast.

"Good morning." She greeted Julia with a smile.

"Good morning." Julia motioned toward the staircase that led to the second floor. "I was just going to use the bathroom."

Rebecca wiped her hands on her apron.

"I'm afraid Gabriel is in it."

"Oh."

"Why don't you knock on the door? He might be finished."

The thought of running into Gabriel, damp from the shower, wrapped in a towel, made Julia's skin grow pink.

"Um, I'll wait. May I?" She gestured to the kitchen sink and, with Rebecca's permission, proceeded to wash her hands. When they were dried, she removed a hair elastic from her purse and pulled her hair into a ponytail.

Rebecca invited her to sit down at the small, round kitchen table. "This house isn't very convenient with only one bathroom. I end up having to climb those stairs several times a day. Even my little house has two bathrooms."

Julia was surprised. "I thought that you lived here."

Rebecca laughed as she retrieved a pitcher of freshly squeezed orange juice from the refrigerator. "I live in Norwood. I used to live with my mother, but she passed away a few months ago."

"I'm sorry." Julia gave Rebecca a sympathetic look as she poured orange juice into two wine glasses.

"She had Alzheimer's," said Rebecca simply before returning to her cooking.

Julia watched as she plugged in an electric waffle maker and proceeded to wash and hull a basket of fresh strawberries and whip some cream. Gabriel had planned the breakfast well.

"It's going to be an adjustment to keep house for a professor after looking after my mother. He's a bit particular, but I like that. Did you know that he's lending me books? I've just started reading *Jane Eyre*. I've never read it before. He says that as long as I keep cooking I can keep borrowing books. Finally, I have a chance to further my education *and* use everything I learned from years of watching the Food Network."

"He's lending you books from his personal library?" Julia sounded incredulous.

"Yes. Isn't that nice? I don't know the professor very well, but I'm already fond of him. He reminds me of my son."

Julia sipped her orange juice and began to eat her breakfast, urged as she was not to wait for Gabriel's arrival.

"I don't know why he bought this house when the kitchen is so small and there's only one bathroom." She spoke between bites of a cinnamon flavored waffle.

Rebecca wore a knowing smile. "He wanted to live in Harvard Square, and he liked the garden. He said that it reminded him of his parents' place back home. He plans to renovate the house to make it more comfortable, but he refused to book a single contractor until you gave your approval."

"My approval?" Julia's fork clattered to the floor.

Rebecca efficiently handed her another one. "He might have said something about selling it if you didn't like it. Although given the language I heard coming from upstairs this morning, I think he has decided to begin his renovations *immediately*."

She passed a plate of crispy bacon to Julia. "I don't know if you've noticed this, but the professor can be a little intense."

Julia laughed loudly. "You have no idea."

She was able to enjoy not one but two waffles before the sound of Gabriel and his Italian shoes came thumping down the stairs.

"Good morning," he greeted her, kissing the top of her head.

"Good morning." Acutely aware of Rebecca's presence, Gabriel and Julia made polite small talk for a moment or two before Julia excused herself to visit the bathroom.

With one look at her face and hair in the mirror, she realized that she needed to have a shower. And that's when she noticed a shopping bag placed neatly on the corner of the vanity.

Inside the bag she found bottles of her old brand of vanilla shampoo and shower gel, along with a new lavender-colored poof. Even more surprisingly, she found a pale yellow summer dress with a matching cardigan. It took a moment or two for her to overcome the sudden, almost overwhelming feeling that passed over her. But she swallowed it back and showered and dressed, making herself presentable.

She was grateful to have clean clothes to wear but slightly irritated at Gabriel's presumption. She wondered if she'd find lingerie in her size hanging in his closet. She wondered if, when he moved the contents of his condo, he kept all the clothes and items she'd left behind.

She swept her hair behind her ears. Grace's earrings were hidden in the back of her underwear drawer with a few other precious things, in her apartment. She knew that putting them away, although it seemed necessary when he left, had injured Gabriel deeply.

They'd wounded each other, and both were in need of forgiveness and healing. But Julia couldn't decide what path would be the best one to take in order for her to mend. The obvious choices in life aren't always the correct ones.

When she finally came downstairs, Rebecca was cleaning up the kitchen and Gabriel was in the garden. She found him sitting in a chair under the shade of a large umbrella.

"Are you all right?" she asked, for his eyes were closed.

He opened his eyes and smiled. "I am now. Join me?" He extended his hand, and she took it, settling herself in the chair adjacent to him.

"That color suits you," he said, appraising her yellow dress with unconcealed delight.

"Thank you for going shopping."

"What would you like to do today?"

Julia tugged the hem of her dress to cover her knees. "I think we should finish our conversation."

He nodded, silently renewing his prayer. He didn't want to lose her. And he knew that her reaction to the next part of his story might bring about just that.

"I know you remember our conversation in the hallway, after the hearing. When John was rude to you, I wanted to break off his finger and feed it to him."

"Why?"

"I don't think you comprehend the depth of my feeling for you. It goes beyond wanting to be near you, or to protect you. I want you to be happy, and I want you to be treated with respect."

"You can't break off people's fingers when they're rude to me."

He made a show of stroking his chin thoughtfully. "I suppose not. What can I do? Strike them with the collected works of Shakespeare?"

"In one sturdy volume? Of course."

They shared a laugh before falling silent for a moment.

"I wanted to communicate what had happened behind closed doors, but I was ordered not to talk to you. That's why I spoke in code. Except I stupidly quoted Abelard, forgetting that you and I had different interpretations of his relationship with Héloise. I should have quoted Dante, Shakespeare, Milton, anyone." He shook his head.

"You were so angry. You accused me of fucking you. *Julianne . . .*" Gabriel's voice broke as he pronounced her name. "Did you really think so lowly of me? To think that was how I would choose to say good-bye?"

Julia looked away, avoiding the intensity of his gaze. "What was I supposed to think? You wouldn't talk to me. You left the next morning without leaving a note. And then at the hearing, suddenly it was over."

"I didn't trust myself to speak with words. When I made love to you, I thought you understood what I was trying to say—that we're one. That we've always been one."

"You were talking about our conversation in the hallway after the hearing," she prompted, eager to change the subject. "I don't understand how they could have forced you to leave the city."

"They couldn't, really. Jeremy simply wanted my word that I'd stop seeing you."

She folded her arms in front of her. "Then why did you leave?"

"Jeremy discovered I broke my promise before we exited the building. He demanded I break things off with you and swear on my honor that I would stay away from you. I'd already told him I'd do anything if he helped us. I had no choice."

Julia thought back to her exit interview with the Dean and Professor Martin, just before graduation. "Why did Jeremy think you broke your promise? You wouldn't talk to me or answer my messages. You sent me an email telling me it was over."

"I know. I'm sorry. I'd hoped you'd read between the lines and realize it was just for the administration. I'd sent you another email before that from my Gmail account, saying it was only temporary."

"No, you didn't."

He retrieved his phone. Scrolling through a few screens, he settled on something. Then he fixed distressed and haunted eyes on hers.

"After the hearing, I ducked into the men's room and quickly sent you an email." He gently took her hand. "Here," he said, giving her the phone.

Julia quickly glanced at the screen.

Beatrice, I love you. Never doubt that. Trust me, please. G.

She blinked several times, trying to assimilate what she saw typed in black and white with what she'd experienced. "I don't understand. I didn't receive this."

Gabriel gave her a tortured expression. "I know."

She looked at the screen again and saw that the date and time of the email corresponded with Gabriel's story. But the addressee of the email was not her. In fact, the actual recipient was someone entirely different.

J.H. Martin.

Julia's eyes widened as the magnitude of Gabriel's error suddenly became very, very clear. Instead of sending the email to Julianne H. Mitchell, he'd sent it to Jeremy H. Martin, the Chair of the Department of Italian Studies.

"Oh my God," she breathed.

He plucked the phone from her hand, muttering curses. "Every time I tried to do something for you, it backfired. I tried to save you, and the hearing officers were suspicious. I tried to give you a clue in conversation, and I made you feel like I'd abandoned you. I tried to email you, and I sent the email to the very person who'd forbidden me to contact you. Honestly, Julia, were it not for the fact that I hoped that someday we would be having this conversation, I would have stepped out into rush hour traffic on Bloor Street and ended it."

"Don't say things like that. Don't even *think* it."

Julia's sudden show of fierceness pleased him, but he found himself back-pedaling quickly. "Losing you was a low point for me. But suicide isn't an option I'd entertain again." He gave her a look that seemed to signify much more than he could say at that moment.

"Jeremy was furious. He'd put his career and his department on the line to help me and I'd gone behind his back two minutes later. Now he had proof, in writing, that I was breaking my agreement with the committee. I had no choice but to do whatever he said. If he sent my email to the Dean, the repercussions would have been devastating for both of us."

At that moment, Gabriel and Julia were interrupted by Rebecca, who joined them on the patio, carrying a pitcher of homemade lemonade garnished with a few frozen raspberries that floated delicately in the cloud of yellow. She served their drinks with an encouraging smile and vanished back into the house.

Gabriel drank greedily, enjoying his reprieve.

"So?" prompted Julia, sipping her lemonade.

"Jeremy told me to stay away from you. I had no choice. He held Damocles's sword in his hand."

"He let you go?"

"With a handshake and a promise." Gabriel grimaced as the memory of that dreadful conversation haunted him. "He showed me mercy. Then more than ever I felt obligated to keep my word. I resolved not to contact you directly until you were already assured your place at Harvard."

Julia shook her head stubbornly. "But what about me, Gabriel? You made a lot of promises to me. Didn't you think about keeping them?"

"Of course. Before I left Toronto, I put the textbook in your mailbox. I thought you'd find the passage in Abelard's letter and read what I wrote on the back of the photograph."

"But I didn't realize it was from you. I didn't even look at it until the night you came to see me. That's why I was running outside. I didn't have an internet connection in my apartment and I wanted to email you."

"What would you have said?"

"I don't know. You have to understand that I thought you'd had enough of me. That you'd decided I wasn't worth the trouble." Tears sprang to Julia's dark eyes, and she brushed them aside.

"I'm the only one in this relationship who was never worth the trouble. I knew I'd put myself in a situation in which I was careless with your heart. But it wasn't done to hurt you. It was pride and bad judgment and mistake after mistake." He looked down at his hands and began to turn the wedding ring around his finger.

"Katherine Picton tried to help me. She said she'd see that the university left you alone during my absence and that she would do everything she could to help you graduate on time. She mentioned that an old friend of hers had left the Department of Romance Studies at Boston University in order to take a position at UCLA. She wanted my permission to nominate me as his replacement. I asked her to go ahead.

"I interviewed for the position, and while I waited for their decision, I went to Italy. I had to do something to shake myself out of my depression before I did something I would regret."

Julia's stomach suddenly tightened. "Something you would regret?"

"Not women. The mere idea of being with someone else made me sick. I was more worried about other—vices."

"Before you go any further, I need to tell you something." Her voice was stronger and more determined than the will behind it.

Gabriel began to watch her carefully, wondering what in the world she was about to reveal.

"When I told you that my relationship with Paul didn't go beyond friendship, what I said was true. Technically."

"Technically?" Gabriel's eyebrows flew up and his voice lowered to a growl.

"He wanted more. He told me he loved me. And we—kissed."

Gabriel was silent for a moment or two, and Julia watched as his knuckles whitened.

"Is Paul who you want?"

"He was a friend to me when I needed one. But I never had romantic feelings for him. I think you know this already, but you ruined me for other men when I was seventeen." Her voice trembled.

"But you kissed him."

"Yes, I did." Julia leaned over and with a gentle hand, brushed a lock of hair away from Gabriel's forehead. "But that's all. I had no idea you were coming back to me, but I still turned him down." She withdrew her hand. "Not because I wouldn't have had a good life with him. But because he wasn't you."

"I'm sure that distressed him." Gabriel sounded sarcastic.

"I broke his heart," said Julia, her shoulders hunching. "And I took no pleasure in doing so."

The sight of Julia's obvious discomfort tugged at him, but he couldn't disguise the relief at her admission that he had no rivals in her affection. He squeezed her shoulder before he spoke.

"I was worried that if we had any contact and Paul found out about it, he'd run and tell Jeremy."

"He wouldn't have done that. He was good to me, even after I broke his heart." Julia smoothed imaginary wrinkles out of her yellow dress. "I know you said you were faithful, and I'm not questioning you on that. But did anyone—kiss you?"

"No." He smiled ruefully. "I'd make a good Dominican or Jesuit, don't you think? With my new virtue of celibacy? Although I discovered during our separation that I don't have the disposition to be a Franciscan."

Julia gave him a quizzical look.

"That's a story for another day."

She squeezed his hand in affection and withdrew it, silently willing him to finish his story.

"If I wasn't offered the position at BU, I was going to resign my job in Toronto. All I had to do was keep myself together until after graduation.

"I wanted to feel close to you, to remember a happier time, so I went to Italy. Truthfully, Julianne, those days with you in Florence and Umbria were the happiest days of my life." He averted his eyes. "I even went to Assisi."

"To become a Franciscan?" She smirked.

"Hardly. I visited the Basilica and I thought I saw you."

He looked over at her hesitantly, wondering if she would think that he was disturbed. "Your *doppelgänger* led me to the lower church and down to the crypt, to the tomb of St. Francis.

"At first, I stared at the young woman, wishing she was you. Wishing I hadn't made so many mistakes. I was confronted by my own failures.

My sin. I'd made an idol of you. I'd worshipped you, like a pagan. Then when I lost you, I was in danger of losing everything. I told myself I needed you to save me, that I was nothing without you.

"I began to see how I'd been given chance after chance. Through no goodness of my own, I'd been given grace and love. And I'd thrown it away or treated it cheaply. I didn't deserve the family who adopted me. I didn't deserve Maia, who was the best part of my relationship with Paulina. I didn't deserve to survive the drugs and graduate from Harvard. I didn't deserve *you*."

He paused and brushed at his eyes again, but this time the moisture didn't abate.

"Grace isn't something we deserve, Gabriel," Julia said softly. "It comes from love. And God wraps the world in second chances and sticky little leaves and mercy, even though some people don't want them."

He kissed the back of her hand. "Precisely."

"In the crypt of the Basilica, something happened. I realized you couldn't save me. And I found—peace."

"Sometimes we search for grace until it catches us."

"How are you not an angel?" he breathed. "Whatever happened to me, it made me want to be good. My experience caused me to focus on God, but also to love you more. I've always been attracted to your goodness, Julianne. But I believe I love you more deeply now than before."

She nodded as her eyes suddenly blurred with salt water.

"I should have told you that I loved you sooner. I should have asked you to marry me. I thought I knew what was best for you. I thought that we had all the time in the world."

Julia tried to speak, but her voice caught in her throat.

"Please tell me that it isn't too late, Julianne. Please tell me I haven't lost you forever."

She stared at him for a moment, and put her arms around him. "I love you, Gabriel. I never stopped. We both made mistakes—with our relationship, with the university, with each other. But I hoped that you would come back to me. That you still loved me."

She kissed him on the lips, and Gabriel felt an overflowing of joy mixed with guilt.

He was embarrassed, she could tell. But Julia also knew that his damp eyes were the result of a myriad of things—exhaustion and frustration, and the pain that lingers from a prolonged depression.

"Then you'll stay?" His voice was soft.

She hesitated just long enough for him to feel worried.

"I want more than what we had before," she said.

"More than I can give you?"

"Not necessarily, but I've changed over these past few month, and I see that you have too. The question is, where do we go from here?"

"Then tell me what you want. Tell me and I'll give it to you."

She shook her head. "I want us to figure things out together. And that will take time."

✱✱ ✱✱

Soon it was too warm to sit outside, so Gabriel and Julia returned to the house and settled themselves in the living room. He reclined on the leather sofa, while Julia made herself comfortable in one of the red velvet chairs.

"Should we address the elephant in the room?" she asked.

He nodded, suddenly tense.

"Um, I'll start. I want to get to know you again. I want to be your partner."

"I want you to be a good deal more than that," whispered Gabriel.

Julia shook her head vehemently. "It's too soon. You took away my choices, Gabriel. You have to stop doing that or we aren't going to get very far."

His face fell.

"What is it?" she asked, dreading his answer.

"I don't regret trying to save your career. I wish we could have come to a consensus about it. But when I saw you in danger, I reacted. And what's more, so would you if I were in danger."

Julia felt her anger rise. "So this whole conversation, your apologies, mean nothing?"

"Of course not! I should have talked to you before I did anything. But if you expect me to be the sort of man who watches the woman he loves lose her dreams, then I can't meet your expectations. I'm sorry."

Julia flushed a brilliant red. "So we're right back where we started?"

"I didn't hold it against you when you went out of your way to protect me from Christa, or from the committee. I didn't hold your harassment email against you, even though we both agree it was a mistake. Can't you give me the same consideration? Can't you give me grace, Julianne? Your grace?"

Despite his pleading tone, Julia wasn't listening. At that moment, all she heard was Gabriel discounting her objections. Again.

She shook her head and walked to the door.

Here was the fork in the road, where the paths diverged. She could walk through the door, and everything with Gabriel would be over. There would be no third chance. Or she could stay, knowing that he refused to see his damned heroics in front of the committee as anything problematic.

She hesitated.

"Let me love you, Julianne. The way that you should be loved."

He stood behind her, his lips vibrating against her ear. She could feel the warmth of his body radiating through her clothes and against her back.

"I am your faithful one, Beatrice. Of course I want to protect you. Nothing will change that."

"I would rather have had you than Harvard."

"Now you can have both."

She turned around. "At what cost? Don't tell me that our situation didn't damage us, possibly irreparably."

He brushed her hair over one shoulder and pressed his lips to the bare side of her neck. "Forgive me. I promise I won't rob you of your dignity or our partnership. But I won't stand by and watch you get hurt when I can prevent it. Don't make me revert to being a selfish bastard."

In stubborn annoyance, Julia took a step toward the door, but Gabriel caught her arm.

"In a perfect world, there would always be communication and consultation between partners. But we don't live in that world. There are emergencies and dangerous, vindictive people. Is my desire to keep you from harm so great a sin that you would leave me over it?"

When she remained silent, he continued. "I will do my utmost to make decisions *with* you and not *for* you. But I make no apologies for wanting you to be safe and happy. I won't be beholden to the rule that I have to consult you before I act in cases of emergency.

"You want me to treat you like an equal. I want the same treatment. That means that you need to trust me to make the best decision I can, given the information I have, without being omniscient. Or perfect."

"I'd rather have you alive and carrying your shield than have you dead and covered by it." She sounded obstinate.

Gabriel laughed. "I think the battle of Thermopylae is behind us, darling. But I share your sentiment and would ask the same of you. *My little warrior.*"

He kissed her neck again. "Take my ring." He quickly slipped the wedding ring from his left hand and held it over her right shoulder. "I wore this to signify the fact that my heart, my life was yours."

She hesitantly took the ring from his hand and slipped it on one of her thumbs.

"I'll sell this damn house. I only bought it to be close to you. But I can find an apartment until we choose a home together."

"You just moved in. And I know you love the garden." Julia sighed.

"Then tell me what you want. We can take our time without making promises about the future. But please forgive me. Teach me, and I promise I will be your most willing student."

When she was silent and unmoving for several minutes, Gabriel took her hand, leading her from the living room upstairs to his bedroom.

"What are you doing?" she asked as they approached the door.

"I need to hold you in my arms, and I think that you need to be held. That damn sofa is too narrow for both of us. Please." He led her to the bed and positioned himself on his back with open arms, inviting her to wrap herself around him.

She hesitated. "What about Rebecca?"

"She won't disturb us."

Julia was unwilling to return to his bed simply because he invited her, and so she looked around for something, anything, to distract him.

"What are these?" She pointed at what looked like two groupings of large picture frames that were leaning against one of the walls and covered by a sheet.

"Look at them."

Julia crouched down on the hardwood floor and removed the sheet. There were about ten large photographs, stacked in two groups of five, all black and white. All featured Julia. Some included Gabriel.

She hadn't seen most of them before as they had been framed after their separation. There were photographs from Belize, from Italy, and posed photographs that had served as part of her Christmas present to Gabriel. All were startlingly beautiful and amative.

"It was difficult for me to look at them when I thought I'd lost you. But as you can see, I kept them."

Gabriel watched as Julia looked through the photographs once more before studying his favorite, a picture of her lying on her stomach on a bed in Belize.

"What happened to the old ones? The ones you had before you met me?"

"Long gone. I didn't need or want them anymore."

She placed the sheet over the pictures before walking to the bed. She looked conflicted.

Gabriel reached out his hand. "Relax. I just want to hold you."

She allowed herself to be pulled into his arms so she could nestle against his chest.

"That's better," he murmured, kissing her forehead. "I want to earn your trust and your respect. I want to be your husband."

Julia was quiet for a moment, holding her breath, as his words sunk into her consciousness. "I want us to take things slowly. No more talk of marriage."

"Fortunately, I can wait." He kissed her once again.

This time, the kiss escalated. Hands roamed to find purchase on muscles and curves, mouths connected determinedly, punctuated by sighs and almost breathless moans, hearts began to beat faster. It was a kiss to mark a reunion, to pledge the continuation of fidelity and love. Gabriel kissed her to show her that he loved her, that he was sorry.

Julia kissed him back to tell him that she could never give her heart to anyone else. That she was hopeful their shared imperfections, once acknowledged and explored, could be ameliorated in order to provide both of them with a healthy, happy life.

She pulled away first. She could hear his quickened breathing, and it cheered her that they still had this spark between them.

"I don't expect our relationship to be perfect. But there are some things we need to work out and whether that takes a therapist or not, I know it's going to take time."

He met her gaze. "I agree. I want to be able to court you as I was unable to back in Toronto. I want to hold your hand as we walk down the street. I'd like to take you to the symphony and kiss you on your front steps."

Julia laughed. "We were lovers, Gabriel. You have photographs of the two of us in bed together, just over there. Would you really be satisfied with simply courting me?"

He wove their fingers together. "I want the chance to make things up to you—to treat you the way I should have treated you all along."

"You were always very generous in bed," she deflected.

"But selfish in other ways. Which is why I won't make love to you until I regain your trust."

Chapter Forty-seven

"*C*ome again?"

At least, that's what Julia wanted to say, but given the context she held her tongue. Somehow, her remark didn't quite seem consonant with his declaration.

"I'm worried that if we have sex, it will short-circuit the kind of changes we need to make."

"So you want to wait?"

He gave her a scorching look. "No, Julianne, I don't *want* to wait. I want to make love to you now and for the rest of the week. I know we *should* wait."

Her eyes widened as she realized that he was serious.

He kissed her tenderly. "If we're going to be partners, there has to be trust. If you don't trust me with your mind, how can you trust me with your body?"

"I think you said that once before."

"We've come full circle." He cleared his throat. "And so there isn't a misunderstanding, when I say trust, I mean completely. I'm hopeful that in time your anger will disappear and you'll forgive me. I'm hopeful that we'll be able to work out our need to protect one another, without causing another crisis." He looked over at her expectantly.

"I should have waited until you were no longer my student before we became involved. I told myself that because we weren't sleeping together, we weren't breaking any rules. But I was wrong. And you're the one who had to pay the price." He searched her eyes. "You don't believe me."

"Oh, no. I believe you. But the Professor Emerson I knew and loved wasn't exactly a proponent of abstinence."

He frowned. "Perhaps you're forgetting how our relationship began. We abstained the night we met and a good many nights afterward."

She kissed his mouth repentantly. "Of course. I'm sorry."

He rolled onto his side, looking into her eyes. "I'm absolutely aching to feel you in my arms, to be joined with you, body and soul. But when I'm inside you, I want you to know that I will never leave you. That you are mine and I am yours, forever." His voice grew rough. "That we're married."

"Come again?"

"I want to marry you. When I make love to you again, I want to be your husband."

When she gaped at him, he continued quickly. "Richard showed me the kind of man I want to become—a man who spends the rest of his life loving one woman. I want to make vows to you before God and stand in front of our families and make promises to you."

"Gabriel, I can't even contemplate marrying you. I need to learn how to be with you again. And frankly, I'm still angry."

"I understand that, and my intention is not to rush you. Do you remember the first time we made love?"

She felt her cheeks flame. "Yes."

"What do you remember?"

She paused, a faraway look in her eyes. "You were very intense, but kind. You planned everything, even down to that ridiculous cranberry juice.

"I remember that you were arched over me, looking into my eyes while you moved, and you said that you loved me. I'll never forget those moments for as long as I live." She hid her face against his soap-scented neck.

"Are you shy now?" he asked, tracing the symmetry of her jaw with a single finger.

"A little."

"Why? You've seen me naked. I've worshipped every beautiful inch of you."

"I miss the connection we had. I haven't felt whole without it."

"I haven't either. But do you think you could make love to me when you don't trust me? You forget, my love, that I know you. You are not the type of woman to place your body where your heart will not go.

"Do you remember our last time together? You told me that you felt like I'd fucked you. The next time I have you naked in my bed, I want you to know without doubt that our union is born of love and not lust."

"That goal can be realized without getting married," she huffed.

"Perhaps. But if you don't think you can ever trust me enough to marry me, maybe you should let me go."

Julia's eyes widened. "Is that an ultimatum?"

"No. But I want to prove myself to you, and you need time to heal." He examined her expression carefully. "I need something permanent."

She gaped at him. "You *want* something permanent or you *need* something permanent?"

He shifted his weight on the bed. "Both. I want you to be my wife, but I also want to be the kind of man I should have been before."

"Gabriel, you are always trying to win me. When are you going to stop?"

"Never."

She threw up her hands in frustration. "Withholding sex so I'll marry you is manipulative."

Gabriel's expression brightened considerably. "I'm not *withholding* sex. If you were declaring that you weren't ready to sleep with me and I tried to pressure you, I'd be a manipulative jackass. Shouldn't I be allowed to wait to have sex until our relationship is repaired, and to have that choice respected? Or does 'no means no' only apply to women?"

"I wouldn't pressure you if you had an objection to having sex," Julia sputtered. "You were more than patient with me when I wasn't ready to sleep with you. But what about make-up sex? Isn't that customary?"

He brought his face very close to hers. "Make-up sex?" The heat of his gaze almost scorched her skin. "Is that what you want?" his voice rasped.

Welcome back, Professor Emerson.

"Um—yes?"

He took a single finger and traced her trembling lower lip. "*Tell me,*" he prompted.

She blinked a few times, if only to break the magnetic pull his dark blue eyes had on her. He'd rendered her speechless.

"I want nothing more than to spend days and nights devoted to your pleasure, exploring your body, worshipping you. And I will. On our honeymoon you will find me the most attentive, inventive lover. All my arts will be at your service, and I will endeavor to undo all wrongs when I take you to my bed, as my wife."

Julia placed her head just over the place where his tattoo lay hidden underneath his crisp white shirt. "How can you be so—cold?"

Gabriel rolled her so she was wholly in his arms and on top of his chest, their upper bodies pressed together.

He kissed her gently at first, soft skin gliding over softer skin before he pulled her lower lip between his, drawing on it slightly. Then as his embrace became more heated, his hand clasped around her neck, stroking up and down until he felt her relax.

The barest tip of his tongue moved forward to tease her upper lip, the act of a gentleman who was unsure how he would be received. He needn't have worried. Julia welcomed him, and he began to explore her mouth with purpose, catching her almost unawares before pulling back without warning.

"Does that seem cold to you?" His warm breath blew across her cheek, a hungry look in his eyes. "Does that feel as if I don't want you?"

She would have shaken her head if she could have found it.

Gabriel moved his lips against her jaw, her chin, and painstakingly slowly down the left side of her neck until he was kissing the hollow at the base of her throat.

"And this? Does this seem cold to you?" His mouth moved against the surface of her skin.

"N-No." She shivered.

He traced his nose up to her ear where he began to nibble, in between whispered adorations.

"How about this?" His right hand slowly descended her side, tracing each rib as if it were precious or perhaps as if he were searching for the primordial one Adam had lost. He shifted her slightly so her thigh slid over his hip, coming into contact with the undeniable evidence of his ardor.

"Can you deny this?"

"No."

Gabriel gazed at her heatedly. "Now that we're clear on that point, I'm interested to hear your response."

Julia found it difficult to reason clasped to his body the way she was. She began to squirm, and he squeezed her more tightly.

"There was no one else. My arms were full even when I was alone. But if you were to tell me you'd fallen in love with someone else and that you were happy, I'd let you go. Even though it would break me." He grimaced and dropped his voice to a whisper. "I'll love you forever, Julianne, whether you love me or not. That's my Heaven. And my Hell."

The room echoed with silence for several minutes, and Julia placed a shaking hand over her mouth. Slow, steady tears poured down her face.

"What is it?" He tugged at her a couple of times before he was able to coax her to cry against his chest. "I didn't mean to hurt you." His voice was desperate, as he quickly rubbed his hand up and down her arm.

It took a few minutes for Julia to be able to compose herself enough to speak. "*You love me.*"

Gabriel's face immediately contorted in confusion. "Is that a question?"

When she didn't respond to him, he began to panic. "You didn't believe that I loved you? But I told you that I loved you over and over again. I tried to show you with my actions, with my words, with my body. Did you not believe me?"

She shook her head from side to side, as if indicating that he didn't understand.

"Did you ever believe me? When we were in Italy? When we were in Belize?" He tugged painfully at his hair. "My God, Julia, did you make me your first thinking that I merely *liked* you?"

"No."

"Then why do you only believe that I love you now?"

"You'd let me go so I could be happy, even if it was with someone else."

Two tears streamed down her cheek, and he caught them with his fingers. "That's what happens when you love someone. You want them to be happy."

She wiped her eyes with the back of her hand, and Gabriel watched a teardrop slide over the wedding ring she was wearing on her thumb.

"When I found the illustration of St. Francis and Guido de Montefeltro, I didn't understand why you put it there. But it's clear to me now. You were worried the university was going to ruin my life. Rather than let it happen, you took my place. You loved me enough to let me go, even though it would break your heart."

"Julia, I . . ." Gabriel's protestation was cut short by the warmth of her lips melting against his. It was chaste and sorrowful, erotic and joyous.

She had never felt herself worthy of *agape* before. It wasn't a goal she aspired to or a grail that she sought. When Gabriel first told her that he loved her, she believed him. But the magnitude and depth of his love was not readily apparent. It had only become clear to her at this moment, and with that revelation came a tremendous sense of awe.

Perhaps Gabriel's love had always been sacrificial. Perhaps it had grown over time, just like the old apple tree that fed them on that night so long ago, and she just hadn't noticed how much it had grown.

At that moment, the genesis of his sacrificial love didn't matter. Having been confronted with what she could only describe as something very deep, she knew that she could never doubt his love now. Gabriel loved her as he knew her, fully, completely, and without question.

He pulled away, pressing his palm to her face. "I'm not a noble man. But the love I have for you can't be turned off. When I came to you at your apartment, my intention was to tell you that I loved you and to see that you were all right. And if you sent me away . . ." He took a deep breath. "I'd go."

"I'm not going to send you away," she whispered. "And I'll do my best to help you any way I can."

"Thank you."

She moved so he was cradling her against his chest.

"I'm sorry I left." He pressed their lips together.

Chapter Forty-eight

In the days and weeks that followed, Julia and Gabriel saw each other as much as they could, but between his preparation for the fall semester and her extended shifts at Peet's, most of their contact was mediated via telephone and email.

Julia continued her counseling sessions with Dr. Walters, which took on a new dimension upon Gabriel's return. Gabriel and Julia began couple's counseling, as well, on a weekly basis, which rapidly morphed into (unofficial) pre-marital preparations.

By the time Julia moved into one of the graduate student residences in August, she and Gabriel had managed to address several of their previous communication problems. But their collective obstinance remained. Gabriel wouldn't sleep with her until they were married, and Julia wished to move their physical relationship forward, incrementally. Gabriel was loath to share a bed with her except on occasion and then only reluctantly, with the grim visage of a martyr.

On one such evening, Julia lay awake in his arms long after he'd fallen asleep. His body was warm and his words had been sweet, but she felt rejected. The passionate Professor hadn't needed much persuasion to reconnect with Paulina when she sought him out. But he wouldn't love Julia with his body, even though he pledged his eternal devotion.

As Gabriel's chest rose and fell beneath her cheek, she contemplated the path her life had taken. She wondered if Beatrice had spent some of her evenings earnestly desiring Dante's presence, yet having to settle for the fact that he would only worship her from afar.

"Julia."

She started at the sound of her name. He muttered something and tightened his grip on her, pulling her closer.

A lone tear escaped her eye.

She knew he loved her. But the knowledge was sharp and sweet. He was trying to let go of the past with Paulina and the other women, and she was paying the price. But perhaps it was no more than the price he'd paid for the shame she'd carried because of Simon.

He mumbled again and this time she whispered in his ear. "I'm here."

She pressed her lips to his tattoo and closed her eyes.

Chapter Forty-nine

Despite the pain of their continued physical separation, Julia recognized that Gabriel was constantly discovering new and ingenious ways to demonstrate his love. Though she found their new situation difficult, she continued to have faith in him.

He refused to even entertain the notion of spending the night inside her small dorm room, but he'd drop in on occasion with flowers or food, and they would picnic on the floor. He took her to the movies (even deigning to see a non-subtitled, domestically produced romantic comedy), and kissed her goodnight on the front steps of her building.

On more than one occasion, he spent a Friday or Saturday evening in the library with her, writing his new book while she prepared for Professor Marinelli's seminar. Julia was being wooed in word and deed, and she liked it. But she was also unsatisfied, craving the closeness that could only be had when making love.

Soon it was August twenty-first and they were flying to Philadelphia to help with the preparations for Rachel and Aaron's wedding. As they walked into the lobby of the Four Seasons hotel, Julia was stunned to find her father sitting in a wing chair, reading the *Philadelphia Inquirer*.

"My dad is here," she hissed, hoping to give Gabriel enough of a head start so he could make it to the elevators before Tom took out one of his hunting rifles and shot him.

"I know. I called him."

She turned to Gabriel in wide-eyed disbelief. "Why would you do that? He wants to kill you."

The Professor pulled himself up to his full height. "I want to marry you. That means that I need to make amends with your father. I want to be able to be in the same room without him attempting to shoot me. Or castrate me."

"This is not a good time to ask him about marrying me," Julia whispered. "If you're lucky, he'll forego castration in order to remove your legs—with his Swiss Army knife."

"I'm not going to ask for his permission to marry you; that decision rests with you. Would you really want to marry a man your father despises?"

Julia began to wring her hands in agitation.

He leaned over to speak in her ear. "Let me do some damage control so it isn't beyond the realm of possibility for him to accept our relationship. You might want him to walk you down the aisle someday."

No sooner had the words left Gabriel's lips then Tom saw the couple standing together. He smiled at his little girl widely, then glanced at Gabriel and scowled. As he stood to his feet, he brushed his jacket back so his hands could rest on his hips. He looked menacing.

O gods of women whose fathers wish to castrate their boyfriend in the lobby of the Four Seasons, please don't let him be carrying anything sharp.

Gabriel boldly leaned over to press his lips to her forehead while staring Tom straight in the eye. Tom fixed him with a murderous expression.

"Dad, hi." Julia walked over and hugged him.

"Hi, Jules." He hugged her back before pulling her behind him protectively. *"Emerson."*

Undeterred by Tom's unfriendly tone, Gabriel stuck his hand out. Tom simply stared at it as if it, like its owner, was felonious.

"I think we should find a quiet corner in the bar. I don't want an audience for what I have to say to you. Jules, do you need help carrying your luggage?"

"No, the porter has it. I'm, um, going to my room. Gabriel, I'll let you check into your room yourself, okay?"

He nodded, noting that Tom's scowl relaxed slightly at the news that his daughter was not currently cohabitating with the Devil.

"Just for the record, I love both of you. So I'd really like it if you didn't injure one another." Julia looked warily between the two men, and when both failed to answer, she shook her head and walked to the front desk. Her first order of business was to find out how well stocked the minibar was.

Later that evening, after a somewhat tense but not unpleasant dinner with her father, Julia availed herself of the gift basket of lavender bath products Gabriel had sent to her room, complete with virginal lavender *poof*. She laughed when she thought of the first time he'd *poofed* her.

She sobered when she realized that he'd purchased lavender items rather than vanilla, despite the fact that he preferred vanilla on her to any other scent. Perhaps this was his way of keeping her at arm's length. Whatever his reason, she'd respect his wishes and hope that he'd change his mind. Soon.

She was soaking in the large, pedestal bathtub when her cell phone rang. Luckily, the accursed device was well within reach.

"What are you doing?" Gabriel's smooth voice filled her ears.

"Just relaxing. Thank you for the gift basket, by the way. How are you?"

"I can't say my conversation with your father was enjoyable, but it was necessary. I gave him the chance to curse me and say that I'm a no-good cokehead who doesn't deserve you. Then I did my best to explain what happened. By the end of our conversation, he begrudgingly bought me a beer."

"You're kidding."

"I'm not."

"I can't imagine Tom paying ten dollars for a Chimay Première."

Gabriel chuckled. "It was Budweiser, actually. And not the original Budweiser Budvar from the Czech Republic. He ordered for me."

"I guess you must love me, if you're willing to give up your pretentious European imports for *appalling bath water*." Julia gave the large bathtub a baleful look. She would rather have been bathing with Gabriel than without him.

"Drinking a domestic beer is the least I could do. I don't think your father will forgive me for hurting you, but hopefully things will improve. I told him that I want to marry you. Did he mention that over dinner?"

She hesitated. "He told me that I was his little girl and that he wanted to protect me. Then he said some things about you that weren't very complimentary.

"But he admitted I'm an adult and that I need to live my own life. He said it was clear to him that you'd changed—even since he'd seen you last. I think you surprised him. And he isn't used to being surprised."

"I'm sorry." Gabriel's voice sounded pained.

"Sorry for what?"

"For not being the kind of man you could bring home to your father."

"Listen, my dad thought the sun shone out of Simon's ass. He isn't exactly the best judge of character. And he doesn't know you as I know you."

"But he's your father."

"I'll handle him."

Gabriel was quiet for a moment as he contemplated her response. "My conversation with Tom was a good warm-up for dinner with my family."

"Oh, no. How did that go?"

He paused. "Talking to Scott on the telephone is one thing, but having dinner with him is something else."

"He's protective of me. I'll talk to him."

"Dad asked me to offer a toast to Mom at the wedding reception."

"Oh, darling. That's going to be difficult. Are you sure you want to do that?"

There was silence on the other end of the line for a moment.

"I have some things I need to say. Things almost thirty years in the making. Now's my chance."

"So you've kissed and made up with everyone?"

"Basically. Dad and I made our peace on the telephone weeks ago."

"Did you meet Tammy's little boy?"

Gabriel snorted into the phone. "He soiled me as soon as I picked him up. Perhaps Scott coached him to make his feelings about me known."

"Quinn peed on you?"

"No, he spilled milk all over my new Armani suit."

Julia dissolved into peals of laughter at the thought of the very elegant, very particular professor being soiled by his brother's girl-friend's son.

"Is it wrong that I didn't care that much? I mean about the suit."

Julia stopped laughing abruptly. "You didn't care? What did you do with it?"

"The concierge sent it to be dry-cleaned. I've been assured that milk will come out of wool crepe, but I'm not holding my breath. Suits can be replaced, people can't."

"You surprise me, Professor."

"How so?"

"You're sweet."

"I try to be sweet with you," he whispered.

"That's true. But I've never seen you around children."

"No," he said quickly. "You'd make beautiful babies, Julianne. Little girls and boys with big brown eyes and pink cheeks."

Julia's sharp intake of breath whistled in Gabriel's ear.

His voice almost caught in his throat. "Is it premature to have this conversation?"

She didn't answer.

"Julianne?"

"My hesitation about marriage isn't over having children. It comes from what happened between us and being a child of divorced parents. They loved each other once, I think, and ended up hating each other."

"My parents were married happily for years."

"That's true. If I could have a marriage like theirs—"

"We *can* have a marriage like theirs," Gabriel corrected her. "That's what I want. And I want it with you."

He tried to communicate with his tone how much he desired a marriage like the one Richard and Grace enjoyed. How he was trying desperately to become the kind of man who could give Julia that kind of marriage.

She exhaled slowly. "If you'd asked me to marry you before, I would have said yes. But I can't right now. There's so much we need to work through, and I'm already stressed out about grad school."

"I don't mean to stress you out." His voice was soft but slightly strained.

"I thought you made your decision about having children."

"There's always adoption." He sounded defensive.

She was quiet for a moment.

"The thought of having a little blue eyed baby with you makes me happy."

"Really?"

"Really. Seeing what Grace and Richard did with you, I'd be interested in adopting someday. Just not while I'm a student."

"The adoption would have to be private. I doubt a respectable agency would place a child with a drug addict."

"Do you really want children?"

"With you? Absolutely. If we were married, I'd consider having my vasectomy reversed. It was done many years ago so I don't know how successful a reversal might be. But once we're married I'd like to try—with your blessing."

"I think it's premature to have that conversation." The arm she was leaning on accidentally slipped off the side of the bathtub, splashing into the water.

Scheisse, she thought, too worn out to call on a god to come to her rescue.

"Are you taking a bath?"

"Yes."

She took comfort in the fact that he groaned into her ear. It was painful that he could resist her, day after day, no matter what.

He sighed. "Well, I'm across the hall feeling lonely and sad, in case you need anything."

"I'm lonely too, Gabriel. Can't we do something about that?"

He hesitated, and Julia felt hopeful.

Gabriel groaned again in frustration. "I'm sorry, I need to go. I love you."

"Good night."

Julia shook her head somewhat resignedly as she ended the call.

❀❀

Despite the absence of her mother, Rachel almost had a fairy-tale wedding. She and Aaron were married in a beautiful garden in Philadelphia, and although Aaron had initially rejected the idea of having fifty doves released at the moment the priest pronounced them husband and wife, Rachel wore him down.

(At least none of his relatives decided to practice their target shooting.)

As maid of honor and groomsman, Julia and Gabriel found themselves standing near the bride and groom, flanked by Scott. Julia spent much of the ceremony peeking over at Gabriel, and he stared at her unashamedly.

After the photographs were taken and the wedding dinner and toasts were complete, Rachel and Aaron enjoyed the first dance. They melted into one another's arms before their parents were invited to join them on the dance floor.

There was a moment of nervousness amongst the guests when Richard stood, alone, before walking over to Julia and asking if she would honor him by being his partner. She was stunned by his request, as she had assumed that he would choose an aging aunt or friend, but she accepted quickly. Ever the consummate gentleman, Richard held Julia firmly but respectfully as he moved her across the dance floor.

"Your father seems to be enjoying himself." He nodded at Tom, who was standing with a drink in his hand and engaged in an animated conversation with one of the female professors from Susquehanna University.

"Thank you for inviting him," she said shyly as they danced to the strains of Etta James's "At Last."

"He's an old friend and a good friend. Grace and I owe him a great deal from when we were having trouble with Gabriel."

Julia nodded and tried to concentrate on her feet, lest she stumble. "Gabriel's toast to Grace was very moving."

Richard smiled. "He's never called us *Mom* and *Dad* before. I'm sure that Grace is watching and that she's very, very happy. I know that part of her happiness is seeing the transformation in our son. You brought that about, Julia. Thank you."

She smiled. "I can't take credit for that. Some things are beyond all of us."

"I don't disagree. But sometimes relationships can be conduits of grace, and I know you've been one for my son. Thank you.

"It took a long time for Gabriel to forgive himself for what happened to Maia and for not being with Grace when she died. He's a very different man than he was a year ago. I hope that I'll be able to dance with you at another wedding in the near future. One in which you and my son take center stage."

An earnest expression came over her face. "We're taking things one day at a time, but I love him."

"Don't wait too long. Life takes unexpected turns, and we don't always have the time we think we have." As the song ended, he kissed her hand and escorted her back to Gabriel.

Julia wiped away a tear as she sat down. Instantly, Gabriel's lips were at her ear. "Is my father making you cry?"

"No. He's just reminding me of what's important." She wound their hands together and brought their connection to her mouth so she could kiss his knuckles. "I love you."

"And I love you, my sweet, sweet girl." He leaned over to kiss her, and for a moment they forgot where they were as she reached up to wind her arm around his neck and pull him closer.

As their lips met and their breath commingled, the noise of the room slipped away. Gabriel pulled Julia so she was leaning across his lap, clasping her to his heart as he kissed her passionately. When they came apart, they were both breathing heavily.

"I had no idea weddings brought out such reactions." He smirked. "Or I would have taken you to one sooner."

After dancing several slow dances with Gabriel, Julia took a turn with Scott and with Aaron, and finally, with her father. It was clear that Tom and Julia had a lot to say to one another, and their expressions weren't always happy ones. But by the end of the dance they seemed to have come to some sort of understanding, and Gabriel felt marginally relieved when she returned to him, wearing a smile.

Near the end of the evening, Aaron requested Marc Cohn's "True Companion" and dedicated it to Rachel. Immediately, a throng of married couples scurried toward the dance floor. Tammy surprised everyone by bringing little Quinn over to Julia and asking her to hold him while she danced with Scott.

Julia was afraid that Quinn wouldn't like her.

"He looks good on you," Gabriel whispered as Quinn fell asleep snuggled into her neck.

"I'm worried he'll wake up."

"He won't." Gabriel reached over to lightly stroke the fine hair that decorated the boy's head, smiling widely as he seemed to offer a contented sigh.

"Why do you want to get married and have children all of a sudden?" Julia blurted.

He shrugged uncomfortably. "Things happened while we were separated. I realized what was important—what I wanted for a happy life. And I went to an orphanage."

"An orphanage? Why?"

"I volunteered with the Franciscans in Florence and they used to bring candy and toys to the children at the orphanage. I went along."

Julia's jaw dropped. "You didn't tell me about that."

"It wasn't a secret. I planned to stay in Assisi indefinitely, but I met an American family who were going to run a medical clinic for the poor in Florence. I decided to join them."

"Did you like it?"

"I wasn't especially good at it. But I found my niche, eventually, telling stories about Dante in Italian."

Julia grinned. "That's a good job for a Dante specialist. What about the orphanage?"

"The children were well looked after, but it was a sad place. They had babies there, some of whom had AIDS or fetal alcohol syndrome. Then there were older children who would never be adopted. Most adoptive parents want younger kids."

Julia placed her hand on his arm. "I'm sorry."

Gabriel turned and gently touched the little boy's head. "When Grace found me, I was at an age that would have been considered unadoptable. She wanted me anyway. I've been blessed."

Julia heard his sudden vulnerability and was struck by how much he'd changed. She couldn't have imagined the old Professor Emerson talking about his blessings, or stroking a little boy's head. Especially if the boy had ruined his new Armani suit.

Just before the last dance, Gabriel walked over to the DJ and spoke to him in hushed tones. Then, with a wide smile, he returned to Julia and extended his hand.

They walked slowly onto the dance floor just as "Return to Me" filled the air.

"I'm surprised you didn't choose 'Besame Mucho,'" she said.

Gabriel gazed into her eyes intensely. "I thought that we needed a new song. A new song for a new chapter."

"I liked the old one."

"We don't have to forget the past," he whispered. "But we can make the future better."

She gave him a half-smile and changed the subject. "I remember the first time we danced."

"I was an ass that evening. When I think of how I behaved . . ." His tone was remorseful. "I had a strong reaction to you but didn't know how to act."

"You know how to act around me now." She touched his face and pressed their lips together before tentatively fingering his black silk bow tie. "I remember admiring your ties when I was just your student. You always dressed impeccably."

Gabriel caught her hand in his and pressed his open mouth to her palm. "Julianne, you were never *just* my student. You're my soul mate. My *bashert*."

He pulled her to his chest, and she hummed against his tuxedo. And when Dean Martin switched to Italian, it was Gabriel's voice that sang in her ear.

❀ ❀

As Gabriel stood outside of Julia's hotel room in the wee hours of the morning, he looked at her appraisingly. Her long, curled hair, her beautiful skin and flushed cheeks, her eyes sparkling with champagne and happiness. The way her dark red strapless dress complemented her figure. His brown-eyed angel still had the power to enchant him.

As he gently caressed her cheek, she gazed up into the hazy blue eyes he was now hiding behind his glasses. He was so handsome in his tuxedo. So very, very sexy.

Boldly, she reached out to pull the edge of his bow tie and felt the silk come apart in her fingers. She wrapped the tie around her hand once to tug his lips to hers.

As they kissed, Julia suddenly realized how difficult it must have been at the beginning of their relationship for Gabriel to keep his hands off her. The boiling of blood and heating of flesh when one knew what lay beyond kissing in the voluptuary dance that was foreplay. She could barely contain her need for him.

"Please," she whispered, straining on tiptoe to place tiny kisses across his neck as she tugged on his tie once again.

He groaned. "Don't tempt me."

"I promise I'll be gentle."

Gabriel laughed gruffly. "This is a stunning reversal."

"We've waited a respectable amount of time. I love you. And I want you."

"Do you trust me?"

"Yes," she said breathlessly.

"Then marry me."

"Gabriel, I—"

He cut her off with his kiss, pulling her against his chest. Somehow his hands were in her hair, clutching her tightly. And then as he gently slid his hands to caress her naked shoulders, he tentatively pressed into her mouth.

Julia released his bow tie to wrap her arms around his neck, tugging him until their bodies were flush against one another. She nibbled his full lower lip and moaned as his tongue slowly traced the curve of her mouth.

Suddenly, his fingers were touching her collarbones and moving to her back, gliding across the surface of her skin as it began to flush and heat.

"Let me do things the right way," he pleaded, his hands cupping her face.

"How could this be wrong?" she whispered back, eyes dark and desperate.

He kissed her again, and this time she shamelessly wound her right leg around his hip, trying to re-create their tango against a wall from the Royal Ontario Museum.

He pressed forward until her back was flush against the door to her room, his hands roaming up and down her thighs, before pulling back suddenly. "I can't."

Julia removed his glasses in order to smooth the creases around his eyes, and saw passion, conflict, and love staring back at her. She unwound her leg from his hip and pressed their lower bodies together.

"*Gabriel.*"

He blinked at the sound of her voice, as if she was awakening him from a dream.

When he didn't move, she placed a few inches between them and handed him his glasses. "Goodnight, Gabriel."

He looked stricken. "I don't mean to hurt you."

"I know."

He remained perfectly still, staring down into eyes that were filled with sadness and longing. "I'm trying to be strong for both of us," he whispered. "But when you look at me like that . . ."

He kissed her lips softly and nodded his acquiescence as she fumbled for her slide card, and the two of them disappeared behind her hotel room door.

❋ ❋

Early the next morning, Julia left the comfort of Gabriel's warm embrace to tiptoe to the washroom. When she returned, she found him wide-awake and gazing at her with concern.

"Are you all right?"

Blushing, she smiled. "Yes."

"Then come here." He opened his arms, and she snuggled close, placing a leg over both of his.

"I'm sorry if I embarrassed you in the hallway."

"You didn't embarrass me." The urgency of his tone took Julia aback. "How could I be embarrassed by the woman I love showing me that she wants me?"

"I think we gave some of the other guests a bit of a show."

"And some inspiration," he spoke against her lips, kissing her.

When they broke apart, she rested her head on his shoulder. "I guess you're serious about waiting until the wedding."

"You weren't complaining last night."

"You know me." She winked at him. "I don't like to complain.

"Thank you for compromising, Gabriel." She tightened her arms around his waist. "Last night was important for me."

"For me too." He smiled. "I could see that you trust me."

"I'm glad, because I've never trusted you more."

He kissed her again, before pushing a lock of hair away from her face. "I have something to tell you," he said, his fingers gently running up and down her neck. "Something strange."

Her eyebrows knit together curiously.

"Go ahead."

"When I was back in Selinsgrove, I saw something. Or rather, something happened to me."

Julia covered his hand with hers, stilling his fingers. "Were you hurt?"

"No." He paused uncomfortably. "Promise me you'll keep an open mind."

"Of course."

"I thought it was a dream. When I woke up, I wondered if it was a vision."

She blinked. "Like when you thought you saw me in Assisi?"

"No. Like what you said about the Gentileschi painting while we were in Florence—about Maia and Grace.

"I saw her. Grace. We were in my old room at my parents' house. And Grace told me . . ." Gabriel's voice broke. He struggled to compose himself. "She told me that she knew that I loved her."

"Of course she did," Julia murmured, hugging him more tightly.

"There's more. She had someone with her. A young woman."

"Who was she?"

Gabriel swallowed roughly. "Maia."

Julia gasped, her eyes wide.

"She told me she was happy."

Julia wiped a stray tear from Gabriel's face. "Was it a dream?"

"Perhaps. I don't know."

"Did you tell Richard? Or Paulina?"

"No. They've both made their peace."

Julia placed her hand against his cheek.

"Maybe you needed this in order to forgive yourself—to see that Grace and Maia forgave you and that they're happy."

He nodded wordlessly, burying his face in her hair.

Chapter Fifty

On their flight back to Boston, Julia surprised Gabriel by telling him that she would welcome his proposal. His happiness could barely be contained in the first class section of the airplane. She expected that he would drop to one knee immediately.

He didn't.

When they arrived in Boston, she expected him to take her shopping for wedding rings.

He made no such plans.

In fact, as September flew by, she wondered if Gabriel was going to propose to her at all. Perhaps it was the case that he merely *assumed* that they were engaged and planned to pick out wedding rings at some later date.

Gabriel warned her that the doctoral program at Harvard was challenging and that the professors were highly demanding. In fact, he remarked more than once that the average faculty member who taught in her program was far more pretentious and ass-like than he had ever been.

(Julia wondered if such astronomical ass-like levels were humanly possible.)

Nevertheless, his warnings hadn't quite prepared her for the amount of work she was required to do on a daily basis. She spent long hours in seminars and also in the library, keeping up with her homework and supplementing the reading from her classes. She met with Professor Marinelli regularly and found that they enjoyed a professional but comfortable rapport. And she worked tirelessly on her Italian and other languages, in preparation for her competency exams.

Gabriel encouraged her, of course, and he did his very best not to pressure her about spending time with him. He was busy with his new position and had immediately taken over the supervision of three doctoral students, having relinquished Paul to Katherine's capable direction. But full professors have more leisure time than graduate students, and so Gabriel spent many an evening and weekend alone.

He began volunteering as a tutor at the Italian Home for Children in Jamaica Plain. Despite his somewhat limited success, under his supervision a small group of teenagers developed a lively interest in Italian art and culture. The Professor promised to send them to Italy if they graduated high school with a respectable grade point average.

Though he kept himself busy, each day ended as it began, with him alone in his now renovated house, missing Julianne.

He seriously contemplated buying a dog. Or a ferret.

Despite her overall busyness with graduate school, which was a welcome distraction, Julia continued to be frustrated. Their separation was unnatural, uncomfortable, *cold*, and she ached to breach that separation and be one with him again. The fact that she couldn't made her terribly sad. All the romantic activities short of intercourse couldn't erase that kind of loneliness. And there were only so many times she could listen to comforting music while lying alone in her single bed.

Sexual desires can be satisfied in many ways, but she longed for the attention that he paid to her when they were making love, the way he lavished single-minded devotion on her as if there were no one and nothing else on earth. She coveted the way she felt when he touched her naked form. For in those moments, she felt beautiful and desirable, despite her innate shyness and unease about her body. She desired the moments after sex, when they were both relaxed and sated, and Gabriel would whisper beautiful words in her ear, and they would simply *be* in one another's arms.

As the days passed, Julia wasn't sure how long she could tolerate their disconnection without lapsing into a depression.

One day at the end of September, Julia opened the door of the Range Rover and silently slid into the passenger seat. She buckled her seatbelt and gazed out the window.

"Sweetheart?" Gabriel reached his hand out to push her hair away from her face.

She stiffened.

He withdrew his hand. "What's wrong? What happened?"

"Sharon," she mumbled.

Gabriel reached over to gently turn her chin in his direction. Her face was puffy, and her skin was blotchy and uneven. She'd been crying for a while.

"Come here." He unfastened her seatbelt and tugged her over the center console and onto his lap, which was no easy feat. "Tell me what happened."

"Dr. Walters brought up all this stuff about my mother. I didn't want to talk about it, but she said that she wasn't doing her job if she let me suppress everything that happened in St. Louis. I took as much as I could take and then I left."

Gabriel grimaced. Dr. Townsend had been making similar comments about his own mother, but he seemed to be closer to making peace with his past since his trip to Italy. Certainly, his continued presence at Narcotics Anonymous meetings seemed to be helping.

"I'm sorry," he offered, kissing the top of her head. "But didn't Nicole address your relationship with your mother?"

"Briefly. Mostly we discussed you."

Gabriel winced. He would always feel guilty for the pain he had caused her, but the fact that he had bumped Sharon off Nicole's priority list for helping Julia made him cringe.

"Is there anything I can do to help?"

Julia laughed mirthlessly as she wiped her tears away. "Find me another therapist."

"I wouldn't be helping you if I did. Any therapist worth her salt would insist that you address what happened with your mother. And her boyfriends."

Julia began to protest, but Gabriel interrupted her. "I understand what you're going through. Even though our mothers were abusive in different ways, I understand."

She wiped her nose with a tissue.

"I'm here to listen, whenever you want to talk about it. But in order to be healthy, you have to deal with your past. I'll do everything I can to help, but this is something only you can do—for yourself and for *us*." He gave her a sympathetic look. "You realize that, don't you? That the healing process not only helps you, it helps us?"

She nodded begrudgingly. "I thought all the angst was behind us. I thought that after everything we'd been through, we'd have our happy ever after."

Gabriel tried to repress a snicker. And failed.

"What? You don't believe in happy ever after?"

He smirked at her and tapped her nose with his finger. "No, I don't believe in *angst*."

"Why not?"

"Because I'm not an Existentialist; I'm a Dantean."

She wrinkled her nose. "Very funny, Professor. With a name like *Emerson*, I would have thought you to be a Transcendentalist."

"Hardly." He kissed her wrinkles affectionately. "I exist in order to please you.

"We will be happy, Julianne, but don't you see that in order to get to the happiness, you have to address the pain of the past?"

She squirmed but didn't respond.

"I was thinking about visiting Maia's grave." He cleared his throat. "I'd like to take you with me." His voice was hesitant and barely above a whisper. "I'd like you to see it. That is, if you wouldn't find it morbid."

"I'd be honored. Of course I'll go with you."

"Thank you." He pressed his lips to her forehead.

"Gabriel?"

"Yes?"

"I didn't tell you everything that happened with Sharon. Or with Simon."

Gabriel rubbed at his eyes. "I didn't tell you everything about my past, either."

"Does it bother you? That we haven't told one another everything?"

"No. I'm willing to listen to anything you have to say. But truthfully, there are some things I don't want to discuss about my life. So I understand your reticence to lay bare your history." He locked eyes with her.

"The important thing is that you address those events with someone. I'm sure that talking things over with Dr. Walters is good enough."

He kissed her once again and held her close, meditating on how far they'd come in their individual journeys and how far they still needed to go.

Chapter Fifty-one

In October, Gabriel persuaded Julia to travel to his house in Selinsgrove for the weekend in order to congregate with their relatives. Rachel and Aaron insisted on doing all the cooking during the weekend, while Tammy's little boy, Quinn, entertained everyone, including Tom, with his smiles.

"How is married life treating you?" Gabriel asked Aaron as he assembled the ingredients for a salad.

"Really well. You should try it sometime." Aaron winked at Julia as he took a long pull from his Corona.

"That's an idea." Gabriel smiled smugly and went back to his salad.

"Cut the crap, Gabriel. When are you going to put a ring on that woman's finger?" Rachel's voice floated across the kitchen from the oven.

"She has one."

Rachel left her chicken Kiev unattended and raced across the kitchen to examine Julia's left hand.

"That doesn't count." She pointed to Julia's thumb, which was encased by Gabriel's platinum band.

Julia and Rachel exchanged a look and shook their heads.

Gabriel regarded the way that Julia's countenance fell and quickly abandoned his salad (which was laden pretentiously with both fruit and nuts), and hastily embraced her.

"Trust me," he whispered, so quietly that no one else could hear.

She murmured her acquiescence, and he squeezed her tightly before kissing her.

"Get a room." Aaron snickered.

"Oh, we have one." Gabriel glanced at him sideways.

"We have two, actually." Julia sighed in resignation.

When they sat down for dinner, Richard asked everyone to hold hands while he said the blessing. He thanked God for his family, for Tammy, Quinn, and Julia, for his new son-in-law, and for the friendship of the Mitchells. He thanked God for his wife and her memory and he pointed out that the seeds she had planted with her children, her husband, and her friends had come to fruition. And when he said "Amen," everyone wiped at their eyes and smiled, more thankful than they could say that the family was together and strong once again.

Chapter Fifty-two

After dinner, Tammy and Scott cleaned up while Rachel and Aaron practiced their parenting skills with Quinn. On the back porch, Richard and Tom smoked cigars and drank Scotch, while watching old Mr. Bancroft carry things from the garage into the woods. Richard gave Tom a knowing look, and the two men clinked glasses.

Inside the house, Gabriel took Julia's hand and led her upstairs. "Wear something warm," he said as they walked into her room. "I want to take you for a walk."

"It isn't that cold out," she remarked, as she pulled on one of Gabriel's old cashmere cardigans.

He'd divested his wardrobe of cardigans after Julia informed him that they made him look like a grandfather.

(Or a PBS host.)

Upon hearing that, Gabriel was only too glad to donate his cardigans to the Salvation Army, with the exception of one or two that Julia rescued.

"I don't want you to catch cold," he protested, tugging playfully on her sweater.

"I have you to warm me," she countered, winking at him.

After winding her Magdalen College scarf around her neck, Gabriel escorted her downstairs, through the kitchen and outside.

"Going for a walk, Emerson?" Tom's voice surprised them.

"With your permission, Mr. Mitchell."

Tom patted the Swiss Army knife in his coat pocket. "If you make her cry, I'll gut you like a fish."

"I'll take good care of her, I promise. And if I make her cry, I'll dry her tears."

Tom snorted and muttered something under his breath.

Julia gazed between Gabriel and Tom quizzically. "What's going on?"

"Gabriel is taking you for a walk, with my blessing." Her father spoke with only the slightest of scowls.

"And mine," interjected Richard, his gray eyes alive with amusement.

"You two need to lay off the Scotch." Julia shook her head at the men as Gabriel pulled her into the dense, thick trees.

"What was that all about?" she asked as they trudged hand in hand toward the remains of the old orchard.

"You'll see." Gabriel kissed the top of her head before quickening their pace. He grinned as he inhaled her scent. "You smell like vanilla."

"I got sick of lavender."

"So did I."

Within minutes they were at the edge of the orchard. Despite the fact that the trees were very thick, Julia saw light streaming through the branches.

"What's going on?"

"Come and find out." He led her through the trees.

There were small white lights decorating some of the branches of the trees overhead and lanterns scattered on the ground containing flameless flickering candles. Amidst the gentle light, which cast a warm glow over the stark, bare trees and the old grass, there stood a white tent. Inside, a bench was spread with a familiar looking blanket and decorated with cushions.

"Oh, Gabriel," she whispered.

He walked with her to the tent, encouraging her to sit down.

"You didn't have to go to so much trouble. I would have been happy with this old blanket and the ground. That's what we used before."

"I like spoiling you." His eyes caught hers, and she lost her breath as a simmering intensity shone from their blue depths. "Would you like a drink?"

He withdrew, walking over to a low table on which rested a champagne bucket and two champagne flutes. She nodded and watched as he expertly opened the champagne bottle and poured two glasses. He returned to her side. "Shall we toast?"

"Of course." She glanced at the alcohol in his hand. "We could drink something else."

"Just a sip for me. *To Julianne, my beloved.*" He raised his glass.

"I think we should drink to us."

"That too. *To us.*" He smiled, and they toasted one another before sipping their champagne.

"How did you do all of this? It must have taken hours." Julia gazed at the spectacle around them.

"Old Mr. Bancroft has been taking care of the house and grounds while I'm away. I asked him to arrange everything while we were eating dinner. May I?" He reached into a bowl of strawberries and chose the largest, ripest one and held it out to her.

Gabriel brought the red fruit to Julia's lips, smiling widely as she took half of it into her mouth before biting down. "You'll find that it complements the taste of the champagne."

Julia laughed as some of the juice from the berry escaped her mouth. She moved to wipe it with her hand, but Gabriel's fingers were faster. He traced her lips slowly, capturing the juice, and transferred his fingers to his own mouth before sucking on them.

"Delicious," he murmured.

As he repeated this ritual, Julia began to feel strangely light-headed. Gabriel's sensuality, even bridled, was dizzying in the extreme.

She reached over to return the favor and was stunned when, after swallowing, he drew one of her fingers into his mouth, swirling his tongue around it before sucking it.

"Sweet like candy," he mused, his voice throaty and thick.

He sat next to her on the bench and placed his arm around her, drawing a single finger across her trembling lower lip.

"Do you have any idea what you do to me? The flush of your cheeks, the warmth of your skin, the speed of your heart . . ." He shook his head. "It's beyond words."

Julia unbuttoned her sweater and placed his palm flush against her chest. "Feel my heart beat. You do this to me, Gabriel."

He glanced down at where his palm was placed. "I intend to elicit that reaction for the rest of my life."

He captured her lips with his in a fiery kiss before withdrawing his hand to hover at her cheek. "I brought you here because this is where it all began. You changed my life that night. I'll never be able to thank you."

"Your love is thanks enough."

He kissed her sweetly.

"Where is the music coming from?" Julia looked around for a stereo system but couldn't find one.

"Mr. Bancroft provided the means to have music."

"It's lovely."

"Not half as lovely as you. You brought beauty to my life the instant I met you." Gabriel tightened his grip around her. "I still can't believe I have you in my arms after all these years, and that you love me."

"I always loved you, Gabriel. Even when you didn't recognize me." Julia pressed her head to his heart as he hummed along to the music.

When the song was replaced by a new one, Gabriel murmured against her skin. "I have a gift for you."

"Just kiss me."

"I'll rain kisses on you once you let me present my gift." He pulled something out of his jacket and handed it to her. It was an announcement written in Italian on very expensive card stock.

"What is it?" She looked up at him.

"Read it," he urged, his eyes alight.

The announcement was from the Uffizi Gallery in Florence and it declared the opening of an exclusive exhibit of an extraordinary collection of Botticelli illustrations of Dante's *Divine Comedy*, some of which had never before been seen in public. The announcement went on to declare that the exhibit was on loan to the Uffizi from Professor Gabriel Emerson, as a gift to his *fidanzata*, Miss Julianne Mitchell.

She gaped at him in surprise. "Gabriel, your illustrations. I can't believe it."

"My happiness has made me generous."

"But what about the legal issues? And how you bought them?"

"My lawyer hired a team of experts to trace the provenance, which ends in the late nineteenth century. After that, no one knows to whom they belonged. And since they were always part of a private collection, I own them legally and rightfully. Now I want to share them."

"That's wonderful." Julia flushed and looked down at the ground. "But my name shouldn't be attached to the exhibition. The illustrations are yours."

"I'm only sharing them because of you."

Julia reached up a hand to touch his jaw. "Thank you. What you're doing is very generous. I always thought that those pictures should be available for people to see and to enjoy."

"You taught me not to be selfish."

She moved to kiss him, eagerly tasting his mouth. "You taught me to accept gifts."

"Then we're a matched set." He cleared his throat as he pushed a lock of hair away from her face. "Will you accompany me to the exhibition? We'll schedule it for the summer. *Dottore* Vitali would like to host a reception for us, similar to the one he held last year for my lecture."

"Of course I will."

"Good. Perhaps we'll be able to find a private corner of the museum so we can . . ."

"I'd like nothing more, Professor." She winked.

Gabriel tugged at his collar involuntarily.

"Do you want to get married in Florence next summer? We could have the wedding while we're visiting the exhibition."

"No."

His eyes sought the ground as disappointment spread across his face.

"Next summer would be far too late. What about next month?"

Gabriel's eyes flew to hers. "I'd marry you tomorrow, if I could. But are you sure? It doesn't leave us much time to plan a wedding."

"I want our wedding to be small. I'm tired of living alone. I want to be with you." She brushed his ear with her lips. *"And it isn't only because I want to have you warm my bed."*

A growl escaped Gabriel's chest, and he kissed her firmly. She sighed into his mouth, and the two embraced warmly before he pulled back.

"What about your studies?"

"Lots of graduate students are married. Even if I only see you in bed at night it will be more than I see you now. Please don't make me wait."

He stroked her cheek with the back of his hand. "As if the waiting wasn't killing me as well. Where should we get married?"

"Assisi. It's always been an important place for me, and I know it's important to you too."

"Then Assisi it is, as soon as possible. Honeymoon to be determined?" He lifted his eyebrows suggestively. "Or is there somewhere particular you'd like to go? Paris? Venice? Belize?"

"Anywhere would be wonderful as long as I'm with you."

He squeezed her tightly. "Bless you for that. I'll make it a surprise, then."

She kissed him again and within moments, felt the world spinning around her. Everything fell away as she melted in his arms.

"I have something else I want to show you," he said at length, dragging his lips from hers.

He clasped her hand in his and walked over to the old apple tree that stood on the edge of the clearing.

He turned to face her, eyes full of feeling. "The first time we met, I picked an apple from this tree."

"I remember."

"The apple represented what my life was like at that time—carnal, selfish, violent, a magnet for sin."

Julia watched as he sank to one knee, pulling a golden apple out of his pocket.

"This apple represents what I've become—full of hope. And love."

She looked at the apple before her eyes sought his.

"Has a man ever asked you to marry him before?"

She shook her head, covering her mouth with her hand.

"Then I'm glad I'm your first."

He opened the apple like a magic box and Julia saw a sparkling diamond ring nestled against a fold of red velvet.

"I want to be your first and your last. I love you, Julianne. I offer you my heart and my life.

"Marry me. Be my wife, my friend, my lover, and my guide. Be my blessed Beatrice and my adored Julianne." His voice wavered slightly. "Say you'll be mine. Forever."

"*Yes*," Julia managed, before the tears overtook her.

Gabriel removed the ring from the apple and placed it gently on her finger before caressing her hand with his lips.

"I chose this ring a long time ago, when I picked out the wedding bands. But it can be returned." His voice was wistful. "I know you might want to choose your own rings."

Julia examined the two-and-a-half-carat, cushion-cut diamond in its platinum setting. The ring was old-fashioned with smaller, bead set diamonds that surrounded the central stone and graduated side stones that decorated the band. Although it was far larger and more ornate than she had ever dreamed of, it was perfect because he chose it for her.

"I choose this one," she said.

He stood up and she flew into his arms.

"I've wanted you forever. Since I first saw your picture," she said as her happy tears spilled onto his chest. "I wanted you even before I knew you."

"I wanted you when I didn't even know your name—just your goodness. And now I get to keep my Beatrice forever."

Chapter Fifty-three

A few days later, Paul received an email from Julia announcing her engagement. It made him ill. Reading and re-reading her words didn't ameliorate his situation. Not one bit. But he did so anyway, if not to torture himself then to have her new status indelibly impressed on his mind.

> Dear Paul,
>
> I hope this email finds you well. I'm sorry it took me so long to answer your last message. Grad school is kicking my butt, and I feel so behind in everything. But I'm loving it. (By the way, thank you for the recommendation of Ross King's books. I don't have much time to read these days, but I'm going to pick up *Brunelleschi's Dome*.)
>
> One of the reasons I don't have much time to read is because I'm engaged. Gabriel has asked me to marry him and I said yes. We'd hoped to get married quickly, but were unable to book the basilica in Assisi until January 21st. Gabriel has personal ties with the Franciscans, which is the only reason we were able to book the basilica in so short a time.
>
> I'm very happy. Please be happy for me.
>
> I'm sending your invitation to your apartment in Toronto. We're also inviting Katherine Picton.
>
> I'll understand if you can't or don't want to attend, but it was important to me to invite the people I care about. Gabriel has rented a house in Umbria for the wedding guests to stay in before and after the wedding. You'd be most welcome. I know my father would be happy to see you again too.

You've been nothing but a good friend to me, and I hope that someday I'll be able to repay the favor.

With affection,

Julia.

P.S. Gabriel didn't want me to mention this, but he's the one who persuaded Professor Picton to supervise your dissertation. I asked her but she refused. Surely he isn't as bad as you thought?

Paul's gratitude for Gabriel's generosity didn't erase the sudden sharp pain he felt at the realization that he'd just lost Julia. Again.

Yes, he'd already lost her, but before Gabriel's return there was the possibility that Julia would change her mind, even if that possibility was remote. Somehow the knowledge that she was going to marry *him* smarted so much more than if she had been marrying, say, some other schmuck called Gabriel. Like *Gabriel-the-plumber* or *Gabriel-the-cable-guy*.

Shortly after she emailed Paul, Julia received a package in her mailbox at Harvard. Seeing that it was postmarked in Essex Junction, Vermont, she opened it eagerly.

Paul had sent her a limited edition copy of *The Velveteen Rabbit*. He'd written a short inscription to her on the flyleaf, which tugged at her heart, and enclosed a letter.

Dear Julia,

I was surprised by your news. Congratulations.

Thanks for inviting me to your wedding but I won't be able to attend. My father had a heart attack a few days ago and is in the hospital. I'm helping out on the farm. (My mother says hello, by the way. She is making something for you as a wedding present. Where should she send it? I'm assuming you won't be living on campus once you're married)

From the first time I met you, I wanted you to be happy. To be more confident. To have a good life. You deserve these things, and I'd hate to see you throw them away.

I wouldn't be your friend if I didn't ask you if Emerson is what you really want. You shouldn't settle for less than the best. And if you have any doubt about it, you shouldn't marry him.

I promise I'm not trying to be an asshole.

Yours,

Paul.

With sadness, Julia folded up Paul's letter and placed it back inside the book.

Chapter Fifty-four

Despite the fact that Tom gave his blessing to Julia and Gabriel (albeit begrudgingly), conflict ensued when the happy couple announced the destination of their wedding.

While the Clarks were only too glad to spend a week in Italy during the winter, Tom, who had never traveled outside of North America, was less than enthused. As the father of the bride, he'd intended on paying for his only daughter's wedding even if he had to mortgage his new house in order to do so. Julia wouldn't hear of him doing such a thing.

Though the wedding would be small, the estimated costs were high enough that they would effectively damage Tom financially if he paid for everything. Gabriel was more than comfortable covering the costs, much to Tom's chagrin. It was more important to Gabriel that Julia have the day of her dreams than for her father to be placated.

Julia tried to smooth over the conflict between the two men by pointing out that there were things that her father could pay for, such as her wedding dress and the flowers.

In late November, she was on Newbury Street in Boston when she saw *the dress* in the window of an elegant boutique. The dress was ivory silk organza with a v-neck and little wisps of sleeves that sat high on the shoulders. While the top was covered in lace, the skirt was full and layered like a cloud.

Without further thought, she walked into the shop and asked to try it on. The shopkeeper complimented her, saying that Monique Lhuillier's gowns were very popular.

Julia didn't recognize the designer's name, and she didn't look at the price tag because there wasn't one. When she stood in front of the mirrors in the dressing room, she knew. *This was her dress*. It was classically beautiful and would complement the color of her skin and the shape of her body. And Gabriel would adore the fact that much of her upper back would be exposed. Tastefully, of course.

She sent a picture of herself in the gown to Tom via her iPhone, asking him what he thought. He called her immediately, telling her that he'd never seen a bride as absolutely beautiful as she.

Tom asked to speak to the boutique manager, and without Julia discovering the substantial price, he made arrangements to purchase the dress. Knowing that he was able to buy his only daughter the dress of her dreams enabled him to accept the fact that Gabriel would be paying for most of the wedding.

After saying good-bye to Tom, Julia spent several hours shopping for the rest of her trousseau. Among other things, she chose a veil that was almost ankle length, a pair of satin heels that she could walk in successfully, and a long, white velvet cape that would protect her and her dress from the January weather in Assisi. Then she went home.

❊ ❊

Two weeks before the wedding, Tom called Julia to ask her an important question. "I know the invitations have been sent out but would there be room for one more?"

Julia was surprised.

"Sure. Is there a long lost cousin I wasn't aware of?"

"Not exactly," hedged Tom.

"Then who?"

He took a very deep breath and held it.

"Dad, spit it out. Who do you want to bring?" Julia closed her eyes and silently begged the gods of daughters whose fathers were single to intervene on her behalf and keep Deb Lundy from attending her wedding or worse—getting back together with her father.

"Um, Diane."

Julia's eyes flew open. "Diane who?"

"Diane Stewart."

"Diane from Kinfolks restaurant?"

"That's right." Tom's gruff reply immediately telegraphed to Julia far more than he realized.

Her jaw dropped in shock.

"Jules? You still there?"

"Yeah, I'm here. Um, sure, I'll add her to the guest list. Uh, is Diane a—special friend of yours?"

Tom fell silent for a moment. "You could say that."

"Huh," said Julia.

Tom ended the conversation quickly and Julia put down her cell phone, wondering which blue plate special had precipitated her father's new romance.

Definitely not the meatloaf, she thought.

Chapter Fifty-five

On January twenty-first, Tom paced nervously at the entrance to the Basilica in Assisi. He was nervous. And the fact that Julia and her bridesmaids were late didn't help matters. He tugged at his bow tie as he waited. Then, a vision in white velvet over organza floated through the front doors like a luminescent cloud.

He was speechless.

"Dad," Julia breathed, smiling with excitement as she walked toward him.

Tammy and Rachel helped divest her of her cape and adjust the layers of her skirt, unfolding the train that extended behind her. Then Christina, the wedding planner who was hovering nearby, handed Rachel and Tammy their bouquets, which were a mixture of irises and white roses, designed to match their iris-colored dresses.

"You look pretty," Tom mumbled, pressing a shy peck to Julia's cheek through her long veil.

"Thank you." She flushed, looking down at her bouquet, which consisted of two dozen white roses and a few springs of holly.

"Could you give us a minute?" he asked the others.

"Of course." Christina pulled Tammy and Rachel to stand at the entrance to the sanctuary, signaling to the organist that the processional was about to begin.

Tom smiled at Julia nervously. "I like your necklace," he said.

Julia's hands flew to the pearls that hung around her neck. "They were Grace's." She fingered the diamonds in her ears too but elected not to reveal their source.

"I wonder what she'd think about you marrying her son."

"I'd like to think that she'd be happy. That she's looking down on us and smiling."

Tom nodded again and shoved his hands into the pockets of his tuxedo. "I'm glad you asked me to walk you down the aisle."

Julia looked puzzled. "I didn't want to get married without you, Dad."

He cleared his throat, shifting awkwardly in his rented shoes. "I should have kept you when I took you away from Sharon the first time. I never should have sent you back." His voice cracked.

"Daddy," she whispered, tears overflowing.

He reached over and hugged her, trying to show her with his embrace what he couldn't say in words.

"I forgave you a long time ago. We don't ever need to speak of it again." She paused, looking up at him. "I'm glad you're here. And I'm glad you're my Dad."

"Jules." Tom gave a strangled cough, then released her with a smile. "You're a good girl."

He turned so he could peer down the long aisle that led to the altar, to where Gabriel was standing with his brother and brother-in-law. All three men were dressed in black Armani tuxedoes, with crisp white shirts. However, Scott and Aaron had eschewed Gabriel's choice of bow ties in favor of regular ones because bow ties were, as Scott put it, "for old men, Young Republicans, or professors."

"Are you sure about this?" Tom asked. "If you have any doubts, I'll call a cab and take you home right now."

Julia squeezed his hand. "No doubts. Gabriel might not be perfect, but he's perfect for me. We belong together."

"I told him that I expected him to take care of my little girl. That if he wasn't prepared to do that, we'd have a problem. He said that if he treated you as anything less than the treasure you are, that I should come after him with my shotgun." Tom grinned. "I said that suited me fine."

"Are you ready?"

Julia took a deep breath. "Yes."

"Then let's do this." He offered Julia his arm, and they nodded to the bridesmaids to begin the processional to J. S. Bach's "Sheep May Safely Graze."

When Julia and Tom entered the Basilica, to the melody of "Jesu, Joy of Man's Desiring," Gabriel's eyes caught hers and a wide smile spread across his features. The January sun peeked through the doors, illuminating the bride from behind and making her look as if a halo shone around her veiled head.

Gabriel couldn't stop smiling. He smiled through the entire Mass, including his vows to worship his wife and the performance of selections from Bach's *Sleepers Awake* and Mozart's *Exsultate, jubilate* by a solo soprano.

After the ceremony, he placed trembling fingers on Julia's veil and lifted it carefully. He swiped his thumbs underneath her eyes, wiping away the happy tears that had trickled down, and kissed her. The kiss was soft and chaste, but full of promise. Then they walked to the lower church and down to the crypt.

They hadn't planned to do so. Somehow, hands entwined, they found themselves approaching the tomb of St. Francis. In the quiet darkness where Gabriel had his ineffable experience months earlier, they knelt in prayer. Each silently thanked God for the other, for the many blessings He had given them, for Grace and Maia, for their fathers and siblings.

When Gabriel finally stood and lit a single candle, each of them asked God for one more blessing. One small miracle out of the lavishness of his grace. As they ended their prayers, a strange but comforting feeling wrapped around them like a blanket.

"Don't cry, sweet girl." Gabriel took her hand to help her to her feet. He wiped her tears away, kissing her. "Please don't cry."

"I'm so happy," she said, smiling up at him. "I love you so much."

"It's the same for me. I keep wondering how this happened. How did I ever find you again and convince you to become my wife?"

"Heaven smiled on us."

She reached up to kiss her husband next to St. Francis's tomb without shame, knowing that her words were truly spoken.

Chapter Fifty-six

Later that evening, they changed into their honeymoon clothes, a dark suit for Gabriel and a purple dress for Julia, and sat side by side in a chauffeured car that he'd hired.

Soon the car was pulling up the drive that led to a villa near Todi. The very same villa that Gabriel had rented when they visited Italy the year before.

"Our house," she whispered, as soon as she caught sight of it.

"Yes." He kissed the back of her hand as he helped her out of the car. Then he was taking her in his arms and carrying her across the threshold.

"Are you disappointed? I thought you'd prefer some quiet time to ourselves, but if not, we can go to Venice or Rome. I'll take you anywhere you want to go." He placed her on her feet.

"This is perfect. I'm so glad you decided to bring us here." She threw her arms around his neck.

At length, he pulled away. "I think I should carry our luggage upstairs. Are you hungry?"

Julia grinned. "I could eat."

"Why don't you see if there's anything tempting in the kitchen, and I'll join you soon."

She leaned forward with a devilish look on her face. "The only thing in the kitchen that would tempt me would be you on top of the kitchen table."

Her sultry suggestion hearkened back to their previous visit, when they'd christened that table several times. With a deep groan, he quickly carried their suitcases upstairs as if someone was chasing him.

In the kitchen, Julia found the pantry to be fully stocked, as was the refrigerator. She laughed when she saw several bottles of cranberry juice lined up on the counter, as if they were waiting for her. She'd just opened a bottle of Perrier and finished preparing a cheese plate when Gabriel returned. He seemed years younger as he raced into the kitchen, boyish even, his eyes bright and his expression cheerful.

"This looks delicious. Thank you." He sat at her side, glancing at the kitchen table significantly. "But I have to say that I'd rather our first few times occur in bed."

Julia felt her skin flush. "This table has happy memories for me."

"For me too. But we have plenty of time to make new ones. Better ones." He gave her a heated look.

She felt the flutterings of desire increase.

"Was the wedding everything you hoped for?" He gazed at her eagerly, pouring two glasses of sparkling water.

"It was better. The Mass, the music—having the wedding in the Basilica was incredible. I felt so at peace there."

Gabriel nodded, for he'd felt that way too.

"I'm glad we only invited family and close friends. I'm sorry I didn't have much of a chance to talk to Katherine Picton, although I saw you dancing with her *twice*." Julia pretended to be offended.

He eyed her in mock surprise. "Really? I danced with her twice? That's pretty impressive for a septuagenarian. I'm surprised she could keep up with me."

Julia rolled her eyes at his pretentious choice of adjectives.

"You danced with Richard twice, Mrs. Emerson. I suppose we're even."

"He's my father now too. And he's an excellent dancer. Very elegant."

"Better than me?" Gabriel feigned jealousy.

"No one is better than you, darling." She leaned over to kiss away his pout. "Do you think that he will ever marry again?"

"No."

"Why not?"

He took her hand in his and caressed her knuckles gently, one by one.

"Because Grace was his Beatrice. When you've experienced a love such as that, anything less would seem like only a shadow." He smiled sadly. "Strangely enough, it was the same in Grace's favorite book, *A Severe Mercy*. Sheldon Vanauken never remarried after his wife died.

"Dante lost Beatrice when she was just twenty-four. He spent the rest of his life mourning her. If I were to lose you, it would be the same for me. There will never be anyone else. Never," he emphasized, a fierce but loving look in his eyes.

"I wonder if my father will marry again."

"Would it trouble you if he did?"

She shrugged. "No. It would take some getting used to, but I'm glad he's dating someone kind. I'd like him to be happy. I'd like him to have someone kind to grow old with."

"I'm looking forward to growing old with you," said Gabriel. "And you are certainly kind."

"I'm looking forward to growing old with you too."

Husband and wife exchanged a look then finished their food in relaxed quietness. Afterward, Gabriel stood and stretched out his hand. "I haven't given you your wedding gifts, yet."

She took his hand and her fingers touched his wedding band. "I thought our gifts were our rings and the inscriptions inside them: *I am my Beloved's and my Beloved is mine.*"

"There's more." He led her to the fireplace and paused.

When they entered the house, Julia hadn't noticed that the artwork that hung over the fireplace previously had been removed. In its place was a large and impressive oil painting of a man and a woman in a passionate embrace.

She took a step closer to the painting, transfixed by the stirring image.

The male and female figures were wrapped around each other, the male naked to the waist and slightly underneath the female as if he were kneeling at her feet, his head resting on her lap. The female figure was bent forward, naked and wrapped carelessly in what appeared to be a bed sheet, clutching the male's back and sides and resting her head between his shoulder blades. In truth, it was difficult to tell where his body began and her body ended, so entwined they were, almost like a circle. Need and desperation leapt off the canvas, as if the couple had just made up after a fight or found each other after an extended absence.

"It's us," breathed Julia as she blinked in shock.

The male's face was partially hidden by the woman's lap, his mouth pressed against her naked thigh. But it was Gabriel's face, of that there could be no doubt. The female's face was Julia's, eyes closed in bliss, a small smile playing at the edge of her full lips as she faced the viewer. She looked happy.

"But how?"

Gabriel stood behind her and placed his arms around her shoulders. "I posed for the artist and provided photographs of you."

"Photographs?"

He leaned forward to kiss the side of her neck. "Don't you recognize your posture? It's a study of some of the pictures I took of you in Belize. Do you remember the morning after you wore your corset for the first time? You were lying in bed . . ."

Julia's eyes widened in remembrance.

"Do you like it?" Gabriel's usually sure tone sounded surprisingly uncertain. "I wanted something—ah—*personal* to commemorate our wedding."

"I love it. I'm just surprised."

His body relaxed.

"Thank you." She took his hand and gently pressed her lips to his palm. "It's a lovely gift."

"I'm glad you like it. But there's one more small thing."

He walked over to the mantelpiece of the fireplace in order to retrieve a familiar looking golden apple.

"How did that get here?" Julia smiled.

"Open it, Mrs. Emerson."

She lifted the lid and found a large, old-fashioned key inside. She met Gabriel's eyes quizzically. "A magic key? To a secret garden? Or to a wardrobe that leads to Narnia?"

"Very funny. Come with me." He caught her wrist and brought it to his lips, hesitating against her skin.

"Where are we going?"

"You'll see."

He led her out the front door, closing it behind them. They stood on the porch, surrounded by darkness that was illuminated only by the lights that hung on the stone walls.

"Try the key."

"What? Here?"

"Just try it." Gabriel rocked back on his heels, trying to hide his sudden anxiety.

Julia put the key in the lock and twisted. She heard the lock click and with a flick of her wrist, it unlocked and the door swung open.

"Thank you for becoming my wife," he whispered. "Welcome home."

She looked over at him incredulously.

"We were happy here," he said softly. "I wanted us to have a place that we could escape to, somewhere with fond memories."

He reached out to lightly touch her arm. "We can spend our holidays here when we aren't in Selinsgrove. You could write your dissertation here, if you want. Although I couldn't bear to be separated from you for more than a day."

Julia kissed him, thanking him over and over again for his lavish gift. They stood there for several minutes, reveling in one another's touch, their heartbeats quickening.

Chapter Fifty-seven

Without breaking the kiss, he picked her up and carried her back inside the house and up the stairs to the master bedroom. He twirled her around, admiring the way the full skirt of her purple dress flared out as she spun.

"I believe I owe you something."

"And what's that?" Julia laughed as Gabriel pressed himself up against her back.

He reached over her shoulder to whisper to her. "Make-up sex."

The tone of his voice goose pimpled her skin.

He rubbed his hands up and down her bare arms. "Are you cold?"

"No. Excited."

"Excellent." He brushed her hair aside so his lips could find her neck, and he began plying her with kisses. "And just so you know, I have a lot to make up for. In fact, I think it will take me all night."

"All night?" asked Julia, coughing slightly.

"All night and into the morning."

She had already begun to melt into his embrace by the time he retreated, pressing his mouth and tongue eagerly to the curve of her shoulder before letting go.

"While you're getting ready for bed I want you to think about all the ways I'm going to please you."

He traced a single finger across her neckline in promise before releasing her with a provocative wink.

Julia gathered her lingerie from her luggage and disappeared into the bathroom. When she went shopping for something to wear on their wedding night, she had been intimidated. She was unsure what to choose that he hadn't seen before.

In a tiny shop on Newbury Street, she had found exactly what she was looking for—a long Merlot colored silk gown with a low neckline. But its crowning glory was the crisscrossing laces in the back, which plunged to an almost indecent level. She chose the gown knowing that he would delight in undoing her. In more ways than one.

She left her hair up and she swiped at her lips with a hint of sheer gloss before stepping into the black stilettos she'd purchased for their honeymoon. Then she opened the bathroom door.

Gabriel was waiting.

The master bedroom was bathed in candlelight, scented with sandalwood, and Julia could hear soft music playing. It was a different playlist than they'd enjoyed before, but she liked it nonetheless.

He approached her in his white shirt and dress pants, his shirt untucked and unbuttoned almost to his waist, his feet bare. He held his hand out, and she joined him, winding her arms around his back.

"You're exquisite," he whispered, his hands almost trembling as they traced the bareness of skin that peeked through her laces. "I'd almost forgotten how lovely you are by candlelight. Almost, but not quite."

She smiled against his chest.

"May I?" He fingered her pinned up hair, and she nodded.

A lesser man would have taken out the hairpins all at once, if he could have found them, freeing the strands quickly so he could move on to something else. But Gabriel was not a lesser man.

Painstakingly, he combed his long fingers through her hair until he alighted on a hairpin and then he gently undid it, letting down a single curl. He repeated this procedure until Julia's hair fell like waves against her pale shoulders and her body was alive with want.

He cupped her cheeks and looked deeply into her eyes. "Tell me what you desire. The night is yours. I'm yours to command."

"No commandments." Julia tasted his lips twice. "Just show me that you love me."

"Julianne, I love you with all four loves. But tonight is a celebration of *eros*."

Gabriel plied her bare shoulders with urgent, heated kisses before standing behind her and stroking the exposed skin of her back. "Thank you for your gift."

"My gift?"

"Your body, alluringly wrapped up just for me." He paused as his eyes swept down to her feet. "And your shoes. Surely after such a long day, they must be uncomfortable."

"I hadn't noticed."

He began to toy with the diamonds in her ears. "And why is that?"

"Because all I could think about was making love with you."

"I've thought of almost nothing else for days. For months." Gabriel inhaled sharply and began running his hands up and down her bare arms. "I'm the only man to see you naked in all your glory and to know the sounds you make when you're pleasured. Your body recognizes me, Julianne. It knows my touch."

Beginning at her lower back, he undid the bow, sliding the satin laces painstakingly through his fingers.

"Are you nervous?" Gabriel reached over to lift her chin to the side so he could see her profile.

"It's been a while."

"I'm going to take my time. The—ah—more *vigorous* activities will come later, after we're sufficiently reacquainted." He pointed his nose in the direction of a blank wall, and Julia felt her skin heat in anticipation.

He slowly pulled the laces open until her back was completely exposed. Then he placed the palms of his hands flat against her skin and began to skim them up and down.

"I burn for you. All these months I've waited, waited to take you to bed."

He turned her so she was facing him and without ceremony pushed the straps of her nightgown down her arms. His eyes followed the sighing silk as it slid down her form before dropping to the floor.

She stood before him naked, her hands at her sides.

"Magnificent," he breathed, his hungry eyes appraising every inch of her with painstaking slowness.

Not content to be the center of attention, she began to unbutton his shirt. She pushed it off his shoulders and pressed her mouth to his tattoo, nipping and kissing across his pectorals before making short work of his trousers.

Soon he was naked also, and she saw evidence of his arousal. He moved to kiss her, but she stopped him.

With eager fingers she began with his hair and explored his body, paying homage with fingertips and lips. His face, his mouth, his jaw, his shoulders, his sculpted chest and abdominal muscles. His arms and thighs and . . .

He caught her hand in his before she could wrap it around him, whispering sweet things against her mouth. Words of devotion in Italian that she recognized as coming from Dante's pen. He picked her up and carried her to the large, canopied bed, where he seated her on the edge. Then he knelt on the floor in front of her.

"Where shall I begin?" he asked, his eyes slightly darkened as his hands traveled across her flat stomach and down her thighs. "Tell me."

Julia inhaled quickly and shook her head.

"Shall I start here?" He leaned forward to trace her lips with the barest touch of his tongue.

"Or here?" He caressed her breasts before letting his mouth take over, licking and teasing them. She closed her eyes and gasped at the sensation.

"What about here?" His finger slowly encircled her navel before he fluttered his mouth across her abdomen.

She moaned and tugged at his hair. "All I want is you."

"Then have me."

She kissed him, and he responded by enjoying her mouth slowly, setting a gentle, languorous pace. When he felt her heartbeat quicken, he took her left foot in his hand and began to remove her shoe.

"Don't you want me to wear them?" she asked, looking down at him. "I bought them for tonight."

"Let's save them for later, when we christen the wall." Gabriel's voice was a throaty whisper.

He slowly removed her shoes and spent a few moments massaging her feet, paying special attention to her arches. Then he pushed her to the center of the bed and reclined beside her.

"Do you trust me?"

"Yes."

He gave her a soft kiss on the lips. "I've waited a long time to hear you say that and to know that you mean it."

"Of course I mean it. The past is behind us."

"Then let's make up for lost time."

Tenderly, he began using his hands to touch and to tease, his movements deliberate but passionate. He added his mouth, nipping and sucking to the tune of her sighs. His heart swelled in gladness at her sounds and the way her body writhed from side to side under his touch.

When her hands moved up and down his back urgently, finally coming to rest on his backside, he spread himself atop her, bringing their bodies into perfect alignment.

Staring down at her, he whispered, *"Behold, thou art fair, my love; thine eyes are as doves . . . Thy lips are like a thread of scarlet, and thy mouth is comely."*

Julia reached up to press their lips together before she responded. "Don't make me wait."

"Are you inviting me inside?"

Julia nodded as a flash of heat raced across the surface of her skin. "My husband."

"My brown-eyed angel."

His tongue played with her mouth as their bodies melted into one another, and soon they were one, their collective sighs muffled by teeth and tongues.

Gabriel's rhythm was slow at first, like the patient lapping of waves upon a beach. He wanted this experience to last forever, for in that moment, as he gazed into the wide and loving eyes of his wife, he realized that their previous experiences, exciting as they were, paled in comparison with the sublimity of their current connection.

She was bone of his bone and flesh of his flesh. She was his soul mate and his wife, and all he wanted was to bring her joy. He was consumed by his adoration of her.

Julia traced his brows, wrinkled as they were in concentration, his eyes now shut tightly.

"I love that look," she murmured.

"What look?"

"Your eyes closed, your eyebrows furrowed, your lips pressed together—you only look like that when you—come."

He opened his eyes, and she saws sparks in their sapphire depths. "Oh, really, Mrs. Emerson?"

"I've missed that look. It's sexy."

"You flatter me." Gabriel sounded embarrassed.

"I want to have a painting or a photograph of that face."

He frowned playfully. "A picture like that might be too much."

Julia laughed. "This is coming from a man who decorated his bedroom with naked photographs of himself."

"The only naked photographs in my bedroom will be of you, my exquisite wife."

His rhythm increased, catching Julia by surprise.

As she panted out her pleasure, Gabriel buried his face in her neck. "You're so enticing. Your hair, your skin."

"Your love makes me beautiful."

"Then let me love you forever."

She arched her back. "Yes, forever. *Please.*"

Gabriel moved apace, his lips playing across her neck, sucking and drawing the skin lightly into his mouth.

In response, her hands grasped his hips, pushing and pulling until she was close, very close.

"Open your eyes," he gasped, moving more quickly.

Julia gazed up into the dark but tender eyes of her husband, so alive with passion and true affection.

"*I love you,*" she said, eyes widening and closing as the sensations overtook her.

This time, Gabriel didn't close his eyes as his brows furrowed in concentration.

"*I love you,*" he breathed with every movement, every glide of skin against naked skin, until they were both sated and still.

Chapter Fifty-eight

Just before sunrise, Julia awoke with a start.

Her handsome husband was by her side, his face boyish in sleep. It was the face of the young man she met on Grace's back porch. She traced his eyebrows and the stubble on his chin, a tremendous feeling of love flowing through her. A tremendous feeling of contentment and joy.

Not wanting to disturb him, she crept from their bed. She picked up his discarded shirt from the floor and put it on before tiptoeing out to the balcony.

The faintest hint of light shimmered from the horizon, over the gently rolling hills of the Umbrian landscape. The air was chilly, far too cold to be outside in anything other than a hot tub, but the view was unspeakably lovely, and she felt the need to drink in its beauty. Alone.

Growing up, she felt so unworthy of having her deepest desires satisfied, of being loved absolutely. She didn't feel that way anymore. This morning, expressions of gratitude bubbled up from her soul, wafting Heavenward.

Gabriel stretched out his hand to Julia's side of the bed, but found only her pillow. It took a moment for him to awake, exhausted as he was with the previous evening and early morning's activities. They'd made love several times and taken turns worshipping one another's bodies with mouths and hands.

He smiled. All her fears and anxieties appeared to have vanished. Was it solely because they were married now? Or was it because enough time had passed that she knew beyond doubt that he wouldn't take advantage of her?

He didn't know. But he was pleased because she had been pleased. And when she gave herself to him in a way that she'd never been able to before, he treasured that gift, knowing that it was given out of love and absolute trust.

Awaking to an empty bed made him nervous, however. So rather than indulge himself in these silent musings, he quickly went in search of his beloved. It didn't take long for him to find her.

"Are you all right?" he called, as he walked out onto the balcony.

"I'm wonderful. I'm happy."

"You'll catch pneumonia," he chided, slipping off his robe and wrapping it around her.

She turned to thank him and noticed that he was naked. "So will you."

He grinned, positioning himself in front of her and opening the robe so it wrapped around both of them. She sighed at the pleasurable feeling of their naked bodies pressed tightly together.

"Was everything to your liking?" Gabriel rubbed her back through the robe.

"You couldn't tell?"

"We didn't have a lot of conversation, if you recall. Perhaps I kept you up too late. I know we were making up but . . ."

"I'm a little out of practice, but deliciously worn out." She flushed. "Last night was even better than our first time together. And certainly, as you put it, more *vigorous*."

He chuckled. "I concur."

"We've been through so much. I feel as if our connection is deeper." She nuzzled his shoulder with her nose. "And I don't have to worry about you disappearing."

"I'm yours," he whispered. "And I feel the connection too. It's what I needed. It's what you deserve. When I touch you, when I look into your eyes, I see our history and our future." He paused and lifted her face so he could see her better. "It's breathtaking."

Julia kissed him delicately and snuggled closer in his arms.

"I spent too long in the shadows." Gabriel's voice brimmed with emotion. "I'm looking forward to being in the light. With you."

She placed a hand on either side of his face, forcing him to see her. "We're in the light now. And I love you."

"As I love you, Julianne. I'm yours for this life and the next."

He kissed her lips once more and led her back into the bedroom.

Acknowledgments

I am indebted to the late Dorothy L. Sayers, the late Charles Williams, Mark Musa, my friend Katherine Picton and The Dante Society of America for their expertise on Dante Alighieri's *The Divine Comedy*, which informs my work. In this novel, I've used the Dante Society's conventions of capitalization for places such as Hell and Paradise.

I've been inspired by Sandro Botticelli's artwork and the incomparable space that is the Uffizi Gallery in Florence. The cities of Toronto, Florence, and Cambridge lent their ambience, along with the borough of Selinsgrove.

I've found several electronic archives to be quite helpful, especially the Digital Dante Project of Columbia University, Danteworlds by the University of Texas at Austin, and the World of Dante by the University of Virginia. I've consulted the Internet Archive site for its version of Dante Gabriel Rossetti's translation of *La Vita Nuova* along with the original Italian, which is cited in this book. I've also cited Henry Wadsworth Longfellow's translation of *The Divine Comedy*. The text from Abelard's letter to Héloise was taken from an anonymous translation dated from 1901.

I am grateful to Jennifer, who read the first draft of this story and offered constructive criticism at every subsequent stage. This book would not exist without her encouragement and friendship. I am grateful also to Nina for her creative input and wisdom. Kris read and offered insightful suggestions on the manuscript during the revision process.

Thanks are due to the fine staff of Omnific, especially Elizabeth, Lynette, CJ, Kim, Coreen, Micha and Enn. It has been a pleasure working with you.

I would also like to thank those who read a previous version of my story and offered criticisms, suggestions and support, especially the Muses, Tori, Elizabeth de Vos, Elena, Marinella, and Erika.

Finally, I would like to thank my readers and my family. Your continued support is inestimable.

—SR

Lent 2012

SYLVAIN REYNARD

GABRIEL'S INFERNO

One man's salvation, one woman's sensual awakening . . .

Gabriel Emerson is a man tortured by his dark past. A highly respected university professor, Gabriel uses his notorious good looks and charm to lead a secret life of pleasure where nothing is out of bounds.

Sweet and innocent, Julia Mitchell enrols as Gabriel's graduate student and his immediate attraction to her, and their powerful and strange connection, threatens to derail his career. Wildly passionate and sinful, *Gabriel's Inferno* is an exploration of the intense power of forbidden love.